PUS
VER
ORIG

PRAISE FOR

THE STOCKHOLM TRILOGY

'*Sin City* meets Raymond Chandler in this atmospheric and compulsive series'   *Attitude*

'A brilliant new talent'   *Sunday Times Crime Club*

'A dark, atmospheric, powerful thriller, the best debut novel I've read in years'   Lynda La Plante

'Holmén has Raymond Chandler's rare ability to evoke a character in a few deft strokes'   *Mail on Sunday*, best crime reads of 2016

'Ferociously noir… If Chandler and Hammett had truly walked on the wild side, it would read like *Clinch*'   Val McDermid

'Gritty, stylish Scandinavian noir from one of Sweden's hottest emerging authors'   *Booklover*

'Atmospheric Scandi retro, but Chandleresque to its core'
                                                Sunday Times Crime Club

'Well-crafted noir that doesn't pull its punches, hitting you in the guts with stark surprises'   *Thriller Books Journal*

'A gritty, stylish debut from a Swedish history teacher and in Kvist he has created a brutal anti-hero quite unlike any seen in crime fiction before'   *Express*

Born in 1974, Martin Holmén studied history, and now teaches at a Stockholm secondary school. *Slugger* is the third thriller in *The Stockholm Trilogy*, after *Clinch* and *Down for the Count*.

Pushkin Vertigo
71–75 Shelton Street
London WC2H 9JQ

Original text © Martin Holmén 2017
Translation © A.A. Prime 2018

First published as *Slugger* by
Albert Bonniers Förlag, Stockholm, Sweden

Published in the English language by arrangement
with Bonnier Rights, Stockholm, Sweden

First published by Pushkin Vertigo in 2018

1 3 5 7 9 8 6 4 2

ISBN 978-1-78227-219-9

Text designed and typeset by Tetragon, London
Printed and bound by CPI Group (UK) Ltd, Croydon CRO 4YY

www.pushkinpress.com

For C.-M. Edenborg and Martin Tistedt

PART ONE

SATURDAY 18 JULY

The wall-lice are thriving in the heat.

There is a bang on the other side of Mosebacke Square as a man in a gas mask flings a window wide open. The reek of hydrogen cyanide spills out into the high-summer air in bitter coils that skulk around the tree trunks in the park, play in the lilies, chase chaffinches and sparrows in flight. They travel farther on a light easterly breeze towards a uniformed Lindholmian seeking shade under the foliage of a tree, causing him to fan his chubby mug with a bundle of National Socialist flyers.

The sharp smell prickles in my nostrils as I sit on a big beast of a radio set in the shade of the doorway to house number 9. I light an eight-öre Meteor cigar to clean out my lungs.

In the flower bed a peacock butterfly is cavorting in the honeysuckle; down at Stadsgård wharf the steam-winches are puffing in the heat. Sweat streams from my forehead, finds channels in the scars on my face and flows down my cheeks.

With the cigar in the corner of my mouth, I take off my hat and wipe the inside rim with a handkerchief. It's hell wearing the same hat all year round. If only I had a straw one for the summer I wouldn't be bathing in sweat the moment I step out the door. The posh blokes in Östermalm flaunt theirs. Wide-brimmed and fashionable. Preferably worn with sunglasses. Well-fed swine.

I put my hat back on. Walking around without it is unthinkable. The heat melts the pomade in my hair and it's not fifteen pissing minutes before it looks like someone has poured a jug

9

of melted lard over my head. It is hotter now than back when I used to heave coal in ships' boiler rooms during my years at sea, and from what I hear it's going to continue for weeks to come.

We are not built for this sort of heat in this country. It drives people to madness. Old folk are dropping like flies, and babies too.

I fiddle lazily with the radio dial, turning through the names of different cities' medium-wave stations with the stump of my severed little finger. I have painted the town red in Marseilles, Bremen and a few of the other cities many times.

I have been cursing the weight of this damned radio since lunchtime. I was sent to collect a debt from a blacksmith in Kungsholmen. He had no money. I worked him over with the handle of an axe I found in the yard and took the radio for my trouble.

'Damn, do I have to sell this thing now?'

My voice echoes in the shade of the empty doorway. I already have a radio. A rather nifty AGA sitting at home in my flat in Sibirien. I look up again and survey the square. A travelling trades-man drives his coarse-limbed mare up the hill on Svartensgatan to the left of the park. The iron-shod hooves strike the paving stones. Lather lines the horse's shoulders like the foam on a Pilsner. The driver snaps the whip across its hindquarters. A cloud of small flies rises from the animal. Horse and carriage turn right at the elementary school, its windows vacant during the holidays, and disappear down Östgötagatan with a two-metre-long dust tail behind them.

The Katarina Church clock tower strikes the quarter-hour. The girl was supposed to be home by two. I hope she hasn't stopped somewhere along the way.

'Five more minutes,' I mumble to myself.

Then it's about damn time for a Pilsner.

I fish out my pocket watch, lift it up and tap the glass with my fingernail. It has been broken for half an eternity but I'm not giving up on it.

I loosen my tie a little and run my forefinger along the inside of my shirt collar. I flick the sweat off my hand, take out the photograph from the inner pocket of my jacket and inspect it for the fifth time.

In the foreground stands the boss himself, squinting into the camera. He is a corpulent fellow in a light summer suit holding a walking cane. His wife stands beside him. She has half a poultry farm on her hat and looks as if her bodice is too tight.

In the background, off to one side, is the housekeeper Evy Granér. Her gaze is downcast and she stands with her hands clasped at the height of what other men would call her glory. Perhaps that is why she appears as exposed as poverty itself.

'Twenty-five years old as I understand it.'

The Lindholmian surrenders to the July heat and sinks down onto his backside against the tree trunk. He puts the flyers down and unfastens the leather strap stretching across his belly and chest.

A woman comes hurrying across the park. I stand up and take one last look at the photograph before putting it back in my pocket.

It must be her.

I kill the cigar under the heel of my shoe.

Miss Granér has left her hat behind, tied a handkerchief around her hair and pinned up her dress. Twists of newspapers and the tops of various root vegetables stick out of the woven basket in her slender hand. Her movements are light and lithe.

No one would be able to tell.

I heave the damn radio onto my shoulder with a sigh. Evy slows down as she catches sight of me and slips into the doorway quietly and slowly like a ferry boat into the dock.

'Miss Granér?'

She stands as still as a picture. Her bright blue eyes are struck with fear. She smells faintly of female sweat. I wrench the basket from her hand, kick open the door and put the groceries down in the stairwell. My back cricks painfully when I straighten up again.

'You're late. You had an appointment with Jensen. Two o'clock.'

'But… my dear sir…'

Her voice trembles like a violin string.

'Your boss has put his foot down. Nothing else to be done.'

Her eyes tear up. My overworked shoulder joint aches under the weight of the radio. I grab hold of her wrist and pull her out into the heat.

Evy's shoes clatter as she stumbles behind me. A few stifled sobs escape her lips. I drag her behind me down Östgötagatan, lined by rental shacks with flaking plaster and beat-up little wooden houses. Sheer curtains billow sleepily from the wide-open windows. Women in aprons can be seen inside, standing at wood stoves like phantoms glistening with sweat. A flock of small birds tweet in an elderflower bush where the blossoms are already withered.

'If he would just listen…'

'Nothing else to be done.'

Two soot-black police cars drive up Högbergsgatan in the direction of the church farther up the hill. I pull Evy alongside me as we wait for them to pass. I fix my gaze on the furniture workshop on the other side of the road. The pulse in Evy's wrist is trilling as intensely as the birds in the elderflower bush. She gasps for breath, and I squeeze her tighter.

'Calm down, lass.'

It would be quicker to take a shortcut via Katarina Church, but I don't want to risk bumping into Reverend August Gabrielsson. We have known each other for twenty-five years, ever since he was a naval chaplain, but if he saw me now he would no doubt lecture me with chidings and the Word of God. Besides, I still owe the sod a few hundred kronor. He would relieve me of a bundle of dough and give me pangs of conscience to boot.

The squad cars pass by, sunshine bouncing off the black lacquer. I drag Evy across the street and continue along the cemetery wall down towards Tjärhovsgatan.

She is crying loudly now, sobbing and sniffling. I push her around the corner just as the Katarina bells hammer out their half-hour strikes. I drive her forward with shoves and slaps. The sun is burning my back, my shirt is sticky and I am puffing like a bellows. Sweat stings my eyes and my throat feels like it's glued shut. I would kill for a Pilsner, and I have killed before, but beer will have to wait until later, when the job is done.

We pass the fire station with its square lantern. The pavement merges into a wide gravel ditch bank. A stench emanates from the outhouses in the yards where the shit has fermented. We skirt around a stray mutt sprawled, exhausted, with its tongue hanging out. It is dying of thirst.

Someone ought to give it a bowl of water.

A couple of blokes are standing at the end of Södermannagatan chatting. I take a few steps to the left, stop and look up at Katarina through the arched gate in the wall. The golden-yellow, black-domed church sits enthroned on her spot high on the hill. If I recall Gabrielsson's words correctly, those walls hold 2,000 God-fearing souls on Sundays.

Emergency lights lash the church façade with red streaks, just like Our Saviour himself, but I see no vehicles from where I am

13

standing. I sniff the air for smoke. The more superstitious folk here in Söder say that Katarina is doomed to burn down twice and that the dome will collapse. That is what people have said ever since the Danish king burned the bodies of his enemies here, during the Stockholm Bloodbath, hundreds of years ago, but from what I know the old dear has only lost her top the once.

So far.

Evy turns to look at me and I look straight back. The municipal water carts have stopped sprinkling the streets due to the watering ban. The street dust clings to her wet cheeks, turning them grey. She opens her mouth, begging like a baby for a tit, but I take a few quick steps and push her on before she can say anything. The force makes her jaws snap sharply shut.

Then finally she gives up. Surrender spreads through her body and soon she lurches limply in front of me in the quivering brilliance of the sunshine, arms dangling loosely, the roadside dirt like a little yellow dust cloud around her worn shoes as she drags them through the gravel. She doesn't say a word and I am getting closer to that Pilsner.

Forty-five minutes, an hour at the most.

Outside the abandoned palace of an elementary school, I haul the radio onto the other shoulder, waving away a stubborn wasp. It flies across the street. On the opposite side of the street is a ramshackle block of flats. The plaster has crumbled to expose a wall that appears to have been repaired with reeds and old rice. The Söder folk have it nice and draughty on a summer day like this. Worse in winter, of course, but they keep each other warm and seem to produce children at a faster rate than death takes them.

'At least that's something.'

'Pardon, sir?'

Evy sniffs and stops as if by command. She begins to turn around. I slap her on the shoulder.

'I didn't say a damn thing. Come on, work those pins.'

We are nearly fifty minutes late by the time we finally arrive at Jensen's surgery. It is located diagonally opposite the trade school in the lifeless part of Tjärhovsgatan. The curtains are shut tight in the windows. I was here just last November when I needed to get a nasty knife wound in my side stitched up. My opponent came out worse, may he rest in peace.

I knock on the door. The sound seems to spread like a jolt through Evy's body, bringing her back to her senses.

'My little precious.'

Her voice barely holds. She is about to turn on the waterworks again. What a shitty fucking job. I bang harder on the door. I hear shuffling steps on the other side and the click of a lock. The door swings open and we are met by a sharp whiff of schnapps.

Evy gasps. The boar of a doctor fills the entire doorway. He removes his round spectacles from his nose and wipes the sweat off his forehead with his sleeve.

'Ah, Kvist, what time do you call this?' he says in Danish. 'You'll have to wait, I have a little problem with a patient.'

Jensen coughs and we are engulfed in more alcohol fumes. The doctor is wearing a shirt with a dirty collar and a white doctor's coat. Like an old field surgeon, he is soiled with blood.

'My little precious,' Evy repeats.

The heavy green sofa in Jensen's sparse waiting room creaks as she rocks back and forth with her hands on her knees. The air is already thick with cigar smoke. I rest my feet on the radio. I might not be able to afford a pair of sunglasses and a summer hat, but I'll be damned if I don't maintain the shiniest shoes in the city.

I take out my handkerchief and try to whip the dust off them. The shoes make the man, and everybody knows one can determine a bloke's standing in life by looking down at his feet. People who claim anything different are poor devils who shine their shoes with soot and coffee grounds.

The protracted female moans coming from the doctor's surgery are interrupted when the Katarina bells announce it is already half past three. Evy looks up and grabs hold of my arm. She is shaking.

'If he would just listen.'

'We're getting rid of it and the boss is paying well.'

'How much do you want?'

'More than you've got.'

'I have money.'

Evy digs out a shabby little coin purse with a brass clasp. She tries to get it open with trembling fingers. A woman's shrill scream issues from inside the abortionist's room. The purse jumps out of her hands and a mass of öre coins roll out on the linoleum floor.

Evy dives to the floor and breaks down again. She sobs as she chases the coins with her arse in the air. Her tears and the coins on the floor are both glinting. My guts feel like they're tangled together. I think I'll have a strong dram with my Pilsner later.

I get up from the sofa and help her. She barely has enough for a meal. I stick my cigar in the corner of my mouth and pull her to her feet. The red-lined purse gapes open like a wide wound in her hand. I drop the coins inside with a jangle. The sofa creaks when I push her back into her seat. I sit down next to her.

Evy sniffs. She wipes her nose with the back of her hand and undoes the top two buttons of her dress. There is plenty to look at if one were so inclined. A blush spreads across her cheeks and she speaks with a tremble in her voice.

'Mr Wirén taught me how the French girls…'

'No need for that.'

'When it's their time of the month.'

'You might as well do up your buttons.'

'You know…? With… their mouths…?'

'For Christ's sake!'

I am invaded by the strange sense of shame that has recently begun to arise when people degrade themselves so openly before me.

The sofa creaks even louder when I lean forward and rest my elbows on my knees. I tap my foot a couple of times against the linoleum floor. It's muggy as hell in this little room. Sweat is pouring down my body.

Don't go soft now, Kvist. You need this pittance.

I get up, walk over to the window, pull back the curtain and hook it up. Another scream rings out from the surgery. It sounds like Jensen is castrating piglets.

I close the window and turn around. Evy is pressing the palms of her hands against her ears. She has resumed rocking.

'What will I do?'

'There's nothing to do.'

'What do you mean?'

'You haven't got the dough for a littl'un.'

For a moment Evy looks confused. She blows her nose in a handkerchief and folds it up. She struggles to find the words.

'If only I could afford a ticket to Motala.'

'What the hell are you going to do there?'

'My sister is married to a farmer in Bråstorp. He has pigs and cows and is chairman of the dairy cooperative.'

'A regular lord, then.'

'Horses too.'

Her voice breaks. She clasps her stomach.

'It's crying inside me,' she screams. 'I can feel it. It's crying!'

I grunt and catch a scent in the air. I think it's the familiar smell of blood. With the cigar in the corner of my mouth, I roll off a few sluggish uppercuts into the air while glaring at the radio set. I should put a sales advertisement in *Social-Demokraten* next time I let a radio get involved in a private detective gig. If no one goes for it I'll have to lug the damned thing to Ström the junk dealer.

Evy calms down and catches her breath.

'Do you have children?'

My mouth fills with tobacco flakes as I near enough bite my cigar in two. I take it out of my mouth and spit on the floor.

'None of your bloody business.'

'Please, be honest.'

'America. A daughter.'

I drag the glob of spit over the linoleum floor with my shoe. The woman inside the surgery has stopped howling. All is quiet.

'So you know.'

'Never hear from her.'

A headache grinds deep inside my skull. I scrunch up my eyes and massage the bridge of my nose between my thumb and forefinger.

'You must know.'

The ache is only getting worse. Once, off the coast of Africa, I was drunk during the day and fell asleep on a pile of hawsers in the forepeak. Afterwards you could have peeled my skin off in large strips, and I had a headache for three whole days. I learnt that it's good to get a few Pilsners under your belt when it's hot so as not to get dehydrated.

I walk over to the sofa and sit down. I take off my hat and use the brim to fan myself. I haven't had a chance to properly tame my hair since I got out of Långholmen Prison in November but for once I don't give a damn. Evy is rubbing her hands together.

'What's your daughter's name?'

'Ida.'

'That's a pretty name. How old?'

I count to myself quietly. It doesn't take long.

'Sixteen in a couple of months.'

My head shakes involuntarily. Her number was almost up before her life had barely begun, from sheer poverty, in a clinic similar to this one. Maybe it would have been better that way. My hand is trembling as it brings the cigar to my mouth.

The memories have largely burned to ashes, and I tend to force the rest out of my head with schnapps, but they are flaring up more often these days, and in the most inconvenient of situations – like now.

Evy shakes me out of my thoughts.

'Why haven't you written to each other?'

Typical nosy bloody woman. I did send a picture of myself when I wrote a line to America last autumn, but no answer came. The cigar crackles as I consume a whole centimetre of tobacco. I glance at the doctor's door. I swallow.

I have taken thousands of knocks both in training and in the boxing ring. I have been persecuted and mocked for my relations with men, and have been beaten by the screws at Långholmen Prison. In this shit line of work I have been stabbed, bitten and slashed, and I probably have more stitches than a mainsail.

Still, nothing can hurt a man like remorse.

I pull the elasticated strap off my wallet, flip it open and look inside. Wirén gave me an advance of 450 kronor to pay Jensen. What the hell can that puff-guts do about it? Demand his money back?

I sigh. Frankly, I am starting to feel too weak for work.

I turn to Evy.

'So what does that bloody ticket to Motala cost?'

I open the door and step headlong into a wall of heat. I stop for a moment to scratch myself.

I hear the faint sounds of traffic coming from Folkungagatan, and crickets that have started their monotonous song. I put down the radio, take my tie out of my trouser pocket, flip up my collar and tie a double Windsor knot.

An elegant gentleman comes sauntering along the pavement with a wide grin plastered across his face. He is wearing a straw hat, pale summer suit and light leather shoes. His beard is fluttering in the dazzling weather. Perhaps he is on his way to amuse himself at the cheap, seedy brothel behind the Navigation School.

The wealthy man gives me a look and crosses the street. I am used to it; they never forget. Some stare at me as if I'm a freak and whisper behind my back; occasionally someone dares to shout abuse at me, others avoid me like the plague.

No big deal.

I walk down Tjärhovsgatan with the radio on my right shoulder. I stop at a crossing and look at the queue of workaday men at the tram stop farther down towards Slussen. They are waiting quietly and soberly in the heat.

With my left hand I fish out my Viking watch. It's still not working. I could really do with that Pilsner. I calculate how I can make time for both a beer and a measurement at Herzog's.

I jog over to the other side of the street. The edge of the radio is thumping on the muscle between my shoulder and neck. There's a beer café called the Stone Angel opposite the rectory that usually serves a tankard that doesn't taste quite as much like stale sawdust and laundry soap as what some other places offer up.

If I cut through the cemetery I might bump into Gabrielsson and get the chance to tell him about my recent good deed. Maybe it'll buy me a place at the Lord's feet. Salvation is probably reserved for those with enough dough to afford good deeds.

'Whereas the hungry take the cage lift down below,' I mutter to myself.

I could also finally pay off a portion of my debt to the rector. He has always looked out for me – a good Samaritan when my need was greatest. We met in Buenos Aires a long time ago. I wasn't much more than a cabin boy. The memory makes me chuckle.

He won't want a Pilsner. Not so early in the day and with a service to give tomorrow.

I walk back along the ditch bank. The air is thick and hard to breathe. The sun is blazing directly in my face. I tilt the brim of my hat over my eyes and breathe heavily. I swap shoulders.

Fifteen years ago I could skip rope for an hour, do another half-hour on the punchbag, spar twelve rounds and finish off with a hundred push-ups. Not any more. Far from it. My body has given up on me, destroyed by violence and hard labour, all before forty. Every joint has nearly seized up and they creak reluctantly with every step I take. My lungs are clawing me apart from the inside out; sometimes it's so bad that I think I'll cough my guts up. This bloody dust will be the death of me.

In the vaulted gate of the cemetery wall, there is a crowd of poor people standing there, mumbling with their heads huddled close together. A slip of a lad in short trousers has a nosebleed and is holding his hand up to his face but none of the adults can be bothered to help him. He is well behaved. I clear my throat;

the cluster of people parts like water for Moses and my feet touch consecrated ground.

The pebbles on the path grumble under my feet. I walk a few metres, stop and explore my pockets with my free hand. With some effort, I light my final cigar with the old one. I mash the butt under my heel with a crunching sound.

Several metres along the path a sparrow has fallen victim to a cat. Its grey down moves back and forth gently in the barely perceptible breeze. Along the left row of crosses on the graves walks a hunched figure, pulling up dandelions.

I look up at the church with its mighty dome. The emergency lights have stopped, but to the left of the building a black police car rears its ugly head. Straight ahead of me, in the dim light between the flights of steps up to the church, I see a couple of rows of brass buttons.

My nerves are prickling with unease but I trudge up to the church as calmly as I can. Some drunk has vomited in the green grass by a grave in the night. The flies tear themselves away from the yellow-brown sludge and whirl up in the air as I pass. I take a deep breath through my mouth.

Constables emerge from the shadows, with pallid complexions not unlike those of the whores in the doorways of Norra Smedjegatan. I shield my face with the brim of my hat and turn the corner around the church. I gasp and stop. A torrential stream of sweat runs down my spine and for one second I forget about the weight of the radio on my shoulder.

Two men are standing outside the west entrance. Facing me is a middle-aged copper in full uniform. He is pasty white despite the heat and looks like he has just forced down a piece of bad meat.

The other one is a slim bloke. A holster sits on his belt holding a revolver. He has a broad-brimmed straw hat and grey hair

22

that cuts across his neck with an exemplary sharp edge. He is wearing a Prussian blue suit with a waistcoat. This year's colour, so I read. His jacket is slung over one arm.

He says something to the uniformed constable, who stiffens and salutes. The pale git nods at me over the other's shoulder and slouches away towards the verdigris copper door. It slams shut with a bang as the well-dressed man turns around.

I look over the familiar wrinkles, the gold-rimmed glasses and the ridiculous thin moustache. He is wearing a light shirt with iron-grey stripes and a white collar. A blue-headed silver pin sticks through his tie knot, matching his cufflinks and reflecting the colour of his eyes. As always, whenever our paths cross, a malicious grin lights up Detective Chief Inspector Alvar Berglund's face.

'Well, shit, if it isn't the city's worst slugger visiting the world beyond prison walls. Has Kvist gone and become a radio trader?'

Berglund's melodic Norrland lilt is audible in his voice. He juts out his chin and rests his hand on the butt of his revolver for a brief moment. I put the radio down by my feet, roll my shoulders and crack my knuckles. I shift my weight and look around. It is so fucking easy to act tough when you've got a firearm and the law to back you up.

'Like hell am I a slugger. *Boxing Monthly!* magazine called my style elegant and technical.'

'Long time ago now.'

'Surely Olsson is still the chief of police? He can vouch for it.'

Berglund is smiling even wider. One minute alone with the bastard and I could squeeze the life out of him. He takes a cigarette from a Carat carton and packs the tobacco down by tapping the end against the box. The back door opens and the pale-faced constable pokes his head out.

'You're needed inside, Inspector. They can't get him free.'

Berglund nods and looks back at me. He shifts his weight to his other leg. The door shuts. Berglund puts the cigarette in the corner of his mouth and pats his pockets. His voice falters as he speaks.

'I always thought that a poof like Kvist would catch fire if he set foot on consecrated ground. Maybe he's here for the confirmation candidates?'

The church bells pound out their thunderous song with four chimes, as if the Lord Himself were joining in the conversation. A murder of crows on a tree takes off and darts into the sky.

Hatred sings in my veins. The blood vessel in my forehead is throbbing with rage. I have half a mind to pick up the apparatus between my feet and smash it over his head, see if I can't tune into the police radio that the coppers have been bragging about so much in the papers lately.

Two, three.

The final strike rings out. I clear my throat and spit.

'Little boys? Like hell. I'm a good friend of the rector himself.'

'Of Gabrielsson?'

I knock the ash off my cigar with my forefinger and stare at the spot where his scrawny neck disappears into his well-starched collar. His loose jowls wobble below his chin. Three years ago I managed to wedge a handcuff chain around that neck and if some fucker hadn't knocked me senseless with a baton, Berglund would have burnt in Gehenna.

I salivate at the memory, and swallow. The inspector takes the cigarette out of his mouth. The official grin fades and his moustache curves downward. Behind the glasses there is a glint in his eyes and Berglund takes on an air of importance again.

'Well, if that's the case, by all means, go in. The priest is at the altar but you will have to forgive him if the conversation is somewhat one-sided. He seems to take his vow of confidentiality deadly seriously.'

Berglund laughs drily and puts the unlit cigarette back in the packet. The pebbles crunch under the inspector's costly summer shoes as he walks to the door. I lift the radio with both hands and follow behind. The headache is back and I need a Pilsner more than anything but it feels urgent that I see Gabrielsson.

Berglund turns to me with one hand on the door. I put the radio down.

I poise the index finger of my left hand against my thumb and flick the glowing tip off the half-smoked cigar. It travels through the air like a firefly. I put the butt in my trouser pocket and follow Berglund through the door.

Katarina wraps me up in her coolness. I breathe out, I breathe in. A familiar scent mixes with Berglund's Aquavera but I can't quite place it.

The Detective Chief Inspector goes first and our steps echo against the stone floor. Farther ahead in the church I hear murmuring voices. We turn to the right and emerge behind the altar.

My eyes wander upward, over the immense organ loft with its gilded pipes and the pompous chandeliers in the cross vaults, but then a strange noise brings my gaze plunging down like a shot bird.

First iron clinks against iron, then a shrill sound screeches through the large room. It sounds like a hinge in need of oil.

'Fucking hell, it's stuck fast!'

'Stubborn as a fly on sugar.'

Between the pews, on the aged oak floorboards before the altar, stands a black cluster of motionless men gathered in a semicircle with their backs to me. A couple wear civilian clothes, some are uniformed. To the side, by the font where my daughter

Ida was christened, stands an older man dressed in a white coat similar to the one I just saw Jensen wearing.

'Make sure the brace board is in place.'

'Is that a seven-inch nail?'

'You have to work the bastard out. Pull it one way, then the other.'

A murmur moves through the group, metal clinks against metal again and the screeching sound cuts through the grey silence of the church.

Berglund clears his throat.

'Gentlemen!'

The men stop what they are doing and a dozen heads turn towards us.

'A good friend of the rector would like to pay a visit.'

My eyes dart down to my shoes as I feel the coppers' eyes sting my skin. I force myself to look up and plaster a smile on my face. The old cigar butt dissolves into crumbs in my pocket.

'The day after payday and half the force in church?'

Nobody laughs. One of them swings a huge crowbar onto his shoulder. Berglund's steps echo on the timber and the black-clad crowd opens up a gap for me. I crane my neck and gasp.

The dark sinkhole of men reveals a pale body. Its naked limbs are lurid against the floorboards. It is angular and knotty from old age, and the skin is stretched taut across the ribs. Its thick white shock of hair is flecked with red like the feathers of a newly beheaded chicken.

I feel as if I've been struck with a hefty right hook. A shudder courses through my limbs. I take an involuntary step forward and accidentally bump my shoulder into one of the men. The colours become more vivid, then fade. I shut my eyes tight, then open them again.

Priest Gabrielsson's face has frozen in a twisted expression with his teeth, yellow with age, showing through his bloodless lips. Someone has driven a substantial rail spike through his skull. Blood and brains have run down into his eye sockets, which now resemble small tar pits. The rector is lying with his arms stretched out, like Jesus Christ, with his bony feet crossed and pierced with iron.

Gabrielsson's genitals seem to have shrivelled from lack of blood supply and in his grey chest hair the red has coagulated like winter frost on a tuft of grass. On the floor above his head is a vivid Star of David drawn in blood. It is his blood, but it feels as if it were my own.

I sink down into a squat in the quiet semicircle of men and take off my hat. I reach out my hand and run my index finger over a black trickle that has dried into a dark and grainy stain on the wooden floor. Everything he has ever thought, felt and experienced flowed out of him several hours ago. I shut my eyes again. My brain is trying to process it all. Hatred burns in my veins like petrol.

My Husqvarna pistol has been at the pawnshop for some weeks now.

It is time to set it free.

SUNDAY 19 JULY

Lundin the undertaker turns the page of his newspaper with difficulty. His iron hand-prosthesis rattles. The cut-throat razor scratches gently as I drag it at an angle across his sunken cheek. I clean off the soap and white hairs in a bowl of water sitting among the plates on the kitchen table. I stretch out his skin between my thumb and forefinger.

'Synagogues on Wahrendorffsgatan and St Paulsgatan too. And they threw a flaming torch into the Jewish jail on Klippgatan. People have changed beyond recognition since the priest's murder.'

His iron hand clinks. The ache in his hand got out of control last Christmas, and the doctor removed it and replaced it with a remarkable construction complete with knuckles and a pair of leather straps to attach it. Obviously it is completely useless and he has refused medical help ever since. He says that otherwise he will end up looking like a total fucking robot.

'His name is Gabrielsson. Was.'

I sigh. The little kitchen smells of shaving soap, coffee and gas.

'We have go back to the riots surroundings the abolition of the Jewish laws in 1838 to find anything comparable,' Lundin reads aloud.

I have to struggle to hold the razor still.

'And why would they be so fucking stupid as to daub their own symbol at the murder scene?' I hiss.

Under the table Dixie growls in her sleep. A single fly drones around a plate of lard. The rhythmic sound of a carpet beater in the courtyard comes in through the window. It weaves in with musical notes when the jazz boy a couple of floors up starts abusing his trumpet. People say he has the gift. By which they mean communication with the spirit world rather than musicianship.

'Gabrielsson was a known anti-Nazi,' I say. 'He wrote in to newspapers kicking up a fuss all the time. Now hold still.'

I work the razor around the undertaker's bushy moustache with small strokes and for a brief moment I manage to get him to shut up, but he's soon off again.

'They're not really like us though, in their thoughts or deeds. And those little caps too. No one knows how they stay in place. There are no two ways about it: they crucified the black-frock just like they crucified Christ once upon a time, you mark my words.'

'I'm going to call my friend Senior Constable Hessler. He usually knows what's going on.'

'And they breed like rabbits, despite cutting off half their penis at birth.'

'Lundin, go to hell. You're talking about them as if they were Gypsies or Finns, or downright bums.'

'At least ten kids per woman and I don't have a single one.'

'Jesus Christ was a Jew as far as I remember, and they have the most generous opening hours in the city. Didn't the tailor just book me in for a measuring? You heard for yourself. Even on a Sunday. What the hell difference does it make how many children they have? Hold still.'

Lundin brushes some crumbs off the table with his good hand. He turns his head and stares out of the window. I snatch the razor's edge away from his skin so as not to cut him.

'I don't give a shit about death. If you've got nobody to take over when the day comes, it doesn't matter how much you've scrimped.' Lundin's voice is thick and he clears his throat. 'I had

29

the odd offer through the years, in my youth, but it was never to be. It's a crying shame.'

I angle his head up towards the light and scrape away some leftover beard hairs from high up on his cheekbone.

'Do you remember that week last autumn when you assisted me in the funeral parlour? That was pleasant, wasn't it, brother?'

I glance out into the courtyard. The carpet beating has ended. Tablecloths and sheets billow lazily on the clothes lines in a gentle breeze.

'When we cut up that bloke so he would fit in the child-size coffin? Delightful memory.'

'He also that is slothful in his work is brother to him that is a great waster,' Lundin quotes the Scriptures.

'Shut up.'

'You may not be the most logical, brother, but you have always got stuck in when it came down to it.'

'Hire an assistant. You've got that Olympian, your cousin's kid.'

'My nephew. Haven't seen him for years and years. And he was something of a slacker before he discovered his talent for shooting.'

'I can track him down. That's my job.'

'It doesn't matter any more.' Lundin stares vacantly ahead. 'Not long to go before the August building inspection. Nilsson says that his cooker is kaput and I think the Good Templars have broken a windowpane, though they're trying to hide it.' He sighs heavily, gathers his strength and continues. 'And let's not forget: I would still like to know who stole timber from the attic to use as firewood last winter. Haven't I always been generous with the heating, damn it?'

'You sure have.'

I moisten a towel in the water and wipe off the shaving cream. A drop of blood trickles down to the tip of his chin, gleaming like a ruby. Lundin looks at himself in the vanity mirror on the table and laughs without a trace of joy.

'Not long now.'

I don't know what to say in response. Instead I pour water into a pot on the hob and feed a gas token into the meter. It soon begins to boil and I fill up the washing-up bowl and place the dishes inside. Lundin takes another snifter from the bottle and sucks his moustache. He mumbles something but the sound is drowned out by the clatter of dishes.

'What are you muttering about now?'

Lundin is staring out the window.

'I just said I'm glad that my brother's back.' He tucks the schnapps bottle under his arm, and unscrews the lid. 'It's not like last winter when you took every act of kindness to be nothing more than an unwelcome interruption to your damned brooding.'

I continue rattling the dishes. Every time last autumn or winter comes up in conversation, I feel a hollowness in my stomach and a sudden wave of nausea. The sensation reminds me of being a child and going hungry for too long.

'I was completely lost.'

I shake the water from my hands. Lundin cups his hand behind his ears.

'Pardon?'

'Just quit your damned blathering.'

I go over to him, lay his arm around my shoulder and pull him up to his feet. Dixie, the half-blind old bitch, wakes up and starts to whimper. I shuffle off with Lundin towards the entrance of the funeral parlour.

With a twinge of bad conscience I stare out across the foyer. A thick layer of dust lies over the desk, the wall mirror and the dead palm leaves, but I can clean another day.

Lundin grumbles as he arranges himself upright in his chair and then turns on the radio. It hisses as he sets the frequency. I check that the chamber pot is in place under the desk.

'I'll put your blankets in the cold room so they'll be cool for tonight.'

'Just forget about that damned dead priest.'

'Of course.'

Lundin nods, tired, and puts on his top hat. The radio crackles as he tunes into the news.

'A telegram received in London around midnight describes the entirety of Spain as a blazing inferno and details a bloody scene of individual acts of violence as well as outright battles.'

I walk over to the wall-mounted telephone and request the police station from the operator girl. The line crackles.

'Large parts of Malaga are burning. New battles have broken out in La Línea, and from Gibraltar we have heard hammering machine guns and the thunder of artillery all night.'

Lundin fumbles with his top shirt buttons and grunts a few incoherent words. A new operator answers with a vacant tone.

'Get me the Anti-Smuggling Section, sweetheart. Chief Constable Hessler.'

'Violent fires rage in Fascist-controlled Seville, bombed by government aircraft during the night,' the radio continues to rasp.

'The sergeant has been dismissed with immediate effect.'

I am taken aback by the girl's monotone voice. I lean closer to the mouthpiece, and a shiver runs down my spine.

'He's gone?'

'Effective immediately. As of yesterday.'

'Why?'

'Unfortunately that is not information I am able to give, sir.'

I turn the crank once round and end the conversation. I face Lundin and grope around my pockets for a cigar.

'In domestic news, this year's general survey of the so-called vagabond community shows that between fifty and sixty thousand of these vagrants populate our streets during summertime. This is substantially fewer than the more severe years we have seen previously.'

Lundin has spilt snuff all over the desk. He is sleeping with his chin on his chest, dreaming about all the clients he might have had, if only people hadn't stopped coming. It is months since the last time the doorbell rang. His moustache flutters when he exhales. His face is slack and drooping.

I bite the end off a Meteor and think about Hessler. It was only November when I saw him last, in relation to my client Elin Johansson and a particularly tricky case. He had risen above the cheap snoops and got his own office and desk. Now he has been dismissed. Something doesn't add up. Since he has a propensity for strong liquor, and often personally confiscated a portion of police seizures of smuggled vodka, I could search for him in the city's bars, if I could be bothered. He has probably already made a fool of himself in one of the harbour pubs. He'll be sitting there staring at the sailors and dockers. After all, that's how we met once upon a time.

I walk over to Lundin, who has jolted out of his sleep. He stares at me like a drunk. I fasten his top two shirt buttons and tie his black tie around his thin neck. He smells of breakfast's coffee grounds, and vinegar. Occasionally I soak his bedlinen in sabadilla vinegar, strong enough to take your skin off, and powder it with insecticides to combat the lice infestation. The smell reminds me of the poorhouse of my childhood and every time I put him to bed it makes my stomach turn. Still, I endure. With so little time left he doesn't need more things to complain about.

Once I am finished clothing him, his chin finally falls down to his chest again. Not enough coffee in his post-breakfast schnapps. I take his brass tin, prise out a pinch of snuff and lay it out for him on the edge of the table for later.

After another conversation with Herzog the tailor on Biblioteksgatan, I strike a match, puff life into a cigar and whistle to Dixie. She pricks up her ears, trying to locate the sound. Half-blind, she takes a few shaky steps in the right direction before sitting back down on her rump. She wags her tail listlessly a couple of times. I sigh, wedge the cigar in the corner of my mouth and pick her up. Her little dog heart flutters against my shirt front as I carry her outside to take a piss. I know I really ought to take the bitch to the park and put a bullet in her head. Put an end to her suffering. I can't do it. Especially not on her birthday. In fact today she is having three porters instead of two.

I heard there are seven dog years to one human year. It sounds like bullshit but it's the honest truth. I sat there trying to work out the numbers in a notebook for an entire afternoon but never managed to get the figures to add up. For simplicity's sake we celebrate every seventh week.

The morning is about as hellishly hot as a log burner. I set Dixie down on the pavement and look around. Roslagsgatan is virtually deserted. The number 6 tram groans up from the south, heading towards the turning point up at the customs office. Rickardsson the gangster comes strolling from the north with his thumbs in his waistcoat like he owns the fucking place. My lungs sting from cigar smoke.

He's a stocky, ugly fucker but impeccably dressed, with his jacket slung over one shoulder. One of Ploman the smuggler king's top men. Known for his ruthlessness.

Dixie carefully sniffs along the wall before crouching down and pissing against it. When she was younger she used to cock her leg like a male but that was before she had problems with her hips. If you press on her rear end she whimpers like a ship dog in a storm.

Rickardsson fixes his eyes on me and starts smirking long before he reaches me. He puffs out his chest to appear stronger than he is. This cocky bastard always seems to want to compare muscle and stares at me wherever I go. I glance at his belt but he appears unarmed. He eyes the waistband of my trousers as well and stops in front of Dixie.

'Hot enough for Kvist? You've sailed the seven seas so you've got something to compare it with.'

The gangster rocks from foot to foot. I stare and take a drag on my cigar. I don't look away. Neither does he.

'So hot my damn watch has stopped. Old man Ström claims to have stopped drinking water completely. Says it'll only come straight out the pores again anyway.'

I nod in the direction of the junk dealer farther up the street.

'Thought I'd pay a visit to Lundin.'

I take a sidestep and stand half in front of the funeral parlour door.

'He isn't doing well. Hasn't seen a corpse in months.'

Rickardsson removes his thumbs from his waistcoat and thrusts out his broad chest.

'Oh, I just wanted to talk for a minute, for old times' sake.'

'You can't demand a percentage of money that the old man doesn't have.'

Rickardsson takes out a silver snuff tin from his trouser pocket and offers me some. The box glints in the sun. I shake my head. He presses his fat lips together but doesn't keep them shut for long.

'What a lovely little dog Kvist has there.'

'Dixie.'

'A miniature schnauzer, right? Wonderful company in the evenings.'

'Just what the hell are you getting at?'

An ache shoots through my skull.

'No fun being alone, is it? Could be very different though, couldn't it?'

Rickardsson gives me a look. I quickly pick up the bitch and hold her tight under my arm. The vein in my forehead is throbbing. My muscle fibres tighten like harp strings. Rickardsson grins.

'Tell Lundin that I'll stop by tomorrow instead.'

He raises his hand to his forehead in a parting gesture and turns back the same way he came. I follow his broad shoulders with my gaze and scratch Dixie behind the ear. Damned thug.

The number 6 tram comes rattling along the street, heading back towards the city, and I open the door and put Dixie back inside. Birthday or not, the world is just too cruel for her today. I start jogging in the direction of the Frejgatan stop.

I swing up onto the back platform of the tram just as it starts rolling away. I work my way through the carriages until I reach the front car, where smoking is allowed. The wheels screech against the shifting grooves of the track and my thoughts return to Gabrielsson. To revenge.

When I visited him to get information for a case last year, someone had drawn a big swastika on the rectory door, which seems like a much more feasible clue than the Star of David. But who the hell cares about politics? I might read the sports pages but I tend to skip the national news.

We roll through the dead city, where every last sod seems to be hiding at home in the shade. The sun casts its glare on the wide-open windows and is reflected all over the streets. The quiet reminds me of Långholmen.

There is nothing I hate more – apart from the pigs, heights and dentists – than a fucking self-nark. Everyone knows, even abroad they all know, all the way down to Turin I would wager, about the shoddy conditions of this city's correctional institution. Still, there are blokes who are released from the jail complex and then want to get straight back in. The institutional air has stifled their spirit and made them feel out of place in the outside world, until finally they rough someone up and squeal on themselves for the sake of quiet company, stagnant routine and clear rules.

We roll on, past the scorched plant beds and bone-dry cement horse troughs. Stockings and underwear are hung out to dry on the windowsills. We pass the spice stalls and clothes shops at the northern end of Regeringsgatan. I am disgusted with myself at the thought, but it has crossed my mind: there have been a couple of occasions this past six months when even I have felt the desire for a cell. Maybe they finally got me after all.

I shudder, but somewhere, happiness flows into the midst of sorrow.

Finally something to do. Something to focus on. Something other than my damned brooding.

I am late out, and in this line of work the trails go cold pretty quickly, but I am convinced that Detective Chief Inspector Berglund and his boys have drawn hasty conclusions. It wasn't the Jews, the poor devils. They have no motive as far as I can see.

Not that I need to understand why; I just need to know who.

'Good enough for me.'

Maybe Herzog the tailor has something to say on the matter. Then as soon as I've been measured for my summer suit I can get started.

Footwork and hard fists, like before.

I dig out my timepiece and tap on the glass. The hands still aren't moving.

'So do we want pockets and fittings? *Knöpfe, ja?*'

I listen to the little tailor's peculiar accent through the rhythmic sighs of the treadle sewing machine. I blink at him and give up on the mental arithmetic. Herzog is peering at me over the sun visor he uses to protect his eyes from his bright desk lamp. He has a red measuring tape around his neck. The lapel of his waistcoat is covered with pins.

I want to explain to him that the details are more a question of price than anything else. The down payment alone has virtually cleaned me out. I just nod sheepishly instead and stroke my chosen fabric on the table in front of me. According to the tailor it is supposed to be lighter than air. If I am not mistaken it is called *mausgrau*. I don't know what that means but it could be a whole lot worse.

I take out my watch, then put it back.

'I show, you wait. Where did I put my file?'

Herzog raises his bushy eyebrows and looks around the workshop. He shouts something in German to his assistant, who is sitting with his back to us at one of the sewing machines. The boy shrugs his shoulders and mumbles in response.

Herzog mutters to himself. He turns around, searches the workbenches, ironing boards and other tools, and lifts up a roll of fabric. When he doesn't find what he is looking for, he walks over to the row of fabric-filled wardrobes that cover the far wall of the workshop.

I stare idly out the window. A young lady passes outside in black riding attire. She is holding her skirt a good half-metre above the ground with one hand, revealing a shiny pair of boots. In the other hand she is holding a riding crop.

Two Östermalm gentlemen stroll past with their chests puffed out like generals or bigwigs of some sort. Both are dressed in light suits and straw hats. One has a twisted moustache and is holding his walking stick like a baton in his fist. They are gesticulating and seem to be absorbed in a heated discussion.

I shut my eyes and am immediately transported back into Katarina Church. I can see the bony rector lying on the floor, as bloody and naked as the day he entered the world. I imagine I can hear the squeaking sound when the coppers tried to pull the rail spikes out of him with a crowbar. I take a deep breath through my nose. The tailor's shop smells of steam-pressed wool.

As soon as Herzog comes back I will ask him about that bloody Jewish star above Gabrielsson's head.

I open my eyes and look back up towards Biblioteksgatan. For a brief moment it feels as though time outside is standing still. Right in front of me, very close, on the other side of the shop window, a youth is standing on the pavement. He stares straight at me with a wild look in his eye. Along his jawline is a flaking row of lice bites. His hand is hanging by his side in an oversized cheviot jacket, like a deformed dead weight. His right hand is high above his head, holding a brick.

I duck and take cover as the windowpane explodes. Shards fly over my head. The brick hits a mannequin and knocks it over. I hear a shrill scream from behind. The youth sticks his head through the window's jagged hole like a lion tamer.

'Jew vermin!'

The boy pulls his head out again and legs it. He disappears northwards, towards Röda Kvarn Picture House and Stureplanen. I get back on my feet. My shoes clatter against the floor. The door opens inward, not outward, and I curse but am soon standing outside on the pavement. I run a few metres towards Mäster Samuelsgatan but then stop.

'Where the fuck did that bastard go?'

My words echo in the silence. The hot air is completely still. Combined with the street dust and soot, it creates a quivering curtain between the façades of the buildings. A couple of cars drive past. A horse clops down one of the side streets. Two ladies standing outside the Svecia Hotel with small chic hats and parasols turn their eyes to the tailor's.

A bloke with a wide gold watch chain over an equally wide belly and a copy of *Svenska Dagbladet* tucked under his arm has stopped next to me. There is a redness to his cheeks as if he has had a few glasses too many with his Sunday roast at the Cecil restaurant on the other side of the street. A group of loitering upper-class kids with grammar school crests on their caps have stopped on the other side of the street to gawp at the tailor's, with massive grins on their faces. People are popping up and vanishing in the windows of the houses above them like a fucking puppet show. Herzog's apprentice stands outside the shop armed with a sleeve board. He is brandishing it like a scythe.

'Bloody cosmopolitans!' shout a couple of the swankily dressed kids. They take a few steps out into the road and the others follow behind. Herzog's assistant backs up to the door and waves his weapon in front of him a few times. The sound of a police whistle travels down from Norrmalmstorg when someone from District 7 gets wind of what has happened.

The kids hesitate and go back to their side of the road, but they don't leave. My jacket, with my wallet, cigars and the pistol I reclaimed earlier today, is still hung up inside. But I don't much fancy going back in if it's about to become a police matter.

The copper arrives. He's a pale bloke with shiny red lips like a neon sign in his doughy white face. He grabs hold of the apprentice's arm and pushes him inside the tailor's. One of the kids lights a cigarette. Another is doubled over in what looks like a fit of giggles.

'What is going on?'

The stout man next to me has a squeaky voice. He takes off his glasses and dabs himself lightly over his face and neck with a handkerchief. He smells of hot toddy in the height of summer. I peer down the sun-broiled street. The drain grates glint gold.

'Someone put a brick through Herzog's window.'

He clucks and folds his handkerchief up into his pocket.

'Just a matter of time before those goggle-eyed types are packed off to America, don't you think?' He puts on his spectacles. 'Pity about all those fine suits.'

The man taps his newspaper on his head in a farewell gesture and saunters north towards Stureplanen. Another copper arrives and stations himself outside the tailor's. I am at a loss and stand there awhile in my shirtsleeves.

A cream-coloured Cadillac with claret mudguards is moving slowly up Biblioteksgatan. I watch it pass. The sun's rays explode all over the lacquer. It rolls past me and parks outside Cecil.

A hefty mitt grabs the car's frame from the inside, and a man heaves himself out. His thin shirt pinches around his broad shoulders and he has metre-long braces running down his chest. His jacket is slung over his arm, at the height of his bulging abdomen, hiding his right hand. He toddles over the crossing and tips the brim of his hat to shield himself from the sunshine.

'Kvist! Well, I'll be damned!'

I recognise the bloke but can't place him. It's happening more and more these days. I look around. The police are still standing outside the tailor's. The corpulent bloke holds his palm up to an old Buick and crosses the street. The sunlight flashes on his gold tiepin. His blue eyes look leaden in the heat. He's a good twenty centimetres taller than me and I back up half a step to even it out.

'Roslagsgatan man, aren't you? We'll drive you home.'

I glance at his hidden hand and take a quick look around. Something about him makes me wish I had got that Husqvarna from the tailor's.

'Like hell. I'm getting measured.'

'Herzog looks a little busy for the time being.'

The huge man slurs his words. He puts his thumb and fore-finger between his lips and blows a whisky-scented whistle down the street. The police officers outside the tailor's look in our direction, nod slightly, put their hand on their sabres and disappear through the door.

'As if by bloody magic, right?'

The man in front of me smiles with his mouth but those leaden eyes radiate violence. He gestures towards his Cadillac with his left hand. On the other side of the crossing someone opens the back door of the car. First I see an ivory cane with a gold tip followed by a pair of crocodile high-heels, and I realise that I have no choice but to do as I am told.

I am standing knee deep in shit.

'In America, it's common for whole families to spend the night out on fire escape platforms during the worst of the heatwaves.'

Ma sticks a cigarette into an ebony-coloured holder and places it between her painted lips. She is wearing a pair of white gloves so thin that one can see the fine blood vessels that run like tattoo ink over the backs of her hands.

I have never met her, but I know who she is.

42

The Cadillac's wheels knock dully like an uninvited guest against the tram tracks as we pass Odengatan and drive into enemy territory. Ma's two sons, Svenne Crowbar and Nix, look from the left pavement to the right and back again. Nix has one hand on the steering wheel, the other on the gearstick, and a revolver in his lap.

They share no similarities to speak of. Nix's face could have been carved out of granite: he's a chiselled and thick-set bloke with a monobrow that makes it look like he has two thin moustaches, one on his brow and one on his upper lip.

Svenne Crowbar's puffy mug keeps appearing in the side mirror. His eyes look about as sly as a cud-chewing cow. Sweat has burnt red furrows into his neck flab. There is a snapping sound as he bites off a fingernail.

The leather back seat creaks with my movements as I try to get a box of matches out of my trouser pocket. Ma is waiting patiently, as if she has never done anything else.

The phosphorous stick rasps against the striking surface. The sudden flame is reflected in Ma's diamond necklace and her deep-green silk dress. It's an exclusive number with lace and frills that fits tightly around her full-figured body, but it probably hasn't been in fashion since the war.

'Is that so?'

Not the slightest tremor in my voice gives me away. She meets my gaze. Her pupils are so large they seem about to take over her blue irises. I lean forward and offer her a light. A heavy scent of perfume washes over me as she puffs on her cigarette and holds out her hand in a polite gesture.

'Of course they have different habits in the heat over there.'

Ma takes a drag. The smoke that fills the passenger compartment is of the same colour as the streaks in her dark hair.

Svenne Crowbar whistles from the front seat and points at the right-hand pavement.

'Rickardsson,' he says, turning to us.

It feels like an ice cube has lodged in my throat when I hear the name. Is Ploman's gangster still out on his walk? I tip the brim of my hat over my eyes. I sure as hell don't want him to see me in this company. Ma cranes her neck and then hides her face behind the hand holding the cigarette.

'Take it easy and turn left into Frejgatan.'

The characteristic double-click of a revolver cylinder turning one notch fills the car, and me.

'If we drive up alongside him I can pick him out,' says Svenne Crowbar.

'Left, I said.'

The tone in Ma's voice sounds as if she were instructing servants. Something that is not foreign to her if the rumours are true. People say she was a vicar's daughter, seduced by the city's most brutal gangsters in the flower of her youth.

'In time. It is important to choose the opportune moment.'

Ma leans forward and slaps Svenne Crowbar on the shoulder. She turns to me.

'Four times they have tried to do me in, and four times they have failed. I have a whole left leg full of metal shards to prove it.' Her cigarette holder flutters slightly between her fingers as she continues. 'And it has cost them dearly every time.'

Nix takes his shaky left hand off the steering wheel and clenches it hard three times. It is unbearably warm in this smoky back seat. My shirt is sticking to the seat. My neck cricks as I stretch it out.

'My jacket and wallet are still at Herzog's.'

'We'll drive you back, soon.'

The car passes my street. I take a look.

Old man Ström is stacking sugar crates outside the junk shop. That blasted Captain Wång is standing at his cigar booth on the other side of the street, fanning himself with his gold-laced hat while entertaining a small crowd of kids outside the tobacco shop. He likes to amuse them with his shaky seaman's English and an occasional tale of thievery from the seven seas, but as far as I know he was never more than the captain of a local archipelago boat.

I also suspect that he is related to Hjalmar Wång, the young socialist who shot the wrong man in Kungsträdgården when the tsar was visiting, but he doesn't dare breathe a word about it. His anaemic, Bible-loving wife would hit the roof.

'Mr Kvist lives here on Roslagsgatan, right?'

Ma lets a thin plume of smoke escape from the corner of her mouth.

'A bit farther up, above Lundin's funeral parlour.'

'Enemy territory for us, home ground for you.'

'I suppose.'

Johannes Church strikes quarter past five. Herzog was kind enough to open for a fitting and now I am afraid he'll be closed.

'My shooter is still at the tailor's.'

'What are you going to do with that?'

'Have to kill someone.'

'Who?'

'Don't know.'

Ma chuckles.

'Kvist lives up to his reputation.'

I stifle a sigh. God knows what this damned bitch is talking about.

'Where are we going?'

'We'll be there soon.'

45

We turn right and follow Sveavägen up along the flower beds of Vanadislunden Park. The pansies are blooming like black eyes after a fight. Nix takes a left by the old emergency shelters. We pass the Getingen area with its shapeless conglomeration of scrapyards, abandoned workshops, warehouses and hovels. Ploman's boys usually dump their bodies here if they can't sink them in the waters of Brunnsviken. I have a shooting pain in my little finger stump at the thought.

Ma takes a brown glass jar out of her handbag.

It's so big that she can hardly get her fingers around it. There is a small spoon inside the lid. She scoops up a little white dust and presses one finger against her nostril. With a whistling sound she snorts the powder up the other nostril, picks up the gold-rimmed pince-nez that is hanging on a silk cord at her bust and places it on the tip of her nose, as if to close it. She pulls out a lace church handkerchief from the sleeve of her dress and dabs her Cupid's bow clean from the remnants that have clung to a few dark downy hairs.

Nix pulls up and parks outside the launderette. The sound of the engine dies, and at once we can hear the birdsong from the narrow garden that splits Ynglingagatan in two. A lone cyclist winds up the street, as you do when you have the whole road to yourself and happen to be in a good mood. He is dressed in work clothes and covered in a fine layer of sawdust. Both Svenne Crowbar and his brother pull their hats down to cover their faces. I instinctively sink down in my seat.

'Perhaps you know the people who work in the moving company up there?'

Ma points past the bonnet ornament to the stone steps at the far side of the garden and sniffs. They lead up to St Erik Park. Some little girls on the pavement below are chalking up a hopscotch. This is a secluded, protected area of the city, far from the centre, but the distant drone of Solnavägen is still audible. I suck in air through my teeth and nod.

'Ploman, Rickardsson and the Reaper.'

'As you know, they control Vasastan, and my boys and I control Östermalm, while Piggen and his crew have Söder, and Belzén of Birka takes care of Kungsholmen.'

'You get ten per cent of everything there.'

'Belzén and I have had a lucrative partnership for many years. Kvist is well informed.'

There is a shooting pain in my little finger stump again. It was the Söder thugs who took off the tip with a pair of pliers and a hammer when I conned them with a fixed fight many years ago. I have always suspected that it was all part of a bigger picture, seeing as it was immediately followed by the breakout of the biggest and most brutal bout of gang violence our nation has seen since the bloody Dacke War. Since that day I have always turned down the big dogs when they ask me to dance.

'Bastards.'

'Excuse me?'

'What?'

'Kvist is mumbling!'

'Didn't say a word.'

Ma shakes her head slightly, sniffs and continues.

'However, our markets have developed, and both Ploman and Piggen have strengthened their positions lately, at our expense. Schnapps might still be the lamp oil Swedes use to face the darkness, but there are other sustainable sources of income now. I am talking foremost about narcotic powders such as cocaine and morphine, and ether, gambling and Jews.'

She is shaking her jar. I take out my timepiece and look at it. The hands are completely still.

'By and large the German refugees arrive into the city on the goods train at Södra Station in the south. That makes them Piggen's and the Söder lads' concern. Ploman controls Karlberg of course, as well as Norra Station in the north, but he wouldn't touch them with a ten-foot pole. Why he turns down those revenues I don't know.'

Svenne Crowbar whistles for the third time in a matter of minutes and gestures towards the steps. Once again the car is filled with the clicking sound of a revolver.

'That was quick.'

Life and movement break out in the car. Ma opens a little hatch on the inside of her door and signals to me to do the same. I fumble around, find a knob and get it open. The latch consists of a centimetre-thick sheet of steel. I stick my hand inside and take out a pistol with Russian lettering and a star embossed on the butt. A Tokarev-30. I think.

'The body of the car is reinforced with fourteen hundred kilos of armour plating and can withstand most things, but keep away from the windows.'

They learnt their lesson when the Reaper rigged Pa's car with dynamite cartridges and blew the head of the family to hell. I slide farther down into my seat as my thumb gropes the pistol to find the safety catch. My nerves are begging for a smoke.

I peek out through the side window. On the bottom step, around thirty metres away, stand two blokes dressed in three-piece suits despite the heat. One, with round glasses on a potato nose, points at our car, and the other starts walking along the opposite fork of the road, partially hidden by the garden between us.

Virtually impossible shot.

'High time we moved. Can Kvisten lift his feet?'

I do as I'm told. Every limb is dripping wet with sweat. My breathing has become irregular. The car stinks of tobacco smoke, perfume and suspense.

There is a snapping sound as Svenne Crowbar bites off another fingernail. The kids by the stairs start playing hopscotch. One of them, with a plaid dress and thin pigtails, stops and stares.

Ma opens an oblong latch in the floor. She picks up a sub-machine gun with a walnut-coloured butt and a drum magazine.

'Ten shots per second.' Her red-painted lips part into a smile. 'In the end life comes down to a question of firepower.'

The Cadillac growls into life and Nix releases the clutch. Slow and controlled, he pulls out and crawls along Ynglingagatan, no faster than the cyclist who just passed us. There is a metallic sound as Ma covers her weapon, ready for battle.

A firecracker of a woman.

'This is a game Kvist has played before. Don't give them a whiff of hesitation. Else you will always lose.'

'Never taken a count.'

My words come out as a hoarse croak. I try to swallow. Maybe it's good that my cigars are at Herzog's. My throat is so dry that it would probably catch on fire if I lit one.

The man by the stairs follows us with his gaze and reaches his right hand into his jacket. The little girls' shoes clack against the pavement. The scent of fresh sawdust wafts from the timber yard farther down the street. The saw blades screech sharply even though it's Sunday. I am squeezing the pistol so hard that I can feel my pulse beating against the butt. A steam engine whistles from Norra Station.

The girl in the plaid dress starts her game. She hops: one, one, two, one, two, one.

The man by the stairs has dark eyes, spectacles and a waxed moustache. We slow down around the left turn. The bloke nods at us with a smirk. One end of his moustache points needle-sharp up to the cloudless sky.

The little girl turns around in the chalked circle at the top of the hopscotch and starts hopping back. Nix picks up speed, we pass the timber yard's howling saws and pick up more speed going south along Upplandsgatan. There isn't much traffic. I take a deep breath and manage to finally swallow the saliva in my bone-dry throat. In the front seat Nix lets out a high-pitched chuckle.

Ma turns her ample body completely around and rests the barrel of the machine gun on the back seat so that she can keep watch through the oval back window.

'Kvist looks a little pale. Would he like a pinch?' She nods to the glass jar between us on the seat, but I grunt 'No' and she continues, 'Now where was I?'

'Piggen likes himself some Jewish gold but Ploman wants nothing to do with them.'

I remember.

'That's right. However, Ploman got involved when the state monopolised gambling a couple of years ago and established the city's two biggest casinos. I refer, of course, to Hälsingegatan 3 and the one on Sätertäppan.'

Her voice is more shrill now and she is speaking faster. It's the powder. I have seen it before. She seems twenty years younger.

'Mm-hmm.'

We turn westward towards Vasa Church and drive along Odengatan, the very boundary between the different territories. The traffic is sparse and it is very quiet. Ma replaces her machine gun in the floor cavity and the steel clunks as I put my Tokarev back in the gap in the door. At once it feels easier to breathe.

'Like I was saying, both Piggen and Ploman have gradually advanced their positions in recent years, and now it seems something is going on. On several occasions Belzén's men have seen a small convoy of vehicles driving across Kungsholmen to Söder in the evening. The question is what these scum are doing there.'

'Why don't they drive through neutral Klara?'

'That, my dear sir, is the next question. And that's where you come in.'

'I have nothing to do with those types. Forget it!'

Ma straightens her gloves as Nix brakes to let a tram pass.

'I know Kvist's story, just like every other idiot in town, the cause célèbre that marked the end of your boxing career *und so weiter*. Look at this as a way to redeem yourself, so that the name Kvist is associated with something other than, well, you know what people say…'

Nix lets out another snigger. He sounds like a snotty little kid. I stare out of the window and resist the urge to curse. In the front seat Svenne Crowbar is going hard at his nails. Shame is throbbing in my blood. A feeling I know all too well.

I gnash my teeth until they hurt and clench my fists, then the words come spilling out of me, against my will.

'They won't let me forget so easily. Nobody looks me in the eye. People turn away in disgust.'

Next to us stands a horse cart. The skinny mare's head is drooping in the heat. We are so close that I can make out the greasy dust stuck in her mane. She wants to go to the slaughter. I can see it in her eyes.

'It's not disgust.'

'What?'

'Pure fear.'

Ma sniffs slightly.

'It's because of the darkness lurking behind those blue eyes. It warns of bloodshed for anyone and everyone who gets in your way. They are afraid. Mr Kvist is illuminated by violence, wherever he sits, walks or stands. It follows you like a shadow. That is why you walk alone. Not because of your weakness for men.'

The nag beside us chews desperately at her bit and the skin of her hindquarters twitches from flies.

'Though your little deviance certainly doesn't help your cause,' Ma adds.

The Vasa bells toll their final chimes. Nix chuckles again, loudly and shrilly, and sets the car into motion. A half whistle sounds through the horse driver's lips and he flicks the whip, sending the road dust flying from the draught animal's hot skin.

Odenplan is quiet and mainly empty in the heat. A shabby man with ulcerated pimples on his face runs out across the hot paving stones of the square. He is dragging something in an old feed bag. A couple of Italian girls are on the prowl with fortunes for sale but there are no customers here. It's the dog days and it bloody well seems like the local residents have rotted away in the heat.

When I stretch my neck I see Nix's face with those dark apertures under his monobrow. He is smirking with one corner of his mouth.

I screw up my eyes for a moment. Ma's words have struck a nerve somewhere inside me. Last autumn I could bask in joy and everything felt easy, but since then I have walked with heavy feet and an even heavier heart. Something happened to me, and I can find no peace; I bear my misery in a way no sensible man would. It is as though I am searching for something, but it's not the sort of civil investigation I am used to. Before, all my other feelings used to stay inert inside me. I preferred it that way.

The haunting eyes of a whole crowd of men rush through my head, scarred for life and so badly injured that they were probably never themselves again. A travelling watch-chain merchant I disfigured beyond recognition. A gouty old man, tangled up in an inheritance dispute, who I was so hard on that the bastard lost his mind. And a young man, up to his ears in debt, with his eyes on the outside of his head like a fucking pike fish. People said he got that way because he was the product of incest. Didn't make a difference to my visit.

We continue down Odengatan through the half-dead city in silence, as if Ma is letting her words sink in. A sturdy red-haired woman is smoking outside Standards corner. Elin Johansson, an old client and a real battleaxe of a woman. She has book smarts and street smarts, and is damned determined to get what she wants. I liked her a lot, and she liked me even more, but we ignore each other when we cross paths, out of fear of retaliation from those higher up, even though it was more than six months ago. She looks away and pretends she doesn't see me, just like everybody else. She could at least give me a little nod of acknowledgement.

I have no one except Lundin. I brush off my trousers with a swishing sound and clasp my hands together like an obliging little confirmation candidate but regret it immediately and crack my knuckles instead.

Nix turns right by Johnsson's Bazaar at the crossroads with my own street. Johnsson is limping around with a broom, hollow-eyed and messed up from beatings. Yet another fucker giving me a bad conscience. Ma's voice saves me from several more bad memories.

'It is getting harder to hire good crew. I blame the state of the economy. Most men have a job to go to. Meanwhile Kvist can move around freely among the different city districts in a way that none of the rest of us is in a position to do. I'm sure you can appreciate that we would be most interested in knowing what is being transported from Ploman's headquarters, via Kungsholmen, to Söder or vice versa.'

Phantom pains shoot through my non-existent little fingertip. I hold what remains of my finger up in the air.

'The last time I got involved with your lot it didn't go well.'

Ma laughs hoarsely.

'One day I will tell you the whole story about that finger of yours.'

I grunt and fumble in vain for a cigar in my sweaty breast pocket. Ma offers me a cigarette and I light it with a match. The soothing smoke: the caress. I cough.

We drive down Birger Jarlsgatan at high speed and pass Humlegården. I hope Herzog's is still open. I stare out through the side window. They are showing the heavyweight match between Max Schmeling and Joe Louis at the Sture Picture House. I should take the time to go and see it. Maybe take Hasse with me, the boy I have been training for six months, and see if the Brown Bomber can teach him a thing or two.

Ma clears her throat.

'It is an incredibly special feeling when one enters a room and everybody stops talking and sits up straight in their chairs. Respect. Yes, you remember what it's like.'

I grunt in response as we turn into Biblioteksgatan and drive towards the tailor's. Fuck knows if the rectory will be open, even though it's the Lord's day, now that one of his servants has gone and got murdered. I am struck by a wave of nausea at the memory and swallow back sour bile. I take a deep drag to get rid of the aftertaste and blow the smoke out the corner of my mouth.

Herzog's apprentice is outside nailing some wide planks across the broken window. His jaw muscles are working at least as hard as his right arm, and his muscles ripple under his skin. A uniformed policeman is still standing posted outside and sweating in the warmth of the evening.

I open the car door slightly.

'Thanks for the ride.'

'You know our place on Kommendörsgatan?'

'It's a couple of years since I was there.'

My fling with Doris Steiner, the film star, immediately flashes into my mind. That didn't end happily either.

'You are welcome to pay us a visit when you have made up your mind.'

'I work alone. I'm busy already.'

'Think it over. It's a question of redemption, for you and for us. We pay well and we don't believe the rumour that Kvist has become sentimental and weak with age. I would very much like to have you on my side. You know where we are. *À bientôt!*'

The door slams shut and the armoured tank of a car drives away. I am left standing on the pavement with anger gripping my heart. Talked down to by an old crone. Would never have happened before last autumn.

With my back to the tailor's I watch the sun devour more and more of the Cadillac's white lacquer before the car turns left onto Norrmalmstorg.

Ma's organisation must really be down on their luck if they are driving around town recruiting has-beens.

I take out the stopped watch. Hammer blows ring out between the house fronts. There is a slight breeze coming down from Nybroviken now. Above my head Herzog's sign screeches on its rusty hinge.

Sounds like a rail spike being pulled out of a priest's corpse.

*

55

Burning in the heat, I walk down towards Norrmalmstorg to take the tram home after visiting Herzog and getting my jacket back. The street is empty but for a youth with a turned-up nose standing and smoking outside the Café Chantant: as flaxen-haired as a little boy, his fringe shiny with oil, a cigarette hanging limply out of the corner of his mouth. He is shielding his face with his hand and leaning his right foot against the wall. When he sees me coming he walks quickly across the street, like the bloke outside Jensen's yesterday.

At least that's something.

I recall Ma's words in the car earlier. My thoughts stray to my twin brother who died of whooping cough when we were little. It infected him suddenly and without warning. Grandma read him the Word of God, threw holy fire out the door two Sundays in a row, massaged his chest with oil blessed by the village priest.

Nothing helped.

Would my brother have grown up to be a brawler like me if he had lived? The shopkeeper on Roslagsgatan talks about Jews and about how character is carried in the blood. Who the hell knows? Maybe my debaucher of a father was a hothead and it runs in the family. If the root is corrupted and something has grown crooked, you sure as hell can't straighten it out.

I turn my head and try to see myself in profile. I'll talk to Lundin about my musings when I come home. He claims to be able to recognise a criminal physiognomy from the shape of a person's head. Maybe it's in my blood and I was born this way.

I pat around my jacket in search of fresh cigars I had in an inside pocket. I locate one, put it in the corner of my mouth and carry on walking as I look for matches.

In Norrmalmstorg the criss-crossing tramlines shine green in the sun. It is practically deserted here too and a cooling breeze brings a little respite. Some men in city suits are brooding in the shade of a bus shelter. In the corner by the grandiose bank stands a youth giving out *Brand* magazine. Despite the heat he is staying true to the anarchist custom of dressing fully in black. Three raucous drunks are staggering around outside Svenska Lifs grey stone palace. It is nice to cool off. Fresh.

'Well, what do you know!' comes a voice behind me, croaky from schnapps. 'Isn't that that fucking sodomite?'

I stop in my tracks. I turn around.

'Damn, it is him!'

A wide grin cleaves the red face in two. His shirt and rigid cap are greasy and the sleeves of his jacket are frayed. He is breathing heavily, and his body is steaming from spirits and the heat.

I know him well. His name is Pålsson, a dirty flesh-pedlar with dozens of street whores working for him. I have stolen one or two from him throughout the years, on a job for the girls' parents or husbands, and he has never forgiven me. Now the bastard has drunk himself into arrogance. People might cross the street when they see me coming, or pretend to study something in a shop window, but it is still very rare that a bloke has the balls to shout straight in my face.

The vein in my head starts to throb violently. My heart begins to race. I smile. Does this fucker think that I am one of his wenches to beat at will? Does he think that I have grown weak with the years?

Behind the pimp, two men stagger into place and smirk. One is a big bloke with a matted beard and booze-induced acne in his sparse oily hair. Probably a lot more muscle than sense. The other is smaller, a pickpocket-type with glazed eyes, shining like those of a small predator in a cone of light. Three against one. The storm troopers of prostitution. I swallow.

It has been a long day.

I indulge myself.

My hand moves towards my shoulder holster, but no, a couple of bullets and death comes too quickly. Besides, my aim is significantly better with my fists. My neck cricks as I warm it up in a sideways stretch. I look around. Not many people.

First Detective Chief Inspector Berglund's mocking, then a youth nearly takes my head off with a brick, then Ma's taunts, and now this gang of tramps. Maybe I have truly lost it. One sign of weakness, and this mob will target it straight away. Maybe it's the heat and the lice, this stubborn sun that refuses to go down at night. Sleepless nights drive people to madness, make them lose all rhyme and reason.

Well, I'll show them. Now it's my turn. And I'm going to pulverise you into bird feed.

Pålsson takes a couple of steps forward. Barely a metre between us. The others don't follow. Perhaps a notch smarter than they look after all.

I bite the end off of my cigar. It is close now, so very close.

Come on then, you bastard.

Come to Kvisten.

The gentle wind caresses the sweat off my neck. Net curtains in the wide-open windows of the surrounding houses flutter like bridal veils. I take a deep breath and can almost feel my lungs fill up with fresh archipelago air. A blackbird is warbling somewhere. To the left of us a kitten meows pitifully.

My gaze wanders over the whoremonger's head, up to the ornate façade of Svenska Lifs, and locks onto the clock tower at the top. I think I hear the mechanism tense its muscles in preparation to slash away at another minute of our lives. The gears lock together, forcing time forward, and one moment later the iron hand points straight up into the cloudless sky. It feels as if the ground vibrates as all the clock towers in the city strike the hour, as clearly as the bell that rings in a new round. The vibrations run through me, making my veins ripple and the match in my hand quiver.

In the boxing ring time stops. Three-minute rounds become a tremulous vacuum, a void, a bit of fucking peace and quiet. I suck in air and bring the Meteor to my lips.

The grey smoke coils up and away as I puff the cigar into life. I peer at Pålsson from under the brim of my hat. He takes one more step towards me and enters my striking range. I widen my stance.

'Well? Did you hear what I said, you fucking poof?'

The words put a smile on my face. I never understand people giving me lip before a fight. Better to keep quiet than try to egg yourself on with a load of big words and swagger. Whoever gets the first punch in wins, nine times out of ten.

With another smirk I flick the burning match towards his face.

Finally.

Fire in the hole.

This bastard's head is going to jerk one way or the other. Whichever he chooses, my anger is going to flow through my arm and meet his jaw through my fist. Right or left, makes no difference. God knows how many virgins he has desecrated over the years. How many poor little girls like Evy Granér he has forced to sell themselves for a fiver and a smoke.

He goes left. A breath of gratitude rushes through my muscles. I have smashed up my right hand far too many times.

A good blow comes from the whole body. You feel its sting and precision long before the fist hits its target.

There is nothing more beautiful than violence's handiwork. Hasse, my boxing protégé, flashes through my mind. Pity he's not here to see this.

It is neither a hook nor an uppercut but a mixture of the two that comes up diagonally from below. This isn't your typical knockout blow that rattles the brain; my aim is to cause as much mess as possible. To break the jawbone and a few molars to boot. Tear the tongue apart with a little luck.

The concentrated force crashes into the pimp. His face shakes, his head bounces back and forth, a cascade of blood and bits of tooth shoot up into the summer evening. His hat spins away like a flying saucer. I grimace with pain. My bloody shoulder.

Still, bloody beautiful.

Pålsson falls heavily onto his back, raising a cloud of dust which then falls back over him like a fine dew. His legs fly up into the air before they thud back down. Both the other lowlifes back up a couple of steps but the rough-cut one stops and then advances again with wild steps. I take the cigar from my mouth and hold up my hand.

'Not ready yet.' The bloke freezes in place. Deep inside the red, sweaty face blink the eyes of a simpleton. 'Far from it,' I add, walking towards the pimp where he is lying on the ground, barely conscious.

By the time I'm done with this fucker, he'll spend the rest of his life in a wheelchair in a mental institution.

Standing here now, I finally feel like myself again.

An older man and a woman stand about forty metres away. He raises his cane and points. A tram pulls into a stop. No coppers in sight.

A couple of young ginger cats are play-fighting and tumbling around by a chestnut tree. They turn somersaults with each other, bounce up in the air, hold each other down and fall on their sides. If it weren't for Dixie I might have taken them home with me. She might be half-blind, deaf and lame but she would probably be able to smell them.

And she doesn't like cats.

Pålsson is lying there whining. I blow on the cigar, jam it in my mouth and straddle his chest. A bubble of blood oozes from his mouth, like the bubbles all these kids are blowing with chewing gum these days. His greasy, slippery hair slides between my fingers but eventually I get a good grip.

'Who are you calling weak, you fucker?'

I pull his head towards me and throw it back onto the rough paving stones as hard as I can. Something cracks. I wrench up his skull, put all my weight on it and drive it down again. Blood pours from the crushed point of contact. I am panting from the effort. Once more, but that's it. I know my job.

'Who are you calling weak?'

The pimp lies lifelessly below me. I cuff him on the ear. I want him awake.

'Weak as a fucking poof, was it?'

I can feel my age: my chest is heaving violently, my lungs hurt. I stare down at Pålsson's ugly but nevertheless inviting nose where it divides his face, full of black pores.

The first time I broke a grown man's nose it was winter.

Thinking of it makes me smile.

Light snowflakes were dancing in the air. I must have been ten, eleven years old. It was between the poorhouse and my years at sea.

It is a unique sensation.

I was working for a mill owner in Eskilstuna. It was the first time I hit back.

The boss beat me all the time. One day in February he walloped me on the backside after I had asked for a stove in my little room. I was undernourished and shivering cold in bed at night. Something inside me snapped. I went up into the barn where I knew there was a broken pitchfork.

I took the wooden shaft and the two-pronged end apart and climbed down again. I drove the bastard up against the wooden partition wall with the prongs and made the shaft whistle through the air with my strikes until he sank to his knees, bloody and wretched, and begged for mercy in the snowstorm. The down-trodden snow around us was coloured orange. One of the working dogs was howling. With my wood-soled poor man's boots I kicked the boss's dirty mug right in the nose. For the first time in my life I heard the magnificent sound of a nose breaking. There is no sweeter music than in that tremulous instant of contact when bone and cartilage yield.

The sound made the blood rush through my skinny little body and has ever since. When I ran away that time I felt like I was flying two centimetres above the ground, so cold, alive and happy. A couple of minutes later I had a rare sense of calm that I had never experienced before. Like coming home. Maybe it built some sort of home inside me.

Who the hell knows.

I raise my fist and drive it straight down into the ponce's kisser. It is a merciful angle, one intending to floor the bastard rather than slam the bone into his brain. The smack resounds between the buildings that line the square. I smirk. The sound reminds me of a foal chewing on a sugar lump. Sweet.

I have always liked foals. So bouncy on those skinny legs with their funny tails hopping behind. Muzzles softer than Japanese velvet.

Somewhere a woman screams. Pålsson's face looks like a bucket of slop. The type you buy from the butcher to feed your dog.

62

My breathing seizes up with effort. It's shit that I hardly have time to beat a man before I am reminded of my body's limitations. The blood that once made my flesh bloom seems to have curdled in my veins. I fold over coughing, phlegm strings quivering down into the red mess that was the pimp's face.

The big bloke takes one step forward but I shake my head.

'Still not ready.'

My voice is wheezing. I recover, clear my throat, take a last drag on my cigar and open Pålsson's right eyelid wide with my thumb and index finger. Red cracks criss-cross the white of his eye; his pupil is an empty black hole. Nobody home.

Let's see if I can wake the fucker up.

By making him half-blind.

Blood is running hot through my limbs after a whole day in the sun. Somewhere behind me comes the sound of tram wheels against the rail points and the driver ringing at the stop. I don't have much time before the passengers get off.

I blow on the glowing cigar tip and bring it closer to his eyeball. A shiver runs through my body but then I stop myself, hesitate. My hand is shaking. The burning orange is reflected in his iris.

I clear my throat, spit and stand up. I throw the cigar away, and stagger around openly in the square. The other two thugs shuffle over and start dragging the lifeless body away.

I look up. In a wide ring around us stand at least a score of witnesses. I can't quite believe it. One second it was deserted, the next second they all pour out, like the tide. A couple of them have their hands over their mouths; some of them are pretending to look away.

I lift my face to the sky and roar as loud as I can.

'Take that!'

MONDAY 20 JULY

The morning sun burns my face, hot as the flames in a ship's boiler. Hungover and thirsty, I am panting as I grasp the iron railing of the stone stairway. It took three days' rations of schnapps to get to sleep last night. I can't escape the image of Gabrielsson's body.

'Need sugar for the fight?'

Undertaker Lundin is hanging on my back, his unshaven chin scratching my neck and rasping in my ear. His breath is sour from his morning coffee with schnapps. We shared breakfast in his kitchen on the ground floor, as usual.

'Go to hell. You're just skin and bone and still heavy as grief.'

Lundin's skinny forearms are stretched around my neck and I can hear his prosthesis rattle. I look up again and survey the reservoir's brick fortress at the crest of Vanadislunden Park. I have already lugged Lundin halfway up the steps on Ingemarsgatan but there are still at least twenty metres to go. My back aches and I stoop under his weight. My thigh muscles are burning as I take one step, then another.

The trees above us reach for each other like seamen in distress. The harsh sunlight is filtered through the foliage. I am getting out of breath.

My trouser pockets are bulging with the contours of Pilsner bottles. A reward for my efforts. I find a rhythm, with Lundin's gammy feet knocking against the steps behind me like logs of wood.

'Soon you will be rid of me, brother.'

'Halfway up to the pearly gates already.'

I take another few steps. I feel the faint rhythm of Lundin's heartbeat against my aching back muscles. My own pump is working all the harder.

This morning I found him in bed in the little room at the back of the funeral parlour, covered in his own piss. I cleaned him up in the washtub and helped him into a fresh suit but he still smells faintly of old man urine.

It's not like before, when he was up early doing morning gymnastics with Colonel Owl on the radio every day. I don't know how old he is. Around seventy-five maybe. Never asked. We don't make a big deal of that kind of thing. You're born, you die, the rest is just numbers.

'What the hell are we going up to the park for?'

'Forgetful, aren't you. Hasse's lunchtime training.'

'The life is draining out of me, what do I care about boxing?'

With the undertaker hanging on my back like a black sack of coal, I heave myself onward with both hands on the railing. There is a rustle as a rat ploughs through the sea of brown grass on the hill. Its tail slides behind it like a mooring rope.

My rotten cough is lurking in my chest. I look up again. Only three flights to go. If I can deck 'The Mallet' Sundström in the last round despite five broken ribs, then surely I can manage this without whinging.

'The Spaniards are at loggerheads with each other.'

'The Spaniards?'

'Do you no longer have a radio, brother?'

'No fewer than two.'

'The southern provinces. Some sort of military uprising.'

I remember a sailor in Malaga a long time ago, with soft brown eyes and a fresh scar across the bridge of his nose. He might have

65

been called Jorge. He was young and strong, and kissed as if it meant something.

It didn't.

The eleven o'clock chimes of St Stefan's Church up in the park egg me on. I grunt and take two steps, then another two. I clench my jaw. Two more.

We wind to the left where the staircase divides and I lug the undertaker farther up the rugged slope behind the reservoir. I am huffing and puffing. The square brick monstrosity affords no shade.

As we approach the south side of the building, I dump the old codger on the grass and stand up straight. I bring my hand to the small of my back and look at him. His face is red with strain and there is a rubbery string of phlegm in his white moustache. He takes a deep breath that spreads through his rickety body before he laboriously rolls onto his back.

I lean my hands on my knees and catch my breath. I would have set Lundin down farther on in the park if I could. I once met with Hiccup, one of Belzén of Birka's henchmen, up here on this scorched, grassy flat. I believe it was the winter of '32.

Bad blood, bad memories.

The weather was different that time: sleet and wind. Hiccup drove to meet me with a couple of battered smugglers in the trunk of his Ford. One was a Söder lad and the other worked for Ploman, the schnapps baron of Vasastan. Their heads were wrapped in bloodstained jute bags, which made them considerably less talkative. Hiccup put three bullets in each, two in the back and one in the head. I remember the sound: the howling in my ears. The shots were louder than usual. Probably due to the rain.

As I understand it, what happened was my fault, but it was bound to have happened to them sooner or later anyway. They deserved it, unlike Gabrielsson. I can't carry the undertaker any longer. Not one metre more.

I look up, squint and shade my eyes with my hand. From up here it looks as though the whole of Vasastan is in flames. The morning sun attacks the rooftops, the flashing rays weave a disorderly pattern, reflected in windowpanes, sheet metal and copper. The poor sods living in the garrets must be boiling alive.

The paths meander like plough lines and the grass is brown from drought. Low groundwater levels have brought about a watering ban for some weeks now. A stray dog with a lolling tongue works its way between the groups of people in search of food and water. The dust whirls around its paws as it trots along.

With its tail between its legs, it circles a group of reclining men playing cards, nearby enough for me to hear their throaty voices. They look like day labourers without a gig. The greasy cards dazzle like mirrors in the sun as they toss them in the pile.

'Whose turn is it?'

'I'm out.'

'Get that fucking dog out of here.'

One of the men picks up an empty beer bottle and throws it. It whistles towards the mutt's head before hitting the ground a couple of metres shy and bouncing a few times. The dog backs up and whimpers before setting off after two tramps who look like they've spent the night in the park. Their rags are full of dry grass and one has twigs and leaves in his beard.

Down by the stone façade of St Stefan's Church, a few make-believe Indians skulk around the bushes. They are dressed up in burlap costumes and carved bows are taut over their backs. A working-class housewife flaps a sheet in the air once more than necessary, so that the other couple of biddies nearby can see how white it is before she spreads it out on the ground. She starts to unpack a picnic from a woven basket.

I take the Pilsner bottles out of my pockets and crouch down next to Lundin. I open the beers and set one of the bottles down next to him. The undertaker tries to pinch out a hefty wad of snuff from his brass box, using his good hand. I take a swig. The beer is lukewarm but it's liquid and it tastes good.

'Have you heard what the Yanks do on hot nights?' I ask.

'You've been talking about America for a dozen years and never done anything about it.'

'What the hell does that have to do with anything?'

'Like some old dear who's been reading too many Californian novels.'

'They take their mattresses outside onto the fire escape platforms.'

'What do you know about it?'

'I was a sandwich man in San Francisco once, for God's sake.'

The mutt lopes to and fro in a cloud of dust. The street dogs are dying of thirst, or they eventually drink sewage, get sick and die. If you're up early you see their paws sticking up out of the tops of rubbish bins. Tomorrow the city is going to start paying compassion bounties to the huntsmen who shorten their suffering. I clear my throat and spit out a clod of dust.

'There's something funny about it.'

'Hush now!'

Lundin raises his iron hand and almost loses his balance as a result. I put the bottle down on the grass and take out a Meteor.

'Something that doesn't add up.'

I spit out tobacco flakes.

'When was the last time anything added up to you?' Lundin asks.

'There's nothing wrong with your mouth, at least.'

'You've been going on about the same thing for hours. Forget it.'

Lundin puts a wad of snuff in his gum and tongues it into place. I light my cigar and take a puff, producing a cloud of tobacco smoke.

'There's something funny about it.'

'What does it concern you? I have seen you like this before, brother. What did it get you but grief, misery and new scars?'

'Dixie?'

He shakes his head.

'A half-dead drunkard of a dog. What does this have to do with you?'

Down the hill the church strikes the quarter-hour. The mongrel comes running towards us and then slows its steps. It's an emaciated bitch with hanging teats. A fresh wound runs across her ear. Her eyes shine like syrup drops in the sunlight. I show her that I have nothing in my hand.

I glance at the undertaker. His yellow, wrinkled skin is stretched like a dried tobacco leaf across his face. My hand begins to tremble slightly. The bitch patters to and fro in front of us.

I take two deep drags. I tap off the ash and take another. I clench my left fist.

'Something happened to me every time I returned to land.'

I stare straight ahead. My words falter and I quieten. My heart is thumping like a punchball in my chest. The bitch slouches away in the direction of the old emergency shelters.

'What are you prattling on about, brother?'

I take a swig of beer. The words return.

'I was one sort of man at sea and another on land. Something happened when I got shore leave.'

'Drunkenness and pox?'

'At sea I was one of the crew, almost. But on land people would stare at me like a scab. It grated on me. Inside somehow.'

'Like heartburn?'

'Can't explain it.'

'And you've always had the gift of the gab. Is the boxer lad late?'

'When I met Gabrielsson in Buenos Aires I was so full of self-hatred I was about ready to hang myself but he took my confession without blinking. It must have been twenty years ago. Or more.'

Lundin starts to hum.

'You did say eleven o'clock?'

'He said that Jesus Christ didn't fit into his time and place either, or something along those lines. Not that I need any consolation from the fucking Bible, but it struck a chord with me.'

A little way down the hill the bitch takes a few wavering steps before collapsing on her side. She is lying there with her tongue out, panting. I take a deep breath. The smell of camomile is hanging heavy in the warm air; it cuts through the cigar smoke.

'You did tell him eleven, right?'

The kids dressed as Indians have laid siege to the white music pavilion below us. I roll the cigar between my thumb and forefinger.

'It has always been eleven.'

I glance at Lundin. The undertaker nods to himself and takes a swig of beer. He extends his iron prosthesis and claps me on the shoulder with a clinking sound. In the scorched clover between his useless legs a bumblebee drones its thirsty song.

My singlet is soaked through. Hasse's wrapped fists jab into my palms with dull, rhythmical thuds, like a barn dance. Every time he makes contact a fine mist of sweat flies from his naked skin and covers his upper body in a glistening dew.

We have been going at it for over an hour and a half. I shout commands and angle my hands for hooks, uppercuts and straight punches. I go backwards, then sideways, and try to make him follow. His right fist cracks against my left palm. He is tired. The power of a right should come from all the way down through the foot. I am tired too but what the hell does that have to do with boxing? I bite my lip to stop myself correcting him.

'Good. Again!' I say instead.

I take a half-step to the side. I have tortured him for over six months, sweated with him, invested my own time and energy. When I manage to get the bastard to listen, he becomes an extension of myself. He has good hooks, fast and hard. My wrists ache, even though he is going at a quarter of his maximum strength.

Sometimes I touch him, to show him an opening, and I feel the sleek warmth of him on my coarse hands and it makes me gasp.

He isn't that way inclined. Few are. I can tell.

'Come on!'

I suck my lower lip in between my teeth. That broad chin could become a problem if the boy doesn't learn to hide it behind his shoulder. He grits his teeth and determination surges through his muscles, forcing them to obey.

His fist meets its target with a smack. Willpower glitters in his eyes and his sharp jaw muscles protrude under his skin. His wide trousers flap as he turns his heel outwards.

That's my boy, give me hell. Go as hard as the Devil himself.

The power runs up his legs, gains momentum at his hips and reaches his naked upper body. It spreads through his oblique abdominal muscles as he turns and puts his shoulder into the movement. His hefty arm and tight fist shoot out from his body.

That's right.

Redeem me.

Hurt me.

My left palm meets his right. He snorts air out through his nose and thunders into me. Drops of sweat fly from his skin. The sunlight makes them glitter around his head like a halo.

This is the one. He doesn't put all of his weight behind it, but still the blow diffuses through my arm and causes my shoulder joint to burn with pain.

'Good!'

I take half a step forward with my left foot and drag my right behind like a slow foxtrot. I am standing up close to him now, with my front leg nearly between his. His staccato breathing pulses against my chest, and I gasp as the acrid smell of sweat penetrates my nostrils. He doesn't notice.

'Uppercuts, let the devils roll.'

One-two, one-two, one-two. My wrists are screaming with pain.

I clinch him and for one moment I feel every contour of his young, muscular body. I twist the youth half a turn starboard and push him away. I am struck by the screaming impulse to smash into him again and again, but I resist. Beauty makes me react that way sometimes. Nothing new.

He is angry now and comes straight back at me.

Poor as a louse, but with a will of stone. It is rare that I meet his gaze but now I can see my own face flicker in his irises. They are blazing like blue welding flames.

I clench my fists too, and stick out my elbows to either receive his blows or deflect them with the inside of my right. I take two sidesteps and make him rip a couple of big holes in the air.

'Why waste the right when the jab didn't find home?'

He chases after me. I counter his right with a left hook, open my fist just before the target and let my palm caress the sweat on his broad chin.

'Hide it behind your shoulder if you don't want a kiss on it, boy. If you hadn't been standing with your feet together, you could have rolled under that without a problem.'

I slap my forehead with my palm and let his sweat mix with mine before flicking it on the ground.

He comes at me again: strong, stubborn as sin, too tired to think straight. My back cracks as I roll away from his fists. I grimace. He tries to break straight through my guard instead of finding the right angles.

'Stop!'

Hasse's arms wither and hang loosely along his sides; he leans his head backwards and staggers on weak legs.

'Finished?'

He is breathing so hard he barely gets the question out.

'Like hell. Round. Do you hear me?'

I gasp for air and fight to keep my voice somewhat steady. I spit phlegm between my feet.

'When will we be done?' the boy groans.

'Hold your arms above your head. Are you listening?'

He nods. Sweat trickles between his bare pectorals, ripples like a wave over the flesh of his stomach and gathers in his navel before being absorbed by the line of hair running up from the waistband of his trousers. I swallow hard.

Behind us I hear Lundin tut.

'Bloody youths, lording it about with their fists, taking them for granted.'

Neither Hasse nor I look in his direction. The old man often joins our training sessions and functions as a sort of commentator.

'We will all be forged out of iron and steel in the future,' he says, rattling his prosthesis. 'Science will turn us into intricate

73

mechanical engines. Then what will become of you and your damned boxing?'

Lundin's grumpy voice is devoured by the silence between me and the boy. I stare down the hill. I feel a pang in my heart every time I have to berate my protégé.

'If you would just learn how to predict your opponent's strikes, it would be so much fucking simpler.'

'Kvist always says that. I don't understand how he does it.'

'With time and patience!'

The youth grimaces, his hands are shaking in front of his face as though cramped and the whites of his eyes are red from the sting of sweat. My own trainer's words ring out from the past.

'There are only so many possible strikes in any given situation. How did I just counter your right?'

He drops his guard somewhat. I bite the end off a fresh Meteor and light it.

'Left... left hook?'

'So you roll under the fucker and hit a hard right.'

I put the cigar in my mouth, hold my fists up again and swipe the odd left above his head. His feet are in the wrong position and he is curtsying like an old widow at her husband's coffin but I spare him the lecture. He has to be allowed to shine a little in the final moments of practice.

'Left, right, duck, right. Good! Very good! Again!'

St Stefan's Church strikes one. I see Hasse's bloodshot eyes light up.

'You were twenty minutes late.'

His chin sinks to his chest. His arms are shaking. I decide to finish off with parries.

'Left, right, left hook.'

The last strike blasts into my hand. My forearm is pushed back at an unnatural angle before rebounding.

'You have power in your fists. Use that force on Thursday and you'll hit your opponent halfway into the dressing room.'

'Are we done?'

'Not yet. Same series fifteen times and then you're carrying Lundin home on your back. The old sod needs shaving and feeding.' For the first time after a two-hour respite, Gabrielsson's body flashes before my eyes again. I raise my fists again. 'And then you and Dixie are coming with me to the Katarina rectory. With any luck you'll get to see how to beat a man like a dusty rug.'

A tall man with large sweat patches under his armpits is pasting red 'No Entry' signs with skulls on them up on the rectory door. The housemaid is next to him. I don't remember her name. She has brazenly unbuttoned the top two buttons of her bodice and is rubbing her hands together.

'It's these muggy nights what draws them out in droves. I find big cakes of them behind the paintings.'

'Both our Zyklon facilities are working day and night. We are fumigating a good fifty homes daily.'

The man moistens his lips with his tongue and produces yet another notice to emphasise the deadly danger of visiting the rectory.

'But we can't get rid of them! They just keep coming back.'

'We are in the process of trialling a heat treatment but for the moment this is our best weapon in the war against the vermin.'

I take a puff on my cigar and shield my eyes with my hands.

'Isn't the rectory considered a crime scene? Are the police finished with their investigations?'

The smug bloke and the housemaid turn to me. She shrugs her shoulders. He pokes his tongue out again and contorts his sweaty face into a grimace.

'And who in the hell are you?'

I clench my fists and squint at the supervisor. One decent right at the opportune moment and the bastard would bite his tongue clean in half. I smile. I widen my stance by a couple of centimetres.

'I was a good friend of Gabrielsson. Who ordered the fumigation?'

'The city takes care of its inhabitants.'

'What the fuck is that supposed to mean?'

His tongue pokes out like a bloody moray eel. My mouth is full of saliva.

Hefty bloke.

I peer over my shoulder to see where Hasse is. He is crouching next to Dixie, red in the face and having trouble breathing in the heat. I told him to be quiet because of the splitting headache that has been harassing me for the past half-hour. It's happening more often. Hope nothing is broken in there. Life plays pranks on a bloke sometimes but that would be too bloody unfair.

'The inspector heard about our problem when he was here and was kind enough to see to it that we got another fumigation,' says the housemaid. 'This is our second in a short time.'

Her eyes dart from side to side before she looks down at her black patent-leather shoes.

'Berglund?' I ask.

'A very considerate gentleman.'

The image of the Detective Chief Inspector's grinning face flashes into my splitting skull. It doesn't help. The last time he brought me in for interrogation was November. He left me to stew with two screws in some sort of meeting room. I remember staring at the table while I waited for him to arrive. Some of Berglund's belongings were laid out on it. I can't recall what they were but it feels important that I remember.

I pinch the bridge of my nose between my thumb and fore-finger and scrunch my eyes closed.

A gas token… a few coins… maybe a bunch of keys? Damn it! This heat has given me memory loss.

When I open my eyes I see a police car creep up the road. Maybe it's the Detective Chief Inspector on a return visit. I nod a quick goodbye, turn my back to the Volvo and signal to Hasse to follow me. I dry my sweaty hat band with my handkerchief. Dixie's tongue is flapping like a rag and she is panting vigorously.

'I think I remember there being a pump in God's garden,' I say, pointing.

A handwritten notice on the door announces that the church is closed. My eyes wander over the brown, scorched lawn and gravestones. I hear the faint hum of an engine on Katarinavägen, a bird warbling somewhere. The dead are silent in their graves.

The old pump handle squeaks, slicing through my ear drums, then a couple of mouthfuls of rust-coloured water cough out into Hasse's cupped hands. Dixie laps it up loudly.

'Maybe Kvisten should talk to the caretaker?'

Hasse gestures with a nod of his broad chin. Farther down towards Tjärhovsgatan a stooped old man is walking along with a weeding fork.

'What the hell is that fossil supposed to know about it?'

'Worth a try?'

'Didn't I tell you to be quiet?'

'Where are we going now?'

77

I light a fresh cigar from the old one, take off my hat and use it to fan my face. I signal to the lad to pick up Dixie. I stroll down the slope with both in tow. Might be worth a try.

The old man is dressed in a grubby linen shirt. His face is sunburnt and flakes of skin are dotted beneath his eyes like white salt deposits. He gently chews a plug of tobacco and spits brown-tinged gob on the scorched grass at regular intervals.

'The only moisture it gets. And they say Women's Week is supposed to be rainy.'

He stamps his spit with his worn shoes as if to press the water into the earth. Dust flies around his feet. I wedge the cigar in my mouth, find my wallet and remove the elasticated strap.

'They're fumigating the rectory now.'

'Lice and fleas should be left in peace. They suck poison out of the body and keep you healthy.'

'Speaking of casualties…'

I leaf through the receipts and find a fiver.

'I wondered if you might consider talking to me.'

The old man squints at us.

'I was the one who raised the alarm.'

I look up again and raise my eyebrows. It doesn't take long for my aching brain to snap into action despite the heat. The strap closes back around the leather wallet with a snap.

'An inquiry of this magnitude takes time.' I wet the nib of my aniline pen with my tongue and turn to an empty page in my notebook instead. The caretaker stares at Hasse. I cough. 'This bloke's here to carry the dog. It was her birthday yesterday. So you were the one who found Gabrielsson?'

The caretaker gives Hasse another look but then turns to me.

'When I came to work. The rector had fixed habits. He was up with the rooster and balanced it out with a nap before supper.'

'I'm not sure I understand.'

'What?'

'Who is the Rooster?'

'Excuse me?'

'Who is this person you call Rooster?'

'It's just what people say. Because they crow at dawn.'

'Surely you don't keep fowl in the rectory, for God's sake?'

I look at the caretaker. He shifts his weight. He's hiding something. Maybe I'll have no choice but to beat it out of him with one of his own damn chickens.

'I would never… I didn't know it was a crime.'

'When did you find the rector?'

'Soon after eight.'

'Then what did you do?'

'Ran to the rectory as fast as my legs could carry me.'

'Who was there?'

'Only Karin.'

'The housemaid? And did you see anyone else? Anyone who might have seen anything?'

'Who lays their hand on a man of God that way?'

The old man sniffs. I look up from my notebook.

'Sometimes people can't help it.'

'What do you mean?'

'Too drunk, fists too quick, it happens.'

'What are you talking about, Inspector?'

'Forget it. Well? No glimpse of someone else who might have seen something?'

'No one. But that afternoon I found the holes and the earth.'

'Blimey, what a discovery.'

'I reckon it's the Bumpkin.'

'Is that a saying too?'

'Everyone here in Söder knows the Bumpkin. The fisherman! Haven't you heard? His son was the first to throw himself from Väster Bridge.'

'Enlighten me.'

The caretaker wipes the sweat from his face with his shirtsleeve and continues.

'Last year, soon after it opened. Split in two when he hit the water, so they say.'

Memories of the inauguration of Väster Bridge make me shudder.

'Enlighten me about the Bumpkin and the holes and the earth. What does this all mean?'

'He started showing up last spring. Said that maggots make the best bait. I shooed him away of course, but lately holes have started showing up here and there in the cemetery.'

I look around. The gold lettering on the gravestones glimmers in the sun.

'I think he sneaks around and digs before I can catch him,' he goes on.

My fingers pinch hard on the pages of the notebook in my hands.

'And you found new holes on the same day as you found Gabrielsson?'

'Correct.'

'A fisherman did you say? Where might I find him?'

'Oh, he won't have any fixed address. He doesn't have much of anything. But he does have a brother who has put up a shooting range tent over by the Rosenlund shelters.'

MONDAY 20 JULY

Five minutes later I am sitting in the shade of a willow tree in Björn's Garden Park with my back to the new milk bar. A duck is quacking its way down the stone steps leading to the park with a gaggle of half-grown ducklings tumbling after. The paddling pool is full of naked little kids and toy boats with white sails. The whippersnappers splash through the syrupy water, the sun is at its zenith, and drops of water glitter on their skin like mother-of-pearl in the bright light. If this pool had been here before I would have brought my Ida. Let the little tyke splash around and get clean in one go.

The trees portion out sun and shade across the park. Stooped workers are gathered in one shady corner, bent under the weight of poverty, as if their hammers and shovels were still pulling their shoulders down.

A man stands beside them. He is dressed entirely in black despite the heat but has a white panama hat on his head. He is squinting at me with small eyes either side of a potato nose. As soon as I make eye contact he looks away and gives up his place in the shade.

Hasse is sitting on the bottom step with his feet in the water. I share a couple of hot dogs with Dixie. Her pleading eyes shine out from under her long fringe. I give her another bite and scratch behind her ear. She needs a haircut.

'The Bumpkin with the maggots.'

I mumble out loud to myself as I watch Blind-Pyttan the street singer walking along with a little girl as escort. The Bumpkin's brother's shooting gallery isn't too far away, and with a little luck I should be able to get hold of the fisherman before evening. Fishermen are creatures of habit, each with their own favourite spot along the shores and harbours. If I can get the brother to talk there shouldn't be any problem.

I am close now; I am getting the scent. Soon Gabrielsson's murderer will lie at my feet and I will be blowing smoke from the barrel of my Husqvarna. It's important to stay stylish, even when the job in hand is cold-blooded murder.

Something flutters inside me. God knows what.

The girl leads Blind-Pyttan into the park and situates her under one of the pear trees on the other side of the pool. The singer is wearing dark glasses and a large sun hat with a drooping brim. The summer revellers sitting on the benches across from me go quiet and twist their bodies to face her. Parents hush their children and the noise subsides, for everyone in Söder knows that Blind-Pyttan's God-given voice can melt even the coldest man's heart and bring women to tears.

The street singer begins and her clear voice shimmers out into the greenery. It is quite an old song that I recall from my childhood but I don't remember the name.

I could hold a tune as a child, before cigars, coal dust and schnapps robbed me of my voice. I don't remember it personally but people told me that my singing was so beautiful it broke my grandma's heart.

After the death of my twin brother she became decrepit and developed cancer in every limb, but continued clinging on to life for some reason. Nobody understood why she chose to remain a burden. I was dressed in a little waistcoat and driven out of the poorhouse where I had stayed for the past six months. They put me at the edge of her bed and I sang 'Children of the Heavenly Father'.

She smiled and died. Everyone praised me for my efforts and I got a butterscotch in payment. They said I should become a musician.

Well, that sure as hell didn't happen.

And after that I had no one to call family.

I open a porter, take a swig, pour some into a cupped hand and hold it out to Dixie. Her rough tongue tickles my palm.

'In honour of your big day. Belatedly.'

I pour some more while watching a newspaper vendor. The youth, twenty-something, works his way through the throng of people to the short side of the pool. His hair is in a well-combed wave across his forehead and he has strong shoulders and arms. He passes another lad who is lazily practising blowing smoke rings, then walks past some kids in sailor uniforms before he nods at a bloke who is holding up his hand. I smack my lips, shake the last drops of beer from my sticky hand and take a swig from the bottle. Dixie whines for more.

Blind-Pyttan raises her voice during the final verse and the very willows seem to hold their breath. Her words flow clear and clean into the cloudless sky:

> See now how the grass full-grown,
> Is cut and turned for haymaking.
> The flower begs not to be mown;
> Now is the end of her short spring.
> See the mighty stalks a-falling
> When the reaper's scythe doth swing,
> But soon an angel comes a-calling
> To rake them up and bring them in.

A lump of unease forms in my throat and I struggle to swallow it down. This song makes me think of Rickardsson, Ploman and the Reaper. I feel a shooting pain in my little finger stump. The lukewarm beer runs down my throat. Applause sweeps across the park and Pyttan's young assistant starts going around with a hat.

With the song over, the paper boy comes closer and starts his announcements.

'Spanish bloodbath continues! Read the latest! Police release statement about priest's murder! Only in *Svenska Dagbladet*!'

Shaking off my fears, I blow out the match, which releases a fine stream of smoke, then I puff the cigar alight and whistle at the youth. He hurries towards me with swift steps. I look him over, pausing at his crotch and chest before meeting his cheery gaze. He has undone a couple of shirt buttons and I catch a glimpse of a suntanned, hairless chest underneath, no doubt as smooth as Pellerin's margarine. I pull my lip with the knuckle of my forefinger, get out a fifty-öre coin and let him keep the change. He toddles on. I watch him go.

'That boy, Dixie. On his knees with his mouth hot and wide open like the gates of hell.'

The bitch flinches when I pat her on the head. I moisten my thumb, flick quickly through the paper, skip the upcoming Berlin Olympics and the ongoing war in Spain until I find the police bulletin in the national news pages. Sure enough, Berglund and the police have found a witness and issued a statement:

> Man, circa 25–45, average to strong build, possibly tall, possibly blue-eyed, with prominent nose, brown-black hair and wearing a dark suit.

'Could have been me,' I say to Dixie, lifting her up and scratching her neck. 'Maybe I should get myself an alibi.' She stretches her neck and nips at my hand. She is probably tipsy. I whistle at Hasse and gesture over to Götgatan.

Just as I'm about to leave, a little girl comes up to me: light-blue dress, white-striped apron, frayed satin ribbons in her golden-brown hair.

'Can I stroke the dog?'

'She's a bit poorly from too much booze.'

'You can have this, uncle.'

In her little hand she is holding a dandelion head. Her nails are dirty. She smiles to reveal dimples and no front teeth. I look around. Five metres away stands a middle-aged woman. The sun glints in her spectacles as she nods at me.

'Oh?'

I take the dandelion. What the hell am I supposed to do with it?

'Blow!'

I clear my throat and do as I am told. The spores spread on the wind. The girl squeals in delight and runs up and down, trying to catch them with outstretched hands. Most stick in her hair. I stand there holding the stalk in my hand awhile before I stick it in my trouser pocket.

'What did uncle wish for?'

'Didn't know I was supposed to.'

'Do it now!'

I think about it a moment.

'I wish I could see you grow up,' I mumble.

The little girl throws back her head and bubbles with laughter, her freshly washed hair shining in the sun, before running back to the woman. I tip my hat to the latter, lumber back to Hasse and give Dixie a stroke. As we wander down towards Södra Bantorget, my wish burns in my trouser pocket.

Götgatan's pavements don't afford much shade, but the porter has chased my headache away and we stroll south at a rapid pace. A shooting gallery, they said. The Bumpkin's brother. Somewhere near the emergency shelters. Please God, don't let it be too far. My shirt is soaked through and I am short of breath.

'It's hot.'

Hasse trots alongside me with nimble steps, smiles and rolls his eyes.

'It's damn hot.'

'National assembly! Three o'clock.'

A small group of shouting Germanophiles are showing off their uniforms and waving flyers a little farther down the street. The smell of the malt house permeates the air. A couple of drops of sweat break loose from my forehead, run around my eyebrows and find open channels in my scars. I blink them away, push back my hat and turn right onto Åsögatan.

'Most of them keep to Strömmen.'

'This city is full of fishing spots, damn it. The bastard could be anywhere.'

'That's where we should go if the brother isn't at the shooting gallery. Nearly everybody hangs around there.'

'Not far till the shelters now.'

Now I find myself hoping the bloke is stubborn so I can rough him up in good conscience. I promised the boy a lesson and if he doesn't get one I've brought him along for no reason.

I glance over my shoulder but the street behind us is dead and deserted. We pass the old nursery school and puff our way up the slope. The road dust swirls around our shoes. The boy can shine them again this afternoon.

Outside the People's House it's buzzing like a beehive. Söder lads in ill-fitting suits run in and out. Someone is hauling a bundle of poles for flags and banners. Gilded buttons sparkle with brilliance in the sunlight. Another man is wearing a snare drum and a third is flapping his arms in the air as if trying to direct the others. A Communist march. It smacks of trouble.

I glance over my shoulder.

The buildings thin out. The little hovels along the street are depressed into their stone foundations, sunken in poverty. Dark sweat patches of wooden wallboards seep through the flaking paint. I stop by one of the mirror-like windows, bend down and straighten my tie. Not a soul behind us but the Communists.

In my unscrupulous piece-of-shit job I have shadowed hundreds of people and at times I have been hounded by plain-clothed goons in bowler hats. One gets a sneaking feeling that lies in wait like a reptile but crawls out when the time is right. Since our lunch break in Björn's Garden I have had the vague impression of being watched. I straighten up and continue.

Under Hasse's arm Dixie soon starts sniffing the scents in the air. The stench of rotting refuse becomes stronger. We are approaching Södermalm's central rubbish dump.

We follow the stink and soon hear the dump's horses neighing in their stable. I scan the open areas, from the orphanage and Rosenlund's old-age home to the homeless shelters. Fashionable area. All that's missing is a paupers' cemetery.

My shoulders shudder involuntarily at the thought of the orphanage. Those ragamuffins could have been me. I could have been them. How randomly one's lot in life is apportioned.

Nobody can control their poverty, nor their wealth. Pensive, I spit out a clod of dust and wipe my lips with the back of my hand.

From a tent of grey awning fabric next to the yellow-painted, two-storey shelters, angry voices can be heard, but it is impossible to distinguish what is being said. Finding no shade, I ask Hasse to tie Dixie to a lamp post. She's scared of loud noises so she wouldn't like visiting a shooting range, and if all goes to plan this won't take long.

I kneel down, undo my tie, roll it up in my pocket and pat the bitch on the head. Her tongue is flapping like a ship's flag. I crack my knuckles.

'This will be quick.'

I walk towards the tent with Hasse in tow.

'Keep an eye on the position of your feet, for God's sake. If you're taller than your opponent you need your right foot outside his. Think about timing and striking angle.'

'I should stay with Dixie. She doesn't do well in the heat.'

'Pay attention, damn it!'

'Timing and angle.'

'If you don't learn to listen you won't learn anything.'

'My girl is coming to watch the match.'

'All the more reason to win.'

Hasse falls back a few steps, I grunt and continue towards the grey tent. As we approach the opening we hear a voice.

'Aspengren is fucking drunk. He couldn't hit a barn wall.'

The tent is divided by a counter consisting of three planks on top of two standing oil drums. Someone has tacked blue fabric around the counter and put a zinc can of fresh flowers and twigs on the left-hand side. Another plank along the back of the tent holds a parade of preserve jars and empty glasses. The proprietor is standing behind the counter. He is a small man dressed in a shirt and waistcoat, with sunburn on his bald head. He is holding a small-bore rifle in his hands. The miserly fucker has sanded down the sight to make it harder to aim.

'I once hit a coin at fifty paces.'

Aspengren's booming slurs well up from the depths of his immense body. A large sweat patch has spread across the back of his shirt. His trousers are dirty and it looks like he has spent the night on a demolition site. He lurches first to the left and then to the right and holds out his arms to find his balance. I walk up to the counter.

'Do you have a brother?' I ask the owner.

'The other day, Aspengren shot on credit for a Pilsner without hitting a thing, and that was when he was sober.'

'The hell I was.'

The proprietor's fingers whiten around the gun; I drop my cigar to the ground and crush it. Birds are trilling somewhere; in the distance a locomotive roars. Perhaps it's another freight train coming into Södra Station with one of Piggen's lucrative loads of Jews. I rap my knuckles hard against the counter three times.

'Stop your damn bickering and listen up! Do you have a brother? One that they call the Bumpkin?'

'Get to the back of the queue.'

Aspengren smacks me hard on the shoulder with a loud thump. The vein in my forehead starts to throb at once, and I check to see if Hasse is watching. I come closer, widen my stance and draw back my right shoulder. The man smells like a spittoon in an alehouse. I could knock the fucker into next week without so much as taking off my waistcoat.

'What was that?' I lower my voice.

'I... was here... first!'

I have a job to do. I have an excuse. I smile.

Aspengren pokes me three times in the chest with his index finger to emphasise his words. A cloud of booze stench washes over me as he speaks. His red-flushed cheeks are shiny with sweat. For a moment all that can be heard is the sleepy drone of insects. The smell of the mustard leaves and wild roses in the can fills the sun-warmed tent. A pale-yellow butterfly rises from the bouquet and strays momentarily between my face and Aspengren's unyielding gaze. He's got balls, I'll give him that. I lower my chin to my chest.

'Do *you* have a brother?'

I bend my knees slightly.

'Like hell. I have three unmarried sisters and…'

My right hook hits him straight in the chin with a dull thud. Pain vibrates up through my fist and bounces back from my elbow; elation shoots into my blood.

A right deck from a trained fighter is like a mule's kick. The bloke's eyes roll back in his head. Time for bed.

I step aside as he falls diagonally forward. His forehead bounces on the counter, making the can jump, and he lands on his side, throwing up a cloud of dust. I shake the pain out of my hand and pull my lips open into a smile. It has been weeks since I delivered a blow like that with such a short striking range. I can't tell whether Hasse is impressed or horrified. He is standing completely still with eyes wide open.

'Look.' I turn to the man behind the counter, bite the end off a cigar and point a foot at the man on the floor. 'See what I did to this bloke, and he doesn't even have a brother.'

The proprietor clutches his rifle. He is red about the ears but otherwise so pale that the dirt in his wrinkles stands out. His left eyelid flickers. He stands on his toes and stretches his neck.

Aspengren is snoozing underneath the counter all the while. Blood runs from a deep gash in his forehead and forms narrow rivulets in the dry soil. I strike a match, light my cigar, roll it between my fingers and bore my eyes into the owner.

'Is he your brother? The Bumpkin?'

My heart is pounding. I'm playing for high stakes but am too close to back down. The man hesitates for two seconds, his weapon shaking in his hands, but soon he brings the rifle down to his side. He swallows a couple of times, then whispers of fraternal betrayal float from his mouth like fine flakes of soot.

'He keeps to the same place, smelt in April, pikeperch in May, all year until it freezes over in winter.'

I clamp the cigar in the corner of my mouth, take my notebook out of my pocket and nod.

'Let's start with his appearance.'

I hope I am the only one who notices that my pen is trembling against the page.

The beautiful union of pain and excitement in equal measure. The union that became my life.

The centre of Old Town. A seagull screeches and swoops towards the rostrum in the middle of the steps up to the Stock Exchange, perhaps mistaking the silver head of the microphone for a glistening herring. With a few metres to spare it changes its course, streaks past the Swedish flags and swastika banners that adorn the façade and sweeps over the men standing packed in Stortorget. Most attendees are wearing suits but some are in uniform.

'The Swedish middle class stand defenceless before the advance of Marxism, which is currently raging against the last lines of defence, of the Fatherland and the Swedish people.'

The speaker takes half a step back from the microphone, straightens his armband and leans forward. He is a thin-haired man with close-set eyes. I recognise him from the press but can't remember his name. There is something simultaneously awkward and brazen about him.

Gabrielsson said that National Socialism was a particularly ugly baby a few years ago, and now it is even uglier but mature enough to step out into the world. The fucking brat has finally grown brave enough to stop hiding behind its mother's skirts and embark on an adventure. If I remember his words correctly.

Probably not.

He didn't fucking swear anyway.

I spit between my shoes pensively. I don't give a damn about the affairs of the state but I know these types. The pillocks can't be reasoned with. The only way to communicate with them is with fists. But I'll be damned if I get involved in politics unnecessarily. Let someone else deal with all that.

I stand at the mouth of Skomakargatan with Hasse and Dixie, next to the corner house with the cannonball embedded in the wall, and we go no farther. The police have cordoned off all roads leading to the square and the hooves of skittish sidestepping police horses clatter on the cobbles in the alleyways. It smells of horse shit and man sweat.

'Remember, practically speaking there is no difference between Social Democracy, in its current corrupt state in our country, and Soviet communism.'

The speaker pauses as the bells of Storkyrkan Cathedral strike a quarter past three. I look around. Maybe we should go back and bypass the square. According to the brother with the shooting gallery tent, the Bumpkin fishes in Strömmen from early morning until early afternoon, and then he goes around the restaurants to sell his catch and maybe get a pot-wash gig to boot. I wonder how much time I have.

'I went on a louse-hunt with a kerosene lamp last night, lifting the wallpaper. At first I thought I was looking at the masonry wall, until it started moving. It was a whole grey mass of vermin.'

'It's that kind of summer.'

Two women next to me are talking with their shawled heads leaning in towards each other. One has an apron that glitters with fish scales. Behind them stands a rag of a man whom I not only recognise but whose name I even remember. He is called Halte Harald. He has tied scraps of cloth over the holes in his knees. His jacket is in tatters and shines with greasy stains in the sunshine. His bushy beard is alive with resident lice. People say that he was an elementary school teacher before a broken heart caused a nervous breakdown and a descent into madness.

'It is clear that our views on race and its significance for the survival of our society and nation necessitate strong opposition to racial intermingling as a political idea and a social system.'

I direct my attention towards the square. I swallow hard and look for a cigar. Opposite us, just a few metres away, on Kåkbrinken, stands Detective Chief Inspector Berglund in conversation with his men. His company includes a tall chap I've never seen before. He is blond and dressed in a superbly well-tailored suit. One of his eyelids hangs a little heavier than the other. He has a cleft chin. A damned stylish gent. I stare for a while.

'We define the Swedish nation by loyalty, a common identity, common language and common culture.'

The thin-haired speaker looks up when the rattle of a snare drum pours out of the narrow alley to the left of the square. He flicks through his papers.

'Judaism has proven to be the most problematic religious creed in co-existence with Swedish culture.'

Brass instruments strike up from the adjacent side streets and the notes of 'The Internationale' swell above the rooftops and up towards the cloudless sky. Feedback cuts across the square like an angry warning sound as the speaker knocks the microphone with his papers. The audience look around. A horse dances in place and whinnies.

'This is going to be another bloodbath.'

The fishwife takes the other woman by the arm and retreats along Skomakargatan. The sound of the trumpets is growing in strength with every second. Inspector Berglund's bony hands gesticulate wildly as he shouts out orders. The uniformed contingent of the public draws to the west side of the square. The batons come out. Someone sets a crowbar to the corner of a paving stone and tries to pry it up. I find a cigar, light it and crane my neck for a better view.

'Get home to Lundin and leave Dixie there,' I say to Hasse and nod in the direction of the German church. 'Don't want you to get hurt three days before the fight.'

Hasse looks almost relieved and immediately starts making his way through the assembly. I watch his back before he is swallowed up by the crowd. I can't figure him out. I turn back to the square.

The climax of 'The Internationale' rings out from the maze of alleyways to the side of the square. It sounds like a half a battalion. They can't be more than one block away. The snare drum is hammering like a machine gun. There is a smash as an empty bottle flies into the square and explodes on the pavement. The speaker slips down from the rostrum and disappears eastward, flanked by bodyguards.

Damned coward.

Music fills the square as the Communist marching band appears on the slope up to Storkyrkan Cathedral opposite me. A hundred young lads gather in front of them, with straight backs and red banners. Some young ruffians among the bystanders rush to join them now that they sense a fight is on its way. The Commies station themselves shoulder to shoulder like beaters in the forest and link arms to form chains.

For a couple of seconds all is quiet but for the rapid roll of the drums. A few pigeons take off from the Stock Exchange roof-ridge. Berglund takes out his revolver.

The trumpeters on the slope bring their instruments to their lips again. The vanguard of the counter-demonstration lower their heads and charge against the police. As if on cue the alleys spew out a rain of stones and empty bottles. The music mingles with the sounds of violence, dampened thuds and smashing glass. People scream. The assembly scatters. The air is filled with black blurs as police swing their batons wildly.

'Attack!'

The Reds let out a collective roar as the police line breaks. They pour out of the alleys like blood from an open wound, rushing forth like stallions in a field. Marlinspikes, straight razors and lifting hooks are revealed from hiding places in jackets. Berglund, the blond man and three constables retreat onto Skomakargatan and I fall back a few metres and hide in a courtyard entrance way so he won't see me. I take a puff of my cigar and peek out at the commotion. My mouth is watering.

A man with a broken nose is raging around a few metres into the square. It looks like someone has slapped a plate of steak tartare on his mug. Strings of blood tremble in his goatee. He bends over a hat, stares at it for a second and throws it over his shoulder before staggering on. Berglund brings a whistle to his mouth. The screeching signal fills the square.

Hooves immediately hurtle across the paving stones and the mounted police charge with riding crops and sabres drawn. The blades flash in the sunlight. Halte Harald has strayed into the square and fallen under the hooves of a brown stallion, which tramples his groin.

That certainly won't help his limp.

Inspector Berglund raises his revolver above his head. The sound of two warning shots cuts through the noise. For a moment things subside; people look around, the trauma of the Ådalen shootings shining in their eyes. A horse rears up. Some of the fighters trickle away down the alleys and the mass in the square thins out.

Then the noise level rises again. One man strikes another between the eyes. A policeman is dragged backwards from his horse but refuses to release his grip on the reins. The nag shies and tosses its head.

A young man comes running in my direction. He has a thin, sharp face and narrow shoulders. A leather strap spans his uniform shirt. He is holding a bloody sheath knife in his hand. A couple of Commies are in hot pursuit.

They surge past Berglund and continue down the street. I take one step from the courtyard entrance way and stretch out my foot.

A sudden pain: the Nazi's shin bashes into mine. With a heavy gasp he lands on his back, winded, his limbs splayed. The knife clatters on the street just beyond his reach.

Damned if I know why I did it.

The Commies pounce on him like a gang of starved farm cats on an injured baby crow. He gets a work boot in his face. There is a crack. He gets another. And another.

I stop smiling when I look up straight into Berglund's eyes.

'Fuck!'

I swear softly to myself and back into the courtyard entrance way. The brown-clad National Socialist remains lying in front of me like a torn piece of jute fabric. His foot is twitching. Blood is coagulating in the dirt. The Communists disappear into the alleys. I push myself up against the doors and hide my eyes under the brim of my hat.

The sound of police boots slamming against the pavement seems to drown out everything else. My heart is hammering, making my entire ribcage vibrate with tension. The pimp from Norrmalmstorg comes to mind. I went hard at that devil. Even if I did refrain from putting my post-fight cigar in his eye.

'Kvist? Well, I'll be buggered!'

Shit.

I look up. Berglund takes a step over the National Socialist who is still lying splayed in the middle of the street. The inspector has three constables with drawn sabres in his entourage. He pulls the handle and one of the doors screeches open.

'In here with him.'

The constables push me through the door and up against the wall of the courtyard inside. It is rough and slightly damp. The chill caresses my back. A stuffy smell of boiled cabbage lingers in the air.

The largest one stands closest to me. He is holding my shirt collar in his left hand and his sabre in the right. He has a furrowed face and grey temples under his uniform cap. His chin droops, and his mouth hangs open like a simpleton's.

'How many times has the slugger done the rounds at Långholmen? Three, four?'

Berglund is still holding the revolver in his hand. I shrug my shoulders but my belly is a knot of tension. Everybody knows that the Malmö police are the worst in the country but the Stockholm pigs sure have their moments, just as sure as the Detective Chief Inspector is motivated by personal malice more than justice.

'Kvist likes a hefty punishment. Unfortunately for you we just don't have the time to bring you to court right now.' Berglund glances through the doorway. 'Let him have it boys. Thoroughly.'

I didn't take beatings well as a child. When the farmer I lived with during those early years took off his belt, I would run and hide in the barn until he had calmed down. I can't say that I feel differently as a grown man, but a life in the ring has trained me. And now I have no choice. The Bumpkin is within reach and on Thursday Hasse will be in the ring.

Do what you have to do.

The gaping-mouthed copper in front of me draws back the handle of his sabre. I manage to clear my throat and gob in his mouth before I push my chin into my chest and shoot my forehead forward. He clocks me with the sabre handle. A bright white light, like an exploding carbide lamp, flashes through my skull. My skin breaks. I fold over a fist in the stomach before getting another in the chest. My mouth fills with viscous iron. I fall through darkness.

Sailors drown in silence, without the slightest sound, as everyone who has seen it with their own eyes knows.

A few whimpers escape my split lips, but inside me all is quiet.

TUESDAY 21 JULY

I slurp a few sips of coffee through busted lips and run my little finger stump over the stitches Dr Jensen gave me yesterday, counting them. Five stitches. Seventy kronor poorer. *Halvfjerds*, as they say in Danish.

You learn something new every day.

Bloody Danes.

Lundin is in front of me, reclining in bed with a newspaper. He licks his thumb, turns the page and then wipes the moisture off on the embroidered collar of his nightshirt. We have had breakfast and sucked a morning dram through a sugar cube but the undertaker refuses to get up. Says it's not worth it.

'Would you rather lie like a dried-up old cow in a barn, starved half to death from eating nothing but old hay and moss?'

He rustles his newspaper.

'The Olympians are taking the night train to Berlin on Friday. They are encouraging people to come to Central Station and wave them off.'

'I'm off out now, but you have a chamber pot under your bed and water, schnapps and playing cards here.'

I point to the bottles on the nightstand. A gentle breath of wind pours in through the open window above the bed and plays in the curtain. Dixie whimpers from the foot of the bed. Her tail beats against the wall.

'Could you help me? We could take a taxi. I want to see if my nephew is part of the team.'

'Maybe, I have a lot to do.'

'Ragnar Lundin, precision pistol.'

'I know. Now, will you be all right?'

'I hope you get your fisherman, brother.'

I pat the undertaker on the shoulder and get up, scraping the chair against the floor tiles. I pick up the bottle from the nightstand and take a mouthful of schnapps that stings my lips. Halfway out the door Lundin calls to me and I turn around.

'What is it?'

'Well, I was wondering. What do they say about me?'

'Who?'

'The tenants. What do they say?'

'They say that you are good about the heating. In the winter. In summer they don't say anything.'

The undertaker perks up, nods and strokes his moustache.

'Quite right. I have allowed a grace period on the rent for those who have needed it and I have never taken payment in kind from the women.'

'That's good.'

'Even though Nilsson the tinsmith's wife tried it on.'

'I'll be back in the evening.'

'Do they know I have an Olympian nephew?'

'You can be damned sure they know that.'

'Good luck with the fisherman.'

Roslagsgatan is bathed in sun. I light a cigar, head south and encounter the screeching number 6 tram. A wild excitement is coursing through my body.

Farther down the street I see that damned Wång and his pious wife outside the cigar shop in the middle of a scrabble of kids. I watch the captain bend down and poke one of them in the stomach with the shaft of his tobacco pipe. Maybe it's one of his own.

They have a whole bunch, named after biblical characters. One of the lads is said to be some sort of musical genius. He stands out on the street sometimes, in his velvet prodigy outfit, playing the violin, but I can't see him there now.

A couple of gunshots resound from up in Vanadislunden Park and I stop in my tracks. The memory of Hiccup doing in those two gangsters judders through me like an electric shock: the bullets blasting into the bodies, the sleet that cleaned off the blood and brain matter. But then I remember that starting from today there is a compassion bounty on offer for hunters who put street dogs out of their misery. I think about the mutt from yesterday. That might have been her meeting her end.

As I approach the cigar stall Wång disappears inside, but seeing as the tram is going to wait awhile up by the Roslags customs office, I think I'll give the kids a genuinely entertaining yarn instead of the captain's lies. I am feeling positive about the day ahead, am in a good mood and feel like taking Wång down a peg or two.

The chattering crowd in short trousers quietens when I approach. I push back my hat, attempt a smile that comes out crooked and stroke my chin. A little lass with a pink bow in her golden blonde hair squats down. She is red around the mouth from cherries.

Wång's devout wife is dressed in a black satin dress buttoned all the way up to the neck. The tight grey knot on her head reminds me of a wasp nest. Her face is wearing that steely expression that religious people get when their Lord has grown tired of their incessant praying and long since stopped listening. I greet her with a nod.

'I hear that the littl'uns like tales of the sea.' I turn to the children. 'Isn't that right kids?'

My split lip and morning drams make me splutter my words slightly. The brats' eyes grow wide and they start fidgeting.

'We like the captain's sweets,' says a short, chubby boy with an unsightly cowlick on his forehead.

'Well, I don't have any, but I'll bet my hat that my stories are more exciting – and true, come to that. Let me tell you about when the Swedish consul had to bail me out in France.'

The little girl with the bow looks up. Mrs Wång takes the two children standing closest and pulls them in to her. Her nostrils quiver.

'I was loitering around Marseilles drinking in bars. One evening I had a couple too many under my belt, well, to be frank, I was completely cockeyed, and I was drifting around the harbour, when I stumbled upon a rather strange sort of establishment.' I chew my lips to get the saliva flowing. 'Fangs were painted around the door as if you were stepping into the mouth of a wild animal, and two blokes were standing outside with their faces hidden behind black cowls. They were chanting in French – a hell of a language that is utterly impossible to understand, even for many natives, or so I hear. Driven by curiosity and booze I decided to go closer and investigate, thinking it was an exotic whorehouse of some sort.'

Mrs Wång gasps for air, and so do I. God knows when was the last time I talked this much. The little girl stands up and fumbles for the woman's kirtle. The chubby little thing screws his face up in a sullen frown. I'll have to pick up the pace or they will lose interest. I move my arms in a swimming motion.

'I enter a narrow corridor with blood-red velvet curtains draped along the walls and get myself tangled up in them. Then suddenly, without warning a terrible creature appears from the curtains, pale as a corpse and with huge fangs in its mouth! Quick as the devil I clout it with a left and smack its sharp fangs clean across the corridor. The vampire collapses to the ground as if staked in the heart.'

The little girl sniffs. Mrs Wång draws her closer in to her as well, her eyes burning with godly fervour.

'Mr Kvist, I don't think…'

I hold up my palm. The best bit is coming up. I need to get to Strömmen and the Bumpkin and don't have time for any interruptions.

'And as if that wasn't enough, next a hunchback comes shuffling along with eyes like an owl and his hairy hump showing through a hole in his shirt. I clip the bastard with a hard right and he tumbles along the ground like a ball of yarn.' I take a deep drag on my cigar and grin. 'I manage to deck another two of these freaks before the police show up and I realise that I wasn't in a whorehouse at all, but some sort of variety theatre.' I laugh loudly. The little girl's tears are now flowing in rivers down her dirty cheeks. I pat her reassuringly on the head. 'There you are, kids, a real sailor's story.'

The brats stand in front of me like a nest of chicks. I get a vague feeling in my gut that I have done something wrong, but I take off my hat and saunter south.

It was probably the lack of sweets as bribes. Spoilt little toerags. Wång must have told some incredible tall tales if that one didn't do the trick. Luckily I have a couple of others in store that are far worse.

I'll try one of those next time. I've always been good with kids.

Just as the number 6 tram pulls into the stop I see a youth approaching with hasty steps. He is around twenty-five, with a wasp waist and broad shoulders, his hair well trimmed, pomaded and waxed. He has probably wandered too far north and ended up in the wrong part of town. I have neither the time nor the inclination to get distracted by beautiful flesh so I avoid eye contact.

The tram screeches to a halt. I am about to step on when someone grabs my shoulder and stops me. I smack the arm away with the back of my right hand and turn around. He is so close that I can smell his expensive cologne and camphor oil, and see the shine of sweat on his right cheekbone. Apparently it is so hot that even the upper class have learnt how to sweat.

My left rams towards his jaw but stops a couple of centimetres from the target. His eyes narrow then widen. He lowers his chin and the bone touches my knuckles. I swallow. His cotton collar is soft and gentle on my hand.

'Don't do that,' I mutter.

I push him back with one hand on his chest. My thumbs leave a decent fingerprint stain on the young man's white shirt. I force myself into calmness. It is as constrictive as a jacket a size too small.

'H-harry Kvist, private detective?' he stutters.

'Don't have time.'

'Please sir, I beg you, it will only take a minute.'

'Have to find a fisherman.'

'I pay well.'

'Sixty seconds, starting now.'

Herzog's *mausgrau* summer suit flashes through my mind. I take out my timepiece and pretend to watch it. The young man interlaces his slender fingers in front of his body and tries to stand up straight, but it doesn't take a detective to see that something is weighing him down.

'I am engaged to be married to a Miss Agnes Anfeldt. I work for her father, as an assistant at Anfeldt's law firm, on account of my difficulties in gaining employment as an engineer, which is my true discipline. Miss Anfeldt and I met at a family event and became engaged last year.'

'Get to the point.'

'There is another gentleman in her life, a childhood friend who has recently moved back to the city after several years as an attaché in Lisbon, and…'

'Tick-tock.'

'My dear sir.' He throws up his hands. 'I fear that Miss Anfeldt is having an affair.'

Hasse's upcoming taxi ride and that tailored suit: an extra couple of coins wouldn't go amiss. My old trainer Axel Albertsson taught me that one should always go to a fight in style. I scratch the tip of my nose and peer at the boy from under the brim of my hat.

'You want him roughed up?'

The youth nods and presses his lips together. I go in hard.

'A hundred kronor, hundred and fifty for both, all in advance.'

'No, for God's sake, not my Agnes.'

'Write down a description, his name and address.'

'You must understand. I fear that the aforementioned child-hood friend is to be found at the lady in question's house right now. On Sturegatan.'

The boy flaps his hands around again like a couple of scared little birds and his voice has a certain theatrical quality to it. I grunt.

'He'll be in hospital by evening.'

The youth flinches at this but takes my notebook and pen. He manages to scribble down the details and returns the para-phernalia with a couple of crisp notes. His hand is shaking. The upper class often react this way, even though they don't have to do a damn thing except pay someone else to do their dirty work.

That is why 1,000-kronor notes look bloodstained around the edges. I have seen them. In real life and close up. Twice even.

I take a look at the description. He'll be easy to spot. I nod in farewell and hasten away. I think of my suddenly very busy agenda and quicken my pace. Excitement surges through my body. Metal bells in the south chime ten ominous strikes, as if counting me down.

The shade of a large chestnut tree, the bark rough against my sweaty back, the grass between my legs still green under the canopy's immense parasol – an oasis among the scorched plant beds of Humlegården.

All this waiting. All my life.

Chevrolet, Mercedes, Cadillac. Cars on Sturegatan pass with the tops down. Youths with their right hand on the steering wheel, elbow on the door frame and a pocket full of their father's cash. In the passenger seat there is always a young lady with painted lips, oval sunglasses and a colourful silk scarf over her hair. Line them all up next to each other and I wouldn't be able to tell one from the next. All alike, slaves to the shifts of fashion.

All this hanging around and not even enough money for a blasted summer hat.

About thirty metres behind me they have set up a cafeteria with round tables and a patch of grass encircled by gravel paths and plants. When I walked past earlier I saw that the menu on the blackboard was chalked up in French. A sweaty little brass band from some Östermalm garrison serves as entertainment and their notes struggle their way through the thick, quivering air.

Few master the difficult art of waiting. You must empty the mind of thoughts. Just stay still and watch.

Bide your time, and then bide some more, in doorways, like the one I am watching, or inside. Waiting in the queue for schnapps. Or for some bloody rain that refuses to fall.

For death.

I hold in a sigh as long as I can without angering my cough. Three plumes of smoke stream upward, blackish grey against the sky, and disperse.

On a blanket to the right of me some young posh types are larking about shamelessly. The number 2 tram groans past with shining windows. The oak front door beyond it remains closed.

A postman is strolling along the pavement with his empty black-lacquered postal bag. According to the Bumpkin's brother, he leaves in the early afternoon to have time to sell his catch.

I'm running out of time.

A couple of lads stop in front of me. They are both covered with brick dust and their hands have been scraped bloody by clay chips. Hoddies on some building site. One of them wants to go for a beer but the other says no, he's broke, better shake a leg and get home. No choice in the matter.

New houses are sprouting up here in Östermalm. Excavators and fucking legal permits have muscled into the unruly shanty town around Träsket Lake and Gropen. Out of the mire of poverty arises a collection of enclaves for the wealthy, circled by broad avenues, water and green spaces, with Birger Jarlsgatan as a razor-sharp barrier against the have-nots, just one block north from Roslagsgatan.

The oak door opposite finally opens and pulls me out of my thoughts. I stretch my neck, grunt, stand up and brush off the seat of my trousers. The man with the eyepatch looks around and dabs his mouth with a handkerchief. Perhaps wiping off lingering female juices. He grabs the middle section of his cane and heads north along Sturegatan. I cross the street behind him.

The man strides along with brisk steps. Fine by me, there are too many people around anyway. I wait until the distance between us grows to ten metres or so. A hurdy-gurdy sings from one of the inner courtyards.

There is something military about the one-eyed man's stature and energetic gait. Not that it matters. He doesn't look like the kind of man who hits back. I loosen my tie and take off the noose.

Here we go again.

This never-ending piece-of-shit job.

I start closing in on my victim, my eyes locked on his back. I can probably run up alongside his blind side when there are fewer people around, and pull him into a stairwell.

I stop whistling abruptly and come to a halt. A feeling I don't fully recognise bubbles ever so gently through my body, a sensation so vague that I cannot really grasp it. The half-melted street sags under my shoes. I see a car company's logo on the pavement, embossed in the asphalt. I force my feet to continue.

'What the hell has he done wrong?'

I mumble to myself and take a deep puff to get rid of the insipid taste in my mouth.

Something feels wrong. I look around. Fewer people here now, no police patrolling either.

So he's stolen himself a little love. It can happen to the best of us.

I think of Miss Evy Granér's weepy, bloodshot eyes, begging helplessly. I'm not sure why. My steps feel heavier, but if I abandon my assignment it will be the second time in a short period that I break an agreement and steal money. Not good for my image or business. Blood fills my mouth as the scab on my lower lip rips open.

I press forward. I am being called on by the savagery I learnt from years in the ring, by the taste of blood. The attaché looks around and crosses Kommendörsgatan. I take a final puff and flick away the cigar butt.

'Bloody captain.'

I spit red. If only that damned Wång hadn't stolen Lind's tobacco shop from under my nose last autumn, everything would have been different. I would have been a shopkeeper with dough in the bank and a new tie every week. I could have even had a charming assistant by my side.

Screeching wheels jerk me out of my thoughts as a Cadillac I recognise all too well brakes in front of me at the crossroads. Over the roof I see the one-eyed man step aside for a couple of younger ladies, bow neatly and saunter on. I inhale deeply and realise I have been holding my breath. My lungs protest, my cough tears at my chest and I end up crouching with my hands on my knees as the back door of the Cadillac opens. I let a magnificent glob of blood smash on the pavement. A couple of well-polished shoes with triangular heels enter my eyeline, and an embroidered church handkerchief appears in front of my nose.

'The young can die, but the old are certain to.'

I press the soft cotton cloth to my bloody mouth and look up: the gold tip on the ivory cane, a light dress that near enough drags in the road dust, some sort of crochet item that looks like a short apron. I clear my throat, spit and stand up straight.

'In which case, the lady and I will meet down below when the day comes.'

I insert a Meteor into my mouth. In the shade of a wide-rimmed hat, a lipstick-red smile slices through the shadows and wrinkles of her face.

'Since that is already established, is it not a question of making a respectable exit?'

'I have an important job at Kungsträdgården.'

Ma emits a sound between a snort and a laugh, then lifts her cane and points to a bench in the park across the street. An elegant executive car with Swedish flags on both corners of the bonnet brakes abruptly as she steps out into the traffic. Maybe it's on its way up to Army Headquarters.

It takes a woman of a certain mettle to dare such a manoeuvre. I glance towards her headquarters farther up on Kommendörsgatan, and then in the direction of the attaché who has disappeared from sight. Then I follow her like a ragged dog, albeit on a long leash.

Ma parks her wide backside on the green bench and pats the slats beside her. The bench creaks as I do what I'm told. We sit quietly for a while. A chaffinch warbles its eternal melody; the sounds of engines intensify and then die away as cars pass. I look at the Cadillac and her sons on the other side of the street.

'For a young man like Kvist death will be sudden, but inside an old crone like me it has long been brewing, in flesh and mind alike. My time is limited and it's ticking away faster than ever.'

'Have to find a fisherman.'

'We'll drive you, like Sunday.'

'Madam is too kind.'

Ma recognises the streak of mocking in my voice and scoffs so loudly the bench timber creaks. She inserts a cigarette into her holder and I shelter a match with my hand though the air is still. The smoke pours from the corner of her mouth like a fine mist. I remember our ride in the Cadillac and want to ask the gangster queen about what she said on the way home. Instead she speaks first.

'I expect Kvist has cheated death at some point.'

'I know all about that ugly fuck.'

I puff on my fresh cigar before the matchstick burns my fingers.

'What went through your mind at the time?'

'How in the hell should I remember? You probably just think you're done for. That the game is up.'

I chuck away the matchstick. Ma points at it with her cane.

'There is time to think while the flames of existence slowly peter out. My mind is full of thoughts about the people who follow life's path, and those who make their own way.' She nods at the Cadillac. Nix has jumped out of the car and is drumming his fingers on the roof, his eyes flitting up and down the street. Ma appears to hesitate before adding: 'Has Kvist anyone to call family?'

I lean forward on my knees, take a deep puff, clear my throat and send a gob of spit through the cloud of smoke. I feel a shudder inside me.

'Like hell.'

'And so perhaps he has nothing to lose?'

A young woman comes strolling along with a little pedigree dog of some description. Her wide trouser legs swish against each other and the sunbeams attack the side row of brass buttons around her boldly swaying hips. The dog stops in front of us and pulls on the leash in the direction of Humlegården. I reach my hand towards it. In the corner of my eye I glimpse the lacklustre young thing's well-painted lips drooping under her wide-brimmed sun hat. She pulls the dog decisively onward. Nix wolf-whistles at her lasciviously from the other side of the street even though it is plain to see that she is the virtuous type, long trousers or no.

I open my mouth to speak but have forgotten what Ma said.

She pats me twice on the thigh with a wrinkled hand.

'One must ask oneself what legacy one is leaving behind,' she continues. 'What is one passing on to the next generation?'

'Debts seem to be the popular choice on my side of town.'

Ma laughs and takes a puff.

'Our position has certainly weakened in recent years, but we won't have it that bad. Perhaps Kvist can appreciate that I am talking about something different. When it all comes to an end, will I be seen as a has-been, withering more with each passing year until I shrivel up completely in bed?'

I think of Lundin and wipe my lips with the handkerchief.

Ma searches my eyes.

'I think it is impossible to foresee the judgement of the after-world,' she continues. 'It probably depends on who writes the obituary. By what yardstick is a woman measured when death comes? And a man?'

'It's the same one. Lundin has one at home.'

Ma blinks, looks away and lifts her cane to the Cadillac where both her sons are now standing on the pavement.

'They fight like cat and dog. I haven't told them yet, and the cocaine helps with the pain.'

'I am telling you, they use the same measuring stick for women as for men. I measured plenty of bodies when I worked at the funeral parlour last year. I might not be good with numbers but I can measure. Accurate to the millimetre every time. Anyone who says differently is a damned liar.'

'I am afraid you don't understand what I mean. It has taken root inside me, dug in its claws.'

'You bet I understand. People tell a whole lot of damned lies. In my years at sea I measured things with foreign measuring systems and in foreign languages.'

'I really don't think…'

My indignant zeal makes me brave enough to interrupt her.

'Kvisten can sure as hell measure anything.' I grip the hand-kerchief hard in my fist. 'I don't give a shit what people say.'

We don't speak for a while. It is nice to have a bit of silence. One can let thoughts come and go.

'Yesterday at dusk Ploman and the Reaper drove to Söder via Kungsholmen again.'

I pinch my little finger stump with the fingers of my other hand and then shake my hand in the air.

'Likely lads out on a nice drive every night.'

'We still need to know where they are going.'

'Maybe up to Fåfängan to enjoy the view?'

'And what they are transporting.'

'Cake and juice?'

I chuckle and look around to check that no one is listening. I lean forward and lower my voice, try to change the subject.

'On Sunday you said that I was illuminated by violence. What did you mean?'

'You're like me. A vicious bull who is best off in the barn, alone, with nothing but gnats and gadflies for company. Does Kvisten understand what I am trying to say?'

I do my best to remember and struggle to find the right words.

'Damn right,' I say in the end.

'It is out of sheer respect that I am asking you to consider this job rather than trying to convince you.'

I swallow and stroke my hand over my chin.

'I'm up to my neck in shit. In four weeks' time maybe.'

I stare straight ahead and drum my fingers on the bench.

'I probably won't be here in a month.'

'Going somewhere nice, are you? These newfangled bloody holidays.'

'Very funny. No. My time is limited.'

Her cane spins in the air before falling back hard on the gravel path. She takes a breath.

Kvisten takes his hat off for no one. Stand up for yourself, you fuck. You don't want to get involved with these types. Already got so many bloody things to do.

I sit as still as one of Humlegården's statues behind us. Like with the kids outside the tobacco shop earlier today, I think I must have said something crazy but don't understand what. I spread my legs, put my arm along the backrest and gaze at Sturegatan. Ma gets up with considerable effort and stands in front of me. The pince-nez dangling on its silk string by her bust glints in the sun.

'Has Kvisten listened to a single word I've said?'

'To each and every one, as attentively as Moses on Mount Sinai.'

Ma taps the gold tip of her cane hard against a wooden slat between my legs, a couple of centimetres from my groin. The vibrations travel through my thighs and make my cock shrivel like a walnut. She looks straight at me, a drip of sweat tunnelling its way through the peach-coloured powder on her right cheekbone.

'Well, listen now. Kvist has a few days to organise his affairs but before the week is over, he is required at Kommendörsgatan to discuss details such as remuneration.'

My clothes are clinging to my body, sweat is stinging the stitches on my forehead. The chaffinch is trilling like a lunatic. I lean forward and kick the gravel but stop when the flying dust clings to the hem of her white dress.

'It's Tuesday.'

'Kvisten is right about that at least.'

'I have a wall calendar. Got it for only ten öre.'

'Work for me and you will be better paid than ever before, I can promise you that.'

I harden.

'On sale. It was already well into February.'

My body rests in Ma's large shadow and I shiver despite the heat. I look around. An emaciated mutt covered in sores and lice is running around after water or food. Chances are it will get a bullet between the eyes.

'There was talk of a lift?'

I hold out the bloody handkerchief but she shakes her head.

'To Kungsträdgården, was it?'

I nod.

'The Bumpkin with the maggots.'

My stomach is fluttering when, ten minutes later, I jump out of the Cadillac at Kungsträdgården and walk along the canal up to the Opera House. The feeling of being watched creeps through my body again. I look around and spot a man in a white panama hat, pottering along the other side of the street. I can't quite place him.

I stop and gaze out over the water, mostly to see whether this bloke will stop too. White smoke rises to the sky from the quay down by the Grand Hotel. The sun glitters on the sewer they call Strömmen. Drums blare from Kungsträdgården as the Royal Guard parade approaches, wearing fine uniforms in the colours of the Oscarian era. I have to wait for them to pass.

I watch a half-rotten yacht sail past, then look up and stare at the end point of the parade: the dirt-brown palace on the other side of the wide canal. I pick up my notebook, open the page with the Bumpkin's description and study it awhile before turning around as quick as a flash.

The man on the other side of the street has also stopped. He is holding the panama hat in front of him. A pair of bright eyes shines above a bony nose. I meet his gaze and hold it until he turns and walks over to a hot dog vendor on the south side of Kungsträdgården.

Someone has definitely put a tail on me.

I flinch at the sound of two gunshots in the park.

The people nearby stare and point. Soon I catch sight of a man with a rifle over his shoulder. In his hand he is holding a small mutt by the hind legs. It is bleeding from two gunshots in its side but is still alive.

Tough to be a dog in this city.

Brass instruments and clattering hooves replace the rattle of the drums. I walk a few steps towards the bridge abutment where the Bumpkin supposedly fishes, then stop again. The man has put his white hat on and turned around and is now walking rapidly towards the tram stop in the park's western corner, hot dog in hand. Probably realises that he has been seen.

Who the hell set him on me?

I grumble to myself and direct my attention to the bridge. Here, where Lake Mälaren rushes into Saltsjön Bay, hopeful anglers stand in a row with their fishing lines in the water. My eyes fix on a skinny bloke with a sun-bleached leather cap swaying near the bridge abutment, not far from the copper lion across the street. He observes the Royal Guard parade for a while before turning around and casting his hook into the water. I know I have seen him here before but don't remember where. Maybe last year.

I remain standing awhile as the sound of the parade approaches. In a few minutes there will be soldiers between us.

I wait.

This eternal waiting.

I rustle around in my pocket and produce a small coin. The fisherman looks like a poor sod and could probably do with the dough. I briefly think of Ma's proposal to track down Ploman and the Reaper's secret transports. God knows I need the money, especially since Jensen the abortionist stitched up my forehead, and I have tailed people before. I turn my head here and there in search of the man in the white hat but see no one I recognise but the Bumpkin.

The drum rolls rattle and I continue westward until I come to Norr Bridge. I undo my tie and look to see where the soldiers have got to. The blue and yellow caterpillar is working its way towards the Royal Palace. Sweat is stinging the soldiers' eyes and turning them red. The austere drum major is the first to turn onto the bridge. I knot the tie and roll it up in my pocket.

God damn it.

The band marches breathlessly past with drums, brass instruments and bright-red faces, and then the horsemen follow brandishing Swedish banners and garrison flags. The sun flashes on their helmets, their brass instruments, the backs of their well-groomed horses and polished silver saddlery.

The fisherman in the leather cap draws up his fishing rod and disappears behind the parade. I crouch down and stare between the horses' legs as they clop past. He baits the hook with a maggot from a jar and gets up. I get up as well, stretch my neck and button up my jacket. Ever since the washerwoman opposite Lundin's died, I have been concerned about my light-coloured shirts and I don't know how cooperative this Bumpkin is going to be, with or without my small change.

The sweetish scent of fresh horse manure spreads on the breeze coming in from the sea, and the final recruits march sweatily on, followed by a trail of boisterous kids. The Bumpkin has got his fishing line in the waves again and is standing and tugging at it gently. I look around, note that there are no police in the vicinity and cross the street.

An old man with a big prophet-like beard is standing by the bridge abutment. He has a box resting on his stomach, hung from a leather strap around his neck. It is filled with cigarettes and multicoloured metal tins of cigars, under which he almost certainly keeps a collection of immoral postcards for those in the mood. This means he wouldn't risk testifying as a witness.

I walk up to the angler, clear my throat and put on my most devilish voice.

'Hear that maggots make the best bait.'

The skinny man in front of me flinches, pulls up his hook and puts the fishing line aside. He looks me up and down quickly with his watery eyes. No indication that he likes what he sees. He pulls his leather cap off his crown and holds it politely with both hands in front of his flea-bitten, badly patched jacket. I bend down and pick a whitish maggot from the jar of earth by his feet. It coils into a fat ring between my thumb and forefinger. I stare at the man. I could blow him down with a sneeze if I had to. I drop the coin back into my pocket with a jangle. I'll be damned if I'll waste any money on him.

'Don't know nothing about it,' the fisherman squeals.

I have been around a long time and know how to spot a liar. Everybody makes the same mistake of looking diagonally upward when they try to fib. Or is it the opposite?

Shit.

I grab the Bumpkin's jaws in my left mitt and press my fingers into his cheeks, forcing his mouth open. He doesn't have many teeth left. I drop the maggot inside and hold my hand over his gob.

'Three days ago. You were digging around in the Katarina cemetery in the wee small hours. I believe you saw someone. If you don't want to end up in the water like your son, you had better talk faster than the Devil himself.'

I have never threatened someone with a maggot before. Say what you like about this pissing job, but it is full of surprises.

The Bumpkin squeezes his eyes shut and shakes like a street dog taking a shit. A few half-choked squeals squeeze out through my fingers. I release his mouth and wipe my palm against his lapel. The maggot lands on the paving stone in a pool of phlegmy saliva.

'Well?'

'Didn't see no one. No one at all.'

Swedes and their rock-hard, stubborn silence. They can be extremely reticent and often need softening up. They take pride in their silence but the only thing it gets them is a worse thrashing. The Bumpkin wipes his mouth with the back of his hand. His eyes are frozen in fear. I grab the bloke by his lapels, lift him straight up and heave him over the bridge's cement railing.

Here we go.

Time to spill.

Or drown.

My back aches as I hold him. The Bumpkin is dangling five, six metres above the water. The sun is glinting on the surface. Excrement and flushed condoms float among the waves. He is kicking his legs.

'I can't swim!'

The man screams as if he is about to explode and it echoes under the bridge. I look around. Too many people around for this kind of move. Some are pointing and staring. The sound of a jacket seam giving up the ghost suddenly breaks through the July heat.

I grip harder but one by one the stitches surrender and the Bumpkin begins to fall towards the water with his hands waving in the air. I still have some reflexes left from my glory days. I let go of the jacket cloth that has remained in my grasp and grab for his wrist. My left shoulder shrieks with pain. I grunt and the Bumpkin screams for help.

'Fuck it!'

The angler's sweaty wrist is slipping through my hand and his thin fingers dig into my flesh. I grab hold with my right too. Blood throbs in my hands. I grunt from the strain. A few seagulls emit a throaty cackle. I pull the fisherman over the railing and think I can hear his legs clattering like castanets against the cement.

The Bumpkin collapses into a gangling heap at my feet. I lean forward with my hands on my knees. Another coughing fit. I pull the fisherman up to his feet. He is as pale-faced as if he had actually spent a week in the water. Brutality seethes in me. I hold my hands up in front of him threateningly.

'You see this fist? Look at the damn thing! Broken it so many times I've lost count. Look at it, I said! What I'm about to do is going to hurt me just as much.'

The Bumpkin looks like he wants to vomit. I take a few small coins out of my pocket again, to soften the blow. He is trembling so hard that tears can't be far off.

'One was the Reaper. P-p-ploman's gangster,' he stutters.

I lean my head back to the cloudless sky and take a deep breath. The sunbeams feel like they are cutting me into small pieces.

The bell of St Stefan's Church announces half past seven with a solitary chime and Johannes responds from the south with a heavy clang. Roslagsgatan, the smoke-ravaged windpipe of Sibirien, cuts across the body of the city, sooty and almost deserted. A single car passes by and old man Ljung is leading one of his hire horses home. The road dust swirls around its hooves.

The city is dying of thirst, withering right in front of my eyes, and flakes from the amber house fronts are blowing in the lukewarm breeze. The undertaker's sign screeches on its rusty fixing.

I stand by the open window with a schnapps glass in my hand. Anger is shrouding my mind in darkness. Poor folk have it worst in the evenings when the long working day is over and we sit alone with our hearts. Then come the thoughts.

On the windowsill is the notebook, the aniline pen and the photograph of Ida weighted down by my Husqvarna pistol. Beside it is a litre of Östgöta Sädes schnapps.

The memory of Evy Granér and her 'precious', the child growing inside her, comes to mind. I don't understand why my thoughts keep turning to that woman. I wonder if she managed to leave the city and get to Motala.

I hope so.

I look up at the brick shack opposite, where Roslags laundry used to be. All is calm in the soft golden-yellow evening light that only a Swedish July can offer. I think of the friendly washerwoman, Sailor-Beda, and her violent death last year.

And now Gabrielsson.

When Lundin takes down his screeching sign I will have no one to call friend. I have so little to lose.

'The Reaper.'

The Bumpkin said he had seen two blokes, on the thin side, in Katarina cemetery the morning of the murder. Both were well dressed and in later middle age, one older than the other. He said he'd recognised one of them as the Reaper.

I don't know his real name but would recognise his skinny frame and sunken cheeks from a hundred metres. And I have heard the stories. Like when he found out that it was Fridolf Five-Bob who hijacked one of his lorries in December of '29. Ploman's gangster sliced a furrow in his belly, from one hip bone

121

to the other. Fridolf Five-Bob carried his own intestines in his arms through a snowstorm for a whole block before he collapsed at the crossroads of Sveavägen and Odengatan and caused the biggest traffic jam of the season.

I shut my eyes again. I see Gabrielsson's dead gaping mouth in my mind, as if he were calling for help. What involvement he had with a smuggler syndicate I can't imagine. A man of God who almost never touched hard liquor, except once in Buenos Aires, which turned into a night we would never forget, but never speak of.

Now that I think about it, I never saw him with a woman, even though there are no rules of abstinence in his faith. Maybe Ploman knew something that made Rickardsson, the Reaper and the others try to blackmail the rector out of some money, which he would certainly have refused them.

It didn't take long to get the Bumpkin with the maggots to talk but there are no more witnesses as far as I know, and finding someone else prepared to squeal about Ploman's gang will be harder than getting a dram during Sunday service.

I hum to myself quietly. Maybe an investigation into Gabrielsson's past would help. If for no other reason than to map out the rector's enemies. I open up a clean page in my notebook with a crisp sound. The list is short:

> *National Socialists*
> *Various rich bastards*
> *The poor sod who tried to nick the church silver a couple*
> *   of summers ago*

The purple letters stare back at me, challenging me. I cross out the last line, then the second to last. Gabrielsson was known for his anti-Nazi stance and criticised them tirelessly, both in newspapers through his letters to the editor and from the pulpit. I drum my fingers against the windowsill.

I would much rather go after one of those little brown-clad scout boys but there's no getting round it. A witness has placed the Reaper at the scene of the crime at the right time, and the gangster is one of the few people in this city who could bring themselves to drive four rail spikes into the body of a priest. The pen scratches against the paper as I strike out the first line too.

Schnapps gurgles in the glass as I fill it one more time. I could stake out Ploman's furniture business up by the end of Ynglingagatan but the place is well guarded, and if I had a run-in with the Reaper there, the whole district would soon be after me.

'The end of Ynglingagatan.' I laugh. 'That's right, Kvisten, we're going to need another nip.'

I throw back my head and drink in an attempt to force some fighting spirit into my broken body. I glance over my shoulder to see if Dixie has heard my merriment. She hasn't, the deaf good-for-nothing. I put down the glass.

Like Ma said: a couple of evenings a week a small convoy led by the Reaper and Ploman drives from their base, through Kungsholmen, to Söder and back. If I can find out when, then I can follow them in Lundin's hearse and put a bullet in the Reaper's heart when they get on enemy territory. That would make the retreat a damn sight simpler. My hand trembles slightly at the thought, holding up a third dram.

'What do you think, Kvisten? Do you have cold-blooded murder in you?'

I light a cigar and blow out great swathes of smoke that colour the summer evening blackish-grey and disappear out through the window. Warmth spreads through my body as the spirits slowly break through the fear.

'Fuck knows but I'll give it a shot.' I take another puff. 'It's not like I got all these scars by falling over in church one Sunday.'

Maybe Danilo's Dance Course can ease my mind. Lundin has torn it out of *Svenska Dagbladet* every Saturday for a decade so that I can keep up my footwork. I dance alone.

'Pissed Kvist the soloist,' I mutter and attempt a little laugh. It comes out as a tired cough. I go over to the writing desk and the pile of yellowed newspaper cuttings. The topmost shows the difference between an ordinary tango and the Argentinian variety with black footsteps and explanatory text. Before I know what I'm doing I have taken all the pages, rolled them up and thrown them in the wastepaper basket. I turn back to the window.

I have managed to get through half a cigar and another two shots when I see a robust bloke come walking along the other side of Roslagsgatan. He has rolled up his shirtsleeves in the heat and is carrying his jacket slung over his shoulder, just like last time. I don't have to look twice to know who he is.

'Well, I'll be damned.'

The words slide around my booze-slippery gob. Rickardsson is out for his evening stroll. I should have thought of this ugly fuck and his contacts earlier. I wedge the cigar in the corner of my mouth.

He must know.

I had better get a bloody move on.

I stumble out into the hall, pick up my hat and put it on my head. Dixie's claws patter fumblingly over the linoleum floor as she carefully sniffs her way out into the hall. My knees hurt as I squat down, stroke her back and slur.

'Bloke stuff. Back soon.'

I crack my knuckles, open the door and step over the pile of post that has gathered on the doormat. With my hand on the polished handrail I stride down the steps. Only when I am out on the street do I remember that the Husqvarna is still on the windowsill.

Damn and blast.

Anyway, I trust my fists more.

Unless I am mistaken, Rickardsson will cross the street down by Odengatan and come back on this side. I run up to the crossing and push my back into the wall of 41. I kill the cigar under my heel and look around. To the left the road winds up to Vanadislunden and the reservoir fortress. If I can drag Lundin all the way up there on my back, then I can sure as hell carry Rickardsson a couple of steps as well.

'Kvisten doesn't take his hat off for anyone.'

From Johannes elementary school comes the incessant distant roar of a football match, which seems determined to continue until sundown. Three cars pass, then a few minutes later the wailing jazz tones start up when the occultist two floors above with his window open starts up his evening practice. I must admit he has made some improvements during the two years he has been at it. The fact that I want to shove the brass down his throat and piss in the horn from time to time, like now, for example, is another matter. I try to listen for footsteps but the music drowns out everything else.

A five-centimetre oblong stone lies at my feet. I bend down and pick it up. It fits perfectly in my left hand and can serve as a backup. I clasp my fingers around it so tightly that I can feel my pulse beating in my palm, as if I were holding a living heart.

The trumpeter's fingers start moving faster on the keys and the tempo increases. Rickardsson steps into my field of view.

He whistles along to the melody as he passes so close by that I can make out the pores on his nose, but he stares straight ahead. Too cocky to be vigilant.

You'll be sorry, you bastard.

A whiff of Aquavera penetrates my nostrils. The notes are flowing out over the street at an even quicker tempo now, drowning out the sound of my approaching steps. I reach out my hand towards Rickardsson's broad back.

Tap a man on the right shoulder and you can bet he will turn on the same foot. Then all you have to do is deck him with your left. The chin is a good point of contact if you want to knock someone out, but if you want to actually talk to them afterwards, you have to hold back to make sure you don't break the jawbone. It's a difficult balance that takes years of training.

Nothing to it.

I know what I am doing.

The occultist squeezes out the notes into some sort of climax. I have a good mind to pull out one of the straps of my braces and let it snap back but no, playtime comes later. I tap my fingertips just above and to the right of the dark sweat patch that has spread between Rickardsson's shoulder blades. He stops. He turns his mug starboard and his body follows.

That's it.

I have decent fists even when I'm drunk. Late one evening after a third-class pub crawl I was staggering past the Salvation Army centre on Långholmsgatan when a Christian soldier opened the door. Meanwhile the rest of the army were inside singing a frightful round of nocturnal hallelujahs that scared the life out of me. Before either of us knew what was going on I had him bloody at my feet. Even as a child the village priest said that salvation wouldn't come easy for me because I was of dishonourable birth, born in sin.

Knocking down a Christian soldier by mistake can hardly be compared to beating up one of the city's toughest gangsters. A thrill rushes through my body. It nearly gives me a hard-on.

You just keep staring at me and puffing yourself up, grinning all the while, cocky as a rooster. You are about to slip into darkness at the hands of Kvisten.

I tighten my grip around the stone and squint one eye to better judge the distance. A flood of saliva gushes down my throat. The trumpet tones ride on a gentle breeze and fall down on the street like a fine, much-needed rain. My muscles stiffen and the excitement is replaced with a rare sense of peace.

With no mother or father I have had to wander rootless through my existence, with a broken rudder, with no chance to mature into morality. Perhaps it was inevitable that I turned out as I did. One thing is sure: you cannot escape yourself.

Rickardsson's profile is in line with his shoulder. His sizeable nose sticks out a good way above his full lips.

I have wanted to get stuck into you for years, you bastard.

Everybody has a wicked streak inside them. On seeing a cat playing with a vole, most people will stop and stare awhile, aroused by the cat's cruelty. Nobody holds it against the cat; it's animal instinct. Brutality both seduces and upsets. Otherwise why had folk paid hard-earned cash to watch me beat another man half to death? When that brick was thrown through Herzog's window, and later when I gave that pimp a thorough seeing-to in the square, the public emerged from the shadows. It was even worse at the National Socialist rally in the square. The average man loves blood, even if it is best kept at a distance, on a movie screen or in the pages of a book.

The power station of a man turns his body to follow his head and is soon nearly facing me.

My fist draws its force from the hip and ploughs through the muggy July evening air. A breeze finds its way into my shirtsleeve and wraps my sweaty flesh in coolness. My forearm is positioned at an angle to my upper arm with my wrist dead straight. Rickardsson's eyes enlarge; a bizarre little peep manages to escape from his thick lips; the corner of my mouth twitches. Just then, the jazz boy can't keep up the tempo and slips on the valves. Accompanied by a shrill, unholy note, my left smashes into Rickardsson's powerful chin. A thick string of snuff-mixed saliva whips out of his gob and gleams down to the dusty pavement. The gangster tumbles onto his back, the trumpet dies and everything goes very quiet.

For one second I think I can hear the stone heart beating in my hand.

The unica box containing ammunition and a jar of gun oil rattles when I shake it. I put a cigar in my mouth, open the lid and take out a single shell. I am sitting in the armchair at my oak writing desk and humming the occultist's jazz ditty. I roll the shell between my fingers.

It only takes one bullet to get the job done.

If that.

I have thrown my sweaty shirt into the corner and am sitting in my singlet. A gentle breeze billows through the thin curtains and cools my clammy neck. Rickardsson weighs as much as two men and my muscles are aching from my neck to my calves. The final heave to get the bastard on the writing desk was almost more than I could handle.

'Lucky there's schnapps for strength and spunk.'

I flick open his wallet in one movement. I rummage through the contents, take out eighty kronor in cash and a photograph. The notes rustle as I shove them in my pocket.

The portrait shows a wrinkly old dear with staring eyes and a high-buttoned dress. I turn it over. A single word in curling letters: 'Mum'. I chuckle.

Rickardsson sighs. I have bent him over my oak writing desk with his chest and stomach against the wood and his arse in the air. His face is in front of me. I have lashed his hands to the table legs with a pair of hemp-rope ends and a couple of brutal knots. No chance that he will get free. I insert the barrel of the Husqvarna into his mouth.

'Time to wake up.'

A fly sits on Rickardsson's well-shaven cheek. He blinks twice and it buzzes away. I push the end of the pistol as far as it will go to encourage him to come round. He makes a few half-choked noises.

There is something special about making a man fellate the barrel of a gun.

I have always liked it.

'Was it you who visited Katarina with the Reaper?'

Rickardsson's physique is inconsistent with the Bumpkin's testimony that referred to two men on the thin side, but it fits with the police statement in the newspaper. I remove the barrel. The shiny black steel glints. He coughs. A few slimy strings tremble from his fat lips. He raises his blood-filled head. How fitting. I bring the gun to his forehead and cock it with my thumb.

'Was it you who nailed Gabrielsson to the floor?'

Rickardsson's red face looks about ready to explode. He presses his lips together and breathes heavily. I take a deep puff on my cigar and blow the smoke in his face.

I pull the trigger.

The Husqvarna clicks. Rickardsson comes to. I hold the shell up in front of him, feed the magazine and press the muzzle against his forehead.

'What days and times do Ploman and the Reaper drive shipments to Söder?'

'Leave me somewhere I'll be found.'

Rickardsson's voice is heavy: breathless and sombre. He spits the rest of his pinch of snuff out onto the linoleum floor.

'What was that?'

'Leave me somewhere my body will be found. And don't let Ploman take care of Anna and the kids.'

'What the hell are you talking about?'

'Oskar, my boy, has an apprenticeship waiting at the manufacturer Enquist. Make sure it works out.'

'How in the hell would I do that?'

'Kvisten owes me that much.'

'I am not planning on killing you.'

'Bollocks. You know what will happen if you let me go.'

The occultist slams his door above us and runs down the stairs. I recognise his steps. He is probably going out on the town. I knock the steel against Rickardsson's forehead.

'You are going to tell me what you know.'

'It's no use. Just get it over with.'

I ease down the hammer with my thumb and put the Husqvarna on the desk. I give Rickardsson a loud smack. I hold a threatening forefinger in front of him and lower my voice.

'I'm going to go at Rickardsson so hard that he won't have any choice.'

The armchair scrapes against the floor. I walk around the desk and into the kitchen, then return with the straight razor, paddle strop and vanity mirror. I sit back down in the chair. Soon the room fills with the rhythmic scraping of steel against strop.

'They say that Ploman took a shine to a whore he won in a poker game. And now she rarely leaves his side. Someone cut out her tongue to stop her blabbing. According to rumour you were the one who held the knife.' I put down the strop, grab hold of

Rickardsson's face and squeeze my fingers so hard against his cheeks that it forces his mouth open. 'Isn't that right?'

A helpless bestial whine escapes his mouth. I test the razor's edge with my thumb and then caress its flat side against his cheek, from ear to upper lip.

'I won't be so kind.'

I put the razor down, pull off one of my socks and force it into his mouth. I take the white-striped tie hanging over the back of the armchair, hook it in the corners of Rickardsson's mouth and knot it hard around the back of his neck.

'We have the whole evening ahead of us. Tough blokes call for tough measures, wouldn't you say?'

I place the vanity mirror in the armchair and angle the mirror towards him. I lean the portrait of his mother against the glass of the mirror.

'Whenever you're ready to talk you just need to look over at mummy dearest. And Rickardsson isn't going to want to let slip a damn word about this evening to anyone. That I am sure of.'

I close the window, secure the hasp and pull down the blind.

With razor in hand I go around the table. My fingers close hard around the mother-of-pearl shaft. My hand is trembling with excitement. I test the edge again with my thumb.

'Sharp enough to castrate piggies. Boars too, if you had to.'

Rickardsson stops breathing. Then he starts again, intensely, through his nose.

'There is a rumour in this town that I have lost my spark. That I have changed.' I laugh shortly. 'Have I, fuck.'

I drag the knife up slowly along his inner thigh. It sounds like a caress as it scrapes against the fabric. When I get all the way up I turn my hand and let the back of the razor stroke his groin painstakingly slowly. Rickardsson freezes still and stops breathing again.

I angle the blade between Rickardsson's belt and clothing, and quickly slice off the belt. In one movement I pull both his trousers and underpants down to his knees.

I back up a step to inspect the goods. Rickardsson's muscular thighs and buttocks look genuinely appealing. It must be all that walking.

With my head cocked to one side I start humming the occultist's melody again. Rickardsson pulls at his ropes so hard that the whole mighty oak desk shakes. His seed-bag dangles, plump and inviting, between his thighs. A robust man, as I said. I drag the flat side of the knife over his hairy scrotum.

'I think Rickardsson needs to shave a little down here.' I snort. 'Neck and chin, and the fucking balls to boot.'

I go to the windowsill, fetch the half-full litre of Östgöta Sädes and take a swig directly from the bottle on the way back. I put the bottle down on the desk, followed by the razor, and I undo my trousers.

'Now we are going to commit some proper sins, so that Our Saviour didn't die on the cross for nothing.' I drop my trousers and underpants to the floor. 'It's been months since I last had a man.'

I spank Rickardsson's backside with a crack. I tentatively squeeze one buttock. He is stock-still and trying to get out some strangled words. Bit late for that. I clear my throat deeply and drop a glob of spit between his buttocks.

'Has Rickardsson heard the story about the bull that refused to mount heifers? The baffled farm boys presented him with one after another, each prettier than the last. He wouldn't even look at them. Then the head farmer came up with the idea that they should try to cover one of the heifers with mud. The bloody bull immediately came running. And the farmer invited all the farm boys to three drams each, which was spoken about in the parish long after.' I laugh. 'Or it might have been a stallion.' I clear my throat. 'In which case it would be mares, of course.'

Out in the courtyard a blackbird is singing with a sort of rippling joy in its song. The dusky half-light shimmers through a fold in the tattered blinds.

'No fucking idea what I am trying to say with that. Maybe that birds of a feather flock together.' I spank his buttock so hard it sets the whole thing aquiver. 'You're going to feel this. The body heals quickly, but the memory will lodge for ever like a rift in your soul.'

Rickardsson is a tad shorter than me and I have to bend a little at the knee. I pull his shirt up high. He has a tuft of black hair in the curve of his back. The strands tickle my palm as I stroke my hand over it carefully. It is as soft as the stuffed hummingbird on the windowsill.

All I brought back from Buenos Aires was Gabrielsson's friendship, that little bird, a coconut and gonorrhoea. I hope I don't have the same bad luck now.

I cup Rickardsson's balls with my left hand and drive my cock decisively towards his arsehole. I look him in the eye in the mirror. His eyes are veiled in hatred and redness is spreading across his cheeks. I smile, grasp tightly around his nuts and pull him closer to me.

'Kvisten, Rickardsson. Rickardsson, Kvisten. A pleasure.'

My voice is as thick as porridge. I feel his considerable body shivering under my hands, and I press down. I swallow hard.

'Isn't this what it's like for her? Ploman's whore? Silent but forced to open her legs when required?'

133

I prepare to ram my cock inside him. I hear a thin snort as I slide in a couple of centimetres. He curves his back slightly in a barely noticeable movement. In the mirror I see him close his eyes. His nostrils flare, sending his breaths as shudders through his flesh.

I let go of his balls and slip my hands between the desk and his thighs. He is rock hard. I lean forward over him and smell his scent of Aquavera and snuff. I loosen his gag and pull the sock out of his mouth.

Tough blokes like it rough.

I tear the gag off with my front teeth, turn his face towards me and kiss him deeply. With a drip of blood running down my chin, I whisper in his ear.

'Oh, you fucker.' I reach for the jar of gun oil. 'So this is why you have been watching me all these years.'

TUESDAY 21 JULY

I hold a cigar in one hand and Rickardsson tight against me with the other. Every millimetre gap between our bodies is sealed with sweat. As I take a puff the glowing tip illuminates our flesh: shiny, bloody, languid and aching after the act. The bed springs creak as he moves and caresses my chest with his hands. Here, shrouded in darkness, we have no secrets.

'Foul play then?'

I bend my arm to reach his hair to stroke it.

'Like hell.'

That knock I gave Rickardsson in the jaw earlier in the evening is making him slur his words. He traces the inky outline of the full-rigger on my chest with his forefinger.

'The Reaper?'

'We've worked together for twenty-five years. Shared Ploman's cut fairly. Now all those years aren't worth an öre.'

'Mmm.'

My heart leaps. Out on the street a handcart rumbles past. The bed squeaks as Rickardsson swings his shaggy legs over the edge. He picks up the bottle from the floor, knocks back a mouthful and wipes his plump lips with the back of his hand.

'How the fuck did this happen?'

I fill my lungs with smoke once more. He looks slumped, a little deflated and even more naked than he is, if that's possible. This great big bloke, vulnerable as a baby bird. His oiled hair has fallen forward and he brushes it away from his eyes. The light of the burning cigar highlights two wide white scars on his fuzzy back. One peeks out from between his two lower ribs, the other runs along his spine, about ten centimetres long from the base of his neck downward. Close call, both times.

A robust man, as I said.

'What's it about?'

'Liquor?' he shrugs his shoulders and blows through his lips. 'I don't fucking know. I think they're doing deals under the table with the Söder boys.'

He reaches for the ashtray and spits in it. Maybe his mouth is coated in the taste of me like a greasy film.

'How?'

'Ploman and the Reaper drive there a couple of times a week with a van and come back a few hours later.'

'Maybe Rickardsson can tag along on the next pick-up?'

'I would never come back. I know how it goes. I know how a story like this begins, and how it ends up. First they shut me out, soon I'll be for the chop, whatever I do.'

'I can help.'

'Lord knows I was under no illusions as to how this life would end. I've been putting something away every week for Anna and the kids. No idea if it'll be enough though. How in hell did it come to this?'

Rickardsson gets to his feet and punches his right fist into his left palm with a smack that resounds between the walls. He stomps hastily to the window, and back and then stops and stands in front of me in all his glory. His eyes burn with rage in the dim light. I feel my muscles contract as if before a fight, but I remain still. He brandishes his finger in front of me, which pleases me somehow. He continues with a tremulous voice.

'What the fuck choice do people born into poverty have? What obligation do us poor bastards have to follow the law? We are stamped down by the educated class, morality is imposed on us and the only thing the damned police are good for is hounding the weak and protecting the rich. And how in the hell is a man supposed to get a real job to support himself honestly when his reputation is blemished by prison sentences?'

'Calm down.'

My voice is still, but inside I am trembling. I don't know why. It is not from fear, not after what we just shared. I take a puff, trying to dispel the feeling with smoke.

The springs complain when Rickardsson slumps on the edge of the bed again. He is staring straight ahead but gropes along my forearm and grips his fingers tight around my wrist. He slides his jaw from side to side to stretch out his swollen mouth.

'Those bastards violate you in every possible way. Throw you behind bars, keep you tethered like a fucking animal, shave your hair so closely you can see the scars on your scalp and cudgel you bloody. Have they ever put you in the isolation cages, in the dark?'

'Too damned right.'

I sink my head into the pillow. It is filled with real down, not sawdust like in the cells of Långholmen.

'You have to fight the rats day and night for your corn gruel and it's as black as a chimney sweep's arsehole.'

'Those were the days.'

'And then comes the prison chaplain preaching that one can have inner riches in the midst of suffering.'

I flinch at his words. I have been listening as though spell-bound for half a minute, but now I am reminded of the reason we ended up here in the first place: Gabrielsson. Rickardsson turns to me.

'Instead violence grows inside you like brushwood. Thorny and miserable. They twist injustice into justice. You start to look at life in a different way. Kvisten understands what I mean.'

'I sure do.'

He nods.

'We are cut from the same fucking cloth, Kvist and I.' He combs his thick fingers through his hair and sighs. 'Take a young man scarred by poverty, anyone at all, treat him like that and see what happens. Most go to pot, but those of us who survive are not to be messed with.' He wipes his mouth again with his wrist. In the corner of his mouth a little blood remains. He sighs. 'Maybe it's no excuse.'

Rickardsson leans forward again and his fringe falls back over his forehead. He fumbles for my hand but takes hold of my wrist instead.

'Probably all over now in any case,' he mumbles. 'The end of the line.'

'Like I said, I think I can help Rickardsson.'

'No point. What would you do?'

'Tail the van and see where they go. At least then you'd know what's going on. Maybe you could give me something? Just the day and time is enough.'

I hold my breath. Rickardsson stares at me for a moment. The grip around my arm tightens, cutting off the blood flow, making my hand throb and my little finger stump ache before he releases it. The scar along his spine stretches as he bends forward and roots around among the clothes on the floor. I take a few deep puffs on my cigar, and his gold pocket watch glints in its glow. The case clicks open.

'Tonight. In fifty minutes.'

*

The engine of the hearse splutters into life and I pull out into the sparse traffic on St Eriksgatan. The Reaper and another bloke I assume to be Ploman have just passed by in a dirty white Ford van with Stockholm plates.

I am tempted to step on the accelerator and force the damn thing off the road but keep my distance, with my hat low on my forehead, and both hands on the wheel. The half-empty litre bottle of schnapps slops about between my thighs. The Husqvarna pistol is on the passenger seat, its magazine fully loaded with death. I'm not sure what smells more of gun oil: the pistol or me.

The Ford has a small oval window in each of the two back doors, and it looks like the bloody van is staring at me. I have a terrible feeling, stinging through me needle-sharp, that it is Rickardsson who has tricked me and not the other way around.

'Fine words seduce a fool.'

I increase the distance between us, fumble with a Meteor and manage to strike a match.

It doesn't pay to trust any devil in this industry.

That much I have learnt.

My new trench coat rustles as I grab hold of the Bakelite again. The poplin coat is too warm but I chose it anyway. If you're going to kill a bloke or two, you might as well do it in style. The plan is to strike as soon as they step out of the car. I am not a good shot at long range and need to make sure I get in close.

I take a deep breath and plonk my right hand on the steering wheel. Wrong damn hand. My fingers spasm with pain.

I keep one car behind the Ford. We turn right, the tyres bounce over the tram tracks and we drive over St Erik Bridge in the direction of Kungsholmen's forest of chimney stacks. The pistol is slipping back and forth on the leather seat with a shuffling sound: a reminder of why I am here. I hit the steering wheel again and grimace. Wrong hand again.

The water under the bridge is as still as the evening air. The willows stretch out their arms, as if they are trying to catch the white-hulled motorboat with green and red lights that is slowly chugging along the canal.

Ploman and the Reaper are now in enemy territory, Belzén's turf, but the van looks like it is slowing down rather than speeding up. I switch to a lower gear and stretch my neck.

At Wiklund's bicycle factory, around where Dahlman, our last state executioner, is said to have been run over by a tram at the end of the war, they slow down, and a black Volvo pulls into the road. It stays close in front of the van. I chew lightly on my lacerated lower lip.

Thankfully, I've never had a run-in with the executioner. When I was younger I never did anything to give him reason to bother with me. During recent years it seems like the reasons have piled up, though, and I am glad they have abolished the death penalty.

A hell of a way to go.

Better like this, with my boots on, if I am going to die now. Ma is right about that. I tremble as I puff on my cigar.

We turn on the deserted Fridhemsgatan. Smoke rises from campfires among the shacks and run-down workshops to our right, but the school's gaping windows are empty and black. I wonder who is in the Volvo and what kind of weapons they are carrying. It hardly seems plausible that Belzén, here in Kungsholmen, and Ploman could have gone into some sort of unholy alliance after decades of waging war.

I twist in my seat and lift one buttock. I am damned sore after Rickardsson's return earlier in the evening. The man knew what he wanted and he had wanted it for a long time. I crack a smile despite the tension. I haven't had a round like that in a dozen years or more. I pull the stopper out of the bottle and guzzle a couple of swigs.

We turn right just a stone's throw from Belzén's headquarters and pick up speed along Väster Bridge towards Södermalm. I glance down at the water and imagine the Bumpkin's son leaping to his death. They will have to set up a real fence here sooner or later, mark my words, but when it comes to protecting the poor, broken and sick of Söder and Kungsholmen, it will no doubt take awhile yet.

We pass Långholmen and the Central Prison. After three stints inside I recognise the distinct smells in my broken nose: dirt, prison sweat, water-damaged concrete and tarred trussing. If I don't play my cards right this evening I will be rattling the bars in there for the rest of my scurvy life. The never-ending shuffling steps in straight rows. Beatings and torment.

I focus my attention as we turn on to Söder Mälarstrand. The quay is a well-known drop-off point for smuggled vodka and, despite what Ma says about gambling and Jews, spirits are still the gangster syndicate's principal source of income. The vehicles are thirty metres or so ahead of me and show no sign of slowing down.

Small, creaking cargo boats are packed close together to our left. The last sunshine of twilight glitters in the water, and a train ploughs south on the connecting rail line, shrouded in the white locomotive smoke. We don't meet many vehicles. I reach for my pistol and place it on my knee.

When they passed me back in Vasastan I saw that the Reaper was in the passenger seat. I might be able to drive up alongside on a straight stretch, empty the magazine through the side window, blow the smoke from the barrel and drive away quicker than quick. I jolt. It's about damn time I put my money where my mouth is. For a second I press down harder on the accelerator, but no, the Mariaberget cliff is to my right, the water to the left, and nowhere to turn off to escape the escort car.

I hold the steering wheel steady with my knee, unscrew the cork and take a whole mouthful of schnapps.

Only when we have passed Slussen and are approaching the big Stadsgård quay, do I realise where we are headed and turn off the lights. Normally the area is teeming with herring girls, dockers, customs officials, interpreters and all the sailors on shore leave speaking foreign tongues, asking for directions to the Old Town's stone labyrinth of taverns and brothels. The place is usually filled with the relentless noise of latches churning over winch gears and the indistinct hum of cranes, but now all is deserted and I daren't follow. Not in a damn hearse.

After a moment of consideration I step on the brake and park next to a shack. I hesitate for a second thinking about the litre bottle. I might need it, but it's too much to carry. I close the door quietly. With my Husqvarna in hand I mash the cigar under the sole of my shoe and set off after the convoy on foot with the back of my trench coat fluttering behind me. The ammunition clinks in my trouser pocket and bounces against my leg.

I follow one of the many train tracks, and my shoes pummel against the sleepers in time with my heartbeat. It is still too light for my liking and I crouch behind one of the many stacks of barrels, crates and kegs that are strewn about. On the track that runs nearest to the edge of the wharf, about thirty metres ahead, stands a long freight train that can offer me some protection. I head towards it.

I glance at the rail spikes along the tracks and conjure up the image of Gabrielsson's skinny corpse in my mind, to stoke up my hatred, feel it burn in my veins. I can't feel it. I don't know any more if I am here for his sake, or my own.

Should have taken the schnapps with me.

I can still hear the sound of the car engines some distance ahead, faint as a breeze. A few seagulls screech, a steam whistle blows hoarsely from somewhere on Saltsjön. I slip but regain my balance and continue with my finger on the trigger and the pistol poised.

I reach the freight train where the shelter of the wagons allows me to pick up the pace. I follow along the embankment, only a couple of metres from the water, lapping against the stone pavement.

I approach a row of familiar cranes. They look like great big giraffes that have come down to drink in the dusk. I listen, but the engine sounds have disappeared and all that can be heard is my own wheezing windpipe.

The van and the escort car are both parked between the train and the northernmost brick building of the customs complex. With more than fifteen metres to spare I slow down and am soon lying flat on the ground. I allow my lungs to recover as I look around. To my left is a ship with a coal-blackened English flag. She is lying in shallow water and has probably not been loaded yet. The ground straight ahead of me is littered with orange peel and to my right are train tracks and wheels. My heart hammers against the ground.

'By all the blue-scorched devils in hell, Kvisten,' I whisper. 'Here goes.'

I crawl laboriously a little farther and squeeze my head under the train. It smells like engine oil. I blink away the sweat from my eyes and look around. The cars are parked diagonally in front of me but there is no one in sight. Maybe they have disappeared into the customs office building.

I am fingering one of the spikes that rivets the rail tight to the sleepers and considering my options when suddenly the rumbling of a heavily loaded trolley resonates through the air. A car door is opened and shut again.

With one hand on my hat I crawl out from under the train and stand up. I hear muted voices from the other side of the train but I can't make out what they are saying. I take a couple of careful steps back and step over the link between two freight wagons. I press my back against the wagon side.

The bleak rippling water laps against the quay; the wind brings sharp, exotic scents from ship holds.

Another car door opens with a creak and soon I hear the shuffling and thuds of boxes being unloaded. I have lifted tons of goods in this harbour myself.

I push my hat back with the barrel and wipe my forehead with the sleeve of my trench coat. I peek around the corner with my pistol outstretched. I suck a breath in through my teeth.

Ploman is a hefty bloke with a square head like a wooden block. He is helping a customs officer aboard with a small wooden crate. The crate is barely thirty centimetres long and wide but it looks as heavy as lead. The customs officer is dressed in full uniform with plenty of brass on his jacket and a peaked cap. Corrupt bastard.

The Reaper is pale even in high summer, clothed entirely in black, with sickly sunken cheeks. Skinny as a starving street cat, with a butt in the corner of his mouth and a monocle dangling on a gold chain. He is holding a significantly larger box in his arms. My little finger stump is aching like a rotten tooth.

I repress a sudden cough reflex and pull my head back around the corner. The irritable impulses start in the sides of my ribs, then push into the centre of my chest and make me arch in discomfort. A few choked sounds escape my tight-pursed lips. This fucking summer and all its dust. I press my left hand over my mouth as my upper body spasms.

I have suffered this damned cough my whole adult life and the only thing that seems to help is a proper spell at Långholmen. The fact that a damp prison cell is the best we have to offer a poor man by way of sanitation says something about this country.

Nevertheless, a twenty-year stint is more than I have the stamina for.

I calm down and take a couple of deep breaths of familiar sea air before peeking around the corner again. Not an easy shot. A moving target in the half-light, ten metres away, partially obscured by the trolley.

I am filled with the same feeling as Evy Granér evoked in me at Dr Jensen's. Maybe it's some sort of flicker of conscience. It has embedded itself in my stomach like a nail.

For fuck's sake, Kvisten.

Can't you see the difference between a poverty-stricken woman and some ruthless bloody murderers? No need to agonise over them.

The customs officer is an inconvenience. He hasn't done a damned thing to me but on the other hand no man with brass on his coat has ever helped me any either. Quite the opposite. He will probably make a run for it, and something tells me the booze smugglers won't alert the police on the way. If he insists on being difficult I'll shoot his kneecap off.

No more than that.

I think.

To the right of us, the sheer side of Katarinaberg drops vertically down to the harbour in darkness. High up, the bells of Gabrielsson's church begin to strike ten o'clock, as if counting down to knockout.

145

'Payment in blood.'

I mumble to myself, lean out slightly and raise the pistol. If I strike now the shots might be partially drowned out by the bell's dull tolls. Three, four.

All the evening's drams have caught up with me, and my finger trembles slightly where it rests on the trigger's seductive curve. My eyes seek out the luminous tip of the Reaper's cigarette. For Gabrielsson. A blueberry right in the kisser.

Five.

I take a deep breath and hold it. For one moment the front sight is locked like a blackjack on the Reaper's pale face. My finger pulls the trigger one millimetre back before he bends down to pick up another box.

A seagull cackles.

I bite my lip.

There is still some bullshit inside me that is resisting.

Katarina's seventh peal urges me on. I blink away a drop of sweat and hold my breath again. My earlier cough reflex remains as a faint tickle in my chest. The Reaper turns his back to me.

'God damn it.'

All I have to do is squeeze the trigger. The ninth chime booms across the grounds. The front door of the escort car opens.

'Fuck.'

Sailors who have spent a few years at sea can usually smell a storm long before it is above the ship. God knows how. For me every storm comes as a complete surprise. A bloody unpleasant one.

My heart leaps. I lower the gun, fold back the hammer with my thumb and crouch down. Detective Chief Inspector Alvar Berglund is well dressed as always. He looks around and rolls the pointy end of his moustache between his fingers.

'You gentlemen had better hurry if you don't want to be late for your little get-together,' he calls to the others.

The customs officer rolls away with the trolley and I still haven't managed to come up with a reasonable plan. Words swoop through my skull like petrels, each gone before I can get a hold of it, to be replaced by the next. It seems I don't have space for more than one thought at a time and the few I do have room for are not getting on well with each other.

'Fucking hell,' I whisper to myself and sink down on my aching behind.

The Husqvarna is shaking in my hand. Out of old habit, I fish out a cigar and shove it in my mouth. The van doors slam. A breath of relief flows through my veins.

It disgusts me.

I peer around the corner in time to see Berglund and the Reaper shake hands. The former puts his left hand on the latter's shoulder. Fucking corrupt coppers. Every one of them seems to be on the smuggling syndicate's payroll; this is not the first time they have offered their escort services. I have heard it happens from time to time as long as the price is right.

I pull my head back again.

'Cop killing.'

I taste the words. Not too bad, if you like the taste of shit. I spit. The whole force would be after me.

One of the men laughs loudly and soon I hear another car door open and shut. One engine starts up, followed by the other. I am going to lose my chance.

A gearbox whines, the sound of the engines rises and falls, the cars roll away. I have worked like a dog in this damned harbour. Heaved 100-kilo sacks of grain on the way to Öhman's or salt to Tempelman's on a backbone of steel. Lugged crates and barrels through rain, snow and baking sun. Ten hours a day, six days a week.

'And still so bloody weak when it matters.'

I peek around the corner of the wagon but quickly pull my head back again. Berglund is doing a U-turn. They are driving back the way they came. The hum of the engine increases, as does my pulse. I chew on the unlit cigar.

My thoughts flow through my head like raindrops: insipid and miserable. Transparent, without substance. I press my back against the wagon. The Volvo's headlights slide into view. The curved fenders spill over the footboard. The car passes so close and slowly that I could step up and hitch a lift with one step.

Sometimes you just have to play it by ear. I learnt that lesson in a fight against Styrbjörn Andersson in autumn 1919. It was my second proper match. I knew that he had smashed some ribs a couple of months earlier. I kept going for his left side even though he beat me off brutally every time. I was just transfixed by those fucking ribs. I was still green and didn't yet know how to adapt and improvise. It nearly cost me the match but I still won, just barely.

'Never been beaten, never even taken a count.'

I have no time to think it over before the van comes rolling along. A match blazes in the darkness of the driver's cab and lights up the Reaper's pale, smoke-haggard profile as he lights a cigarette.

I finally let my hunger for revenge lead the way.

I toss the cigar over my shoulder, run out into the open and set off after the Ford. Gravel crunches under the wheels and the fleeting blue exhaust caresses the road, filling my lungs and angering them further. I make one final effort. Stumbling, I grab hold of the handle of the left back door. It slides open and I dive in sideways and land on the floor with a thud.

I look around. No window between the driver's cab and the cargo space. I bury my face in my crossed arms. My body spasms with coughs. I am dripping with sweat.

The tar cavities of my lungs calm down. I get up on all fours and shove the Husqvarna into my coat pocket. I turn around to close the door. The van lurches, I fall back on my side and the door swings wide open and slams shut again. I get up on my knees and peek through the right-hand oval window. The silhouette of the upper storeys of the Drottsgården skyscraper is etched against the backdrop of the summer sky.

I turn towards the driver's cab again and squint to see better. It is dark but the back windows let in a flickering lustre. Crates of booze line the side of the van. They are made of unplaned wooden boards, free from text, with lids nailed shut. Hemp-rope handles droop on either side.

I creep to the front of the cargo space, stand up and place my left hand on the cool metal. I take out the Husqvarna and aim it at the place where the Reaper's back should be. The bodywork of the vehicle vibrates, causing the muzzle of the pistol to tap gently against the metal, and making my hand shake.

God knows if the bullet can break through the van as well as his body. I've heard that Husqvarna lead is about as powerful as a sleepy bumblebee but it's worth a try. I grit my teeth so hard it makes my skull ache.

'Bloody hell.'

The pitiful whisper slips out from my cracked lips but is swallowed up by the hum of the engine and the wheels against the road. I clutch the butt so hard that I can feel its every groove. The van lurches and I lose my footing. I drop one knee to the floor.

Deep down it feels like a relief.

'Damn!'

I stand up again as the van swerves. Streaks of light flicker across the floor. Slouched like an old farmer's widow, I work my way to the rear windows and peek out. We are driving back along the Söder Mälarstrand embankment, passing the animal pens where the abattoir vehicles fill their cargo. We will soon reach Väster Bridge.

Maybe it is better to wait until we have driven the whole way to Vasastan. Berglund will most likely leave the convoy at around the same place as he joined. The police station is not far from there and on the other side of the bridge we are back on Ploman's territory. I smack my lips. The thought of that schnapps lying in Lundin's coffin carrier is making my mouth water.

'One bullet in the Reaper, one in Ploman, and then Kvisten gets a little something as reward.'

My voice echoes faintly. I sit down on the floor with my back against the van's side. When I first met Gabrielsson he didn't have a church of his own but spread his gospel from a flat not far from the Buenos Aires docklands. More than twenty years have passed since then.

'Your oldest friend for fuck's sake.'

I shake my head. Rickardsson, the ice-cold bastard, said we were cut from the same cloth. No way in hell can I reconcile myself with that. I hang my head and feel strain in my neck.

'Kvisten's run out of spunk.'

I clear my throat and try to spit out the taste. At times fury has taken over, and I have killed, but only in self-defence and I am not sure that counts. Shooting a man in the back in cold blood is a different matter altogether, that much is clear now.

I creep over to the doors again, stand up and look out. We are driving down Fridhemsgatan, first past the school and then the slums on the right. They are clearly driving back via the exact same route. If my assumptions are correct Berglund will leave the convoy soon.

I don't have much time to pluck up the courage.

I was right. As soon as we turn off and onto St Eriksgatan I see Berglund's black Volvo disappear in the opposite direction.

The hour is at hand.

A flash of fear sings in my limbs. I see my own face reflected in the window: a vicious hound who finally learnt how to be a good dog in his old age. All he needs now is one of those compassionate gunshots.

The factories down in the Atlas area are keeping quiet. This is the rag-girl hour, when all manner of human refuse creeps out to sniff around in the cool, dusky late evening. A tramp rifles around in the bins outside the tobacco shop on St Eriksplan; three streetwalkers are absorbed in a discussion with sweeping gestures, pale from alcohol, diseased blood and hatred, coarse and cruel, with shrill sneers and screeches. A man is kneeling in the corner of the square with a large neck swelling and a stubborn beggarly hand held out in front of him. The other is gripping a bottle.

I bear no grudge against them. We all do what we must to put food on the table. I have been where they are now and with a bit of bad luck I could end up back there tomorrow.

If I get out of this alive.

I press down the handle and open the door. A warmish breath of petrol penetrates the van. We are driving too fast. If I were to give up on myself and Gabrielsson by jumping out of the back, my body would be crushed on the pavement.

The hollow-eyed face of the Jewel flashes among the other girls and I blink. She used to be a neighbour of mine, and she was renowned for her riotous nature and unbridled, joyful indulgences, but she calmed down when she popped a tot. Was supposed to be apprenticed to a milliner, so they say. But the kid soon got sick and died because she left him in a draught. Now she wanders around here: a frail grey moth, hoping to return home with a couple of notes in her stockings once the night and the men are finished.

When the inhabitants of Sibirien fall, they fall hard.

I should know, if anybody does.

My rambling thoughts vanish as the van slows down and we turn left. I grip the side to steady myself. We swing right.

Where the hell are we going now?

The vehicle stops with a screeching sound and I gasp for air. Creeping back a few steps, I lean my weight on one knee and raise the Husqvarna towards the back window. The left front door opens. Rapid steps clatter across the pavement. It must be the Reaper.

If I am going to abandon my task, I should do it now while we are standing still. I try to reconstruct our journey to figure out where we are now. My collar feels too tight and I rip off my tie. My throat is as dry as snuff and I wish more than ever that I had a dram to lubricate my thoughts. A door slams somewhere and someone comes running back.

Too slow on the uptake.

As usual.

You blockheaded bastard.

The motor growls into life, we back up at high speed and I almost fall on my face. We turn around a corner and set off forward again. If ever I had an opportunity to get out of this quandary, I just missed it.

One more turn and the car accelerates even more. I stand up

and look outside. We are back on St Eriksgatan driving north. We probably stopped outside Ploman's casino on Sätertäppan. It's not far to his headquarters now. If I am going to do it, it has to be within the next couple of minutes. My pulse is so furious that it feels like a thumping drum beat in my head. I conjure up the mental image of Gabrielsson again, naked and bony, nailed to the floor of his own church.

Death shouldn't bother me any more. Everybody disappears from my life in one way or another. Everything I touch turns to shit. When Lundin croaks there won't be a living soul left who can stand me.

'What the hell am I going to do?'

There is nothing convincing about my whisper. I smack my dry lips. The pistol weighs heavily in my hand. More than anything I just I want to drop it to the floor. Instead I look around the little space.

The crates.

How did I not think of it before?

Maybe they're right when they say that I'm as thick as two short planks. In all likelihood I am literally surrounded by fine imported spirits on their way to Ploman's den. A mouthful or two should make my balls grow back.

I prise out the blade of my pocketknife and set the tip into a crack in one of the wooden crates. There is a muffled thud as I push the blade farther in with my palm.

That's it.

I lean my weight on the shaft. With a creaking sound, much like the one that resonated between the walls of Katarina Church last Saturday, the wood releases its nails.

I pry off the board and reach my hand inside. I immediately feel something metallic in the straw-filled box. It is no bottle.

I take out the object.

I gulp.

The machine gun is a model I have never seen before. I run my fingers over it. The magazine is inserted from the side. I angle the barrel up towards the flickering light and touch the marking with my thumb. MP35. Means nothing to me.

According to Ma, Ploman has been growing stronger recently. If all the other crates contain the same thing it would appear that he is planning a full-scale war.

I peek out through the back window. The shop signs for a real estate agency, a gentleman's outfitters and Liljan's café rush by. If my pulse doesn't calm down I am going to have a heart attack. Which isn't really how I imagined my end would come. A has-been with a failed heart in the back of a fucking van.

The magazines and ammunition must be in the smaller boxes.

I put the weapon back in the crate and fall to my knees by the crate nearest the door. I fumble with my pocketknife as I try to get some air in my lungs. It feels as though someone has twisted a strap around my chest and pulled it tight.

The board creaks as I rip it off. I gasp. Rows of gold bars glitter in tight rows packed with straw. The sender's address is stamped at the top. The German eagle clutching a ring surrounding a swastika.

In the flickering light it looks as though its wings are poised, about to take flight.

The van rocks on its suspension. I am sitting with my shoulders pressed against the driver's cab and my legs stretched out in front of me. I hold my Husqvarna with both hands, aimed at the doors. My coat pockets are sagging with the weight of a gold bar each. They must weigh four, five kilos apiece.

I have tied my dirty handkerchief over my nose and mouth. Sweat is flowing from this bastard hat down my forehead and stinging my eyes. My heart is racing. I would skin someone for a cigar.

If I come out of this alive I'll buy the latest model of car, collect the suit at Herzog's the tailor and invite Hasse to the Grand, all out of a day's earnings.

A door slams shut, followed by a second. The vehicle sways. I listen to murmuring voices. There is a thump as someone kicks the front tyre.

I hear steps crunch against dry gravel and murmurs moving along the right side of the van. I cock the trigger with a soft click.

'Little Ida,' I whisper into the darkness.

Somehow I have always believed that we would meet again, father and daughter. God knows how. Regardless, I have always considered it an inevitability. Something to hold on to in the absence of much else. If I find a way out of this I can send some proper dough across the Atlantic. Enough to buy her a big house with a sun lounge and all the trimmings she fancies. She will want for nothing. Maybe it will release me from the guilt of what happened, free me from my nocturnal penitence.

Someone kicks the back tyre. The vibrations spread through the vehicle. I whimper like a newborn.

'We'll have someone refill the petrol and pump the tyres tomorrow.'

The voice is hoarse, ravaged by smoke. A thin wisp of a man passes first the left back window and then the right. I follow him with the front sight.

Footsteps scuff the gravel and die away. I gasp for breath through my handkerchief and creep over to the doors. I peek out through the sooty windows. No one there.

I carefully open one door and slide out. It has got darker, but is still too light. I sink to my knees and listen hard with the pistol in my hand.

The large gravel yard is enclosed by three brick warehouses and a high fence along the road. All the windows in the main building are lit up.

It doesn't make it any more inviting.

There is a gateway in the fence about twenty metres away guarded by four blokes, each with a weapon hanging over his shoulder.

I am certainly not getting out that way.

Ploman's compound is packed with vehicles of all descriptions. I crouch and shuffle my way over to a well-polished Chevrolet, then I look around again. A fence separates the compound from the road, with a wooden walkway running along the top. Belzén of Birka has a similar set-up at Kungsholmen. Shielded by the fence, they can defend themselves from enemies in the street below with the additional benefit of a better view. If I could find a way to get up onto it I could sneak above the guards' heads, heave myself over the fence and jump down to the street. It doesn't look much more than three metres high.

The bullion weighs down the pockets of my trench coat as I move quietly from car to car, along the side of the yard and well away from the centre. I search for a ladder or staircase of some sort. There is a large lorry parked next to the corner of the main building, so I suppose it must be hidden behind there.

A sudden blare of applause and shouts makes me dive onto my stomach next to an Oldsmobile.

I wind myself.

A shiver runs down my back.

Down in the harbour, Detective Chief Inspector Berglund said something about a get-together. It doesn't exactly sound like a quiet poker evening in there. More like a football match.

I get up, work my way in a crouching position towards the lorry in the corner and slip around it. Just as I had hoped, there is a wooden staircase leading up to the ramp. The first step creaks but I continue, as quietly as I can.

To my right the metre-wide ramp leads along the main building and then curves towards the road. I have to crawl under two overhanging windows, open in this heat, then turn right and work my way along until I'm right above the guards' heads. The wood creaks beneath my feet as I begin to slowly make my way towards Ynglingagatan, freedom and wealth.

Another round of applause bursts into the clear, warm summer night. I freeze. The sound of men chanting in unison flows through the open windows. From the racket they're making I'd guess there are several hundred of them.

'*Heil* Ploman! *Heil, heil, heil!*'

Are they holding a fucking Viking feast in there? Drinking mead and reciting verse? One look can't hurt. I blink away a drop of sweat and creep as quietly as a cat towards the window where the yellow light is spilling out on the wood like lemon slices.

Snatches of speech in a gruff voice sail out into the evening as a plank complains under my right shoe. I glance at the guards. One of them is lighting a cigarette, another is kicking at the gravel. I swallow.

I am only a few metres from the window when a door screeches open under me. I fall to my knees and stretch out headlong on the floor. The gold bullion in my coat pockets hits the wood with a dull thud and pain shoots through my right thigh as one of the bars jabs my hip bone. My hat falls off.

As if in slow motion I watch it roll towards the edge of the ramp.

Steps crunch below me.

I grind gritty road dust between my teeth. I stretch out my arms.

The hat's red silk lining shines as it spins over the grey boards. It is more than halfway over the edge when my fingers grab the brim. I snatch it back.

That was a close one.

I hold my breath. My heart is pumping so hard it is making me feel sick. It seems to almost drown out the harsh voice coming from the open windows.

'...plan into action, much of the police force and the officer corps are behind our cause, and in a few days, when the Swedish people take part in the Olympic opening ceremony, National Socialism will stand out as the only real front against Marxism and Judaism.'

More steps crunch below me and a tall bloke comes into view. He is wearing well-polished black boots and black breeches with a strap across his broad back. He stops around two metres below and to the right of me.

'...because in the chaos that arises in the wake of Jew murders and a Marxist terror bombing, our protection, gentlemen, is the only alternative that can bring about order.'

The man below turns around and I hold my breath. I recognise him and that dimple in his chin. He has a lurid red swastika armband on his arm. Under the black uniform cap I see a few blond curls. He is standing so close that I can hear the little clasp on his cigarette case click open. I have seen him somewhere very recently but I can't remember where.

If he looks up I am done for.

'...In a week the men will be sorted from the boys.'

The cigarette case snaps shut, a match rasps, a flame flashes on the skull emblem of his cap.

I cock the hammer soundlessly with my thumb by carefully pulling the trigger back with my forefinger at the same time. The man below me is using a long ivory-coloured cigarette holder. A few quick breaths, three puffs of smoke that chase after one another in the night, a light cough. I retain the tension in my left hand. As slowly as possible, I roll over onto my back, out of his sight.

The gravel crunches under his combat boots as he goes inside again and the door slams. I take a deep breath.

It judders with fear.

I get up onto my knees and peek at the figures by the gate. It has darkened somewhat and they are moving around but I can see one of them lay his rifle across his shoulders like a yoke and rest his forearms on it.

I approach the window in two silent moves. Light spills out on the ramp in a hazy semicircle.

'…and with that I will hand over to our German friend Helmut Kunz.'

Applause rips through the stuffy summer evening. I straighten up a little and peek inside. On the podium on the farthest side of the large premises stands the Reaper. He applauds with a cigarette dangling from his lips. Ploman is standing at a rostrum draped with Swedish and German swastika banners.

The German officer makes his way between the perfectly straight rows of the audience. They are all dressed in brown shirts with leather straps.

'*Heil* Kunz,' calls the Reaper and the attendees respond as one. As if on cue, a hundred right arms stretch diagonally up towards the ceiling three times. Their hands are completely straight, as if they are trying to slice existence itself in two.

*

Darkness descends slowly over the city like a sparse rain of soot. One of the guards switches his hunting rifle to the other shoulder, pulls the soft cap off his head and uses it as a cloth to wipe his face and neck. Another presses his index finger against one nostril and snorts a blob of snot onto the ground.

I continue at a slow pace on all fours, pressed tight up against the building. It has taken at least ten minutes to creep along the façade and I have just a few metres left until I reach the walkway that runs directly above the guards' heads. The ammunition rattles gently in my trouser pocket as I edge half a metre on, weighted down by the gold.

A heavy humming bumblebee flies straight into my face on translucent wings. I bite my lip under my handkerchief. I creep forward a little, stand up, creep a little farther, trembling with terror.

I finally reach the corner, get onto my knees, grab hold of the top of the fence and stand up. A silent breeze breathes in my face. It is lucky that they don't have barbed wire over the fence like Belzén of Birka.

I peer down.

Around a three-metre drop.

I hear the distant hum of traffic from Solnavägen and a whole choir of crickets singing in the park opposite. Diagonally below me, hidden under the ramp, the guard clears his nose again.

'It's so damn hot you gotta drench your nightshirt in cold water to get any relief. And then you get a bloody cold.'

I carefully place my left hand and right foot on the edge of the fence. A board creaks on its nail as I lay my weight on it.

This is fucking it, Kvisten. Down Ynglingagatan, through Vanadislunden and home. In barely fifteen minutes you will be a wealthy man. The latest Cadillac, lunch at Cecil's and a Havana in your mouth. I got an intoxicating whiff of wealth for a few weeks around Christmas of '32.

It didn't last.

I brace myself and leap over the fence. My left foot hooks the edge and I spin around mid-air. I hit the ground heavily like a slaughtered hog cut down after bleeding dry. A gunshot blasts in my ears. An intense pain explodes across my ribcage.

I turn onto my back. I groan and blink in a cloud of gunpowder. My ears are ringing. I stare dumbfounded at the Husqvarna in my grasp. The shot is still reverberating as a gentle tickling in my hand.

'What the hell?'

'Up on the walkway!'

I feel my chest but I'm not bleeding. That fucking gold bar must have jammed into my ribcage when I landed. I find a Meteor. I put it in my mouth and get up to my feet with a sigh. I stagger and pat my pockets for a match. The trench coat's shoulder seam has split and the fabric is flapping like an open wound.

'The fuck did I put them?' I mutter to myself.

I bite the end off the cigar and spit it out. I grimace. One rib is broken, maybe several.

My eyes dart around: the street is a puzzle of grey stone, a dark streak of cloud cuts the moon in two, wilting bluebells are bending in the scorched grass of the roadside verge.

The ringing in my ears changes frequency. My brain is struggling to re-enter reality. It hurts, as usual. The clearer my head, the more it hurts. I fold over my injured ribcage and whimper, still dizzy and confused.

Then come the footsteps and the men.

I hear them now.

161

Angry boots beat against the wooden planks of the walkway, orders and shouts ring out from inside the compound. I look up and head for where the street ends in a flight of steps ten metres away. The entrance is shrouded in leafy bushes. I take a few tentative steps and then speed up. The ammunition rattles like marbles in my trouser pocket and the gold bars slam against my thighs. I am dragging a hell of a lot of ballast along with me.

As I pass the main gate I hear the familiar sound of a barrier being pulled away. I lift my right arm and fire two shots blindly, leaving a bullet hole in either side of the gate. For a moment everything is quiet but for the eternal nagging of the crickets.

With every step I take the vibrations jolt up into my battered ribcage. I reach the steps just as the gate opens behind me. I turn around.

Three men: a revolver, a hunting rifle and a machine gun that might be the same model as the one I found in the van.

I fire another couple of shots. The man with the machine gun flinches, then raises his weapon to waist height.

I turn around and hurl myself down the steps just as the concert begins and the very air around me explodes. The machine gun chops its monotonous requiem and bullets whistle above my head, raining a torrent of leaves, bark and twigs down on me.

My broken ribs scream. I reach the first of the staircase's two landings and collapse to my knees with a groan. The firing has stopped and I hear steps approach from both above and below. I raise the Husqvarna. A solitary leaf lingers in the air, drifting gently down to the steps like a feather. The sound of footsteps is getting louder. From below appears a bowler hat, then a pair of round gold-rimmed glasses; the Husqvarna flashes, the recoil jerks my wrist and strikes my injured chest. One shot remains, no time to reload.

The round glasses lie gleaming on the landing. The left lens is missing, the right is splashed with blood. I stand up, jump over the corpse that is lying motionless on the stairs and out into the street below. Somewhere above and behind me a pair of tyres screech to a halt. They are going to have to drive around the whole block if they want to catch up with me.

The sleeve of my trench coat has ripped free and is sagging around my forearm as I run along the middle of the road. My legs are already numb and my lungs are wheezing in protest. The gold bars must weigh thirty kilos each.

I'm coming up to an intersection when another shot cuts through the night. The dull bang of the elk rifle ripples between the houses. In the same moment there is the sound of screeching brakes and then an engine revving up. More pursuers.

Getingen stretches out to the left: the vast, brutal district of warehouses, hovels, abandoned cars and all sorts of tramps, which we drove past on Sunday.

My best chance. I see three campfires flicker like a series of beacons among warehouses with roofs of corrugated iron, and I head towards them.

I cut across Norrtullsgatan as a car turns around the corner about ten metres from me. I decide to go for it and fire my final shot. I manage at least to hit the windscreen. The car lurches, the tyres scream, the vehicle skids and stops.

There is a rhythmical tapping coming from somewhere above me, sort of like when Ström the junk dealer sits at home straightening out nails with his little hammer. Behind me I hear the car doors open and steps drum against the street. My feet kick up dust as I turn the corner of a crumbling wall, wheezing all the while. I'm slowing down. This damn handkerchief isn't helping my breathing.

I step on a pallet, but a rotten plank gives in and my foot goes through. I pull my leg out but the bastard pallet wants to come with me. As I try to shake it off jagged splinters tear holes in my wide trousers and scratch my calf but I eventually get free and continue on breathlessly.

Two tramps are sitting by a fire in an old zinc bucket, each holding a hammer. The flames are licking like mad through a hole in the side of the pail.

So much madness.

The vagabonds have a pile of old bricks in a wheelbarrow. Behind them stands a neat stack of chipped-clean bricks. Two pairs of flabbergasted eyes shine out from their bearded faces.

'Stop!'

The voice comes from a few metres behind me. I take a few steps and jump behind the pile of bricks. Shots ring out, small clouds of pulverised, burnt clay explode like blisters into the night air; the bucket clatters over in a shower of sparks, and the tramps yell hoarsely.

I take out one of the gold bars, chuck it next to the brick pile to shed some weight and crawl clumsily under a low wall to an abandoned farrier stall. It smells like wet horse. My chest is about to explode with pain.

In the distance I hear police sirens. I crawl under another wall, come out round the back of the farrier's, squeeze through a tarpaulin tent packed with rolls of rusty barbed wire, and soon I am making dust fly, stumbling through foliage, dirt and sun-scorched tall grass. I emerge on a gravel road and stagger east. My legs are as heavy as iron bars.

To my right the police car's flashing lights colour Ynglinga-gatan's façades blood-red: more enemies.

I slow down a little, take out the second gold bar and look

around for a place to hide it. It is weighing me down and I can't carry it much longer.

The hunting rifle bangs behind me again. Panic sets my muscles on fire. I pick up speed once more.

'Fuck!'

So damn weak when I need strength.

I am crying, and my salty tears sting my gasping mouth. There is a bang as the gold bar hits a burnt-out oil barrel. My mouth tastes as if I have a bunch of small screws in my jaw. I pull the handkerchief off my face.

'Fucking hell!'

Another bullet whistles past my head. I think I can hear someone behind me feeding another cartridge into the rifle. I stumble, drop my hat, and the bullet sails through the summer night, just above my head.

They are closing in.

I rush towards Vanadislunden in tatters. Above me the bell of St Stefan's Church strikes the half-hour, as if ringing in the final act of a tragedy.

PART TWO

PART TWO

WEDNESDAY 22 JULY

'Is a man supposed to go bareheaded in this heat? Huh? What sort of infernal notion is that?'

Dixie sits down on her backside and turns towards my voice. She tilts her head to one side and whimpers.

'It's just not going to work.'

Tuesday became Wednesday just an hour ago. I manage to pull Dixie a couple of metres farther along quiet Roslagsgatan before she barks and sits down again. I hear the odd car drive up Vallhallavägen one block to the east. The sound of an engine rises and falls, dies away and returns, as if the city were breathing deeply in its sleep.

'I'd rather walk around with a damned paper cone on my head.'

My ribcage aches as I look to the north with a sigh. The white beams of the street lights converge into a single point up by the tram turning loop. A breath of wind, lukewarm like a Bengal breeze, becomes trapped between the façades and exhales in my face. I try to remember whether I was stupid enough to mark the lining of my hat with my name.

Fuck knows.

Dixie sniffs the air. The sour-sweet smell of sun-warmed refuse seeps from the bins in the courtyard and out across the neighbourhood. The close, musty atmosphere reminds me of prison and the stench spread by fellow inmates, even though everyone can wash at least once a month nowadays.

I can't say I am tempted to send a thank-you note, but it occurs to me that this must be the first time the law has ever done me any favours. Just as the police appeared at Getingen, Ploman's gangsters retreated and allowed me to escape the labyrinth of shacks and storehouses. Staying to find the gold bars was out of the question. The vein in my forehead begins throbbing with rage. I tug Dixie's leash and mutter to myself.

'Such is the nature of this country: they expect you to toil and sweat, and be grateful for the privilege, while someone else enjoys the fruits of your labour, and you don't have a hope in hell of receiving Fortuna's good grace.'

I light a cigar and force the smoke out my nostrils.

'How in the hell is one lonely man supposed to take on a whole conspiracy of gangsters, coppers and fuck knows what else?' I shout to Dixie.

The bitch tilts her head to one side and swishes her tail. The cigar crackles as I take a drag. My ribs are tightly bound with bandages, which makes it difficult to inhale the smoke as deeply as I would like.

We hobble on while thoughts of the Reaper, Gabrielsson and the crate of gold continue to swirl around my brain. My thoughts have sunk into a hopelessly stagnant backwater, unable to move on. Lundin often says that I am at odds with logic at times, but that is mainly when I am drunk. Emma, my wife, used to tease me by saying I had developed a habit of talking to myself, but I don't know if it is true.

'Why the hell would anyone pay that much attention to themselves?'

The darkness has finally defeated the sun. I wait for Dixie, looking at the stars and contemplating the gold bars. I have seen glittering spring whales in the North Atlantic, snake charmers in Bombay and a strike-breaking scab bled dry and swinging from a crane in Cherbourg. Once I saw two Creoles joined at the hip in a circus, and once at the market in Malaga I saw a sailor boxing a bear.

Still, I don't think I have ever been as dumbfounded as when I opened that box of Nazi gold.

Something creaks as I bend down and pat Dixie.

'What the hell do the affairs of the state have to do with us? We'd do best to stay away.'

Emma was a Social Democrat and tried to trick me into going to the May Day march a few times, and I did go, even though I had to fight the urge to march against the current.

I haven't been welcome there either, not since I fell into disrepute. I'll be damned if I get involved in national politics. Especially if Ploman's gang is involved.

Pain shoots along my back when I straighten up. I put the cigar in my mouth, and we hobble farther north.

Once we have reached Johannes elementary school, I see a stoic old draught animal standing stock-still in front of its cart a couple of metres into the courtyard. The driver is nowhere to be seen. I think it's Balder or Loke, one of old man Ljung's more ancient hire horses. For a moment the stationary scene fills me with unease, with some sort of memory, but then I tie Dixie's leash to a fence and approach the nag. For a moment I think I can see a star glinting in its blue-glazed pupil, but then realise it is only the glowing tip of my cigar.

The horse shows its yellow gnashers when it snorts but its smile is friendly. I press my cheek against its silky soft nose. Its warm breath caresses my face. I don't know if the horse's muzzle is making my face moist or if my own tears are taking me by surprise.

I sniff, stroke the old beast across the withers and return to Dixie.

'You've done enough work for one day. I'll carry you now.'

I let a deep puff tear at my lungs, grimace and look around. Rickardsson lives with his family in one of these houses. The memory of our evening spreads hotly inside me and eases my misery. When I was younger I mainly spent time with older men who would take care of me or slip me a coin, but in recent years it has been the other way around. That is how it works: it is practically obligatory. I think about it but can't remember ever bunking up with someone of my own age. Not for any length of time anyway. Even less with a bloke of a similar coarse calibre. I chew my lips listlessly and turn back towards my shabby home.

A shooting star scores through space.

I make my wish.

The stairwell brings coolness. With Dixie in one hand and the other on the handrail, I lumber up to the flat. Fatigue courses through my body and my skull feels like it weighs a ton. Like when I downed some palm wine laced with poppy buds in Rangoon.

A powerful odour of cigars seeps out of the flat through the door grate. Dixie stops in the long narrow corridor with her leash trailing behind. With a grimace of pain I bend down and gather up the letters on the floor. The road dust feels like it has penetrated every hinge in my body and all my joints creak in protest.

The past four days have been taken up with avenging Gabrielsson and I have neglected my work, but the truth is that I am as skint as a louse and need every job I can get if I ever want to release my Herzog suit, or, for that matter, pay next month's rent. I let my advertisement roll on in the daily newspaper last

172

week. An evening nip and a good night's sleep and then it's time to get to work.

I switch on the lamp and flip through the envelopes. I stop at one marked 'Sweden' in faded pencil. For a moment I think my broken rib has pierced straight into my heart. I can't tell whether the earth is quaking, or if it is just me. I stay standing for a long while until the ground stops shaking and settles beneath my feet. The back of the envelope reads:

Ida Kvist, Grand Forks, North Dakota, USA

I lie in the dark, tossing and turning, like a farmer in the barn where his only cow is about to calve. Every movement hurts my ribs, but I keep forgetting and repeating the same mistake. I mechanically count the church bells' quarter, half and hourly tolls.

The occultist has managed to charm some wanton jazz fan with his trumpet, and for half an hour I hear joyful rutting cries from his flat upstairs. Wonder if Rickardsson and I made such a fucking racket. I think about banging on the ceiling with a broom but change my mind. Let them have their fun. I turn onto my side with a sigh and grope gingerly for the schnapps bottle on the floor. Spirits don't help a damn on a night like this but I'll give it a good go.

I take a mouthful, put the bottle back and pick up the letter. The torn envelope trembles in my hand. I consider reading it, but can't bring myself to. Not again. There's no need. The graphite has already etched its way into me: the neat handwriting, the peculiar mix of English and Swedish. I flick bedbugs off my sweaty neck.

If only these fucking lice would leave me in peace, maybe I could sleep. I am sure I can hear them crawling along the water pipes between the flats.

I lean back and strike a match. The smoke hurts my ribcage. Through the open windows I hear two yard cats fly at each other. The roller blind claps in the wind. Ma told me Americans were allowed to take their mattresses out to the fire escape platforms on summer nights. In this poor backwater country we don't have any fire escapes to help us one way or another.

'Here we just burn to death.'

Dixie responds with a whimper from the foot of the bed. With no illumination other than the cigar, I lie and stare at the ceiling. I feel like I have a pile of bricks on my shattered chest. Movement murmurs from the shared water closet in the stairwell.

I try briefly to focus my thoughts on Rickardsson in the hope that self-defilement will give me a few moments of peace, but my mind won't cooperate. I brush away the cigar ash from the full-rigger tattoo on my chest. I take another swig.

It is extraordinary how certain memories fade with time while others remain burnt into the mind's eye everywhere one goes.

And wherever I look now, I see Emma.

We met at the Social Democratic Youth Association's Walpurgis Night dance. It was soon after the war and I had signed off for good. I've always been good at footwork, even when I'm drunk, and I could really swing her around.

The Swedish year should begin on May Day and not in the middle of the grim, cold winter.

Poverty had only allowed me a second-hand suit with a mis-shapen waistcoat but Emma couldn't care less. Her rose-patterned black shawl swirled like a flower garland in the spring night. Now it whips at the mire of my mind.

I shut my eyes. I can clearly recall the notes of the accordion, the poor people's shoes slamming against the wooden dance floor, and her exuberant laughter as I took hold of her waist and swung her around, her soft gasp in my sweaty face when my lips, emboldened by booze, first dared to seek out hers.

The recollections weigh like lead. The city clock tower strikes three, then four, and soon the blackbirds begin to sing from the trees up in Vanadislunden. The sun bleeds through the gaps in the tattered blind and the rubbish man bangs the metal bins in the courtyard. I take the green cloth rag from the desk drawer where I keep newspaper clippings and old memories. I press it hard over my nose and mouth, as if it were drenched in chloroform and could send me to sleep.

As it got dark, we were enveloped in the spring chill, but the glowing ashes of the bonfire still warmed the blood. And yet, when Emma took hold of my arm and stopped me from launching myself into the evening's obligatory fist fight, I experienced a rare sense of peace, despite the schnapps vapour and scent of violence.

The old newspaper hag's steps thunder on the stairs and the sound of banging letter boxes mixes with cooing pigeons on the gutter pipes.

It worked for me and for her, and the next winter she fell pregnant and we had to hurry the marriage along. To afford the rings I took a gig at the mill outside Norrtälje. Three weeks later I was on shift work, and though I had sworn never to walk the country roads like a tramp, I had to walk halfway home to save money. One cold evening a raging snowstorm was very nearly the death of me but I found a farm, surrendered my matches and thankfully, got a place to stay overnight in the barn.

When I came home I thawed out, swapped my chaff-covered clothes for my Sunday best and ventured a proposal. I had the engagement gifts with me, wrapped in a piece of linen to sew baby clothes with. She had tears in her eyes that day, and she stroked my cheek and smiled, and said that at least I could have shaved. I probably should have, but there were so many damn things to think about.

'How the fuck could I forget something like that?'

I smack my palm into the mattress and a muffled thwack resounds in the room. I turn the bottle upside down a couple of times and give it a shake. One lonely drop trickles into the line of hair than runs between my chest and crotch.

Forgetting to shave when I'm about to propose marriage. So fucking stupid when it matters most. They got that much right about me.

An alarm clock blares distantly somewhere and life begins to stir in the house. Soon there are feet shuffling across linoleum floors, the smell of the coffee pots and the sound of lice being beaten from the bedclothes out in the courtyard. I had hoped that the schnapps would knock me out. Instead it seems to have cleaned out my brain channels to allow my memories to flow more easily than ever. The spirits make my sweat sting my skin, as if my own filthy interior were leaking out through the pores. A headache is sawing through my skull.

All I ask is that I can sleep inside this hell.

I married a good woman. The times when I had to stay home and rest after injury, broken and wretched the day after a match, she would rush out to rinse bottles at the brewery next door, or carry mortar to the building sites while I stayed at home and saw to the little one. She had to get up at half past four to get breakfast on the table because the workers' whistle called the mason women in on the stroke of six. There was no other choice.

There was some sort of love. Those were the good years of my life. They didn't last.

There is a murmur of movement and I hear a few clunking metallic sounds coming from outside, as if someone were chasing after a rat and trying to hit it with a shovel. Flat doors fly open, and brackets rattle as children on school holiday whiz down the banisters amid all the hustle and bustle. Before long the iron heels of work boots sing their monotonous song against the stone steps.

Grief grips my insides. I drape my forearm over my eyes.

The courtyard doors slam. Mats rustle as they are hung up on their stands. The first beat makes me wince, the second smacks my head to one side and rattles my skull. Fragments of the old crones' gossip drift in through the window.

How they gossiped, when I came home to the empty flat that time, and my betrayal became a certainty. Grand finale. My eyes well up for the second time tonight.

Another pair of muffled thwacks makes my whole body flinch, and soon a hellish whipping resounds across the grounds. I twist my head frantically from side to side, causing lice to jump out of the pillow seams. Exhausted from schnapps and lack of sleep, I turn onto my good side and sob.

My ribcage explodes over and over, and over again.

The schnapps stings my blotchy palms, runs reddish along the scars on my knees and itches. A long night of drinking versus the morning after. There is nothing to do about it either, apart from take a break for a few hours to give my body enough of a rest for the schnapps to have a kick again.

Somewhere outside I hear children laughing and small birds singing in the courtyard, as if my problems didn't matter a damn.

They probably don't. The generation before me starved, the generation before them had the wars.

'No cause to complain. Time to work.'

I sit hollow-eyed and miserable at the desk and squint to focus on the columns in my notebook

One new hat	- 20 kronor
One wool coat	+ 20 kronor
One Husqvarna pistol	+ 40 kronor
One pair of autumn boots	+ 5 kronor (after a polish)
Pocket watch (Viking)	+ 10 kronor (poss. 12)
Five suits	+ 7–15 kronor each
Five shirts	+ 2.50 kronor each
Three silk ties in various colours	+ 1 krona each
A pigskin punchbag	?

I take out the timepiece and tap on the glass. To my surprise I hear an irregular ticking when I bring it to my ear but the hands are still stuck. I might be able to convince someone that it works. I grab my pen and raise the price by a fiver.

I was seven years old when I made my first business deal. The farmer who won me with the starting bid at the paupers' auction liked to have a brimming cup of lingonberries each morning. I lived in the barn, in a pig sty that was divided with a metre-high plank wall, and was woken up in the wee hours every morning by the boar scratching himself against the boards.

I would get up early and managed to pick an extra litre, which I sold to the woman at the neighbouring farm. Soon I made enough to buy a hen with nine eggs. Not long after that I had six chickens living under my bed. They were good company, and I cried the day I wrung their necks. I sold the meat, took the money, packed my belongings in a handkerchief, hit the road and never looked back.

With a sweeping glance I take an inventory of the sailor souvenirs in my room. The ashtray with a hula-dancing figurine, a stuffed hummingbird from Rio so small that it fits in the palm of my hand, a box decorated with mother-of-pearl and a flagship made by a German donkeyman I once knew. Ström the junk dealer might give me a small lump sum for the lot. The hall mirror should be worth a couple of notes.

It's still not nearly enough. Maybe Lundin is right when he says that I don't have a nose for business.

I take the hummingbird in my hand and close my fingers around it. The feathers are soft against my palm. I want to crush it into pieces.

I take a swig of java to chase the schnapps out of my body. The beans are ground in my grandmother's mill and the coffee is weak but good. I'm not fussy. In the poorhouse we got coffee every other day. On the other days we got coffee grounds with a knob of butter to eat with a spoon.

Born destitute, for ever destitute.

I rip the page out of my notebook and crumple it up. I judge the distance by eye and throw it at the wastepaper basket, where the remains of Danilo's Dance Course are still sticking out.

'Well you're good at missing, at least.' The words ring out in the lonely room.

Lundin's Amerikaur clock strikes ten times from the flat below. It's high time I go and check on the old man. I stagger to my feet and tap the barometer on the wall. The indicator confirms the relentless heat. I wouldn't wear a jacket if I didn't have to conceal my shoulder holster.

Out of habit I grope futilely for my hat on the shelf on the way out. I almost trip on the doormat, fumble with the key in search of the keyhole and nearly fall over again as I turn to go down to Lundin's. I find my balance and stand still. Through the flood of schnapps an idiotic notion floats to the surface and before I know it I am dashing up the stairs.

I knock twice, thrice, before the youth opens. He is wearing elasticated underpants and has his undershirt on inside out. He

179

has his arms wrapped around his body and looks decidedly cold despite the summer heat. His face is ashen and he seems to be suffering a severe case of Klara Malaria, the special hangover caused by the combination of spirits and amphetamines, which harvests its victims primarily among artist types and writers.

'Kvisten? What the hell?' the boy greets me mid-yawn and is suddenly wide awake. He straightens up and clears his throat. 'Um, I'm sorry if I kept Mr Kvist awake. If that's why you're here.'

'I hear you come from a family of fortune-tellers?'

I am still slurring my words. I stretch out my jaws to make the words come out right. The lad looks at me.

'My father had dealings with spirits, it's true, but not me. I've got the gift, all right, but I haven't done that in a long time now.'

The youth indulges in another yawn. Cocky sod. Even my own neighbours have lost respect. I shift up a gear.

'You've got birds standing in a damn queue outside morning and night.'

'I have visitors. I'm sure Kvist understands…'

I look him over. He backs up half a step, lowers his voice.

'Female visitors.'

I stand there quietly and let my battered face do the talking. Sometimes it is a blessing to look like you've been run over by a sled. He squirms, glances back inside the flat and stifles a sigh.

'What's it about?'

'My wife.'

The hinges in his jaw appear to be suddenly incapable of holding up his chin. It drops to his chest as if I had just broken his jawbone. He searches for the right words and plucks up the courage to produce a barely audible whisper.

'I didn't know that Kvist was married.'

Grief shoots through me like black fever. I clench my fists so hard that my nails cut into my flesh. Another word from this pallid fuck and he's going to get a proper box on the ear. I step in and force him back inside.

I stand in place for a moment and look around the dimly lit flat. Heavy silk curtains obscure the windows. I squint. Every wall is covered with oil portraits, landscape paintings, pictures with battle motifs, gold-framed mirrors and a bunch of old weapons. A bookshelf displays a huge array of expensive-looking leather-bound books. A cardboard ouija board is attached to the divan table. In one corner I spy a horn gramophone. The bloke seems to have stuffed an upper-class apartment from the nineteenth century into forty square metres in Sibirien.

'What was your wife's name?'

'Emma.'

'Do you have your rings?'

'Our engagement rings?'

'Yes.'

''Fraid not.'

The fact that I pawned the gold and drank the money in my boozing years is information I keep to myself. I peer at a drinks cabinet full of bottles of whisky and gin. I stroke my unshaven chin and wet my lips.

'Any other keepsakes?'

'Nothing.'

I hear sounds coming from the bedroom and soon a young woman appears, with bobbed hair and a plaid dress with wide lapels across the bosom. She is holding stockings of the thinnest silk in her hand. She nods and looks away. A smile flashes across her face as she pads out to the hall. The occultist and I wait in silence until the front door is closed again.

'When did your wife pass away?'

'Recently.'

'How did she die?'

The letter from America burns in the inside pocket of my jacket.

'Lung fever, as far as I can tell.'

'I am sorry for your loss.'

'I'm in a hurry.'

The youth gestures towards a card table draped in a blanket. I sway as I walk and stretch out my arms and regain balance. The chairs scrape against the parquet floor. The occultist lights a paraffin candle in a bronze candlestick in the middle of the table, rubs the cards together and hands them to me across the blanket. Those wrists wouldn't last half an hour at a ship's boiler.

I take hold of his slender hands. The candlelight flickers over his bare arms. He looks me straight in the eye. He clears his throat and there is a tremble in his voice as he speaks.

'We have come here today to make contact by means of psychic trance with Mr Kvist's wife Emma, who has sadly passed to the other side. If sir would be so kind as to close his eyes.'

I do as I'm told. I feel slightly dizzy. I don't understand why I came here. Bloody mumbo-jumbo. I swallow hard. My hangover is creeping in and clinging to me like a half-dead climbing plant. A gentle shudder runs through me. The youth's breathing becomes heavy.

I open one eye and sneak a peek at him. His eyes are shut but his eyelids are flickering. His mouth is half open and his lips are curved. He is holding his head tilted to one side and facing up to the ceiling with a mischievous expression.

'Give us a sign.'

I scoff, even though I feel a streak of superstitious fear at his voice. Nothing happens. My arms feel heavy.

'Give us a sign, Emma.'

His voice has something solemn about it, almost like a minister speaking to his congregation. Outside I hear the number 6 tram drive past. A few female voices drift in from the street. I glance at his eyelids again. The candle has gone out. A dark wisp of smoke coils towards the ceiling.

All my pores open and sweat runs down my body. Maybe he blew it out while my eyes were closed. Fucking smoke and mirrors. If I know Emma she would definitely make her voice heard and I would be in big trouble.

'She is here.'

I squeeze the lad's hands and try to breathe calmly. A hand, so cold it makes my blood turn to ice, caresses my sweaty neck. The skin on my back is taut. The chair falls backwards as I leap up and flap my arms as if a nest of hornets were after me.

'Be gone servants of Satan! Be gone, I say!'

I spin away like a madman, stumble over the divan table and fall heavily on my back. One of the paintings jumps off its nail and takes another with it on its way down. They hit the floor with a crash. I am lying on the floor, hugging my ribs. The sharp contours of the Husqvarna dig into my side. I whimper as I get up onto all fours.

'It was my fault.'

My voice is trembling.

'Don't worry, sir. Everybody has a different reaction to contact with the spirit world.'

'It was my fault.'

I slam my fist into the tiled floor and bite my lip hard. I get up, my legs shaking, and push away the youth when he rushes to help me.

'Keep your filthy ghost-talking trap shut!' I threaten him and stagger out into the hall. The jazz boy calls something after me but I can't hear what. Residents are slamming doors. I tumble down the stairs and grope for a cigar. Terror – the ice-cold embrace.

The sharp smell of sabadilla vinegar from Lundin's bed makes me feel sick. I breathe through my mouth as I sit on the carved chair next to it. The undertaker is struggling to get a bite of a fried egg onto his fork. He has a bit of yolk in his bushy white moustache. He gives up, throws down his fork with a clatter and pushes the plate away. The corners of his mouth droop downward.

'My father, the old curmudgeon, turned a hundred and received a telegram from the King.'

'Thought His Majesty preferred younger blokes.'

Exhaustion surges through my body and makes my eyelids twitch. I scoop the egg up on the fork and hold it out to him.

'What was that?'

He opens his mouth and I feed him.

'Nothing.'

I take his plate and shovel some in my mouth too. My hand is unsteady and the porcelain clinks.

'What a to-do you caused last night, brother. Did you have company?'

I shake my head so hard my brain rattles between the bones of my skull. It feels like my hangover has multiplied in this God-forsaken heat. The more liquid you pour in, the drier your mouth becomes. I can't even begin to understand how that works. I pinch the bridge of my nose as Lundin looks out the window. The curtains bulge inward lazily in the wind.

With trembling hands I begin to shuffle his red-chequered pack of cards, but I drop a few on the floor and fumble to pick them up. Lundin takes the deck from me.

'How old is your daughter now?' he says in a breathy wheeze.

'Ida.'

'How old?'

'Almost sixteen.'

Lundin nods and continues as if he is speaking to someone out in the street.

'I'm sure she is coping. Women cope.'

My heart strikes my broken tuning fork of a rib. I screw up my eyes. Hope the bastard will move on soon so I don't have to deal with his horseshit. He starts talking about a young love of his but I'm not listening.

He sets his cards out in his lap for another round of patience and nods at them.

'It's called Idiot's Delight. It's near impossible to win, like life.'

'What the hell are you blathering on about?'

I lean my elbows on my knees and hold my head in my hands. It's still spinning.

'I thought that you would probably go first, brother, the way you romp round. I'm glad that is not the case. There is no space in the future for the likes of us, you mark my words. The older generation.' Lundin picks up the queen of spades and turns his head but I catch a glint in his eye.

'Can you ask Good Templar Wetterström to shuffle his way down and bear witness to my will? It concerns the business and the building itself. The whole damn shebang.'

'Can't I do that?'

Lundin laughs and shakes his head.

'That wouldn't be right.'

Wrong fucking day to talk about death. I can feel myself welling up, and look over at the newspaper on the nightstand. 'Rebel army 50km from Madrid' reads the headline. I try to comfort myself with the memory of Jorge, the seaman I met in the harbour market in Malaga. He looked up at me while he was on his knees; his gaze was pure and intoxicated like a calf between the club and the knife. I want to stop my mind, get some respite from all the bad news and my money worries, but Lundin has fallen back into bitterness over lost love.

'And Sigrid, what a temptress of a lass she was. Her figure was the envy of many an Östermalm lady, despite the corset-maker's efforts.'

'Hell!'

I get up and scrabble together the greasy cards in his lap. My blood is racing.

'You need to calm down, brother. What is the matter?'

'Malaga! A memory artist. Could remember all the cards in a pack. I've never seen anyone rake in so much dough!'

'What the hell are you plotting now?'

'I'm no worse than him in my own way. You're always saying there's something wrong with my memory. I'd wager my hat that I could *forget* every last one of them.'

'You don't even have a blasted hat, brother.'

'That's hardly the point.'

'You think people would shell out to see your crummy mind at work?'

'Exactly.'

'You have no nose for business, just like I've always said.'

'What the fuck is that supposed to mean?'

'My brother's brain isn't equipped for handling complex situations.'

186

Lundin stares at me, and I stare back. I don't understand. He sighs.

'God help those with no good sense, and not a coin in recompense. It is as if the minimal logic you did have has melted away in the heat.'

'Isn't remembering nothing whatsoever at least as respectable as remembering everything?'

'One moment my brother is coming out with the most idiotic of notions, and the next you turn around and beat up poor weaklings as easily as ordinary folk pick flowers on the common. And every time I see you, you are even more beat up than before. When all the while you could be helping me out and working off your debts. He who lives without law, dies without honour.'

'You've damn well pedalled schnapps to the entire neighbourhood for decades! And there's nothing to do here, besides.'

I sink down on the chair and lean back. Lundin tries to scratch himself with the fingers of his left hand. There is a clink as his iron hand falls back on the mattress. He sighs and shuts his eyes.

'It was different during the influenza outbreak,' he mumbles. 'We had to dig the paupers' graveyard from both directions at once to manage.'

'Maybe things'll turn around?'

I lean farther back. The ceiling paint has yellowed over the years.

'Yes, they will.' Lundin looks out through the window. 'With water shortages comes cholera, with cholera comes honest work.'

I put the cards back and get up. I struggle to find my balance. I stick a cigar in the corner of my lips and pick up Dixie under my arm.

'I have an errand in Kommendörsgatan, but then I'm coming home.'

'Are you in a fit state?'

'Like hell.'

Lundin seems to hesitate before speaking.

'Brother, can you ask the general store manager to come here with his Kodak to take our portrait?'

'What for?'

'For your memory.'

A whistling shadow passes on the other side of the curtains. I bid farewell to the undertaker and leave him alone with his vinegar-smelling bed sheets.

Dixie will have her morning porter at Bruntell's general store before I take the number 6 to Slussen, and then I can ask about the photograph. I am staggering as I walk out. I hold the bitch more firmly and focus on the embroidered wall-hanging above the shop door: *Order in all things.* The little bell jingles and we step out into the relentless heat of the dog days.

We near enough bash into Rickardsson. A familiar smell of Aquavera and snuff creeps into my broken nose. I stumble to find my balance and put Dixie down on the street. I straighten up and stroke my chin. I could have had a fucking bath. I adjust my tie to hide a lost collar button.

'So Rickardsson's out for a walk in this dazzling weather, I see?'

'Oh, yes.'

He is having difficulty moving his jaw when he speaks. He takes out his silver box of snuff, smacks it against his hand a few times and looks over at Ström's junk shop.

'Is Kvist on the go? Or does he have time for a coffee and a schnapps? Up at your place?'

'I have a pressing job up in Östermalm.'

'Then you should visit Nyström's barbers first. And get your clothes stitched up.'

'No time for that.'

'And get a hat.'

I glower down the sun-drenched street. It is empty save for a couple of leisurely mooching types walking along and dragging their feet.

The air is trembling as if it wants to dissipate.

We stand still for a moment. My thoughts stray to the many men he must have murdered, and the odd few I have killed, and the evening we shared. I wonder which one of us would have to make way for the other if we met on a narrow staircase?

Probably me.

These days.

Rickardsson sucks in some snuff juice and I feel a stirring in my groin. I gasp for air and my knees feel as though they are crumbling under the weight of my body. Rickardsson kicks a crumpled packet of Stamboul cigarettes, then turns to face me. Dixie whimpers and I give the leash a tug to quieten her.

'As Kvist knows, I go for a walk here every evening. Around seven or eight. Yes, eight, shall we say.'

There is a brief silence, as if the very sun, the very heat between us, were a cruel fire consuming every breath, melting down every letter of every word.

He pushes back his hat in that way that men do when they are about to get on their knees for another man. Finally the saliva starts to flow in my dry mouth and I swallow. Out of habit I take out my pocket watch. To my surprise the hands are moving again. I bring it to my ear. Deep inside the mechanism is ticking like the heart of an unplanned foetus.

'I know.'

'Good.'

Rickardsson nods goodbye. As he turns away, the hairy back of his hand strokes mine, seemingly by accident. The sound of the clacking of his American rhino shoes slowly dies away in the heat. I watch him from behind: his back as powerful as a parliamentarian, his hairy arms and his hands hanging like battledores from his wrists. It feels as though the heat of the sun is burning straight through me.

A handsome devil though.

Above me a window creaks and bangs open.

'Kvist?'

I look up at the building. The occultist is leaning out of his window.

'What the fuck do you want?'

'You disappeared in such a rush that I didn't get a chance to warn you. I had a premonition. Kvist must be careful about joining forces with people he doesn't know. It will bring you misfortune.'

I nod absent-mindedly and stare at Rickardsson's broad back until he dissolves into the sunshine.

WEDNESDAY 22 JULY

The hatch closes with a bang that is a touch too reminiscent of the procedure at Långholmen. Someone pushes and pulls the handle inside and the letter box with a gob full of gold rattles out a mocking guffaw. Maybe it is directed at me, unshaven and hatless as I am.

Eventually the door to the exclusive speakeasy on Kommendörsgatan opens and I am looking down the barrel of a pistol. Svenne Crowbar holds out his enormous left mitt. The cuff of his stark white shirt rides up, revealing a tattoo on his wrist. A date: 7/2.

'The shooter.'

I stick my cigar in the corner of my lips, look around and take the Husqvarna out of its holster. Svenne Crowbar stuffs it in his trouser pocket.

'Anything else?'

I shake my head and follow the big gangster down a narrow corridor with walls draped in thick red curtains. An oriental-patterned carpet dampens the sound of our footsteps. The last time I was here was Christmas of '32. A client of mine, the former film star Doris Steiner, exchanged luxurious furs for some form of liquid opium. If I hadn't had that madcap beauty on my arm, I doubt I would have been admitted. Times are different now.

I must have the upper hand.

The empty bar hasn't changed. We pass the booths and tables on our right. Last time there was a jazz quintet playing on the little stage and the large dance floor was packed with upper-class ladies, transvestites and drunken Östermalm villains. Flashes of all imaginable colours chased each other wildly across the dance floor, the bodies and tables. Now our steps echo in the deserted room. I wonder if I can ask him to get the light machine going.

'Grog?'

Svenne Crowbar grins and gestures towards the American bar and the shelves of bottles.

'Thanks.'

I smack my dry lips and climb onto one of the round bar stools. The paraffin candles in the lanterns along the bar have burnt out. Svenne Crowbar mixes whisky with Pommac fruit pop in two tumblers and I cast my gaze across the portraits of boxers hung high on the wall. All of the fighters are as white as cold corpses. They should add Joe Louis to the ranks. I take my drink and don't mention it.

'Last time I got a little umbrella in my drink.'

'Well, fuck, of course my good sir Kvisten must have an umbrella.'

The gangster roots around under the bar, finds one and sticks it in the glass. This time it is yellow. I pick it up. You can open and close the umbrella by moving a little paper cylinder up and down. I do it a few times and hear a hollow guffaw that I suppose must be coming from me.

'Do you think they've seen these things in America?'

'Course they fucking have.'

I look at him, purse my lips, place the folded umbrella in my shirt pocket and hop down from the stool.

'Ma?'

Svenne Crowbar lifts the telephone receiver, presses a button and doesn't request a number before speaking.

'Kvist is here. Says he's got information about those fucking shipments. Yes. No. He changed his mind, apparently. No, I didn't swear. I did not. Okay.'

Svenne Crowbar gestures towards the door to the right of the bar. There was a gorilla stationed there last time. Maybe it was him.

'Follow the corridor to the iron door at the end.'

I drain the grog and ask for another. The primary focus of the remainder of the day will be finding the right balance between inebriation and hangover. Then early to bed and I'll be myself again in the morning.

I walk through the dimly lit, red-painted corridor, with dark panels and four doors on each side. They are numbered with gold digits like in a hotel. From Room 3 light spills out across the floor of the corridor in the shape of a peacock's arse; from Room 4 opposite I hear a radio playing a jazz song I actually recognise even though I don't know what it is called.

I hear the babbling of a child somewhere. The combination of smells is one I recognise all too well: ingrained tobacco smoke, sickly sweet intoxicating drinks, heavy perfume and the scent of desecrated female bodies.

I go over to Room 3 and peek inside: a proper wardrobe, white enamel washbasin, vanity table with mirror, hair-curling rod and various small jars, and a nightstand with a glaring lamp and an overflowing ashtray. No windows. Under the bed there is an assortment of high-heeled shoes and a couple of empty bottles.

The woman in the bed is a full-figured lady dressed in a negligee made of some sort of flimsy material. It has ridden halfway up her thigh. She is smoking and staring at a weekly magazine. On the floor sits a little toddler ripping pages out of another magazine with its chubby hands. The paper swirls round its head, half-covered with thin hair. The little one laughs. The woman looks up and I slap my forehead.

'Shall I close the door?'

'No need.'

Her voice is hoarse.

'Are you awaiting a visitor?'

'No.'

'I've got you under my skin,' sings another woman from behind door number 4. I think I understand the words but am still not sure what it means. My English isn't what it used to be, but it will come back to me quickly. Just as soon as I'm on the other side of the pond.

'Half my life at sea.'

'What was that?'

'Nothing.'

The woman snorts smoke out through her nose and returns to her magazine. Within a few steps I am standing in front of the hefty iron door hanging heavy on its hinges at the farthest end of the corridor.

'Right in the lion's den.'

I take a deep breath that threatens to burst my lungs.

Interactions with the upper class can either heat you up or burn you down. Something I have experienced before.

I need a straw hat, a pair of sunglasses and to claim that suit from Herzog. Then I want a passport, visa and tickets to America. Maybe I have enough information to go first class. Hopefully I'll get the Reaper killed to boot.

I slug back the grog and knock.

'Gold, you say? Gold and machine guns?'

The tapping of the ivory cane's ferrule reverberates between the walls of the spacious office. I am sitting in front of the heavy desk. The chair is armless with a fringe that caresses the floor underneath. In the other chair sits Nix, his eyes narrowed under his monobrow. Ma gives me an ashtray and parks her substantial backside on the tabletop. She is dressed in a shiny, emerald-coloured satin dress with double rows of buttons. Her hat is the size of a millstone and covered with feathers and frills.

'So they are planning some sort of bomb attack.'

Ma's eyes are glittering.

Pure, clean-cut hatred.

I like what I see.

'And when is this supposed to happen?'

For a second my eyes dart up to the golden chandelier with its shining prisms. I think about it.

'Soon. Straight after the Olympic inauguration, I believe. Something political.'

'Bullshit!' Nix crosses arms on his chest. 'There's no way in hell Ploman would be involved in that sort of thing!'

He is really acting the tough guy. I inspect him. A few drops of red stand out from the whiteness of his right cuff, and I notice a certain redness to his knuckles. He may well have just beaten someone up, but what I find impressive is his appearance. He is dressed in a pinstripe suit and a striped waistcoat with a watch chain.

Bold.

Ma gives her son a look that makes him sit up straight. In the silence that follows I hear nothing but the scratching of the horn gramophone and the clinking of the pianist.

She has control over her sons. With an elegant movement she takes a cigarette and sticks it in her long holder. I find my matches, get up and offer her a light, like during our car ride on Sunday. She nods thanks, leans back and lifts the receiver of her desk telephone.

'Forget the grog. Kvist is here with news.'

Nix scoffs. No idea why he is so peevish, I can't figure him out. He throws a piece of sugar candy into his mouth and chews it with a crunch.

The heavy iron door complains like a broken violin and Ma grimaces, deepening the wrinkles around her eyes and mouth. Svenne Crowbar comes into the office.

'How many times have I told you to oil those hinges?'

'Nix said he would do it.'

'Like fuck did I say that!'

'Language!'

Ma drums her cane on the table, making the telephone receiver rattle on its stand.

'It makes no difference who does it as long as it gets done.' A flush of vexation spreads across her cheeks, she takes a deep breath and lowers her voice again. 'Listen carefully now while Kvist describes the route.' She gestures towards a map of the city hanging on the wall behind the desk, picks up her pince-nez and pinches it onto the tip of her nose.

Both Nix and I get up. We walk around the desk from opposite directions and converge in front of the map. Nix points out Ploman's den on Ynglingagatan. On his wrist is the same tattoo as his brother's: 7/2.

'The shipment comes from headquarters,' says Nix.

'Right. But the police first join here.'

I point at the crossing between St Eriksgatan and Fleminggatan and continue to describe the journey to Stadsgård quay in as much detail as I can. The small group listens attentively and enquires about the gold and guns.

'Does Kvist have any proof of his story?'

Nix glowers at me. I bite my tongue and struggle to keep calm.

Ma taps ashes off her cigarette.

'He has no reason to bear false witness.'

'Revenge.'

'What the hell are you talking about?'

I shift my weight to the other foot to protect my broken rib from Nix, and clench my right hand into a fist.

'Maybe you want to avenge the black-coat. A friend of yours? Gabrielsson, right? Maybe you invented all these stories about machine guns and fuck knows what because you don't have the guts to take care of the problem yourself.'

'Now listen here!'

With a sharpness in her voice, Ma pokes Nix in the chest across the table with her cane.

Nix glowers at me for another second before smacking the cane away with the back of his hand and backing up a few steps. He mutters something inaudible. The needle on the gramophone scratches. The pianist seems to have suddenly become bored, because the tempo increases and the piece doesn't seem to hang together any more. Maybe he's under the influence.

'Maybe Kvist does have his own battle to fight,' Ma continues, 'but we should still be grateful that he came to us. It gives us a chance to act in time. Are we to assume that Kvisten has heard of the Munck Corps?'

'The street in Old Town?'

Ma looks at me over her pince-nez and furrows her brows before she resumes speaking.

'I am, of course, referring to the paramilitary group that was formed with the blessing of the police force to assist said authority in defending society in the event of riots or left-wing uprisings. The members were recruited en masse from the National Socialists and worked incognito – naturally – in obscurity.'

'That sounds vaguely familiar.'

'Does Kvist know why this so-called protection corps was finally dissolved?'

'Let me guess, that's also a secret?'

'It was revealed that Munck and his minions had got their hands on hundreds of firearms. From Germany.'

'And how in the hell does the lady know all this?'

'I read the newspaper. The whole thing played out in the open just four years ago.'

I think, but can't remember shit.

'We will consider what Kvisten has said.'

Ma puts down her cane, takes the pince-nez off the tip of her nose, picks up the little brown jar with the spoon and turns to Nix.

'Make sure Kvist gets his hat and suit. Then take our guest for his visa and passport. He should want for nothing. And check the underside of the automobile just in case. If dynamite is on the cards.'

I grin and blink at Nix. That shut the bastard up.

Ma shovels a small amount of powder from the jar with the built-in teaspoon, presses her index finger with a red-painted nail to one nostril and sniffs.

'Do you remember the burning of the Reichstag in Berlin three years ago, the very starting point for the establishment of the National Socialist regime? Though they accused *die Roten*, it immediately became apparent that it was the Brownshirts under the direction of Karl Ernst himself who started the fire. Soon Hitler, Goebbels and Goering were in place to watch the drama play out first hand. However, I must admit that this is hearsay and nothing I can guarantee to be true.' She sniffs. 'We are meeting for supper this evening at half past seven, so Kvist can tell us more then. Regular table, number 10, at the Grand.'

She swings her cigarette holder out in front of her in time with the trilling of the piano.

'Schumann, a living testimony of how circumstances can intervene and suddenly turn an accident into a blessing.' She shuts her eyes. 'Not like the Negro music that we have to play on the weekends when it happens to be in vogue. Is Kvist a music lover?'

I take a puff.

'I could hold a tune as a kid.'

Ma sniffs and looks me over. I squirm under her gaze.

'Supper at the Grand then.' A stream of smoke drifts up to the ceiling when she stubs out her cigarette. 'I read an interesting article in a science journal not long ago.' She looks at me from under the brim of her hat. 'Did Kvist know that sweat is acidic and bactericidal, but if uncouth people let it remain on their body too long, then it becomes favourable soil for bacteria and the carrier gets sick?'

Ma closes her eyes and rocks gently back and forth. My cheeks flush and I begin to cough.

'This damned water ban…'

'I'm sure Kvist is advised about his stench often enough,' says Nix with an expression like a screw taking delivery of a new inmate. He takes the Husqvarna from Svenne Crowbar and passes it to me.

I check the safety and holster the shooter. I gesture goodbye but Ma is still sitting with her eyes closed and her red lips drawn in a wide smile, lost in a pleasing memory. I nod to Svenne Crowbar and follow Nix out.

We emerge into the gloomy corridor. I take out a cigar and place it between my lips. The gangster stops at Room 1 and opens it with a grin.

'Boy?'

Inside lies a youth of around twenty, sleeping in his under-pants and a flimsy undershirt. He is a beautiful example of a good, old-fashioned Swedish native: sharp, strong features, unruly mop of blond hair, broad shoulders. I can clearly see the bulge of his cock in his underpants. I yawn and drily smack my lips.

'Maybe later.'

I fix my gaze on Nix and hold it until he looks away first. He snorts air out through his nostrils and slams the door.

Sometime, somewhere, it will just be him and me facing each other, alone with our rage.

I look forward to that day.

I walk over to the bulletproof Cadillac while I puff on my last Meteor.

'We need to stop at a cigar kiosk.'

'On the way to the petrol station.'

I stand, shifting my weight from foot to foot, observing as Nix carefully checks the underside for dynamite, and quietly wonder-ing to myself what the fuck I have got myself into.

The attendant at the petrol station on Vallhallavägen mops the sweat from his forehead with his free hand and wipes it on his stained overalls. There is a hollow clunk in the tank as he shakes off the last drops of petrol. He bows slightly, Nix starts the car and we leave the station behind in a cloud of smoke. I purse my lips and stare at him.

'The payment?'

'Next time.'

Artillerigatan's fashionable shacks pass by at high speed and I place my hand on the dashboard. Nix lets go of the wheel to light a filter cigarette and has to grab hold of it again at the last second to turn left onto Östermalmsgatan. He only slows down when we catch sight of the guards outside the Army Headquarters.

I glance at the looming grey building and scoff.

'Why the hell have they chosen an inscription in Italian on the façade?'

'Latin.'

'That doesn't explain it.'

'*Exercitus sine duce, corpus est sine spiritu.*'

Ma seems to have done a better job with this son than with that other boozer.

'They're busy in there at the moment, I bet. Maps and the like.'

'An army without a leader is like a body without a mind.'

'I've never been one for maps. Don't trust them. They're wrong too often.'

'They're the ones that are wrong?' Nix snorts and clenches his left fist in the air. 'Stupidity and the desire for revenge are not a combination that has ever won any wars. On the other hand: organisation, leadership, the ability to adapt and plan according to the situations of allies and enemies.'

'Heard plenty about that place.'

I ignore his grumbling and point with my cigar at an establishment farther away. Nix strokes his moustache and changes to a higher gear, and the tyres vibrate more rapidly against the road.

The restaurant is closed for summer. Someone has drawn a swastika in the thick layer of dust on the shop window.

'You used to receive training in an organisation such as ours. The youngsters can run errands, do the simpler pick-ups and deliveries, and when it's time to join the nightwatch you get a confirmation suit tailored to conceal a shoulder holster. The best, in terms of intelligence, loyalty and toughness, rise above the others.'

'Quite.'

Nix is very roused all of a sudden.

'How the fuck can a grown man have a brain like a walnut? He might be the elder but he has always been a little backwards.'

The bastard is acting tough again. One more word and I have half a mind to throw him out of the moving car. I run my tongue along the inside of my mouth. It feels like sandpaper against dehydrated wood.

'The goat that bleats the loudest is milked the least,' he concludes.

We turn right onto Strandvägen. The sun is pouring its golden beams over the rich men's apartments in the luxury buildings. From our left the lake winds blow against the side window, and along the quay the boats' masts flutter in the blue sky. Dockers stagger under a load of bricks due for shipment. A fiery mask has been painted onto their sweaty faces, making them look like redskins. The gangplank bends under their weight and concentrated silence. On the quay the bricks are piled in high squares by muscular blokes with battered hands for a couple of kronor and a sandwich in the evening. I have been one of them myself.

'Once we had hundreds of men ready and armed, various cops and several judges on our payroll, but now we have to run around the city hiring all sorts of new people.'

'That's a good place for a stop. In the evening.'

I gesture to *The Widow*, a white-washed steamboat that serves as an illicit drinking den. Nix doesn't seem to hear me. He speeds up even more.

Reflections fly from all the gold around the entrance to the Royal Dramatic Theatre as we pass Berzelii Park. The spot near the grey mass of the statue in the middle of the park, hidden among the dark shadows of the trees, used to be frequented by promiscuous youths schooled in the twenty arts, ready to sell their arse for a fiver. A couple are there still, despite the vice squad's efforts. They share it with a few of the city's youngest hussies, fourteen-year-old girls that nobody wants due to their age and lack of experience. I see one of them kneeling in her much-too-high heels. Her painted lips quiver like a death twitch when she tries to smile in that conspiratorial way that is the secret greeting of whores.

God knows where all the rest have gone.

Just before Norrmalmstorg a house cat, with a red collar and a belly full of kittens near enough touching the ground, runs across the street. Nix turns hard on the wheel. I hold myself in my seat.

'Watch out!'

The cigar that was fixed in my mouth tumbles onto my lap. There is a bump as Nix hits the cat with the front wheel. A barely perceptible shock moves through the body of the vehicle.

'Bullseye.'

Nix's voice is barely a whisper. I pick up my Meteor, dust the ash off my trousers and glare at him.

A smile spreads across his chiselled profile. His gaze lingers in the rear-view mirror for half a second, he clicks into a lower gear, the motor changes its note and we slow down.

A tense silence inside the car. I cough, open my mouth to speak, close it again. The seat creaks as I lean forward. Nix lets go of the wheel and makes a helpless gesture with his hand, but seems at a loss for words. Part of me wants to beat him into oblivion.

He looks over at me. His eyes sparkle darkly with mischief. I take a deep puff on my Meteor that tears at my windpipe and stare out through the side window. The car lurches into a right turn and the plant beds on Birger Jarlsgatan rush past. Tension migrates from my abdomen to my head, my hangover headache flickers in my forehead and we turn left.

The door of Herzog's the tailor has its window intact, but the shop front is still boarded up with rough planks. The words 'JEW DEVILS' bleed in red dripping letters on the boards. The paint can is still in the gutter.

Nix finds a parking spot outside the tailor's and turns off the engine. He lights a new cigarette with the old.

'Kvist must understand…' He chucks ashes into the street through the side window. 'That fat fucking cat was in no state to be running around in city traffic. It didn't know any better, so just followed its impulse. So the fucker got run over.'

A bubbling, childish giggle spills from his mouth. The sound is at odds with his appearance and distorts his sharp facial features. I nod dumbly, press the door handle and jump out into the street. The harsh bang of the car door cuts off the giggling. On the mudguard and the underside of the running board, I see viscous drops of blood.

I hasten towards Herzog's, away from the maniac in the Cadillac. I open the door to the tailor's with one hand and pinch the bridge of my nose with the other. The clapper hits the bell with a hollow, half-hearted tinkle.

I am struck by the emptiness. The work table is free of tools, only one of the machines is in place on the short side of the premises and the wardrobes gape open with no rolls of fabric inside. Even the smell of the steam-pressed wool has been expelled by the fan.

On a decapitated wooden mannequin in the middle of the workshop hangs my suit, grey with chalked lines. The unease I felt in the car intensifies further, as does my pounding hangover, and I feel like turning around and forgetting the whole thing, *mausgrau* or not. I pluck the cigar from my lips.

The door at the back of the room creaks and the skinny little tailor creeps in wearing felt slippers. Just like on Sunday, he is wearing a visor on his head and a red measuring tape tied in a loop around his neck, but now the look in his eyes is of an old pauper who wants nothing more than to leave his earthly existence behind. The apprentice is nowhere to be seen.

He nods at me with a wearied expression.

Some weeks must be tougher than others.

'The suit will be ready first thing tomorrow.'

'There was talk of additional measurements?'

'How silly of me.' He gestures towards the mannequin. 'Of course.'

His tongue twists angularly around the words. I puff greedily on my cigar. The thick smoke billows out as if from a chimney. There is nowhere to tap off the ash.

I take off my jacket, look for somewhere to put my shoulder holster and rags but the tailor relieves me of my clothes, folds them expertly and excuses himself before disappearing into the back.

I carefully lift the jacket and waistcoat off the mannequin. They are hanging together with tacking thread. First one arm, then the other, then the same again. I do a few shoulder rolls, then I try out a couple of uppercuts and a straight blow. Cigar ash drifts to the floor. The jacket fabric follows my movement and fits close around my muscles without diminishing the motion. I undress and stand there in my elasticated underwear, socks and suspenders.

It's cold in the shadow of the boarded-up window, despite the persistent heat outside. I shiver. I contemplate the dead vacancy of the tailor's shop. There are traces of life on the walls: screws, nail holes, colour variations on the wallpaper where notices and promotional posters for various suits and mannequins once were. Another deep puff on my Meteor dissolves it all into smoke.

The back door creaks, shuffling steps reveal Herzog and I turn around. He has the trousers over his arm. Under his bushy eyebrows his brown eyes are as exhausted as a starving dog. He moistens his lips.

'*Gejn forojs*, please, Mr Kvist.'

I carefully pull on the trousers. Herzog watches me in silence, kneels down and digs out a box of pins from his pocket. With steady, spindly fingers he begins to pin them up. Words run through my head though there isn't much to say.

Finally I break the silence.

'So, closing up?'

'In exile I will miss the customers. The people in the city. The city as it was.' The tailor mumbles something in his guttural native tongue, lets a double sigh escape his lips and continues with clipped consonants.

'Young Baroness Heening and her exquisite feel for quality. *Schließen, ja?* Cheerful mood despite the burden of her rank, but decisive concerning clothing. The housemaid always had fresh breakfast bread as a gift. *Broyt.*'

Herzog switches to the other trouser leg.

'Even though it was often long after twelve. Hold out your arms, please.'

He puts a couple of pins between his lips, pulls gently at the fabric and continues speaking through the corner of his mouth.

'One must assume that the Baroness had late habits.'

I take the cigar out of my mouth.

'The dynasty has its privileges.'

'Dr Henck and the coats with fur collars.' He whispers something in his own language and then speaks more loudly: 'Treat themselves to a new one every winter, *der Hochstapler*, in the same design as the previous one, regardless of changes in fashion and the weather. The last day of November for the past twenty years.'

Herzog gets up with a certain amount of effort and looks me up and down.

'Two sons, one administrator at the university and one do-nothing at the dance palace. I got the impression that the doctor preferred the… *shlefer*… how do you say… layabout, yes?'

I smack my lips and try to muster a little saliva in my bone-dry gob. Herzog signals to me to turn around and I obey.

'The gentleman is a little uneven around the shoulders.'

'Right-handed, walk with the left first.'

'You will be my last customer in this country.'

'An honour.'

Herzog clucks and gestures for me to take off my new suit and put on the old one. The Jew moistens his lips again.

'It was not long ago that I was known as the best tailor in the city, *Baruch HaShem*, but in one day everything changed.'

A lump wedges in my throat. Herzog sheds a glittering tear that sits in the wrinkles under his eye before he wipes it away with the knuckle of his forefinger. I try to relax the knot in my stomach with a couple of drags. The hangover is making my hand tremble.

'The clients don't come any more,' Herzog continues. 'Not even the ones who left a deposit. *Ratevet*. Afraid.'

'The Führer's fault.'

'*Zol men oysnitsn zayne kishkes oyftsuhengen dem vesh.*' The tailor swallows. 'May his guts be used as a washing line.'

The skinny man shakes his head and the tape measure round his neck glints. An image from last autumn flashes through my shattered mind: a good friend, innocent as a maid, his throat cut from ear to ear. I take a few steps towards the door but turn around. I swallow hard.

'Where are you going?' I wheeze.

'Relatives in Warsaw.'

'I've never been there.'

'Edit… Edyta, and Sara,' mumbles the tailor. 'And little Eli.'

'Guaranteed to be better there.'

'*Baruch HaShem*,' repeats Herzog. 'If He wishes it.'

'The people in this city are nervous sheep.' I raise my voice into a roar. 'Always so fucking quick to point the finger at someone else to avoid staring into the dirty depths of their own selves. The truth is that they are the ones who need us.'

'Us?'

'If we weren't here they'd find others. And still more in their place.'

The tailor raises his eyebrows, looks down at his felt slippers for a moment and then looks up again.

'Mr Kvist can have his suit for free. Tomorrow. *Morgen, ja?*'

I swallow. Just in time for Hasse's match. Sometimes people's kindness hits harder than a right hook. I mumble a thank you but don't know if he hears.

I look out at the street and see Nix standing in the sun, smoking. Two young ladies are walking arm in arm along the pavement. One has round copper plates in her ears and the other has some sort of comb stuck in the back of her hair. Nix's wolf-whistle cuts through the window in the shop door to where I am standing with my hand on the handle. His teeth flash under his moustache as he grins and the girls hurry up the steps. I am shaking anxiously but I pull the handle.

'Make sure you brand the inner pocket,' I say over my shoulder.

'It will be a pleasure to see the lapel with your name every time I hang up my jacket.'

I open the door and take a couple of steps out into the street. It is as hot as a blast furnace. With a few strides I am next to Nix and the car. He drops his butt into the gutter.

'Kvist took his sweet time.'

'A lot of adjustments.'

'We'll need to hurry if we're going to have time to buy a hat and sunglasses and visit Thulin.'

'Like hell, the Prince is around the corner. I need a drink.'

His eyes narrow, his fingers fasten his single jacket button and his hand touches his shoulder holster. I don't look away.

'Out in the open. Good luck explaining that to Ma.'

I turn my back on the erratic git and walk up Biblioteksgatan. Anxiety makes the hairs on my neck stand on end and sets my limbs atremble. My lungs cry out for oxygen but I can't seem to get any.

Don't back down.

Kvisten never backs down.

Rushing steps: Nix slides up next to me and I look at him. His face is bright red and sweat gleams on his brow. He is holding his shaking left hand to get control over it. I exhale, duck into Mäster Samuelsgatan and point at the Prince.

'It's a constant fucking counting game with you boys,' Nix hisses. 'When did I have my last nip and when can I get the next? Can I have two and still be in a fit state? The answer is no. A drinker is never in a fit state to get the job done, whether they prefer cheap schnapps or top-shelf whisky.'

'You're paying,' I say and open the door to the tobacco smoke, the clatter of porcelain, the boisterous male voices and the spirits vapours that are soon to envelop me in peace.

*

The leather of the passenger seat creaks as I stretch my neck and take a look around. To my right is a dispatch counter and Hotel Bellman's façade signage. To my left is Café Élégance, a beer café that keeps a brightly coloured parrot in a cage and is a favourite haunt among the ladyboys of the city. I know it all too well. The boys have a full set of women's underwear underneath their suits and perform their dirty deeds much like the girl-whores do, with powder and make-up and God knows what. When the sun has gone down they go traipsing around the neighbourhood, wiggling their arses and making eyes at everyone they meet. I have been here more times than I can count. The parrot is pretty fun too. It can swear like a sailor.

Nix checks the rear-view mirror. He pulls back the catch on the revolver, flicks the cylinder out with one quick wrist action, flicks it in again and holsters it.

'Does Kvist have his shooter to hand?'

It's the first time the bastard has opened his trap since we walked into the Prince. Just as well, I prefer drinking alone, never with shipmates. It's a rule of survival.

'Course I do.'

I slur my words, my jaw loose. A drinker, like hell. He should have seen me a decade ago, when a deluge of schnapps couldn't drown my sorrows, but I gave it a good go, on my travels here and there.

'Farther down the street. The stamp shop.'

We climb out of the car, and Nix takes another cautious look around as he locks the door. He has every reason to be cautious. Violence reigns here, despite police efforts. The Klara district is neutral ground for the gangster syndicates. Here, on streets that seem to consist solely of gutters, there is a flood of amphetamines, and spirits that taste like fusel oil from the moonshine apparatus of Dalarna, plus the whores are cheaper than on Kungsgatan or in the fashionable dance clubs. There are no laws to take into account, no unwritten rules, no code of honour. Pimps stand outside the plethora of hotels, ready to lure out-of-towners with marked cards. If the conmen fail, along comes a carefully painted decoy to flatter them into a shady alley where a bloke is waiting with baton at the ready.

I straighten my shoulder holster, glance behind me one more time and follow Nix westward. We pass a couple of people. The vagrants here are more numerous than anywhere else in the city. They have no work and no possibility of escaping the heat of the concrete jungle, so they just amble listlessly around in search of a gig. The wooden soles of the poor men's boots make a hollow clatter against the pavement. Lundin often refers to this part of the city as 'Sodom and Gomorrah'.

Nausea is bubbling in my stomach. I cover my mouth and nose with a handkerchief. Cat piss and rubbish in the gutters have mellowed in the heat, and the sharp odour of sabadilla vinegar reeks out of each and every window, reminding me once again of the poorhouse where I spent several years as a child.

Tattered sheets flutter like spectres on the washing lines hung between the façades, and their shadows dance on the pavement. Nix and I walk along the row of the hopelessly empty window frames.

We stop at an inconspicuous door. Behind the grille in the shop window rows of stamps are displayed on yellowed fabric. Nix knocks: three long, three short and another long.

I take off my new straw hat and hastily drag a comb through my hair. I would have worn a different shirt if I knew I was going to have my photograph taken. I'm unshaven too. Rickardsson was right: I should have made time for barber Nyström to take care of my beard stubble before rushing off.

I hear the sound of heavy footsteps, then a bolt is drawn and the doorway is filled with an older, heavy-set bloke. His brown eyes peer out like raisins from a glazed saffron bun. He sticks his plump thumbs inside his braces.

'Ma telephoned and said that you needed a passport and American visa. Is that right?'

'This gentleman is keen to cross the ocean in a hurry,' Nix replies.

'No need for secrecy. Unfortunately, anyone would know Kvist's face a mile off. Anyway, follow me.'

The bloke has full, womanly hips. We come into a dim workshop with a camera on a tripod. It smells of dust, old books and adhesive. On a table under the harsh light of a work lamp, the forger's tools are all spread out: tweezers, scalpel and small glue brushes. The dust dances in the cone of light.

Despite his fat fingers, Thulin is renowned as the best forger in the city and is even said to be employed by the police themselves when necessary. I have also heard that he is an expert in safe-deposit boxes and has taught an entire guild of masters.

Next to a typewriter and a pile of discarded German passports is a large adult tomcat in a cardboard box. He is all black but for a white patch like a shirt front between his forelegs. He immediately begins to purr loudly. The stamp dealer strokes his back.

'This is Beelzebub.'

I scratch the Prince of Darkness under his chin. His fangs are exposed, and it looks like he is smiling. The purring intensifies. It makes me think of the cat that Nix did in.

'You need Kvist out of the country in a matter of days from what I hear? Not much time.'

I stop scratching the kitty. My heart lurches. With a little luck I'll be standing face to face with my daughter this time next week.

The idea makes me feel warm inside, but it also clenches my stomach into rebellion. Beelzebub flexes his claws and tentatively paws at my arm.

'We'll pay whatever it costs.'

'Busy times. The queue is longer than the one for that new escalator at Slussen.'

Thulin makes a sweeping gesture over the work table. I scoff. I don't understand what's so damn special about that escalator. Went on it four times in a row a while ago. Didn't think there was much to it.

Nix pulls a thick roll of banknotes from his pocket.

'We'll pay double the usual fee.'

'Now that's more like it. Let's start with the portrait. What name do you want on your new document?'

'Same as now. Easier to remember. Same name, new photograph.'

I stumble to the side. Maybe one schnapps too many at the Prince after all. The stocky forger squints at me and smiles.

'Kvist lives up to his reputation. If I may say so, I would recommend using another name.'

'You're the expert.'

It doesn't take long. Nix peels the notes from a roll and soon we are standing out on the street again.

'Kvist can find his own way home. I'm sure you appreciate that I'm not keen to drive through Ploman's territory alone.'

'I don't care.'

'The Grand restaurant tonight. Half past seven.' Nix looks me up and down. 'That should give you enough time for a bath and a shave.'

I sneer, and something catches my attention that makes my muscles stiffen. Over Nix's shoulder I see a bloke approaching

213

in worn-out shoes. A wide grin shines out of greying beard stubble. I gesture with my chin and Nix turns around. I take one step forward so that we are standing shoulder to shoulder.

'Get out of here!'

The man's voice is barely more than a croak. His clothes are crying out for a scrub and an iron. In his left hand he holds a broken bottle with sharp edges; with his right he pulls a bread knife out of his trouser lining. It has no shaft and the handle is taped on. I see his blood throbbing in a vein under his sparse grey fringe.

I grunt, move my left foot forward and draw my head in between my shoulders. Nix giggles just like he did in the car. Like a little girl being tickled in the belly.

Nix and I look at each other and grin. For half a second I feel some sort of solidarity with the bastard. His snake eyes narrow in the shade of his hat brim; a drop of sweat shines on the pointy tip of his nose, fat and quivering above his moustache. The tip of his tongue flicks over his top lip, stops in the left corner of his mouth and stays there.

He knows just as well as I do that we have probably found ourselves on this old man's section of the pavement. In territories that rarely span more than twenty-odd metres, the street people and sewer rats rule. Thieves, ragamuffins and miscreants can have free passage, but as soon as anyone shows up who could pose a threat, the territory must be defended.

The old man has stopped a couple of metres in front of us and is swinging his knife and bottle in line with the waist of his trousers, which are secured with a bright girl's button. Maybe he doesn't realise who we are. Maybe he has nothing to lose.

It doesn't matter. Not to us, nor him. The outcome will be the same.

I play with the thought of letting Nix take care of the problem by himself. To see what he's made of, and maybe get him scratched up in the bargain, but no, that could jeopardise the whole plan.

'Get lost.'

The vagrant takes a step forward as the hoarse words tumble out of his trap. He is slow, run-down by age, schnapps and hunger. I step forward and to the side; better if we approach from different directions.

A sudden bang, trapped between the buildings, blasts my eardrums. The man flies backwards a metre and lands on his back. The bottle smashes on the paving stones. I leap to the side and take cover.

Four gleaming grey pigeons flap in the sunshine. As the distinctive smell of burnt gunpowder enters my broken nose, I stand up and immediately pat my pockets for a cigar. A shrill but pitiful wheezing comes from the old man, like the sound little kids with whooping cough make when it's just a matter of time.

And from what I can tell this is also just a matter of time. Red-brown blood streams out of his abdomen, taking his life along with it. It was probably the liver that got it.

Nix is still standing with the smoking revolver at waist height. His mouth is half open, his faces just droops, revealing no emotion, and his eyes are a couple of narrow slits. Then his left hand starts to shake; he opens his jacket, holsters his revolver and grips his trembling hand with his other. I look around. Not a single person remains on the street.

The old man has rolled over onto his side, drawn his knees into his body and folded his arms around his stomach. The dark blood forms a pool on the paving stones. He opens his mouth to reveal a gaping hole of broken teeth.

'Help,' he whimpers. 'Help me.'

I put the unlit cigar in my mouth and take a step towards the broken heap of a man.

'Not a chance.' Nix massages his hand. It has stopped shaking. 'Nothing to be done. That's why I like shooting in the guts. It's slow but it works, every time.'

I stare at Nix, he gestures towards the car and starts to jog to it. I take one more look at the old man, then turn around and trundle after. Every step reverberates ominously between the house fronts.

'Help!'

Somehow the old man has managed to gasp a breath of air. His hoarse cry rings out along the street as our footsteps quicken. I find my new sunglasses and press them onto my nose. Behind us I hear another pleading cry.

When we get back to the car I look around. Not a soul, not a cat, not a bird, only the bedlinen on the washing lines flapping in a breeze. The old man has gone quiet in his pool of blood.

Nix meets my gaze above the white car roof. Both the car's lacquer and his teeth glint in the sun.

'It's probably best if I drive Kvist home after all.' He has stopped smiling and is stroking his moustache. 'Now that there's a little static on the line.'

I stride briskly along the east avenue of Kungsträdgården Park and pass Wahrendorffsgatan, where the smell of burning from the synagogue still hangs thickly in the dog-day evening.

I take off my sunglasses and try once again to bend the small saddle-shaped plates on the inside. They pinch my nose too tightly and leave a mark.

I fold them up and put them in the inner pocket of my jacket. This old Herzog suit is still going strong despite repairs following a knife fight in the winter of '32, and the steel-grey shirt looks rather splendid together with the silver-striped silk tie. I shined the shoes myself with junk-dealer Ström's oil concoction. Hasse is meeting his girl tonight, apparently.

A hell of a waste of energy the day before the match.

A southerly wind makes the water quiver in the sunshine. It splashes gently at the quayside, and the docked ferry boats creak a lingering, wistful melody. On the roof of the German legation a swastika flag flaps limply on its pole. A bunch of carefree gulls squawk around an overloaded rubbish barge moving through the waves between the National Museum and the oldest parts of the city. I check my Viking timepiece and sidestep a tramp who has gathered up hairpins, matchboxes and other bits of tat found in the gutter, and wrapped them up in a newspaper. I quicken my pace.

The long-established hotel is enthroned stoutly and majestically on the waterfront, on the west side of its islet with a view over Old Town, the palace and parliament. A black row of tightly packed taxicabs stands outside, clean and shining, each waiting for some liquored-up gentleman or business traveller of means going out on the town.

A doorman wearing a jacket heavy with gold stands in my way.

'As I am sure you are aware, Monsieur, our least expensive room costs six kronor a night.'

What in the hell? Doesn't he see that I'm wearing a straw hat of the very latest style? Can't he see the careful shave barber Nyström gave me? I washed pretty recently too. I feel a snarl of anger deep inside me.

'Here for the tuck.'

'And who might the gentleman be meeting?'

217

The half-hour chimes weakly from Skeppsholmen Church. I stand still for a moment. I don't know their real names.

'The head of the family is a lady they call Ma.'

That makes the bastard stand up straight. The glass door opens.

'Certainly. Forgive me, sir. I didn't recognise you.'

I give a reserved little nod and walk with my fists still clenched into a foyer filled with stuffed bears. Damned pretentious rubbish. Hang a bunch of metal on a man and he will immediately expect people to bow to him. No doubt the doorman makes a handsome salary with all the twenty-five-öre coins tossed at him in tips, but that is hardly a reason to get cocky.

Another concierge jackanapes tries to take my hat, but I keep it on out of old-fashioned peasant custom.

'Kvisten doesn't take his hat off for anyone.'

'Forgive me, sir, but I must insist.'

Go ahead and insist. But get out of my way.

'Like hell.'

With jerky, exaggerated gestures and a white cloth over his forearm, the maître d'hôtel leads me to a round table placed out of the way, on the farthest side of the spacious hall. Ma meets my gaze and makes a courteous, dainty movement with her hand. She is wearing black gloves up to the elbows. Her fingers glitter with a bunch of gemstones. She is flanked by her sons, and there is a giant bloke sitting with his back to me. He looks about a head taller than Svenne Crowbar.

A pianist caresses a perfunctory, almost bland melody. The dinner guests stare at me. Fragile, thoroughbred aristocrats, uniformed cavalry officers, suited and booted businessmen with faces red from schnapps, honeymoon couples – they are all craning their necks so hard their heads might come off. As soon as I make eye contact they look intently elsewhere, as if deeply fascinated by the enormous chandeliers, the silverware, the white tablecloths or the arched windows to the street.

'Thus the task of the employers' association shall be...'

A man goes silent abruptly in mid-speech and becomes as still as an ice sculpture, holding a brimming schnapps glass by his second waistcoat button.

I have a mind to put my sunglasses back on. Doris Steiner took me here, and to Cecil and the Continental, but that was years ago. Since then I have only seen the inside of the hourly hotels on Stora Nygatan and Norra Smedjegatan.

I take a deep breath. The smorgasbord's aromas of smoked salmon, goose breast and anchovy mingle with expensive perfumes and the thick smoke of Havana cigars. My stomach is growling louder than Thulin's cat's purring.

Svenne Crowbar has already picked up his cutlery and tucked in his napkin like a bib, though the food is yet to be served. Ma extends her hand with palm facing down. It is an awkward handshake.

'Kvist has met Mr Blom before, as I understand it.'

'I certainly have.'

Hiccup, the cold-blooded murderer of Kungsholmen, extends his giant bear paw of a hand. The last time we shook hands it was over a corpse up in Vanadislunden four years ago. His grip has not softened with the years. Mine has weakened.

'As the transit crosses Kungsholmen, we thought it advisable to involve Belzén of Birka. He was kind enough to loan out Hiccup here.'

A hell of a lot of violence gathered at one table. I greet the two sons with a casual salute and then take my seat next to Svenne Crowbar. Nix is wearing a shirt as red as the devil himself. Narrow collared and ironed. At first glance it looks ridiculous but then I feel a sting of envy. The bloke knows how to dress at least. My thoughts are interrupted by the maître d'hôtel, who sashays over with four drams. Ma gets a man's dose as well.

'And a grog of whisky and Pommac for the gentleman.'

He puts down a square glass in front of Svenne Crowbar and excuses himself with a slight bow.

'I must say I find it fascinating when people mix Pommac with spirits,' says Ma. 'It ruins the drink. The grog becomes diluted, and you lose the alcoholic taste.'

She flicks her napkin.

'Soda water also works with whisky but can go wrong if you're too cautious. The drink dies and loses all pleasure.'

She spreads the linen over her lap.

'Citrus flavour is the commoner among mineral waters. Only choose it if you wish to appear uneducated.'

Finally she raises her glass.

'Welcome, friends and sons. Help yourself to the smorgasbord first to abate your hunger. Then we shall discuss business. Cheers, and enjoy.'

The spirit is warm as it runs down my chest and into my stomach. We all nod in unison at Ma's words, then get up and follow Svenne Crowbar, who races over to the plentiful buffet table. Soon I have goose liver melting on my tongue and I sigh with pleasure. Makes a change from the herring rissoles and mincemeat I ate in my childhood, when I got anything to eat at all.

Svenne Crowbar shovels salmon into his gob and chews with his mouth open despite Ma's disapproval. Nix has some Strassburger pâté in his moustache. I have glanced in his direction a few times but the fact that he killed a vagrant today doesn't seem to have dampened his appetite – quite the opposite. Hiccup is sitting in his chair, big and stout and quiet. He is working methodically through his gigantic portion, from the left edge of the plate to the right.

I bring the fork to my mouth with care. Ever since the launderette opposite closed last year, I usually eat in my underwear at home so I don't spill on my shirt and cause unnecessary costs. It is safe to assume that I am the only one here who does that. I might be able to afford a reputation stained with prison sentences, but I worry about my clothes.

When the initial gluttony is sated I check my pocket watch under the table. If it is to be trusted, it's already ten past eight. I go completely weak at the knees when I think of Rickardsson, that bastard. My heart, cold and inert since last winter, seems to have reawakened.

He is probably already out for his evening stroll. I can picture him now in my big cast-iron bed. I would rather be at home in Sibirien licking the scent of schnapps off his chin than sitting here at the Grand. What a time to encounter a handsome man, in these dangerous days.

'A good feast soothes the soul.' I am shaken out of my thoughts. Ma dabs her lips with a corner of her napkin. 'First they restricted the Swedes' right to a little nip at lunchtime, and then they impeded the use of narcotic powder, gambling and the gee-gees, but we gave the people what they wanted. When the vice squad persecuted the whore girls and prostitute boys under vagrancy laws, they turned to us for protection. If only they forbade man's right to food our success would be utter and absolute. Cheers to law enforcement!'

Hiccup clucks and Ma's sons hum in agreement. She picks up a compact mirror shining with mother-of-pearl, opens it and touches up her lipstick.

The menu is in French. I point to the top line but the waiter informs me that the words mean 'starter'. I go for his recommendation, which is some sort of winged delicacy. Ma orders a few bottles of Bordeaux. That's somewhere I've been at least, even if I didn't get shore leave that time.

'So Kvist is going to the States,' she says once her glass is filled. 'I hear that they drink iced water with their food over there, even in the finer establishments, and no one is interested in wine.' The deep-red liquid rolls around her glass. 'A bizarre people.'

'Perhaps.'

'However, as I have said, they know how to tackle the heat. And apparently in the winter they set up hot chocolate vending machines on street corners for anyone to use.'

'Is that so?'

'We intend to hijack the van.'

Four pairs of eyes are on me. The sounds of clinking glasses and howls of laughter from a table of snobby youths cut through the tinkling of the piano.

'Nothing to do with me.'

'We want Kvisten to take part in our little operation.'

My glass trembles as I take a swig of wine. I stroke my well-shaven chin. I can't help but think about the occultist's premonition of impending misfortune.

'I have a lot to do and would like to cross the ocean as soon as possible.'

'What did I tell you?' says Nix, the fucking robin redbreast, waving his hand and glowering into the distance. Ma looks like she wants to give him a smack with her cane but instead she turns to me.

'We would never suspect Kvist of lying, but we live in turbulent times. People have changed. The tiniest suspicion that you were duping us to escape from the country would be enough. Or even worse, that you were leading us into a trap.'

'But my daughter…'

I fumble for my wallet to show them a photograph of Ida.

'Daughters!' Hiccup opens his mouth for the first time since the starters. 'Those little creatures are impossible to understand. There's no fucking logic to their actions.'

Ma interrupts.

'Kvist was seen in conversation with Rickardsson not long before you came to see us. We have eyes and ears everywhere.'

The man in the white panama hat comes to mind. I wonder just how long they have been keeping track of me.

Nix lowers his hand beneath the tabletop. I swallow involuntarily and feel the hand gripping my wine glass begin to shake. It wouldn't surprise me if he had a revolver pointed at my guts. This volatile man likes to shoot defenceless men in their soft parts. My mind struggles to find the words.

'A coincidence. We live on the same street for Christ's sake.' I raise my glass, even though it feels like it weighs more than the gold bullion I was forced to abandon yesterday evening. The men are flaying me with their eyes. It feels as if my skin is slipping from my face. My cheeks are stinging. Not much of a choice. I sigh.

'Okay.' I take a big swig, try to suppress a shudder in my shoulders. 'Count me in.'

Ma smiles as two waiters approach with food laid on silver platters.

'Kvist has plenty of fight in him. We might need your fists.'

I look at the gangster queen. One moment she praises me, the next she implies I have gone soft. She changes positions as quickly as my old trainer Albertsson and I don't understand why. The aim seems to be simply to confuse me.

'I hear you have a twin brother,' she continues with a smile.

'How the hell did you know that?'

'As I said, we've mapped you thoroughly. Is he of the same calibre as Kvist himself? Hijacking this transport will mean war. We're going to need every man we can get in the aftermath. In this economic climate the factories seem to have swallowed them all up.'

'Well, not him. He's as dead as those bears in the foyer.'

'I am sorry.'

'Long time ago now.'

I taste the food and try to think of something else to talk about. I don't know what it is I am eating and can't decide whether I like it. I wash it down with a couple of swigs of wine and refill my glass.

'Maybe you would like to hear the story about when the consul bailed me out in Marseilles?'

I tell the anecdote about the monsters and the whorehouse that was really a vaudeville theatre. The audience is more obliging than those snotty kids on Roslagsgatan. Even Hiccup and Nix snigger. Svenne Crowbar guffaws until he chokes and the maître d'hôtel has to rush over with a jug of water. Not far behind him come three black-and-white-clad waiters in a row with the main courses on silver dishes. They look like penguins.

I saw a small procession of penguins once. With binoculars, off the coast of Chile, from the deck. I thought about bringing one home, but someone told me that, even though they could survive in the Nordic climate, they would die on board on the way over.

Dixie wouldn't have liked it anyway.

On my plate lie two breaded birds facing breast up with their skinny legs in the air. Svenne Crowbar pokes at them with his knife and laughs. Drunkards often see humour in places that sensible men can't understand. I stare at the plate for a moment. The little bodies are wrapped in American streaky bacon. I tear a piece of meat from one of the babies. It smells good. It tastes good too.

Other than a few grunts and sighs from the men around the table, we eat in painfully prolonged silence. Cutlery clatters against porcelain, Svenne Crowbar smacks his lips, and at one point I think he breaks wind, even though I don't hear it. Hiccup looks up from his plate, frowns and sniffs. Ma looks in another direction and ignores it, but I can see her cheeks redden beneath her make-up.

In come the coffee and desserts. Ma lights a cigarette and emits a thin stream of smoke through the corner of her mouth.

'We would prefer to hit the Kungsholm side but the police headquarters is obviously a problem. There are probably more officers than just Berglund involved with Ploman.'

'What about Hiccup's daughter? Doesn't she work for the police?'

Nix is slurring his words and Svenne Crowbar laughs again.

'The young lady is only a typist and interpreter,' says Ma.

Hiccup laces his fingers, rests his hands on the table, and the words spill forth.

'I'll never understand why the hell she went to work for them. I have raised her single-handedly since our other daughter died and her wildcat of a mother ran away. When she got older I arranged a separate apartment for her in the house. This is the thanks I get. Fucking stubborn women.' He screws his eyes shut and opens them again. 'I shouldn't have taken her to work that time.'

Ma interrupts his muttering by tapping her teaspoon against a saucer.

'Gentlemen. If I had followed my father's advice we wouldn't be sitting here enjoying this feast today. A woman must be able to walk her own path, just like a man.'

I clear my throat to speak.

'I am acquainted with the constable in charge of the Anti-Smuggling Section, Chief Constable Hessler. He has been dismissed but may still have contacts.'

'*Persona non grata.*'

Ma stubs out her cigarette in the ashtray. A thick coil of smoke rises to the ceiling.

'Sorry, what?'

My eyes wander around the table. Nix leans forward.

'He is no longer welcome there,' he hissed. 'Kvist knows the story better than most. That fucking snake had to leave when word got out that he was canoodling with men on the sly.'

Ma leans forward and gives Nix a box on the ear. There is a loud smack as her son's head recoils. It all happens so quickly that I am quite shocked. The pianist stops playing; the clattering porcelain goes silent. The whole restaurant is holding its breath.

A flush as scarlet as his shirt spreads across Nix's cheeks. Perhaps it is more from resentment than the sting of the smack. There is a thick tension in the air.

'Now be quiet.' Ma pulls ups her gloves. 'Stay quiet until we get home.'

The table rattles as Nix pushes himself up with his hands and shoots out of his seat. The white linen napkin flaps over his shoulder and then swoops to the floor like a gunned-down seagull. A few guests with plates full of buffet food hurry out of his way as he resolutely strides through the restaurant.

Ma takes a few deep breaths and collects herself.

'He gets his fiery temper from his father.'

Svenne Crowbar coughs and goes as red in the cheeks as Nix did five seconds ago. His coffee cup rattles against the saucer when he puts it down. I can't for the life of me understand what is going on.

The pianist resumes playing. The light is beginning to fade. Rickardsson has probably finished his walk by now. Maybe he looked up at my window along the way. Ma inserts another cigarette into her holder.

'I used to think that Ploman, the Reaper, Rickardsson and their rabble were working to become the most powerful organisation in the city. Now it has become apparent that they won't be satisfied with anything less than the entire nation, with the help of their high-ranking friends and the Third Reich itself.'

I strike one of the restaurant's matches, lean over and light Ma's cigarette for at least the third time in the last few days. The smoke streams out of the corner of her lips and she makes an elegant sweeping gesture about the room with her cigarette holder.

'Look around. Look at the cream of the Swedish elite and establishment, and then look at us. Notice that they don't feast, they are merely resting in all the comfort that they, and their predecessors, have usurped over the years, at the expense of others. How ironic that it is we, and not they, who are going to prevent a *coup d'état*.'

I have followed her cigarette holder with my eyes and looked wearily around the restaurant. Ma leans forward.

'We have a plan, seeing as the convoy always follows the same route.' She lowers her voice. 'We strike just before they reach their home turf, on Fridhemsgatan. We let the police vehicle turn the corner onto Alströmergatan and we separate the cars, possibly with a baby pram crossing the street. One of the boys and I will take the van, and the rest of you will be parked on Fleminggatan in the bulletproof Cadillac, ready to take care of Berglund if necessary, although we hope the Detective Chief Inspector will play it safe and go back to headquarters. Then we drive the convoy to Belzén of Birka for unloading. Kvist leaves Swedish soil on the same day. You realise what this entails for the Reaper, Ploman and possibly the inspector as well?'

I do realise. I nod and stare down at my hands where they rest on the table and the scars that criss-cross my knuckles. Like the runes of our ancestors, etched into stone, they tell a history of violence and wild escapades. Somewhere in the restaurant the cork pops from a bottle of champagne. I clear my throat.

'They're going to die.'

'Yes.' Ma's red-painted lips draw apart into a smile. 'We're going to kill them.'

THURSDAY 23 JULY

I fall asleep as soon as I get home, exhausted from lack of sleep, schnapps and rich food, lying on my good side. About an hour before dawn Dixie crawls up from the foot of the bed. She gives me a tentative kiss and curls up into a ball between my thighs and belly. I lay a clumsy hand on her. The skin on her back twitches a couple of times as if she is shaking off a fly, but that's it.

When I open my eyes in the morning, she is cold and dead.

I recoil as though she might be infectious, and back away.

'Oh, fuck.'

I move over to the punchbag in the corner of the room. The dust dances in the light streaming through the window. I snatch the bottle of Kron from the desk, and pace back and forth without taking my eyes off her.

Under her bushy brows her eyes are closed. Her body lies like a rigid, charred pretzel in the middle of the white bed sheets.

I take a couple of proper breakfast swigs, put the bottle down on the nightstand, tear the bed sheets off from both ends and lift her up.

Bloody mutt dying on me like this without any warning. Maybe this was the misfortune the clairvoyant upstairs foresaw in his trance. I put the bundled sheet in an old jute sugar sack.

Roslagsgatan seems to narrow in the bright sunlight and runs like a stone-grey line between the worn façades. I walk south with Dixie's body. I try to remember the first time I met her. Nothing comes to mind.

The junk shop smells of rat shit and turpentine. The owner Ström stands behind a counter of stacked sugar crates, scratching his big beard. He looks like an old man, forgotten on the sidelines of life. He clears his throat and spits on the dirt floor.

'To think that it could be this damned hot in Sibirien,' he says. 'Twenty-nine degrees in the shade yesterday. Soon the thermometer won't go high enough.'

'And so many fucking lice that even the upper-class ladies have to drop their airs and scratch themselves sometimes.'

'Has Kvist ever known a worse July?'

'Did a summer at Långholmen.'

'Was it this hot?'

'My cell was above the barrels where they emptied the prisoners' chamber pots.'

'Oh, Jesus.'

'Yes, sir.'

The junk dealer stares out of the window and scratches himself a few more times.

'It makes the beard curl,' he says into thin air, before turning back to me. 'Has Lundin gone west yet?'

I shake my head.

'Wondering if I could borrow a spade.'

I take off my hat and dry off the sweatband with part of the sheet.

'Is Kvist a digger now?'

'My dog died.'

I hold up the bundle with Dixie inside. It is the first time I've said it out loud. Grief cuts through me like black lightning. For a moment I shut my eyes.

'The asylum nurse, may he rest in peace, used to have a miniature schnauzer. Walked the dog with a spoon in his pocket

230

in case her eye popped out when the gang boys kicked her up the arse.'

I recall Wallin, who used to live up the street. He died in all his vileness last autumn.

Dust billows up when old man Ström kicks at the ground. Something sparkles in his eyes but he avoids my gaze.

'He sold the corpse to me when the day came and I paid well.'

'What for?'

'Dog fat, of course. A little sod like that can be cooked down to half a litre if one knows how.'

'What in the hell? So it's really dog fat, that stuff? I thought it was just a name.'

'Speaking of which, it's a long time since you bought a jar. Has Kvist stopped caring about a bit of spit and polish?'

'Had a shoeshine boy to take care of it for a while.'

Ström scratches his beard for the third time, more violently than before. Dry skin flakes fall like snow over his already dirty shirt front. He lays his hand on one of the sugar crates.

'What does Kvisten think of my new counter?'

'It looks damned proper.'

'Stack them on one side and they're too low, on the other side they're too high.' Ström runs his hands over the crates. 'Well, I gave Wallin decent money anyway.'

The junk dealer looks at me and adds quietly, 'I pay the best in the city.'

I look him over.

'Like hell.'

'Sure?'

'Never on my honour.'

I soon leave the junk dealer, sack and spade in hand, and march up the street. Dog fat for Christ's sake. She will be buried on the south side of the water fortress, in the same spot where I sat with Lundin four days ago and where Hiccup killed those two men in '32. It's beautiful up there.

As I lumber up the stone steps, I contemplate how one's life can be completely turned upside down within a few days. First my oldest friend was murdered, I met a man made of the right stuff, then for a few minutes I was unfathomably rich, then I got a sign of life from Ida, and was forced to get involved with a gangster syndicate. Finally the dog dies. If all goes to plan the next few days should offer an equal amount of drama.

Or more.

'Far from over.'

The soles of my shoes clap heavily on the stone steps. Once in the park I pick up her little body. I stroke her head. I regret leaving her unclipped and letting her suffer in the heat for the past few weeks.

'I mean, you were practically blind,' I mutter and lay her down on the grass. 'I didn't suppose you gave a damn what you looked like.'

As I walk down to get Lundin, I think that Dixie's death is a bad omen for Hasse's match tonight.

Swearing and cursing, I haul the undertaker up the stairs. I heave him down onto the grass and soon I am holding the spade and sweating. There isn't much to say about it. She was a friend. It can be that way sometimes with friendship: you don't have to talk about it all the damn time.

I take my shirt off, and curse as I use the spade to chop through a few tough roots. The earth throws up dust and sticks in the sweat that covers my skin like a fine film. When I was young I could shovel coal for hours at a stretch at the ship's boilers, but my muscles don't really obey me any more.

'Calm yourself and take a drink.'

Lundin holds up his hip flask.

'I am calm.'

'Like hell. I know you, brother. You get yourself fired up in silence and then it all spills out. Take two.'

I accept the flask, stand up straight and stretch out my spine a little. I stare out over the park's scorched grass lawns and the part of the city that makes up Ploman's little empire.

It does feel sort of good, in a way, that Ma will be the one to send the Reaper to the other side.

I give the schnapps back and carry on digging. I have obviously had fragile nerves recently; I didn't even manage to shoot him in the van. I can't say for sure if I'll manage next time either. But I have nothing against watching.

The hole is big enough. I drive the spade deep into the grass so that Lundin has something to lean against. The jute sack's coarse fabric in my hands; the little dog's body stiff inside. I lower Dixie down into the hole and help the undertaker to his feet.

'Are you going to say a few words, brother?'

'There isn't much to say.'

'Do you want me to?'

'You're used to it.'

He passes me the flask again and leans on the spade handle with both hands. He clears his throat.

'We have gathered here today to bid farewell to Kvisten's dog Dixie. You lived a tumultuous life, little dog. You were born into wealth on Strandvägen...'

'Nobelgatan.'

I run my thumb over the undertaker's inscription on the hip flask.

'...into wealth on Nobelgatan, with pâté for breakfast and rubies in your collar, but life was unkind to you. You ended up

233

with Kvisten up in Sibirien and it wasn't long before you took to the bottle. You were truly a booze-hound. You drank yourself blind, and now you're dead. May you rest at the Lord's feet. You were good company. We remember how your bones hit the floor tiles when you were scratching at your fleas; we remember how helpful you were when we cut up that big bastard of a bloke last autumn. Rest in peace.'

I bite my lower lip, raise the flask at the grave but can't force out a single word. I take a mouthful and send the schnapps back to Lundin. In the wrinkles around his left eye a tear glitters in the sunshine. I pick up a handful of dry earth and sprinkle it over the sack.

'From birth you came.' I empty my fist. 'And to the earth you shall return.'

'What was that?'

Lundin falters and for a moment it looks as if he might topple headlong into the grave. I brace him.

'What?'

'From the *earth* you came.'

I stare at the old fool trying to steady himself, half-lame and ravaged by age and epilepsy, and God knows what.

'Earth? What kind of stupid idea is that? How the hell does that work?'

Lundin thrusts the flask under his moustache and then passes it to me. His iron hand rattles as he places it on my shoulder.

'My brother has never been much of a thinker, but one hears the truth from children and fools.' He wipes his moustache with the other hand. 'To think I have heard wrong all these years.'

I nod, take a sip and give the flask back to Lundin.

'Hell, I should know. They said that we split our mother in half at birth, my twin and I.' I stare straight into the sun without squinting. It burns. 'Tomorrow evening I'll take you to the station myself. To see the Olympians.'

There is a soft rattling sound as the undertaker pats me on the shoulder. The old man leans on me for support and we stand drinking quietly until the flask is empty, listening to the insects droning and the grass silently dying of thirst.

Kungsholmen is deserted, as though ravaged by a mysterious plague. The traders, who usually stand in the doorways gabbing at this time of year, have retreated into their shops for shade. The ground, which is usually vibrating with the roar of industry, lies fallow. Everything is heavy and still. A mutt pants along the pavement with its tongue lolling out.

'Detective Chief Inspector Berglund joined them down on St Eriksgatan, near the Shoe Coop, but on the way back the cars separated here, is that right?'

Belzén of Birka clears his throat, takes off his glasses and polishes them with a deep-blue silk handkerchief. His eyes are like two peppercorns on either side of his little rose-hip nose. The slender smuggler king gives the impression of being harmless, as tall as three stacked apples and hard of hearing as he is. But, according to rumour, he is even worse than his old man. And his old man was a violent bloke of the old-fashioned sort, who killed his way across two whole provinces, and was chased through forest and fen, before a police chief with a hunting party trapped him out on the ice just north of Sundsvall one winter late last century. At least if one is to believe the chapbooks. I wouldn't get cocky with Belzén any more than I would challenge Ma. Never in my life. He looks at me with his coal-black eyes and smiles widely enough to curve the scars that run from his eye down to his dark beard stubble.

'The risk is that they will take more men with them this time, maybe change their route.'

I point with my cigar over the city map that is spread out on the bonnet of the Cadillac. Nix checks his wristwatch.

'It's a gamble, but a risk we must take,' says Ma. She sweeps her ostrich-feather boa over her shoulder.

Our group is standing gathered on Fridhemsgatan, not far from the florist at the crossing of Alströmergatan.

'Once we have figured out which evening the transport is going, Sture or Sven will keep watch from one of the doorways.'

It is the first time I have heard her son's real names. Ma gestures down the street. The neighbourhood looks about ready for demolition. The houses are practically bending under their own weight, and weeping golden-yellow, poison-green and snuff-brown wall plaster. The window frames are rotted and flaking in the burning sun. Hiccup sprinkles tobacco into a cigarette paper.

'I'll do it,' says Svenne Crowbar.

'Like hell!' Nix's face darkens. 'I was a damned sniper in military service.'

'Calm down, boys. I haven't made up my mind yet,' Ma tells them, then turns back to us. 'As soon as the inspector comes round the corner, I'll roll the pram into the street and make the Reaper stop. The rest of you have to make sure you keep your heads down until I have fired both of my shots into the windscreen. Buckshot.' She smiles with her lipstick-red mouth. 'Oh, how I have waited for this. I feel thirty years younger.'

She leans her cane against the car and fishes the brown glass jar out of her handbag.

A few street sweepers come by, dragging their heels. They are walking with their eyes on the ground and resignation hanging like a veil over their heads and shoulders. Maybe they're on their way to the City Mission's workers' home a few blocks away. We keep quiet until they have passed. There is a gentle rustling sound as Hiccup rolls his cigarette. A tram bell rings down on St Eriksgatan. Ma takes a little shot of powder in each nostril.

There are a couple of clunks as a ground-floor window opens. Ominous, indistinct tones from a radio stream through the window and out into the street. Ma sniffs and the corner of her lip twitches.

'Wagner.' She takes a church handkerchief out from her sleeve and dabs the area between her mouth and nose, staring ahead with hollow eyes. She sighs deeply.

'Georg never understood music but he was going to take me to the Opera House to see *Don Giovanni* that night. There was a winter storm, early February, our wedding anniversary. Your father was wearing his big overcoat with a fur collar.

'We had barely moved ten metres before the explosives detonated and nearly took my leg off. Georg was thrown from the car. I found him in a snowdrift, mutilated beyond recognition. Then the police found a trouser button and a box of snus fifteen metres away.' Her shoulders are shaking. 'I have been biding my time, waiting for years, and now finally the day has come. *Sento in petto sol vendetta parlar, rabbia e dispetto.*'

We stand in silence. The road dust whirls up as Svenne Crowbar drags his foot in an arc in front of him. Ma is shaken out of her thoughts. She looks at each of us individually and speaks with a sharpness in her voice.

'Hiccup, Kvist and one of the boys will wait in the Cadillac on Fleminggatan, ready to take the inspector if he turns back. I will drive the van to Belzén's headquarters.'

Ma dabs away some powdery remains with her handkerchief. Hiccup licks the gummy strip of his cigarette paper and exchanges a glance with his boss. I get the feeling there is something fishy about them but suppress it. Belzén hates Ploman and has worked with Ma for nearly fifteen years.

'We should have a disguise,' Svenne Crowbar says, slurring his words even though it is barely one o'clock.

There is a snapping sound as he bites off a nail.

'Don't fucking start with that damned hot dog vendor idea again,' Nix snaps.

He is dressed in a light summer suit made of thin linen. When he waves his hand, a gold square cufflink shines in the sun. Such a damned snob. I take another big puff and inspect Svenne instead. I hope the brothers fulfil their part of the bargain. Ma gives her sons a look and they immediately stand up straight and stop bickering. She continues.

'While we are hijacking the transport, Belzén will be coming from the other side of the bridge with two rubbish trucks filled with men. The aim is to shoot up, and then firebomb Ploman's gambling dens at Hälsingegatan and Sätertäppan.'

'Rubbish trucks?'

I raise one eyebrow.

'Exactly,' Belzén answers. 'The modern kind. The container on the back has a side that can be swung up like a door. Eight armed men can fit inside shoulder to shoulder. You only need to drive up alongside, hoist it up and open fire.'

I try to picture it. The tactic makes me think of warship broadsides with cannons.

'Furthermore,' Belzén continues, 'we have a couple of men waiting for Rickardsson to go on his evening walk in Sibirien.'

The orchestra rests a beat before the timpani and trumpets explode one after the other, like two heavy knocks on the gates of hell.

I cough. It feels as if Hiccup has punched his enormous fist into my stomach. I stroke my chin and stare down the street. The sharp rays of sun seem to plane the air into strips.

'The bloke has three kids.'

I step on my cigar butt and drag the tobacco over the paving stone with my shoe. I can feel the whole group staring at me. Svenne Crowbar spits out a half-dozen fingernail fragments. A couple of them end up on the tip of my shoe. I clear my throat.

'He doesn't have much to do with Ploman's business any more.'

'So it's true what people say, that Kvist has gone soft?' Belzén squints at me. 'We are fighting on several fronts at the same time. The aim is to crush Ploman's organisation completely. We have been preparing for this for a long time, and we mean it to be final. That's that.'

Up on Fleminggatan the number 11 tram jolts past on its way up towards the hospital. The radio orchestra increases its tempo and sounds like it's mixing in every sodding instrument at once. I clear my throat again.

'Rickardsson is the source.'

'What do you mean?'

'He's the one who talked.'

I immediately regret it. Everyone in the small congregation freezes. Belzén leans forward to hear better. Ma's fingers whiten around her ivory cane.

'And why in the hell would he do that?'

Belzén is staring me straight in the eye. My ears go hot.

'We have been neighbours for as long as I can remember. Home on Roslagsgatan. In Sibirien.' I pull on the cigar and look away towards the intersection. 'Nearly up by the tram turning loop.'

The last sentence was little more than a hoarse whisper, hanging lonely in the air between us before disappearing in a cloud of smoke.

'And Kvist doesn't think that he might have been lured into a trap? That he is a pawn in a bigger game? It wouldn't be the first time.'

Belzén extends his little finger and wags it with a smile. It seems I am the only person who doesn't know the background story of that fucking finger. For a moment I am transported back, lying beaten to the ground by sticks and chains, feeling the dull iron teeth of the pliers biting through my flesh and bone. My stump aches as usual.

'I'm damn sure.'

'Then Kvist can find out when the next transport is planned,' says Ma. 'If he is so anxious to cross the Atlantic.'

The pavement tremors beneath me. She rolls up the map, wedges it under her arm, picks out a couple of car keys from her handbag and dangles them in front of me like a fishing lure shining in the sun.

'Kvist's getaway car,' she continues. 'We will notify you where it is parked at a later date.'

I stroke my chin as my eyes dart around. A girl of about fourteen or fifteen comes out of the florist on the corner and throws a bucket of brown water from mopping into the street. She has already developed a feminine shape and is dressed like a grown-up with a light blouse tucked into a long, black skirt. A few strands of hair have escaped her golden plait. She glances at us, cricks her neck and turns to go back in. Anxiety spreads through my guts.

I bite the end off a cigar, spit on the street and take the bait.

'His boy has an apprenticeship waiting with the manufacturer Enquist.'

'Good. We'll also give the wife adequate compensation and a funeral wreath.'

The keys are glittering in the air. I take them. Ma knocks the rolled-up map twice on the body of the car.

'Finally the time has come.' She makes a gesture towards the open window, where music continues to stream out. 'Siegfried was born to fulfil his destiny.'

She smiles widely and holds the map up like a marshal's baton.

'Gentlemen, we are going to war.'

THURSDAY 23 JULY

Finally.

The sound of clinking beer bottles spills into the dressing room and reverberates on the metal lockers and elongated zinc washbasin.

We can hear the murmurs of the spectators outside and the occasional guffaw of laughter. Coils of cigarette smoke seep in through the cracks around the door and cut through the pungent odour of Sloan's liniment. I am crouching in front of Hasse and wrapping his black-flecked hands.

'Are you sure you want me in there?'

I run my tongue over the salty scab on my bottom lip, look up from what I am doing and meet his gaze. A streak of doubt or indecision shoots across his baby-blues. His ribcage is motionless for a second.

'Of course Kvist should be there.'

I nod, run the grey wrap between his fingers and thumb, and pull it carefully. Hasse is sitting on one of the wooden benches that runs along the dressing-room wall. In the absence of a dressing gown I have wrapped him in a white sheet to keep him warm. His face is the same shade as the bedlinen; he's pale with nerves. I finish what I'm doing and pat him a few times on his broad chin.

'Time to wake up, lad!'

Hasse gives a start and stares at me as if he has never seen me before.

'When the hook hits home you have to be the one to follow up. High and low.'

Hasse slips his hands into his gloves and I lace them up tight. I try to catch his eye. He is still miles away. I can't say whether it is a good or a bad thing. Everyone prepares differently and some only properly wake up when the first gong sounds. In any case it is time to snap out of it. I click my fingers in front of his face. He gives a start again.

'My girl Josefin is here,' he mumbles. 'Her girlfriends too.'

'Don't think about that now.'

Every match must be more important than life and death. I have pissed blood for weeks afterwards and never had to ask myself if it was worth it. Without that attitude, fear takes a hold of you, and then you are in serious danger.

His legs carry him, but the young man moves as though in a trance. I make him jog from one wall to the other and throw uppercuts into the air. I look him over. Loneliness swells in my breast. I light a cigar just as there is a knock and the door opens.

It is time.

I throw a towel over my shoulder and grab a bottle of water. Expectancy flutters inside me.

This is fucking it.

It is about damn time to fucking show them.

Kvisten has still got it.

I walk behind the boy. We are met by a wall of humid heat. I take a deep breath through my broken nose.

I am finally back where it all went belly up, but this time it will end differently.

Hasse stops in the doorway and paces on the spot a few times before stepping into the room. The Kungsholm club has no seating but there is a gangway running through a black mass of people. Fifty-odd men turn to look at us in unison.

They are fanning their mugs with daily newspapers and hat brims.

I smile internally.

I am home.

We start making our way through. Various situations and strike combinations flash through my mind accompanied by the public's cheers, as if I were the one about to go into the ring.

We have what it takes. I've never gone down, never even taken a fucking count. I don't intend to start now. We've got this in the fucking bag, with sequins and bells on.

It has gone quiet. The buzz has subsided, as has the sound of clinking from smuggled-in Pilsner bottles. I look up. The lights from a dozen glowing cigarette tips intensify only to immediately fade into darkness. In the gloom I see a white summer dress, and a pair of round cheeks with a straight nose and rosy mouth in between. Her front teeth are biting her lower lip. She has a bunch of flowers in her arms and a couple of other young women on either side. That must be Josefin, Hasse's girl.

Smoke and solemnity hang heavy in the room. My heart starts pounding. I take a deep drag on my cigar. Our shoes make a lonesome echo on the floor tiles. The ten metres to our destination feel horrendously long.

What the fuck is going to happen?

A wave of noise seems to push us forward. As we move towards the ring we hear a ripple of whispers following behind our backs. Someone coughs, someone else scrapes their foot against the floor, a couple of people laugh quietly. With every step the noise levels intensify.

We have almost reached the ring when a scrunched up cigarette packet flies past the brim of my hat and hits Hasse in the back of the head. A few men laugh.

'Who let that fucking queer in?'

A guttural Skåne accent cuts through the room. The laughter multiplies. I clench my fists. The vein in my forehead begins to throb and I swallow several times. I place my left palm between Hasse's shoulder blades and push him gently ahead of me.

'We'll show them. We'll show them in there.'

I point at the ring with my cigar. The referee is already standing in the middle of the square but the opponent hasn't shown up yet. I slap Hasse on the back.

'Step into the ring with your left foot first. Always helped me.'

'Take the boy to a dance instead!'

That same Skåne bastard. Hideous memories blaze in my brain. It's as if the insults sink down to the sludgy bottom of my consciousness and unearth recollections I thought I had drowned in schnapps years ago. I shrink under the jeers; my whole body seems to contract.

I step up onto the platform, move away a three-legged stool with flaking paint and part the ring ropes. They are wrapped in dingy material so as not to chafe the boxers' skin. The referee nods at us. He has all the characteristics of a fighter himself. His nose is crooked, his ears are battered and violence has carved its marks around his eyes.

He stares at me. Maybe I met him during my down-and-out years. Chiselled my hobo symbols into his mug.

Who the hell knows.

Doesn't matter.

Not now.

When Hasse is about to step through the ropes, he stumbles and is close to falling face first. Laughter patters like hailstones behind my back. The redness of shame creeps across the young boxer's cheeks, which are shining with sweat. His knees are shaking; his eyes are darting around for something to latch onto.

'Keep moving, keep yourself warm and supple, and listen to me. Look at me.'

Hasse obeys and begins to jog on the spot.

'Not a single one of them… no, look at me, I said! That's right. Listen! Not a single one of them would dare step into the ring with you. Keep warm!'

I pinch the cigar in the corner of my lips and massage Hasse's neck muscles with both hands. I am trembling but I hope he doesn't notice. He rolls his muscular shoulders back and punches a few tired strikes into the air.

'Once you're in there, nobody exists but you and your opponent. Do as we have trained and show those bastards.'

Thunderous applause tears my attention away. I chew on the cigar and peer over my shoulder. I swallow tobacco.

I can tell a man's weight to the kilo, whenever, wherever, and I'll be damned if our thick-necked opponent falls within the welterweight division. He must have had to angle himself sideways just to fit through the door, and his powerful shoulders slope sharply inward to his waist. There are a whole lot of weight cheats at this level. Still, you've got to handle the heavier opponents just like any other: knock them in the chops and say goodnight. Nothing else to do, even if you're bound to receive the odd blow on the way.

There is a knot in my stomach. I have never been so nervous before a match. In a few minutes the referee will raise Hasse's hand to the ceiling and it will feel as if it were my own. I take the cigar out of my mouth and turn to face the boy.

'Movement and speed, in and out the whole time. You have a good hook. Use it. Even if you miss, you'll get him with your elbow with a bit of luck.'

'What is Kvist saying?'

'In the clinch you hold his head down with one hand and give him an uppercut with the other. And why not cut his eyes up with your glove laces while you're there.'

Our opponent steps into the ring amid whoops from the crowd. He is grinning so widely his mouth guard is about to burst out of his gob. I grab hold of my boy's neck and pull him close to my face.

'When you have the referee on the wrong side, give him a body punch. Make sure you make contact just below the hip. It stuns the leg lame like hell. Gives you a few seconds to do whatever you want. Headbutt him if worst comes to worst but make it look like an accident.'

The bell rings and the referee waves the boxers into the middle. The sound of the bell fades, but it has struck something inside me.

I fought my first proper match a few months after I had signed off for good, soon after the end of the war, with no other qualifications whatsoever. Ever since my time as cabin boy, I had fought bouts with my fists wrapped in sailcloth for bets. Countless hours with a shovel in the boiler room and at the turning wheel made my shoulders and arms strong and my wrists as hard as steel. The instinctive desire to cause harm also helped. I was probably born with liquid violence in the veins.

I won that first time, though just barely. I had a good couple of years, climbing over bodies on my way to the top. I was somebody. The people at home believed in me. People wanted to buy me a beer, pat me on the back and shake my hand. I got a reputation as something of an artist, with knockout power in both my right and my left, and as a thoroughly entertaining boxer who could also take a hell of a lot of blows.

This isn't the first time the odds have been against me. I was tipped to lose against Tord 'Hässelby' Thulin out in the

Fjäderholmarna Islands early in the summer of 1920 but won despite a broken hand. It cost me a place in the Olympics a few weeks later. Another Harry, a Brit, won the middleweight gold.

Everybody said it should have been me.

Then the legendary Axel Albertsson took me under his wing and formed me into a true technician. He said that a good boxer has to be shrewd, and that I had everything it took, with a mind as quick as my fists.

I often danced around with ravenous ferocity to break the opponent's mind before I unleashed my combinations to break his body. It was more entertaining that way, for me and the audience. I didn't go for the light switch earlier than necessary. The audience loved it.

They loved me.

If everything hadn't gone to hell in the autumn of '23, I would have gone professional. Maybe I still would be today. Thirty-nine is no age for a fighter, but it's impossible to know for sure. Some have a hundred matches in them, others have ten. No one can know in advance.

I open my eyes when Hasse comes back to the corner of the ring. I pour a little water down his throat. My own trainer's words echo through me.

'Move and keep moving. Finish your combinations with a hook.'

The gong sounds again and the boxers begin to circle one another. Hasse is trying to bite his bottom lip through his mouth guard. Our opponent rushes past the centre of the ring and meets him a few metres from our corner.

Not a good sign.

The other bloke does a double jab, finds the right distance and follows up with a hard right. Hasse takes the blows on his guard.

The strikes' dull thuds resound through the premises, and the crowd jeers. A left in the belly makes Hasse stumble backward. My knuckles whiten around the ropes.

'Move, I said!'

A similar combination concludes with two hard blows to his body, and Hasse tumbles towards the rope to the left of me with his hands firmly covering his face. The opponent is above him immediately and raining down punches. It is as if he has ten arms. A vicious ancient Indian god.

'Counter for fuck's sake! Move!'

I can tell the quality of a boxer's footwork just by listening to the squeaks and swishes of his feet against the canvas floor. This time it seems totally damn quiet. For one moment the opponent stops hitting and appears to be considering his options. Light feet and a light heart, a small superior smile on his lips.

Devil take him.

I have a good mind to climb into the ring myself, but instead I scream: 'Now! Now!'

Hasse doesn't hear me; he just stays with his feet nailed to the floor. I can't for the life of me understand what is wrong with his bloody ears. He just has to do what I say.

His opponent is on him again, with strikes so swift they make the ropes sing. His muscles move like well-fed snakes under his skin, and his fists drive into Hasse's trunk over and over again. Hasse stands pressed against the rope, about as dynamic as a sea stack, and absorbs them. It is only a question of time before he drops his guard. The crowd roars with excitement, the scent of blood in their nostrils.

'Go in red-hot! Clinch the bastard!'

Tobacco flakes and saliva spray out of my mouth as I shout. It is as hot as a fucking Turkish bath and he is varnished in sweat.

The opponent jabs at his head and chest, smacks a straight right into his guard and twists a left into his liver.

Those bastards will have hurt.

Hasse's elbows slip down. I instinctively raise my hands in front of my face. The next right hook hits him hard in the eye. His neck muscles surrender. His head practically hits his shoulder before bouncing back.

I grab hold of the ropes and squeeze them. It feels like every damn blow I've ever taken hits me in one single strike. I gasp, and my cigar almost falls out of my mouth, but I manage to catch it.

Hasse slumps diagonally forward, already out of the game. His opponent seizes him by his left forearm and heaves him towards the ropes. Another right meets his beautiful jaws and smacks the mouth guard clean out of his gob. The left misses because the boy crashes to the floor nose first. A deafening cheer raises the roof, and I close my eyes and sink my head.

We didn't even get a single punch.

Not even a fucking jab.

At last, the mob keeps their mouths shut and the count inhabits the same ghostly silence it always does. At three I am back, at five I lift my head, at seven I open my eyes. I let the chewed-up cigar fall towards the canvas and stamp on it. The darkness of brewed disappointment wells up in my breast. I kick the stool with a clatter.

I step down from the platform. By number ten cheers explode and I reach Hasse. He is still unconscious. A trickle of blood is running from his nose.

I reach for his limp left arm. His body makes a shuffling sound against the floor as I drag him under the ropes.

I turn the youth over onto his back. It hurts when I lift him into my arms, in my back and my soul. I swing around holding the hot, limp body and direct my gaze at the door on the other side of the passageway between the men. I grit my teeth and start walking.

The corridor of bodies smells sharply of sweat, liniment and cheap tobacco. I walk. Life gradually returns to the boy's numbed body. His legs twitch, he moves his head slightly and groans.

'Like a bride over the threshold.'

The Skåne bloke again. A guffaw ripples through the audience. Someone leans forward and spits in front of my shoes. Soon the insults are flying thick and fast through the air, as quick, dark and unpredictable as bats. I slow down and look into the crowd's eyes. There is hatred there.

'Off to the bedroom.'

I attempt an insolent smile but fail. Several gobs of snuff-spotted spit land in our path. Mouths are gaping wide open from sunburnt faces, mouths full of broken poor men's teeth: a gauntlet of jeers.

Four metres left.

Hasse's girl is covering her face in her hands. Her shame implants itself in me, runs red-hot under my skin. The flowers lie strewn on the floor. One of her girlfriends has her arm around her and whispers something in her ear.

What the hell is there to say?

I don't know.

All sixty-five kilos of the boy begin to make my arm muscles ache. He sniffs and hides his face against my breast. I peer down at him and hold him tighter around his torso. He is quiet but his shoulders are twitching slightly and my shirt front is damp with blood and tears.

When I look up again I am looking straight into a pair of familiar green eyes. Memories whirl in my head. Nausea pinches at my guts. My intestines coil like reptiles.

It's been over a decade since we last saw each other, in a boxing club much like this one. He is standing at the farthest end of the final row of men. His hairline has crept up a bit, and age has broken furrows in his high forehead, but his bulky boxer's physique remains. I gasp for air but do not break eye contact.

Two metres.

He opens his mouth as if to speak and I stand up straight, like before the village priest back home. I don't know what I am expecting, maybe one of the long harangues of equal parts praise and scolding that he used to deliver, but he says nothing. Then he looks away, as though in disgust, and I pass by with my fighter in my arms.

I'm not about to give up on my own, not again. I've got him.

Whatever happens.

I hold him tight.

Four labourers get on at Kungsholmstorg. One of them is holding a rolled-up newspaper, another has an unica box. The wooden benches creak as they spread themselves out in the window seats and the conductor calls for departure. As the tramcar rolls slowly forward, a bearded man in a dirty, collarless shirt and notched braces tries to hail it.

'Hey!'

The conductor reaches through the front door and locks hands with the tramp, who manages to swing himself up into the car with considerable effort. He takes off his cap and bows before looking around. Slowly he starts to make his way across the dark carriage floor littered with white tickets. The ceiling straps above his head sway with the lurches of the tram.

Hasse and I are sitting on the lengthwise seat at the back. He is leaning his elbows on his knees and hanging his head. The driver pushes the front crank and we rattle at full speed down Hantverkargatan. In one hand I am clutching the green scrap of cloth from my desk drawer. God knows why I took it. Supposed to be lucky. It wasn't. I put it away.

I wrestle with my words for a while before speaking.

'I saw my old trainer in there. When I was dragging you out. Haven't seen him in over a decade.'

Hasse turns his head, to hear me better perhaps, but doesn't look at me. He hasn't looked me in the eye since he regained consciousness.

Just as well.

'I'm sure you've heard the rumours.' I clear my throat. 'Now I'm going to tell you what really happened.'

Hasse scrapes his foot against the floor. I lean back against the backrest so that he can't see me, tip back my hat and take out a cigar. My body is crying out for tobacco. Non-smoking carriages are an invention of the Devil.

The conductor goes around taking fares from those newly boarded. The tramp is limping behind him and presenting something to the passengers, who all shake their heads guardedly or stare out the window. I push my hat farther back and carefully touch the wound on my forehead with the palm of my hand. Sweat stings in the stitches. Each word is a struggle, but I force myself to continue.

'Axel Albertsson.'

I focus on one point on Hasse's neck. His skin is sunburnt and peeling. He has spent too much of this summer bent over shoes. The cigar aches between my fingers. I hold it under my nose and inhale its scent. The conductor leans against one of the poles, removes his cap and dabs his face with a handkerchief.

'I was already a hell of a fighter when I signed off but it was

Albertsson who taught me to box. We spent many hours together, sweating half to death.'

The tram rattles and jerks into the next stop. I pinch the cigar between my lips, remove the elasticated strap off my wallet and take out a photograph. Creased grooves criss-cross the yellowing image like whiplashes. My little girl was only a couple of years old when I was carrying her on my shoulders in this picture. She is mainly her mother's daughter but I think she has my nose, or the nose I used to have once upon a time.

A woman in a light bodice sits down three seats in front of us. She takes out a compact mirror and powders her red cheeks. I hold out the photograph and Hasse takes it.

'Her name is Ida. My daughter.'

The words catch in my throat. The tram wheels thump hard against the rail points, and so does my heart against my ribcage. I squeeze the cigar near enough in two between my index and middle fingers.

'I never let them go hungry, not for a single day. We had food and fuel in winter. Every morning by the stroke of six I was unloading down at the harbour. I had my Friday binges, and they say that the last dram brings the first smack, but we never quarrelled, her mother Emma and I, and I never hit her, even with an open hand.'

The letter from America is burning in my pocket.

'Get lost, you damned tramp!'

The bloke five seats in front of us swings his rolled-up newspaper at the vagrant, who shuffles back a couple of steps. Hasse is sitting as stiff as a bargepole but the photograph in his fingers is quivering slightly.

'They were my blood kingdom.'

I don't even know if that's a real expression. I look out the window. We are approaching City Hall, with its turrets steadfastly

254

towering up into the bright summer evening sky. From the corner of my eye I see Hasse take out a handkerchief with his other hand and bring it to his face.

'Don't blow your nose, for God's sake. It'll make those blue bruises under your eyes go black.'

Hasse obeys. I notice two men changing a street light outside Kungsholm Church.

'They travelled to America in autumn '23. I was supposed to join them a couple of months later as a professional boxer. That was the plan. Written in the stars it felt, from what people said.'

The stench of sweat and poverty makes me look up again. The tramp is extending his filthy paws, holding a few badly sharpened razor blades and a poorly forged mortgage deed. His brown eyes are weary from hardship and humiliation. I shake my head and suggest with a cursory nod that he go back down the gangway.

'Just one match.' I force the words out. 'A big international gala at Cirkus. A yank by the name of Kid Brownie.' I sigh. 'He was unbeaten, like me, but no great threat from what I understood. Mostly a formality before the professional contract could be signed.' I scoff and mumble: 'That fucking Kid Brownie.'

A slim middle-aged man jumps on at the Seraphim Hospital. He is dressed in trousers with well-pressed creases and a straw hat. He has tied a long-sleeved jumper around his neck. He has an elegant air about him, and he looks like has come straight from a tennis match, though he doesn't have a racket as far as I can see. He grabs hold of one of the ceiling straps a few metres in front of us and starts to whistle.

The tram picks up speed along Stadshus Bridge, which is practically empty in the July heat. There is usually a lot of congestion around here at this time of day but not now. I fix my gaze on the jagged silhouette of Strömbadet bathhouse and the spires and towers of Riddarfjärden. A seagull on the bridge railing spreads its wings as if about to take off, but doesn't.

'You can never get away from yourself,' I mutter into the soot-streaked window. 'Some things are beyond your control, like schnapps, or the weather.'

I suck on my bottom lip but resist the impulse to rip off the scab. The tram swerves slightly to the right and the wheels screech against the tracks.

'My main sparring partner during training was a youth from Birkastan. Early twenties, like me.' I glance at Hasse. 'And just as lonely.'

The photograph flutters like an insect wing in his uninjured hand. His teeth strain a whistling breath.

'It was something I learnt as a lad. At sea. It took. Once ashore, I tried to rid myself of the habit, but I couldn't fucking do it. It is what it is. It isn't something you can just force yourself to stop just like that.'

We follow the quayside and overtake a lorry loaded with crates of bottles. Two blokes on bikes are getting a free ride, with one hand on the handlebars and the other on the side of the lorry. For one moment I shut my eyes. The memories flash through my brain. I grimace.

'Three days before the match my trainer caught us in the dressing room. And that's all I have to say about that.'

The words clump together like porridge. Hasse's hand is shaking as though from fever. I swallow twice and clench my fist so hard that I mash the cigar. The discordant tones of the whistling man slice through my ears.

'Within a few hours word had spread to half the city. Soon the damned gossip column of *Fäderneslandet* got wind of the story.'

My mouth is twitching spasmodically like a retard's. 'I didn't save those clippings.'

My moist eyes dart around the carriage. That damned fitness fanatic is still whistling. Only a madman would play tennis in this heat. I blame all this talk of progress. It makes people obsess over vitamins and idiotic antics. Progress and the heat. People never used to take time off in the middle of summer to devote to leisure activities.

'Going into the ring again was out of the question. And sure enough I was dismissed from the harbour as well.'

The vein in my forehead is throbbing. I punch my fist against my thigh.

'A man has to work for God's sake!' I bellow.

The man stops whistling. The woman with the powder compact and the man with the newspaper stare over at us.

I look past Hasse's head. The clear summer evening is extinguishing nearly all the light from the pale neon sign of Centralpalats. I remember how people would whisper about me when the scandal came out, and how their eyes ground me to dust. Self-hatred spread like pus in a knife wound and it took years to recover.

Hasse returns the photograph and I put it back in my wallet. We travel in silence staring straight ahead. The carriage's irregular jerks make our shoulders touch. We rattle past Norr Bridge.

The Bumpkin with the maggots is nowhere to be seen. I hope he didn't come to any harm beyond the fright I gave him.

We get off at Kungsträdgården to change. I'm going north and Hasse is going south. I strike a match, finally able to smoke a Meteor. My lungs fill with singeing smoke and calm.

In the park on the other side of the street the National Socialists have drummed up another gang. I used to sit here in summertime and stare at the bare-chested sailors who would saunter around with swaying walks and curious eyes.

Times are different now.

Labourers with hands stiff from chalk dust and cement rub shoulders with elegant gentlemen wearing suits of the latest fashion. A few brown-shirted blokes in boots stand in a line with a wide stance, left hands behind their backs, and the right holding blue-and-yellow swastika flags. They are guarded by about thirty coppers, despite the ban on political uniforms. The fish rots from the head down and it is no secret that priests and policemen and half the officer corps have embraced the doctrine.

Some sort of mini-Führer stands in front of the gathering and rattles off some rubbish about the Jews. God only knows what is so bad about the Jews. They stay open for their loyal customers even on a Sunday and none of them has ever shouted insults at me.

Not that I know of, at least.

Not like other people in this city.

Out in the country there is animosity between the villages, because one earths up their potatoes on a different date, or plants their seeds in a different way from the next village over. At the Friday dances, these trifles start fights between the farm-hands, fuelled by fusel and malice, that can get so vicious that some of the lads are never the same again. Since Gabrielsson's murder a similar sickness has infected the city, and when one group gets angry, the same anger soon spreads to their enemies. I distinctly remember the priest himself calling it a spiritual epidemic when I visited him for the last time, some time in November.

Hasse and I stand shoulder to shoulder and look at the gathering. I let my eyes stray to the statue of Karl XXII. The warrior king conquered and died with his boots on before the age of thirty-five. I would have preferred that. I have barely achieved a thing in my thirty-nine years.

Between the tree trunks and the lemonade kiosks in the park, I spot Hasse's tram come chugging along. I take a puff that almost devours half the cigar.

'I continued to fight for my bread and butter, in backyards and alleys, with the crowd as the ring rope,' I say straight out into thin air. 'Sometimes I was so drunk that I had no recollection of it the following day, except for the bruises and broken fists. Often on an empty stomach. There wasn't much choice.' I glance at Hasse, who is staring at the National Socialists. 'Going to America was out of the question.'

The youth clears his throat and gestures towards the park.

'If this continues we'll end up like Spain.'

I shrug my shoulders. The number 10 veers around the bend and works its way quickly towards our stop. Hasse extends his hand and I take it. Our eyes meet for the first time since the fight. A decent bruise is growing around his left eye.

'I owe Kvist my thanks.'

The tram rings its bell as it pulls up. I don't want to let go of his hand.

'I never had the opportunity to pick myself up and come back,' I say.

Hasse bites his bottom lip and nods dumbly.

'Stuff this defeat, and spit in those bastards' faces next time.'

From the corner of my eye I see the disembarking passengers float around us like shadowy spectres. The conductor calls for departure. Hasse jumps aboard and works his way farther down the carriage. I back up a few steps to try to catch sight of him through the back window but I can't. I grunt.

Another person disappearing from my life. I already know that he isn't coming back. This is how it ends.

The same damned story every time.

I swear weakly to myself and tramp over to the platform for the number 6 home to Sibirien.

As the son of a whore, I've had to survive on my own, and since my trainer left me in the lurch, there haven't been many people with the guts to stand by my side.

I let my gaze wander from the palace to the other side of the water and over the rocks of impoverished Söder. High up there, among the worn-out apartment buildings, the tumble-down little shacks, the places of worship and beer cafés, Katarina Church watches over her flock. The occasional white cloud rises from the factories. I sigh and put a cigar between my lips.

Never accomplished shit. Nothing of lasting value anyway. Every street I have walked down has been a dead end. That's just how it is.

I never went to any of his sermons, but I heard that Gabrielsson always wove some humour in to make the congregation laugh. Lord knows they rarely laugh up in Katarinaberg otherwise, where the children are many and the need is great. There was a certain tenderness to the priest, and anybody who wanted to could bask in his warmth. Even a bloke like me. He didn't whip virtue into the bratty kids either; he wasn't like the others, who preach patriotism and fear of God instead of forgiveness.

The Skeppsholmen clock tower peals across the water, calling the sailors home for the evening. The familiar sea air fills my lungs. It reminds me of the old salty me. With one exhalation I rid myself of all the self-doubt from the boxing club and stand up straight. Like hell am I going to let them defeat me with their taunts and abuse.

I look up. A little farther along the platform, one of the brown-clad National Socialists is glaring at me with a sneer.

'What the fuck are you looking at?' I raise my fist at him. 'Get lost before I put you into a coma for so long that you'll wake up in an outdated uniform!'

I puff angrily on my Meteor. I have no idea what's going to happen but I feel a surge through my veins.

'You've still got it in you, Kvisten.'

Nothing to lose. It is time. I've still never taken a count. I'll show those bastards.

The time for revenge is now.

A gust of wind comes through the window and cools my sweaty upper body as I sit on a wooden chair staring out onto the street. I have Harlock's Swedish–English dictionary in one hand, a notebook in the other and a pen in my mouth. A fully packed seabag leans against the wall, containing a change of clothes and the new suit from Herzog's. I can get it pressed when I arrive.

With a final glance out on the street I return my attention to the book and flick from the letter A to P.

'Press,' I mutter to myself. 'It's the same in both languages. I can remember that.'

I stare out at Roslagsgatan again, and wait. Nisse's Eva toddles slowly up Ingemarsgatan on the way to her bakery. Kullberg locks the door to the haulage company on the other side, glances up at my flat and catches sight of me. He rushes off down the pavement, heading south.

Another poor devil I've been too hard on in my time.

I put the dictionary down on the windowsill and thumb through my notebook. Some of the words, like 'apple' and 'animal', I knew already. Others, like 'address', 'automobile', 'alibi' and 'aquavit', look more or less the same as in Swedish, but plenty of the others look impossible to pronounce.

I hear raised voices on the street and lean out of the window. The air is still hot and carries the stench of sun-heated rubbish. When I was up in the loft earlier looking for my old seabag, the walls smelt like resin under the metal roof.

'A strike? When the confirmation suit needs paying for on top of everything?'

One-Eyed Lasse's old bat is standing down on the pavement giving her husband a talking to. God knows where the stevedore got his nickname, considering the fact that he has both peepers fully intact. I don't know the wife's name, but the fact that her only wedding dowry was a guardsman's child with a cleft palate is common knowledge in these parts, as is her stern temper. Maybe that's the kid who has grown old enough to leave the nest.

'Do you want us to work our fingers to the bone for a lower wage than we got before?'

'You're just following the others like a dog!'

'I'm a union representative, for God's sake!'

'And you get sod all for that.'

My gaze moves northward up the street: nothing but a shuffling vagrant dragging something along past the house where asylum nurse Wallin hanged himself last autumn.

Or whatever it was that happened.

'They are shipping over three hundred riff-raff from the harbours of England. Am I supposed to work opposite them?'

'Oh, you...! When one of us dies I'll finally be able to open that café.'

The old bag picks up the sides of her skirt and storms south. One-Eyed Lasse slouches after her, and I sigh with relief. The fewer people who see me talk to Rickardsson the better.

The church bells chime eight o'clock. Somewhere in the house a woman laughs and outside in the courtyard the door to the potato cellar slams shut. I take out my watch and check that it is still working properly.

He should be going for his walk soon. It's not only my broken rib that is making my chest ache: it is clear that I have to choose between my little girl and Rickardsson.

'Life is harder than any cock.'

I lean out of the window again.

I can't see him yet.

The skinny vagrant is laboriously dragging a dead mutt past Kullberg's on the other side of the street. He is holding its body by the hind legs. There is a cloud of dust and flies around the mongrel's crushed skull, and small accumulations of blood on the pavement show where the bum has paused for a breather. I can't see any rifle. He probably smashed the mutt's head in with a rock or a sturdy cane.

I sigh.

It was bound to happen sooner or later. There isn't exactly a long life expectancy in Rickardsson's field of work, and judging by his clothes, his family will probably have a healthy inheritance to look forward to. There is nothing I can do for him. It is how it is. I will have to continue dancing alone for a while yet.

My eyes rest on every blood pool along the pavement, and I imagine him stumbling home, leaking like a sieve, groping along the house fronts on the other side of the street.

I put my schnapps glass down on the photograph and pick up the Husqvarna. I open the magazine, see that it is empty, slot it back in and raise the pistol. The comfortable weight of the weapon tugs at my arm muscles. The front sight sweeps across the street, stopping in turn on the golden pretzel outside

Ingemarsgatan bakery, old man Ljung's back, then to Bruntell's general store, where the manager has put up a sign saying 'NO JEWS OR HALF-JEWS', before I let it merge into the paintwork of a black Plymouth that is slowly driving northward. The bonnet is open to prevent the engine from overheating.

I glance back at my timepiece. Don't trust the bastard. It was as still as eternity itself for over half a year before it started ticking just as adamantly as ever. The hands say five minutes past.

My thumb trembles as I fold down a page corner in the notebook. I strike a match and thick cigar smoke billows out through the window. I shut my eyes and try to conjure up that distinct aroma of Aquavera, sweat and snuff that can only come from a Swedish man. I am going to miss it on the other side of the pond.

'I could take a hectogram of Ljunglöf's snuff to sprinkle the bed sheets with.'

I chuckle to myself and glance over my shoulder to see if Dixie has heard. She hasn't. She is dead.

There is nothing keeping me here. It's just like Ma says: it's only a question of making a respectable exit, in one way or another.

I look back down at the street with emptiness in my heart. The tram transports four passengers up to the turning point. The occultist starts up his evening practice with a slow, moody melody, similar to the one he performed when I was giving Rickardsson a good hammering.

I won't need my hard fists tonight; I'm relying on my wits. Albertsson did always say that a good boxer needs a good head on his shoulders.

And I was damned good.

I raise a dram. As soon as I meet my match, everything falls apart. I down the drink and run my fingers over my short hair.

It doesn't matter. Not any more. It has to be done. For a moment I feel that same stagnant sensation from the boxing club earlier moving through my limbs. I smack myself hard on the cheek with a loud crack. I get up and pace to and fro across the floor in rhythm with the occultist's little ditty a couple of times. I stop in front of the punchbag and wedge the cigar in my mouth. I shut my eyes and recall the moment when Hasse's opponent stood still for the briefest moment, thinking over his options.

I punch three jabs in quick succession with my eyes still shut. With every strike I turn my front foot a quarter turn and roll my head like a fucking owl. I listen to the rattling chain, feel the faint draught of wind when the punchbag swings back. The sound of my right hook reverberates through the flat; the straight left makes everything go quiet.

I could have smashed that bloke into pieces with my eyes shut. I bury my face in my aching hands. I feel on the verge of tears.

When the bell strikes the quarter-hour, he appears. He is walking south with a decisive, swaying gait. He is dressed in a brown shirt and black waistcoat but has left his jacket behind.

I watch the condemned man. For a moment I play with the thought of warning him and giving him a head start. He could leave town by tonight, but Ma and the others would smell a rat.

I put on my sunglasses. It isn't necessary in the dusky twilight but I don't want Rickardsson to look me in the eye while I am sealing his doom. I lean out through the window and purse my lips to whistle, but there is no need, he has already noticed me. He takes off his hat, waves with it and hastens along the pavement like a bull to the slaughterhouse.

Kvist must be careful about joining forces with people he doesn't know.

The occultist's prophecy sears through my mind like one of his dodgy trumpet notes. If that bastard would just take a break from his dodgy music, maybe I could concentrate on my dodgy dealings. I bury my face in my arm and sink deeper into the pillow. Every limb is stiff, except the exact one that was intended to play the leading role in this scene.

A sudden chill: my cock slides out of Rickardsson's mouth with a slurping sound. My member is soft and slack like warm gutta-percha. He gives my saliva-moistened dick a shake, and slaps the blasted thing against my thigh.

'Is Kvisten not in the mood?'

He chuckles and flicks my flaccid cock against my thigh muscle again. Every joint in my body is trembling with shame. In the mood, like hell. Part of me wants to punch him but I daren't meet his gaze.

As soon as my mind begins to regain the slightest control, my body becomes completely useless.

The bed springs creak when he gives up on me. He sits back against the iron bed frame, takes his hat off the bedpost and puts it on his head. He nods at the silver box of snuff on the bedside table.

There is no disappointment in his eyes. I take a breath so deep it makes my ribcage hurt, and I pass him the box. He holds it tight in his right.

'It happens,' he says as he prises out a pinch. 'With schnapps and this fucking job.'

'I lost Ploman's convoy after Väster Bridge the day before yesterday, but the devils are definitely driving around Söder for some reason.'

I press my lips together and fiddle with a cigar. That was too direct. A shiver of deceit runs along my arm and makes the flame dance as I draw the matchstick towards my Meteor. I take a puff, twist the cigar a half-turn and puff again, squinting through a curtain of smoke.

'Thought Kvist had signed off for good? Is he setting sail again?'

Rickardsson grins and gestures to the seabag of clothes. My muscles tense up, and my ravaged lungs feel like they are on fire when I hold my breath too long, before I finally squeeze out a response.

'Laundry.'

Rickardsson smiles, bites his top lip and strokes my leg. A few greasy flakes of snuff stick in the hair on my calf. The jazz boy upstairs starts playing something a little livelier and soon the notes are wailing as loudly as cats in heat. The music makes the blood pump a little more easily through my veins in any case.

'Kvist knows how to wear a suit. I've always thought so. Good haircut too.'

I feel my cheeks flush and my eyes flit upward and lock onto the ceiling lights: six yellow light bulbs in a circle, most with burnt brown patches. I run my hand through my hair.

'Can't get any shape into the bastard even with half a hecto-gram of Fandango.'

'I must admit, I'm a sucker for that prison cut.'

'Hell of a way to treat a grown man.'

'It is punishable by law for a man to love another man. People like Kvist and I can only fulfil our hearts' and bodies' desires in secrecy and shame. Funny, isn't it? That they try to force us out of it by threatening the clink, which is filled with a thousand other lonely men?'

Rickardsson snorts. He moves his hand ten centimetres farther up my leg and cups it over my knee.

'And what does Rickardsson use?'

'Pomade, you mean? Triumf. What the hell does it matter?'

'I am considering buying a pure red shirt.'

I close my eyelids.

'Red? I'll be damned.' His hand is working its way gradually higher. 'Well, I'm sure a man like Kvisten can get away with anything.'

The creases in my cheeks and skin deepen as I squeeze my eyes even harder. How did I get here? They forced me onto the wrong side of the law from the start. They took everything away from me. They took my daughter away, and now she needs her father. Rickardsson, of all people, should understand. I want to try to explain it to him, but it is impossible. There is no way out of this other than betrayal.

I am going to get him killed as a result. I can picture him now, riddled with bullet holes. The thought of it makes me feel sick.

His damned children.

Versus mine.

'Does Kvist remember when he was discharged last autumn? We bumped into each other in the stairwell of number 41. Your crown was as smooth as a peach, but the rest of you was as sour as a lemon.'

'Thought you wanted a fight.'

'I offered to walk you home.'

'Thought you wanted to compare fists.'

'And when you refused I suggested a walk to somewhere private in the park.'

'Did you already know then?'

'I've always known.'

'Always?'

'Since the first time I saw you.'

'That's why you always stared at me.'

'Hell, you always gawked back.'

I scrabble among the clothes on the floor for my wallet to show him the photograph of Ida, as some sort of apology or explanation for what must be done. The bed springs complain as I tear loose from his grip and swing my feet over the edge.

'Maybe I would have been safer in Långholmen, the way things are looking these days,' I hear him mumble behind my back as I stand up. I shudder.

I turn around with a quart of moonshine in a beer bottle. The condemned man has the right to a final drink. After a mouthful I pass the bottle to him and suck on my Meteor as greedily as Rickardsson just sucked on me.

I stand naked before him, take the cigar out of my mouth but hesitate and take another few considerable drags to gather my strength.

'If only I hadn't lost Ploman's damned van in Söder…'

Dark grey coils trail from our cigars and hang between us like gun smoke. I move my hand down to my cock, to hook the bait, though my nerves definitely won't allow any hanky-panky now.

'Maybe their little trips aren't that important anyway. I don't know. I'm sure I could figure out a plan but the more I think about it, the more hopeless it feels.'

His voice has become hoarse. He wipes his hand across his plump lips, then looks at my crotch and takes another swig.

I close my eyes, and pull at myself.

'Rickardsson did say before that it's probably important.'

He reaches for the ashtray, takes out his snuff and tips his hat farther back on his head. I thrust my hips forward a couple of centimetres. His Adam's apple moves as he swallows.

Men. When their blood is up you can steer them any way you like. My work would be so much bloody easier if more men shared my preference. Then I wouldn't have to chase them halfway round the city and beat them into submission.

My blood surges when I think about it. Rickardsson sucks his fat lower lip into his mouth for a moment but then looks away.

'There is no way out,' he says. 'Only here and now.'

The condemned man's words burrow into my skin. I sink down a couple of centimetres. Betrayal, after all we have shared.

'I'm sure we can figure out a plan together, but let's start with the van. Does Rickardsson know when the next transport is planned?'

Half a minute later I tear into the funeral parlour, with my shirt done up wrong and in shoes without socks. With my notebook in one hand and the telephone receiver in the other I request the number to the drinking den on Kommendörsgatan. Svenne Crowbar answers, like last time. Just as I am about to communicate my message, a coughing fit tears through my body. It feels as if my lungs are going to burst. I lean my forehead against the wall.

'The last transport.' I wheeze. 'Tomorrow evening. Our only chance.'

I end the conversation as another hacking cough ravages my ribcage. I wait out the spasms. I stare up at the ceiling in a cold sweat, with tears running down my cheeks. I can hear Rickardsson's shuffling steps as he paces around my flat on the second floor.

Maybe there are some tears of sorrow mixed in with the tears of pain.

If Ma and Belzén have their way, then he has barely twenty-four hours left to live.

My wallet and the photograph are still in my jacket. I try to summon the image of Ida but my thoughts are filled with the gangster upstairs.

I close my eyes and recall the brief times we managed to snatch together. Each one of his words caresses me as intimately as his calloused hands.

'We are cut from the same cloth.'

I wipe my face with my shirtsleeve.

'We met only to be separated.'

It sounds like a fucking film. I think about him and me, and about his kids and my daughter. Then I throw open the funeral parlour door and step out into the evening heat and the stench of rubbish. It sure feels as if my whole wretched existence has gone rotten.

FRIDAY 24 JULY

It is still early when I enter the bakery up the hill the next day.
I've got my old boxing gloves hanging by their laces around my
neck. The smell of leather and ingrained sweat mixes with the
enticing aroma of newly baked bread, cinnamon and butter.

I am going to say goodbye to Lundin this morning.

I take the heavy seabag off my shoulder and it lands with a
thud. I push back my hat and wipe the sweat from my forehead
with my shirtsleeve. Nisse's Eva, the baker's wife, is loading
trays with freshly baked loaves. She brushes the flour from
her fingers and strong arms. Her chubby round face breaks
into a smile.

'Has old Lundin given up the ghost yet?'

'Still some grit in the bloke.'

Nisse's Eva rubs her hands on her apron.

'Naturally the women have already laid claim to his corpse
needles.'

'I didn't know that Nisse's Eva was interested in the occult.'

'I sew Småland pouches in the evenings.'

'Well, leather is leather.'

A smile moves across Nisse's Eva's lips before settling as a
smirk in the right-hand corner.

'What can I do for the sombre Kvisten?'

'Bloody stupid really.'

I search for a cigar and wonder how I am going to fulfil
my task.

'Well, I was wondering, would it be possible to order a couple of soft-bread sandwiches, with meat and everything, to wrap in paper and take away with me?'

'Take them away? What do you mean?'

'Home to Lundin. I'll pay extra for the topping and for your trouble.'

'We don't usually do that. Down in town maybe, but not here.'

'Just a thought that occurred to me.'

'In paper did you say?'

'Possibly a cardboard box.'

'We don't usually do that.'

'Sure.'

'Could fry some eggs to go in them.'

'That would be very kind.'

'Maybe you'd like to have a look at our American cash register while you wait. A Patterson. You didn't have time when you were last here.'

'I'll do that.'

Despite her reservations, it's not long before I am walking back down the hill with two egg sandwiches wrapped in green crêpe paper. A skinny rat runs along the gutter. The seabag burdens my shoulder like grief but the smell of the boxing gloves reminds me of victories past.

The doorbell chimes. I set down my paraphernalia in the foyer of the funeral parlour and take a couple of deep breaths before entering the living quarters.

Lundin has nodded off and is snoring with his mouth open. His untrimmed moustache flutters as he breathes. I swipe away a louse that is crawling across his forehead but he doesn't wake up. The bottle on the table is empty. He is probably sleeping off the booze.

273

I put the sandwiches down on the bedside table and leave the room. I open the door to the cool room and let my steps echo between the fully tiled walls. The room is empty but for the white child's coffin. I open it. It used to be brimming with bottles, including sweet liquors for the ladies. Now there is just one bottle of O. P. Anderson left, right at the bottom.

During the Spanish flu, in Lundin's heyday, the tram seats were scrubbed with alcohol at each turning point to stop infection, and those who survived the influenza pandemic at least got a taste for schnapps. Now he has no customers, for funerals or booze. I pick up a liquor bottle and go back.

He is still sleeping. A buzzing fly is beating against the dusty window. I find his engraved silver-plated hip flask in the pocket of his jacket hanging on the bedpost. There is a glugging sound as I fill it with aquavit. I put it in my inside pocket. Lundin grunts and I am afraid that he will wake up but he soon begins to breathe heavily again.

I put Mr Andersson down and puff up the pillow so that Lundin's head is a little better supported, then move the wooden chair and sit down next to his bed. I can taste sweat. I dry off my face with the sleeve of my jacket.

'I remember when you first took me in.' I clear my throat. 'I said, I remember when you took me in.' My hand reaches for the bottle again. 'Nobody wanted to rent above a funeral parlour, of course. And you couldn't very well turn down the money either.'

After a swig I unwrap one of the sandwiches and start to eat it, continuing to speak between chews.

'You should know that I could have had a two-room flat in Birkastan.' I tear off a bit of bread between my front teeth and chew. 'But what the fuck would I do with two rooms? Corniced ceilings but a blockage in the stove from what I understood.' I put the last bit in my mouth, chew and swallow. 'There, I finally said it.'

I lean over the bed and open the window to get a little air into the muggy room. The fly escapes.

Warm silence fills the bedroom. I sit down again, take the snuffbox, open it and pinch out a decent wad. I slowly shape it into a ball, as big and smooth as a bullet.

'It's finally time to go now.' I pinch out another ration from the box. 'The past few days have turned my whole life upside down. I didn't say anything. You've had plenty to think about, what with dying, and the funeral parlour and everything.'

I put the snuff on my knee, reach for the bottle, swallow a couple of swigs of aquavit and suck my lips clean before I continue doling out the snuff.

'I'm sorry that I left you alone last Christmas. When those damned screws let me out last autumn, I was on top of the world. Then when it all went to hell I just couldn't cope.'

My voice breaks, but I pull myself together.

'People in the building say that you smell like your corpses, but I never noticed. You're good about the heating. Your brother raised the telephone tower, and your nephew is going to the Olympics. That's more than can be said for the rest of them.' I cough and clear my throat. 'I went up to Wetterström's and asked him to come down and witness your will this afternoon.'

Quietly and carefully, I line up the snuff until a dozen pinches are set out along the edge of the bedside table like a rosary.

'One for each year.'

I brush the breadcrumbs from my trousers. The chair legs scratch along the floor as I stand up.

'If you ever think of me, just know that I am doing well. If I don't die on the way.' I have to pull my sticky shirt free from my back. 'God knows what will happen next.'

I take the stuffed hummingbird out of my jacket pocket, lean over the bed and put it down on the windowsill. The words get stuck in my throat.

'Sleep well, old man.'

I turn my back on him.

Like always.

I turn my back on them all.

Enough now.

On the way out I stop in the doorway for a moment. I know that I will never come back, unless it's feet first. I want to say something else but nothing occurs to me. I unscrew the lid from the hip flask and raise it to him.

'Thank you Lundin.'

I leave him there in his room, lying in the warm silence.

Bruntell's general store, Ström's junk shop, the captain's cigar shop and Nyström's barbers. I don't look around, I just place one foot in front of the other hurriedly, my wide brown trousers flapping around my dusty shoes, the boxing gloves bouncing against my chest.

It is time for my comeback.

I stand at the crossing for a while. I stare up at Goering's old place and Wernersson's Velocipedes. For a moment I wonder whether I should go and say goodbye to my old employer, and thank him for all the debt collection jobs he gave me through the years but I turn towards the library instead.

They thought they had me. They thought I would surrender, but Kvisten always gets back on his feet, just like in the fight against 'The Mallet' Sundström. Half the match against the rope, then it was the last round and I had six broken ribs, a smashed cheekbone and crushed nose. But I fucking floored him.

And I'll fucking floor you all.

I smirk and quicken my pace. Old man Johnsson is limping out of his bazaar, moving display boxes. There have been no fewer than three occasions when I have had to see him about a debt in the last few years. A strong and obstinate bloke. So I beat him, mainly to see how much punishment he could take. You can't influence a man like that with kindness. He hasn't been able to hear properly since and he limps like he has gout.

Johnsson catches sight of me when I am a couple of metres away from him. He drops the box he is holding. A bunch of scrubbing brushes of the cheapest variety spill out onto the dusty street.

I take the bag off my shoulder and help him to pick them up. They have for some reason painted the brushes in the colours of the flag, so that some old dear can feel patriotic as she scrubs the floor on her hands and knees. As if there wasn't enough filth in the folds of the flag already.

I drop the brushes back down into the box. Johnsson meets my gaze. There is still fear in his eyes, and they dart around more than ever, but he puts on a brave face.

'Kvist is certainly in a better mood than last time.'

'I'm not here on business.'

'Three times you've paid a visit.'

Johnsson stands up straight, apparently confusing confidence with strength.

'I've never come across such a stubborn man.'

'I don't know. My father was a stubborn man. Didn't bend for anyone.'

'Believe me, during my time I have never encountered anyone like you, Johnsson.'

The old man sticks out his chest as if I'm about to pin a medal of honour on him.

'Mr Kvist is too kind.'

'Don't know about that.' I meet his gaze. In his crossed eyes I see the insatiability of my desire for violence. Nausea is bubbling in my stomach and I breathe deeply to be able to take in all my brutality. 'Tonight damn it, Johnsson. Tonight is the night.'

'Certainly is, but it's an away game against Norrköping. Won't be easy.'

An old woman comes hobbling along with two zinc buckets of water on a yoke. Three bangs from a rifle roll out from somewhere across the street and I flinch. I look around but don't see anything. I take the cigar out of my mouth.

'Kvisten has won a few away matches.'

'Football's not like boxing.'

I laugh and touch the brim of my hat.

'Take care now.'

Johnsson nods, and I heave the sack up on my shoulder and continue along the pavement. A couple of blocks to the west I see my old client Elin Johansson standing and smoking outside Standards clothes boutique.

I cut across Odengatan to avoid her but she has already focused her attention elsewhere. If I managed to stay alive last autumn I can sure as hell survive tonight as well. That time I was in a clinch with more powerful enemies than the Reaper and Detective Chief Inspector Berglund. Plus this time I have Hiccup, Ma and her entourage to help me, instead of a damned clothes shop assistant.

'Child's play.'

I put a cigar in the corner of my lips and light it as I peer from under the brim of my hat over at the steps up to the City Library. There is a wall hiding the boy from me. I jog across the road through the light traffic on Sveavägen and reach the other side. I loosen my tie and shirt collar.

Hasse is sitting idly on his wooden stool but he stands to attention when he sees me.

'Kvist?'

'Wanted to get my shoes shined one last time.'

'Last?'

'Let an old man sit down.'

He offers me the stool and almost trips over his own box when he backs up a couple of steps. After a glance around he picks up one of his rags and bends to one knee by my feet.

'Dixie is dead.'

'I'm sorry to hear that. She was a good dog.'

He concentrates on his work without looking at me. The bruises on his face are as black as plague spots.

'Damn it, I told you not to blow your nose after the fight.'

Hasse speeds up his work, rubbing as if he were starting a fire. With a deep breath, I begin. The smell of the nearby tobacco roasters hangs heavy in the warm air.

'I was in there a couple of years ago, you know.' I nod towards the orange library with its gigantic round pillbox of a roof. 'Because of Dixie.'

'They're nice in there.'

'Of course I've been in there more times than that.'

'Really?'

'There was one time I asked up and down Roslagsgatan but no one had ever got a volume B in the encyclopedia's fucking scam of a subscription. So I came here.'

'What for?'

'Always been curious. Have you ever tried looking up the word "schnauzer" in a book where everything begins with S?'

''Fraid not.'

'Well, trust me. It takes a certain type of man.'

'Sounds tricky.'

'And did you know that there are three completely different varieties of the same dog? You have the giant schnauzer, the standard schnauzer, and you have Dixie, the smallest.'

'I don't really understand what Kvist is getting at.'

'It's fundamentally the same dog, but in slightly different sizes and shapes, and with different personalities. It was the Germans who arranged them according to their differences. Hence the fucking spelling.'

'Sorry, I still don't understand.'

I laugh and dare to ruffle his hair a little.

'They're all schnauzers. No matter what people say.'

An empty ballast lorry chugs past. The clouds aren't moving, but I think I can hear the noise of an aeroplane. I look down again, seeking out his eyes in vain. No good.

'Maybe you should take a look in a book sometime too?' I say.

'Probably should.'

My lungs ache as I take a deep breath.

'This time you have to really listen.'

'I always do.'

'Well, listen to this, once and for all. It wasn't your fault. I put you in too early, tried to get you to do my dirty work.' Hasse looks up as me as he continues his work. I blow smoke out of the corner of my lips. 'My fight is a different one.'

'I don't understand.'

'I mean that you have damned fine hooks.' I take my old boxing gloves off my neck and dangle them in front of him by the laces. 'Nobody has ever lost wearing these.'

'I can't accept those. Kvist has done enough.'

'I don't need them where I'm going.'

Hasse changes shoe and carries on working in silence. The gloves land on the pavement with a thud. The hubbub of children playing is coming from the paddling pool in the park on the other side of Restaurant Corso. A bloke is walking along the pavement, kicking a football. I try to recall the sounds of San Francisco from the brief time I spent there. All cities seem to have their own song.

I consider my words. On the other side of the street, the sun is making it look as though the golden bullhead above the butcher's shop is on fire. A few labourers with overalls stiff from work grime lumber past.

'Lundin is a peevish bastard.'

'He seems all right.'

'Bloody moody.'

'I like him.'

'But when you get to know him you will realise that he is a true friend, no matter what. Frank and fair. So stingy that he wipes his nose and arse with the same bit of newspaper. But he still needs an assistant, though he refuses to admit it.'

'Where is Kvisten going?'

'I'm not coming back.'

I fan myself with my hat brim and look over the boy's head, down towards Rådmansgatan and Arsehole-Pelle's scab agency.

Hasse angles up my right foot and works another cloth over it vertically to get a proper sheen. I am going to need a new pair of shoes to go with the suit from Herzog's but that can wait until I'm on the other side of the Atlantic. The main thing is that Ida isn't ashamed of her old man, now that he is finally making the crossing. I take my keys from my pocket and jangle them.

'One is to the funeral parlour and the other is to my flat. It is fully furnished, with gas and wood stoves, and an ice cupboard too. Bed has proper bolsters. Big enough for you and your girl.'

Hasse's shoulders shake and he hides his face under the brim of his cap. A tear falls down on the tip of my shoe and trembles there, shining like a herring eye in the sunshine, before he wipes it away with the rag. I spit out a gob of dusty phlegm which sucks up even more dust when it hits the pavement.

'At nine o'clock this evening the final Olympians take the night train to Berlin. Go with Lundin to wave them off.'

'I don't know what to say.'

'Then keep your mouth shut.'

I place one hand on his muscular shoulder and give it a firm squeeze. Then I leave him, and walk the short, sweaty stretch to Thulin's.

The walk only takes a few minutes, but Thulin's stamp shop is closed. A slip of paper taped up on the door informs me that the forger will be back soon. I study the stamps in the window and quietly wonder if they are genuine, before stepping into the shadow of the doorway on the other side.

In the grid carved out by the paving stones, in the spot where the tramp bled to death the day before yesterday, rust-red remnants still glisten in the sunlight. I wonder how much blood will spill tonight. I wonder what will happen with Nix, the trigger-happy bastard. Both brothers seem damned temperamental, each in their own way. I notice that I am dancing in place and try to shake off my nerves.

'Kvisten bloody well knows how to wait.'

I force myself to whistle a tune as I watch two hollow-eyed prostitutes pass on the opposite side of the road. Their worn heels clack against the pavement. It will be nice not to have to run around after them all the time. Even though Central Station, a few blocks south from here, doesn't spew out farmers' daughters at quite the same rate as it did during the lean years, the flow continues. Seduced by promises of the city's splendour, they will soon discover the truth about life in the sludgy bed of this marshy swamp. A drunkard in ill-fitting clothes sways down the street, following the whores. Behind them a man with a bare chest stands on a ladder leaning against a lamp post. His skin is as pink as a piglet. Here too, every fucking square centimetre is fully illuminated, even during the short summer nights. The ones who try to hide in the shadows may as well stand naked in their own miserable doom.

One cigar later I see a driver leading a draught animal by the mane, and waddling along behind it is none other than Thulin. My face breaks into a smile. I throw the butt into the gutter and step out from the cool of the doorway.

Once inside the poky little workshop I get Beelzebub purring with a good scratch under the chin. Thulin hands me the visa and bends down with a sigh in front of his safe.

'I understand that Kvist is leaving tomorrow?'

The master forger throws the question over his shoulder while he clicks in the code to open the safe. I stop scratching the cat and the purring dies away. The thick door of the safe opens and Thulin roots around among the German–Jewish passports.

'That's right.'

The old man finds the right one, turns around and gives me the document.

'What's the route?'

'Norway to Canada via England.'

'Good luck then, with whatever you are going to do.'

'Thanks.'

'You're going to need it.'

Fuck. For half a second I get the feeling that this bloke knows too much, but I just nod a short goodbye and turn to leave.

Once I am out on the street I take a deep breath. The oxygen floods through me like a sense of peace. A boy walks past Café Élégance, made up with powder on his face and wearing trousers that are far too short. He nods to me and I tip my hat brim. I think I have seen him somewhere before but I'm not sure where. I take out my passport to appear busy.

Apparently my name is Ola Andersson and I look like a professional criminal in the photograph. But I've done my homework. As long as I can answer 'no' when they ask me whether I am an anarchist or polygamist at the American border control, I should get into the country without a problem. I for one can't distinguish the passport from a real one, and from what I've heard the Swedish quota isn't filled yet.

The name has bad associations for me. A few years ago an Ola Andersson had the misfortune of receiving a visit from Kvist. He ended up looking a lot worse than I do in this photo. A pity and a shame. He was a stylish bloke.

'Better name than Thulin anyway,' I say into thin air. 'Who names their child after a make of car?'

With the seabag slung over my shoulder, I walk up to Hötorget with a spring in my step, walk around the concert hall with its new Milles statue that caused such a hubbub at the inauguration and head for NORMA on the other side of the street. Might as well take the opportunity. Who the hell knows when my next meal will be.

After pork sausage, mashed turnips and a couple of Pilsners, I continue down to Stureplanen with its jumble of glittering tram tracks. It is mainly deserted, as if the residents have embraced the Spanish tradition of siesta.

'Though they've got a lot to deal with down there now. Maybe they don't even have time for it any more.'

A couple of Östermalm fops stroll towards the baths on the other side of the square. I look down towards Three Whores Field, as it is known, and up Birger Jarlsgatan before I cross.

Two muscular tram men with bare torsos sit opposite each other on one of the tram tracks, pulling a plane between them. I drink it in.

A couple of others are standing a little farther away, nailing down a rail with a railway spike. The sledgehammer hits the head with a loud clunk and Gabrielsson's still, dead face flashes through my mind. Strange that nobody heard the blows from Katarina Church on Saturday morning.

I stop in my tracks. The singing of the hammer sets my limbs aquiver. The Bumpkin witnessed two men, both slim and well dressed. I close my eyes, and recall Detective Chief Inspector Berglund shaking hands with the Reaper down by the Stadsgård wharf as clearly as if they were in front of me.

Fucking turncoat pig.

The cigar crumbles apart in my fingers. I stomp resolutely towards Humlegården and my getaway car. With every step the anger and conviction in my heart intensify. It is time to visit the Bumpkin with the maggots one last time.

As agreed, Nix has parked the car on Sturegatan in Ma's territory, not far from the pontoon on the south-east corner of Humlegården. It's a beige two-door Dodge with soft, flowing lines, and dark-brown mudguards. I dig out the keys Ma gave me and unlock the vehicle before walking around it and checking the air in the tyres.

I throw in my seabag. The leather in the driver's seat creaks under my weight. I pat my clothes to check I have my wallet, passport, visa, cigars and, in my chest pocket, the little cocktail umbrella. In the passenger seat, as promised, is a large unica box with two long-barrelled revolvers and a double shoulder holster. I take out my scrap of green fabric, unfold it and conceal the box.

My fingers fumble for a space under the dashboard by the passenger seat. I take out my Husqvarna and pull a roll of sticky tape out of my bag. I bend down and use a few decent strips of tape to stick the pistol to the bottom right corner of the space.

If life has taught me anything it is to always have a backup plan. Especially when you are dealing with the most powerful gangster syndicates in the city. A backup escape route, a little extra lead in your magazine, a fucking horseshoe in your boxing glove.

Can't hurt.

I put on my sunglasses and push down the clutch. The engine roars to life at once. There isn't enough juice to drive the whole way to Norway but I already know where I'm going to fill up. The petrol station on Valhallavägen stays open in the evenings.

My breath quickens with anticipation just thinking about it.

I place my hand on the gearstick between my knees, click into first and steer towards the neutral Klara district to park the car. The fewer people that know where the car is, the better. And I don't see eye to eye with that Nix. Can't trust the bastard. I've dealt with Hiccup before, and there's nothing wrong with Ma, but there is something fishy about the younger son. And the elder for that matter.

As soon as I pass Kungsträdgården I see that the Bumpkin is still in the same place. I park around the corner from the Opera House and crack my knuckles. Whistling 'Yankee Doodle', I saunter over to the fisherman. He is standing with his line in the water. His face seems significantly more sunken than on Tuesday. My insides are gripped by the same feeling as when I shadowed that amorous attaché. The thought of that stubborn Evy with her fucking foetus doesn't help either. It is some sort of flickering conscience.

I pull the elasticated strap off my wallet and take out a fiver. Whether I've gone soft or not, there is no need to go at it like a bloody steamroller every time.

The Bumpkin's eyes are focused on the fishing float and he doesn't see me coming. I fold the note lengthwise, hold it up between my index and middle fingers and clear my throat.

'For your good memory.'

The old man looks as though he is about to faint and I haven't even laid a hand on him. His face twists into a grimace, the fishing rod falls to the ground and he grabs hold of the bridge railing. I wave the fiver.

'You mentioned two slim, well-dressed blokes last time. You recognised one of them as the Reaper. I am interested in the other one. He had grey hair, didn't he?'

'D-dunno. Had a hat.'

'A white little fucking pointy moustache, right?'

The Bumpkin looks around as if weighing up his chances of escape. I shake my head.

'Older than the Reaper?'

'Right.'

'And the moustache?'

The Bumpkin nods. 'White as dead moss.'

He grabs hungrily at the note I am holding out. I blink at him. 'For your bad memory.'

On the way back to the car I think about the Reaper and Berglund's handshake at the harbour, and how one can certainly earn a coin with a poor mind, despite what Lundin says. I open the car door and put on my sunglasses.

I would like to test the power in the engine but the rambling lanes of the Klara district don't offer the opportunity. I would also like to test the power of the guns. Something tells me that they kick back hard but a life at sea and in the ring has toughened my arms so the recoil shouldn't be a problem. Deep down, part of me hopes that the Detective Chief Inspector does follow us tonight so I can blow the bastard into smithereens in good conscience. And part of me hopes he just stays away.

I find a deserted back street not far from Lindkvist's casino in the Sköldpaddan district. I sit and smoke in the driver's seat for a long time. I like smoking in a new car. I turn the evening's plan over in my mind. If all goes well I am soon to be a very happy man.

The door slams. I go around to the passenger side and step on the cigar butt. A few labourer youths slink past with their Friday litres and their girls. They are already ravaged by hard graft, with lopsided bodies that they must have inherited from generations of working men.

I feel a hankering for schnapps, but the contents of the hip flask will probably benefit me more later. An old jailbird like me isn't trusted by the damned schnapps company any more, and there is no time to hunt for contraband.

During the lean years, when I was a proper boozer, I might have fleeced one of those lads out of his litre, but that was before I became weak and withered.

It was Gabrielsson who helped set me straight, and I have honoured the promises I made him ever since. It is very rare that I have any hard liquor between my breakfast nips and the three o'clock full ration at the restaurants.

I wait until they have passed, take off my shirt and waistcoat and open the door. With a glance down the sun-drenched street, I put on my double shoulder holster and the jacket over it. I crouch into the car and take out the black-shining revolvers: two heavy Smith & Wessons with twenty-centimetre-long barrels. I open the cylinders to check that they are filled. According to Ma, they take a new kind of cartridge that the police use in America to pierce gangsters' cars.

This is going to be beautiful.

I holster the shooting irons and fasten one button. I let a handful of cartridges rattle in my trouser pocket but leave some in the box. They might come in handy.

Soon we shall see. Tonight is the first night of the rest of my life – or my last.

I walk towards Drottninggatan, with the sun on my back. I take out my pocket watch in my left hand.

Assuming it is correct, it's less than twenty-four hours until the boat sets sail from Oslo.

I clear my throat and spit in the bone-dry gutter.

'Kvisten's final round.'

FRIDAY 24 JULY

Ma and I don't meet many people as we amble along the avenue between the lanes of Karlavägen. The residents of Östermalm have probably left the bustle of the city to spend the warm weeks in the countryside or the archipelago. Utterly deserted, like a salt flat, except for the black-clad gatekeepers standing to attention at every other house looking like sweat rags. In the trembling sunlight the air is still and hard to breathe.

'Peace hangs like a threadbare mantle around Svea's shoulders. People are flitting from one branch to another like frightened birds. We are living in truly uncertain times.'

I agree absently and finger the letter from America in my pocket. I haven't summoned up the strength to read it again, let alone throw it away.

A lady in fine livery with a short riding crop trots past. The sun's rays filter through the leaves of the linden trees and play in Ma's silk dress. Patches of light dance on the gravel path as we walk.

I am close now. I can feel it. Part of me is there already.

Ma glances in my direction.

'Cross a poor victim of the arrows of Mammon and he will become dangerous. We have chosen a shady business where loyalties shift quickly, even if trust is the only guiding principle we have.' Ma breathes smoke out of her nose. 'If you've got a full trough there will always be some piglets who come along for a nibble.' She takes another drag. 'The only thing one can trust is one's own blood, but I see Kvist as a mixture of both my sons. A mixture of their more reprehensible qualities.'

She laughs. I leave the letter alone and feel instead to check I still have the little cocktail umbrella in my breast pocket. There have been several times over the past six months when I have bitterly imagined death as a blessing. Once, at my worst, I considered ending it all by my own hand. I have seen fellow inmates in Långholmen, at least as sane as me, throw themselves off the suicide walkway, down into the three-storey-deep cement valley.

All those thoughts are gone. Now, with happiness within reach, death frightens me. The stakes are too high. This morning I felt exhilarated; now I want nothing more than to wake up tomorrow.

We approach an old lady sitting on a wooden bench on the level of the secondary grammar school. Life has carved razor-sharp lines in her sunburnt face. She dunks an old crust of bread in milk and shoves it in her mouth. She holds out a cupped hand as we pass. A moist, slovenly sound comes from her toothless mouth, almost like when you poke some bastard's eyeball. Ma avoids a steaming pile of horse shit.

'Is Kvist listening?' she says suddenly.

'What did you say?'

'Well, I said that my father was a man of the cloth who couldn't handle my wilful ways. I fell pregnant. Had a healthy girl. After the birth he took the child, wangled the church records and drove me out of the rectory with nothing but a tirade of expletives to live on. I was as alone, as I believe Kvist has been.' I kick at a stone. 'Here comes the Baroness with her first and second chambermaids.'

I look up and see a lady with a parasol. A woman in uniform walks one metre behind her, and another follows a metre behind her.

'At that time it was unthinkable for a woman to be independent, and I must admit that I traded my body for a while. Father was probably right when he said that sin originated in women, and so continually seeks to return to its source.' She coughs lightly. 'And it's true that I rarely turned down a little *Nachtspiel* when it was offered, it has to be said. One might choose to see that as a weakness. In a woman.'

Ma nods in greeting to a gathering of several gentlemen dressed in very dapper summer suits, each with a little dog on a leash.

'I couldn't trust my own father, but I got another in recompense. Georg was good to me; not once in all our years did he raise a hand to me. It could have been because he knew I would leave and never return, but I think it was a case of that oh-so-complicated yet simple phenomenon: we grew to love each other.'

'Mmm.'

My eyes wander aimlessly. The sun reflectors in the ground-floor windows shine across the pavement on the other side of the street. A horse and carriage pass by. The carriage's rubber wheels glint in the sun. It smells like summer. Gay piano notes come from an open window above the Swedish–American tailor's, and mix with the hammer blows from the construction site up ahead.

'Georg came from a long line of butchers but had Finnish blood in his veins. Maybe that was what drove him onto the criminal path. Poor folk go where the road takes them. For my own part, perhaps I had no excuse.'

'Mmm.'

I glance sidelong at her. Strange that she is confiding in me all of a sudden.

'One thing that Kvist and I have in common is the thirst for revenge.'

She drags her ivory cane along the low iron fence that runs the length of the avenue. The hollow clanging is so loud that the horse up ahead takes a few skittish sidesteps and the lady has to pull on the reins. Ma stops and turns to me.

'I have issued dozens of death sentences but never personally taken a man's life.' For a moment she seems to look straight through me. 'It does something to a person, I have come to realise. In some ways it is two lives extinguished in one go.' The gravel crunches under our shoes as we resume our walk. 'It makes no difference to me. In a way, I was already extinguished with that car bomb on the seventh of February 1924.' Ma taps the cigarette out of her holder with her forefinger, stretches out her lame leg and crushes the butt under her shoe. 'I will probably be gone before this year is through.'

I check the time.

'Something happened to me in November last year,' I mutter.

I peer at the building over her shoulder. I hear the rhythmical blows of hammer against rivet and watch the trainee masons balancing on wooden frames with shovels in their belts. A couple of painters in paper hats mix up the paint. Someone is shouting orders.

'What do you mean?'

'It was a Wednesday.' My voice feels thick. I clear my throat. 'I remember.'

Ma chuckles.

'Kvist is a strange one, but that doesn't bother me. Do you know Otto Weininger?'

'Had a donkeyman called something similar once.'

'Weininger was a German, or maybe Austrian, philosopher.'

'A whizz at making ships in bottles.'

'Committed suicide by shooting himself in the heart. In the same hotel room where Beethoven died, of all places.'

'Got one of his at home.'

293

'He proved quite clearly that there is no such thing as masculine and feminine, but that every individual, to varying degrees, is a mixture of the two. The idea spoke to me, and perhaps it speaks to you too.'

I stop.

'What the hell are you saying?'

'We are both obstinate in our ways, and perhaps we go contrary to what is expected of us.'

'Perhaps.'

She lifts her cane and uses it to pat the back of my thigh, kind of like one does to get an old gelding moving. I obey and we continue.

'There is something else that we have in common.' Our shuffling walk has brought us nearly all the way to the Karlaplan roundabout with its big fountain. 'Kvisten's mind can be of use. I expect you have sent the odd man to the other side.'

'They're starting to pile up.'

'And people still think that you have lost your edge recently. Look at this as revenge. People are going to talk about Kvist, however it turns out, but the talk will be different from what it was before.'

I hum absent-mindedly. Ma stops and pats me firmly on the cheek, like I did to Hasse in the dressing room yesterday.

'Time to wake up, lad!'

I blink, tense up and look her in the eye. She is squinting at me. There is gravity in her voice.

'Your associations with Rickardsson have made the boys mistrust you.'

Words fail me. I rub my broken hands hard against my forehead.

'Oh, for God's sake! Didn't I fucking say that we have been neighbours for as long as I can remember?'

I rummage for a cigar.

'I know. I believe you, of course. I am glad you will be by my side.'

It feels like a spring thaw in my mind when I finally grasp what Ma means. A cold, fatal terror floods through me from head to toe like a bucket of ice water. Ma locks her eyes on mine.

'You have a lot to lose, but that cannot be helped. Kvist and I will take the van, Ploman and his murderous *Mädchen für alles*.'

The street is sun-drenched and sleepy. The Cadillac is filled with tobacco smoke and tension as we sit parked on Fleminggatan, a hundred or so metres from the scene of our planned ambush. The sleek mudguards have been lacquered in a deep shade of blue and the number plates have been swapped. The sun's shimmering rays play on the white body.

From the driver's seat I can hear Svenne Crowbar biting his nails. He smells of grog and aftershave. The barrel of a machine gun sticks up between his thighs. He has hung his jacket over it.

There is a click from the passenger side as Hiccup opens the drum once more to examine his large-calibre revolver. Then, for the first time since we got into the car, he opens his mouth.

'Hope the Detective Chief Inspector chases after us so I can shoot the bastard in the face. That'll be something to tell Lily over Sunday lunch.' He holsters his weapon. 'She makes an excellent veal steak.'

I stare at his flabby neck. You could stick a coin in there and it would get lost in the folds. Belzén's right-hand man hooks his massive forefinger in the trigger guard and lets the revolver swing, as though weighing it. A wide, deep scar runs vertically across his palm.

'Typist for the police,' he continues, then looks out the side window with a snort. 'Didn't I sing for her every night after her damned mother went crazy?' He lowers his voice: 'Hush little baby, don't you cry. If you live through spring you'll have your daddy's eyes.'

I am sitting in the back seat and flicking through the tickets and food coupons I have just been given by Ma. The journey is from Oslo, via Hull and Liverpool, to Halifax in Nova Scotia. I have been to Liverpool before. Maybe Hull too.

Who the hell knows.

I'll get myself over the American border somewhere. Once I'm there Chicago will be my first stop. People say that it's almost like home, with Småland folk everywhere.

In the envelope there are also two crisp $100 bills. I pull the elasticated strap off my wallet and put them inside.

'Make sure the street stays empty now,' says Ma. 'We don't want any innocent people involved.'

Without make-up, her true age shows through, with wrinkles and liver spots. She is dressed in a servant's floor-length grey uniform with apron. She has hidden her hair under a stiff white headscarf folded over her forehead. Only her shiny nail polish reveals her true identity.

A sharp whistle cuts through the yellowing summer evening. I lay my arm across the seat and peer out through the back window. Nix, who is standing posted farther down the street, turns his back to the road and studies the display window of Augustsson's Second-hand Bookshop. I crouch down in the back seat when I see a black police car driving straight towards us.

Hatred for the police blazes inside me. It is far stronger than the hatred I feel towards the Reaper. All my life I have been hounded by the pigs and especially by Berglund. Like Hiccup, I would gladly see the Detective Chief Inspector full of bullet holes, but I am not prepared to risk my life for it. I shut my eyes and feel the car vibrate as the police vehicle passes. It makes my breathing vibrate too.

The convoy has barely disappeared around the corner before Nix rushes over from the bookshop and opens the door on Ma's side with urgency.

'That was them. Police car and van, no more vehicles. But the cop car has a new driver.'

'One more man makes little difference.'

Ma takes the little glass jar out of her apron pocket.

'Gentlemen, in about half an hour, it is time.'

My chest feels tight. I need fresh air. I open the door and step out onto the pavement. Nix's suntanned face immediately sticks up over the roof.

'Where are you going?'

'Stretching my legs.'

'Don't go anywhere.'

'I'm not going anywhere.'

I put on my sunglasses and bite the end off a cigar. In the street the tram tracks shine green in the last of the daylight. A lanky man in a bowler hat, collarless shirt and buttoned blazer comes strolling along the pavement. He walks slowly with splayed-out feet, as if he has no aim or purpose to his walk, but his eyes oscillate alertly back and forth over the crossing where we are parked. He is carrying a violin case in his hand. I think I recognise him but can't remember where from. It happens sometimes. I unscrew the lid of the hip flask and take a mouthful.

The man passes between me and the car. He bends slightly as if to peek into the driver's seat. It's not strange that a well-polished Cadillac draws a certain amount of attention here in Kungsholmen, but there is something about him that gives me the creeps. He stands up and his jacket puckers.

Maybe it's a weapon, maybe it's a half-litre bought at the liquor shop on St Eriksgatan. My heart contracts.

I fix my eyes on the bastard's back, put my right hand into my jacket and grab hold of the butt of my pistol. The bloke cuts across the road. He stops a little way in front of Fridhemsgatan, facing us. Nix hurries over the street and says something to him. After a minute or so of gesturing the stranger in the bowler hat walks on.

A group of scruffy street kids romp past. The whole gang need a good scrubbing. They are armed with slingshots and sticks. The biggest of them is holding a run-over street cat by the tail. Not long after them limps a little one in leg braces. Maybe they are on their way to start a fight with the lads in the next district. I watch them. Doomed to pilfer and make mischief. In a couple of years they will run past feeble men and snatch their watches from their chains.

'Jailbirds in the making.'

I turn around and take a few steps towards Vilan's locked café. The chairs are upturned on the tables inside, covered with a layer of dust. A sun-bleached notice on the shop window announces that they are closed for holidays. My memory darts back to last Sunday, the pimp and his mincemeat face.

'Kvisten has still got it.'

I light a cigar.

'Just need to show it.'

I see my own face reflected in the dazzling glass.

I am dressed in my pinstripe chocolate-brown suit with an ill-fitting waistcoat, light-brown shirt and red spotted tie.

It has been a long time since I last saw myself in the mirror and felt any kind of pride. I examine my broken face. Among the scars I see worry lines in the hardened skin.

The only good thing that came from that catastrophe in the dressing room was that I no longer had to disguise myself, hide my true self. I didn't have to act according to other people's words and deeds. On the other hand, there was no one left to hide from.

There were a few years when I managed not to give a fuck about people and hold my head high, but Lord knows they got to me in the end. Time to turn it all around now.

I know this feeling. I have been burdened with it for over half a year. It's like the state of mind that comes from being arrested and locked up in a musty custody cell. At first you are occupied with tobacco cravings, but then you start thinking too much. Your nerves tangle together like a fucking skein of wool, and you spook yourself like a stallion. After a few days in custody you long for the connections and company of prison. Between push-ups and self-flagellation, you sit and listen to the hollow silence in your head, and wait. You resign yourself.

'Never again. You hear what I said, you ugly fuck? Not another second at the hands of their brutality.'

If my blood spills over these sun-warmed cobblestones in half an hour, at least I will die with dignity. Nobody can take that away from me. I agree with Ma on that point.

My reflection dissolves in a heavy cloud of cigar smoke. I close my eyes and picture Ida again, as she looks now. Almost old enough to get married. It is impossible to fathom.

I have been striving for this moment for fifteen years. I must admit that I have veered wrong countless times, and I have wasted my money on suits, schnapps and boy-whores, but I believe that was partially down to the loneliness inside me that I was trying to lance. A poor excuse, but now I have a chance to redeem myself.

I think of the housekeeper, Evy Granér, who was willing to leave everything behind her to save her unborn child. I think about the sailor in Malaga who had the stupidity and the nerve to go into the ring against a circus bear. I think of all my victories inside the ropes. A verse I learnt as a child echoes in my ears. It sounds like a prayer.

> *Sharpen up the knives,*
> *The farmers go to slaughter,*
> *Display the bloody shirts,*
> *Four fresh carcasses in the hall.*

The car door opens and shuts again behind me and I know it is time. I shove a cigar in my mouth, pull the elasticated strap off my wallet and take out the folded photograph.

God only knows how something so pure and beautiful could have come from me. I hold up the picture, and tilt it back and forth, letting the evening sun play in the creases.

We walk.

We don't speak.

Not now.

Nothing to say.

Ma is pushing a wicker pram along Fridhemsgatan. One of the wheels needs oiling and is squeaking shrilly and rhythmically between the run-down façades. The sound sears through my consciousness, dragging images along with it: a copper with a crowbar, Gabrielsson's corpse lying gaunt and ashen on the floor, the rail spikes with their nebulous bouquets of coagulated blood.

The shotgun is poking out from under a blanket in the pram. The butt has been sawn off and taped up and now resembles a revolver handle. The barrels have been shortened too, to get a wider blast.

We drift along with lingering steps, much like when one enters a church. The street lies empty. We have the sun on our back, casting long shadows over the grey stones of Fridhemsgatan. Ma is limping and we are walking slowly. I have the double shoulder holster tight across my back and a load of ammunition rattling in my trouser pocket. My heart is beating so hard I can feel the pulse in my skull, and my legs are restless and shaking. I want to get this over with.

We have made it halfway to the junction with Alströmergatan, where we are supposed to separate the police car from Ploman's convoy. I take out my pocket watch.

'We should have another quarter-hour. I'll drive the van from here afterwards,' says Ma.

The heels of her shiny shoes are clacking quietly. A steady breeze makes the heat bearable. The perfume factory is several blocks away but I can still smell the dense scent of hair lotions and cosmetics. I take a deep puff on my cigar to fend off the sickly smell. I try to recall the lust for revenge I felt the evening after Hasse's defeat, but the occultist's premonition will not leave me in peace.

'Today is the day I die. Fall at the finish line. Like I always do.'

Ma chuckles.

'Better than dying of booze and bad humour.'

'The clairvoyant at home had a premonition.'

'Nonsense. You need a snifter.'

'It's a fine day to die.'

'You drink, Harry, I'll drive.'

Industry code of conduct: co-conspirators to murder are on a first-name basis. I get out my hip flask and take a hefty swig.

'Take another, you're a little pale.'

When the most powerful woman in the city gives you advice, it's best to do as you're told. The spirit trickles into my stomach and spreads warmth. I clear my throat and spit.

'One time I saw a film called *Duel at Dusk*.'

'Who won?'

'I don't bloody remember.'

Ma chuckles. She looks and me and takes a breath.

'Maybe we'll get a few drops of rain at last.'

She is standing ten or so metres from the Alströmergatan junction and points at a vaulted doorway on her left. It is next to the window where the same radio is blasting out music again. I peek in as we walk past: a typical Kungsholm flat with peeling wallpaper and tatty furniture. If I survive the night, it'll be a pleasure to leave this impoverished shithole of a country behind.

'We conclude this broadcast with the latest news from Spain,' says a throaty radio announcer. 'The French government have decided not to provide the Republican forces with fighter aircraft.'

It is cool in the doorway. The space between the pavement and the oak door is at least half a metre deep and provides good cover. Ma remains on the pavement.

'You stay back as they approach, but as soon as the van has passed you move out here.' Ma points to the left at the uneven stone walls. 'Do we need to go over everything one more time?'

'Nothing to it.'

'And now: Brahms's *Requiem*,' rasps the voice on the radio. There are two seconds of silence before the slow violin notes flow out onto the street. Someone turns up the volume even more.

'How fitting.' Ma smiles with her unpainted lips. 'How unbelievably fitting.'

The choir join in, first the women, then the men. Ma closes her eyes and nods her head. My pulse slows.

'Brahms worked for years on this piece, abandoned it, then only completed it on his mother's passing.' She opens her eyes. '*Denn alles Fleisch, ist wie Gras.*'

I take the cigar out of my mouth and raise one eyebrow.

'All flesh is grass.' Ma pats me on the arm. 'Georg never understood music either.' She glances down the street and shades her eyes with her hand. 'Today I am delivering justice. I have waited for a dozen years.'

'Long time.'

'Georg isn't Sture's father.'

Ma gazes at the Cadillac. I take a drag that's deep enough to paint my lungs black.

'I never told Georg,' she continues. 'But Sture is very well aware of my transgression. It eats him from the inside out. To be honest, I am worried about what will happen when I am gone.'

She turns to face me and examines me with her blue eyes.

'That is also one of the reasons why Kvisten is standing here with me now instead of either of my sons. I'm glad it turned out this way.' She lowers her voice. 'Something must be very wrong when you cannot truly trust your own flesh and blood.' I cough to conceal my confusion, and Ma raises her voice again. 'Finish your flask now.'

I nod and unscrew the lid off the hip flask. I offer some to Ma but she shakes her head. Instead she takes the little brown jar out of her uniform pocket, digs out a couple of decent spoonfuls and snorts one in each nostril.

'Follow the plan and everything will go splendidly,' she says in an unwavering voice.

I attempt a smile as I raise the flask, but my nerves won't allow it. A small trickle of blood leaks from Ma's right nostril, follows the groove down to her Cupid's bow and then the contours of her lips. A few white grains sail along the red liquid. She takes the church handkerchief from the pocket of her apron and wipes it off. She takes hold of the pram handlebar.

'Good luck.'

The pram wheels start squeaking again and Ma hobbles off to her position near the junction. Outside the florist on the corner is a display of zinc buckets filled with roses, carnations and white lilies.

I pour the dregs of aquavit down my throat and stare at Lundin's engraved initials before putting the hip flask back in my pocket. Anxiety is tightening its hold on me. The tempo and intensity of the music increase.

I am so damned alone. I undo my tie, take the timepiece out of my waistcoat pocket, unhook the watch chain and add it to the jangling collection of ammunition in my trouser pocket. If Ma's calculation is correct we have five minutes to go. If everything goes according to plan I will be sitting in my getaway car within the hour, and after the petrol station on Vallhallavägen, it'll be straight west.

I peek out of the doorway in the direction of the Cadillac. Ma's words have hardly allayed my concerns about Nix, the volatile bastard. His doolally giggles echo in my mind. A shudder runs through me. It is so intense that it makes the hair on my arms stand on end.

The choir dies away with one long final note, followed by a few harp chords, and then the radio goes quiet. A whistle cuts through the evening air. My muscles tense, my breathing catches in my throat, my little finger stump aches.

The time has come.

I think again about the occultist's prophecy and spit three times just in case. The orchestra on the radio starts up the second movement. I stick my head out and scan the dead-straight street. Far away, I spot the convoy approaching in a yellow cloud of road dust, backlit by the sunset. I pull my head into the shadows and unfurl my green rag. I hold it over my mouth and nose like a mask, and inhale as hard as I can to try to get the scent.

I can't smell anything.

Someone pokes out of the opposite doorway. Above the door is a crescent-shaped red-glass window. It looks like a segment of a blood orange.

A golden-blond little boy of about ten steps out onto the pavement. He is wearing short trousers and long socks that are falling down. He has purple bruises on his knees and a grubby mouth. In his hand he is holding a half-metre piece of steel reinforcing bar. I feel sweat break out on my forehead.

In two steps he reaches the edge of the pavement and sets about hitting it with the steel. He makes little impression but at least he has rhythm, and the blows strike in time with the increasing tempo of the radio symphony.

'Go inside to your mum!'

The idiot child doesn't seem to hear. The strikes continue to emit their monotonous musical accompaniment. Ma peeks out of her doorway near the crossing.

'Go inside for God's sake!'

'I don't live here.'

I peek out from the doorway and can clearly see the cars coming towards us. Dust is dancing around the tyres. I have fifteen seconds, if that.

My scrabbling shoes clatter on the pavement. My shoulder holster chafes with my hasty movements. I grab hold of his collar and the steel bar crashes to the ground. The door creaks open. The boy whimpers as I throw him into the stairwell.

'Come out again and I will beat you to a pulp.'

I push myself flat against the wall and pull out both revolvers.

The humming of the engines can be heard over the ominous music that swells with emotion and intensity. I resist the impulse to take out my wallet and look at Ida's photograph one last time. My breathing is unsteady and I am clutching the guns so hard it's making my hands sweat. A warm trickle runs down my spine. At the same time it feels as though I have put my little finger stump in a glass of ice water.

The warm summer air flows through the scrap of fabric. Maybe there is a little sweet scent left in it after all.

I used to soak this rag in sugar water and give it to Ida to suck on when she needed comforting or when I couldn't afford to go to the toffee women in Mariahallen on a Saturday. It works as a mask.

The black squad car drives past the doorway. Berglund's chiselled profile is a metre from me: the grey, well-combed hair, the waxed tips of his moustache, the wattle hanging below his chin, and that scrawny neck, adorned by a shimmering green, knotted silk tie. Fucking filth. My nerves dissipate like mist. My index fingers itch.

This is fucking it, Kvisten. It is about damn time to reclaim yourself.

The van is following about ten metres behind the Volvo. They have left the bonnet slightly open to keep the engine cool in the heat. I slam into the opposite wall with the long-barrelled revolvers at the ready. I lean out and extend the left one.

The police car disappears around the corner to Alströmergatan. The rusty pram wheel squeaks on its axle as Ma rolls it out into the street. Tyres screech. A bloke sticks his head out of a window on the second floor.

The radio orchestra rears up like a spooked stallion, inflamed with drums and violins. The van has skidded somewhat askew on its sudden braking. Ma's face breaks into a smile. It looks as though all the rays of the evening sun are converging on her, making her white headscarf dazzling bright. The black double barrel of the shotgun glints. The polyphonic choir fires first, disciplined as a German artillery regime. I hide my head in the doorway.

Everything explodes. The shotgun emits a double bang, the symphony bursts into a crescendo, a boy screams in one of the flats overhead.

I leave my hiding place and move quickly in an arc around the van. I reach the door of the driver's seat. The windscreen is perforated with small holes. Ploman is coughing and clutching at his body. He turns his square head to face me. He has blood in his moustache. I raise both revolvers. Fear glitters in his eyes. Now I am smiling under my makeshift mask.

Finally.

With straight arms I pump six bullets into the driver's cab. The recoil hammers against my wrists and shoulders, the revolvers flash and the body closest to me jolts and twitches. Red slop dances around the cab and splatters over the windows. The dampened orchestra tones flow out through the window behind me, leaving their home to be crushed together between the house fronts and forced up towards the sky, taking the echoing gunshots with them.

The smoke stings my nose; the bangs hurt my ear canals. I back up a couple of steps, turn around and hurry back around the rear of the car. Ma limps forward as she reloads her shotgun. The passenger door opens and the Reaper clambers down over the running board. Below him hangs a monocle on its chain. He tumbles onto the street and falls on his back. His white shirt is red with blood. My bullets had probably hit both men. I am glad he is alive. With arms outstretched I aim my left revolver towards his head and the right one down the street.

The Reaper hugs himself a little and reaches one shaking hand for the gun in his belt holster as his right foot scrapes against the paving stones, trying to get some purchase. The choir on the radio eases off. The smoke has cleared and I can smell hair lotion again.

The bastard's finger reaches the butt of the pistol. I cock the hammer with my left thumb. The Reaper manages to pull his shooter out, but the weight is too much for him. His hand opens and the weapon clatters onto the street. His head is shaking uncontrollably. Bubbles of blood ooze from his mouth with each exhalation. They catch the last of the sun's rays, glitter and diverge.

All this beauty.

Ma arrives in time to witness a hint of life in his mangled body. The fingers of his right hand seek the pistol. She steps on his forearm, pins it down and pushes the shotgun barrels into his hand. The first shot slices the radio music in two. Everything goes quiet. A bald old man sticks his head out the window. I aim my right-hand revolver at him. He jerks his head back in.

The Reaper raises his bloody stump of a forearm to the sky. There is a click as Ma cocks the hammer for a second time. Her bottom lip is quivering but she is smiling. Her eyes shine as she pushes the gun barrels into his forehead. A single tear runs down her cheek.

'Denn alles Fleisch, ist wie Gras.'

Little more than greasy red mincemeat remains where the Reaper's head once was. His skull has been crushed from the tip of his nose up, forming a sludgy swamp hole, with his brain lying splattered in the gutter. All is quiet.

My heart is beating so hard it feels like it might burst. I hurry to the passenger side of the van, place my shoe on the running board and open the door. Ploman has leaked everywhere. It looks as though most of his blood has already been pumped out. His head leans back on the headrest, his face ashen. His mouth forms a grinning rift in the pallid skin. One shot has ripped open his thick neck. I stare at the flesh hole for a few moments. It gapes back at me.

Bullet holes never stop staring back. You can't escape them.

Ma sweeps bloods and laminated glass from the sunken driver's seat.

'The dog has pissed himself.' She leans in, sets her shotgun on the floor and gives the robust dead body a shove. 'Get to it, Kvisten.'

I take hold of the corpse's upper arm and wrap his tie around my other hand. I pull and Ma pushes. The cadaver's head hits its shoulder and the brown hat drops off.

The ravaged body hits the ground with a muted thump. The front seat is drenched in blood and covered with glass shards. The steering wheel and dashboard are sodden and the windscreen looks like a red-stained sieve.

I get in. Crushed glass crunches under the weight of me. Ma clicks open her shotgun, passes it to me and sits down in the driver's seat. She tosses four cartridges into my lap.

'Break the window and reload.'

She starts the car and I bash the windscreen with the taped shotgun butt. The gearbox vibrates, the car jolts forward and the engine dies.

'God damn it.'

Not like her to swear. I bash again and the rest of the windscreen gives in, scattering over the gleaming bonnet that still isn't fully shut. Ma repeats the procedure, gets the engine going and finds the right gear. Looking in the side mirror, she begins to reverse. The van bounces as we drive over the Reaper's leg.

Red cartridges with brass yellow caps. I feed them into the double barrels as we pick up speed. Frenzied screams and curses come from the buildings around us. I close the shotgun and glance in the side mirror. A boy of about ten years old runs straight out into the street. His short trousers flap above his knees, his Vega cap blows off and for a moment he hesitates mid-step.

My breath catches in my stinging trachea. I grab hold of Ma's sturdy forearm but I don't have time to warn her. I screw up my eyes and wait for a thump that doesn't come. I see the boy sneak into a doorway to the left of us.

I rest the shotgun's barrels on the ledge where the windscreen was. The tyres screech as Ma backs around the corner and up to Fleminggatan. At the junction I catch sight of the other side of Fridhemsgatan, up towards the school and the timber district. The man in the bowler hat who passed our car half an hour ago is loping along so fast that the road dust is whirling around his Chaplinesque feet. He is still carrying his violin case but is trying to open it on the fly.

Something doesn't add up.

We stop opposite the Cadillac parked about fifteen metres farther down the road. The southerly wind blows straight into the driver's cab. Far away, above Lake Mälaren, some pale-grey clouds are forming at last.

Hiccup, who is a head taller than both of Ma's sons, stands a little behind them. He has put a feedbag with cut-out eye holes over his head. The straps are tied in a neat bow around his neck. He looks like an executioner. Nix has tied a handkerchief over his face. Svenne Crowbar hasn't bothered.

Ma struggles with the gearstick and we reverse another few metres. She probably hasn't driven in years. Stubborn bitch. She should have let me drive. Still, if we pick up speed we can be at Belzén of Birka's place in a few minutes.

My eyes oscillate between the three gangsters on one side of the street and the workers' home on the other. Two men are standing there in shabby suits with bowler hats askew. They look as if their eyes are about to pop out of their heads.

Ma manages to get into first gear and get the van moving. Svenne Crowbar waves his machine gun in the air. He has a gaping, idiotic smile on his face. Behind him, like an enormous shadow, Hiccup approaches with the bag over his head. He raises his large-calibre revolver and makes it flash in a cloud of powder and noise. He shoots Svenne in the neck: an execution.

A shining bouquet of red and white spills from Svenne's grinning lips. The machine gun drops from his hands and his body falls forward, with his arms stretched up in the air, like a surrendering soldier. Nix has time to turn around before the second bang. Hiccup's bullet meets him smack in the forehead. Fragments of skull and brain slop red, grey and amber across the Cadillac's shining white bonnet. Nix slumps on the car and falls on his side. A wisp of blue smoke rises from the revolver in Hiccup's hand.

He moves quickly for a man of his size, plunging forward and picking the machine gun up off the pavement. Ma's words from Sunday echo in my mind: 'Ten shots per second.' A whole fucking armed platoon in one man.

I point the shotgun in his direction and let rip without taking aim. The Cadillac bodywork takes most of the barrage, but the display window of Vilan's café behind it shatters with a crash. The van speeds towards Hiccup. On the other side of the road the two men are ducking down with their hands over their heads. Pale terror dances silently across their faces.

Hiccup takes cover behind the bulletproof car but soon pops up again like a fucking Punch puppet. He rests the butt on his shoulder. The gun hammers out lead so quickly that all the bangs seem to condense into a single angry blast. Ma flinches in the driver's seat as bullets ricochet around the cab. I fire my second shot and the Cadillac's front wheel bursts, throwing up a cloud of road dust. Hiccup ducks down again. As we race past I see the feedbag bobbing behind the window like an unusually ugly fish in an aquarium. He works his way towards the back end of the car.

Ma sounds the horn. Hiccup blasts out his hammering scorn in another three short bursts of lead behind us.

That fucker tricked us all. Bullets fly all around us and hit the back doors of the van with muffled bangs.

The sky-blue nose of a tram comes into view down at the St Eriksgatan crossing. A stray bullet shatters one of the side windows and the driver accelerates. I click open the smoking shotgun and take out the cartridges.

'Belzén of Birka,' Ma growls.

She has tears in her eyes. Her fingers whiten around the large steering wheel. A deep-red stain is seeping from her belly through her dress and white apron. She floors the accelerator. We are approaching the crossroads with breathtaking speed.

'Look out, for Christ's sake!'

'Kvisten drinks, I drive, like I said.'

I probably would have given my other little finger for a drop of schnapps.

I brace my feet against the floor as we approach the crossing. A woman in the rear carriage of the tram presses her hands against the window. The glass bead on her hat pin is green. A bloke with bad teeth emits a silent, wide-mouthed scream and another ducks down in his seat. The van's bonnet is still ajar and trembles in the wind. If it flies up now it will obscure the windscreen.

And then we are toast.

The tram struggles forward like a caterpillar. Ma turns a hard right onto St Eriksgatan in the nick of time. Her hands slip on the blood-drenched Bakelite, but she finds her grip again. The bonnet remains in place but we're in the wrong lane. I glance down the street ahead of us. About fifty metres away, level with the plant beds at the next intersection, are two motionless rubbish trucks.

The modern kind.

Suddenly Ma swings back left to avoid an oncoming car. We're heading back towards the tram again. The passengers run from the windows. We are going to crash.

'Fucking occultist!'

Right at the back, a boy is cadging a ride on the tram's back coupler. His greasy hair shines in the evening light. He has a satchel on his back. He presses forward to avoid the van.

I gasp for breath. Ma treads on the pedals like she's playing a church organ. We miss him by a thumb's width.

'Slow down, for fuck's sake!'

'Language!'

'Slow down!'

'You're going to the States. That was the agreement.'

A patrolling police officer blows shrilly on his whistle. Ma swerves into the left lane and I drop one of the shotguns shells on the floor. I look over at her. She is pale and coughing. I lean towards her and press my hand against her doughy stomach. She pushes it away.

'Keep your hands to yourself.'

I obey and open the cylinders of the revolvers, shaking the empty shells onto the floor before reloading with fresh lead.

'That fucking Belzén!'

Ma hits the steering wheel with her palm. I remember the look Hiccup gave his boss when we were planning the hijack yesterday. This is the second time in a dozen years that that half-deaf gangster has started a full-scale war. It worked for him last time and he managed to take control of the whole of Kungsholmen. Ma and her Östermalm men helped him and gained ten per cent of his income for ever more. Maybe he has grown tired of paying out. Maybe he has got bigger plans.

The sounds of emergency sirens slices through my ears. I glance in the side mirror and see a black Volvo with flashing lights. My voice is little more than a whisper.

'Police.'

'Berglund?'

'Think so.'

Bastard copper. For years you've chased me around like a hungry hound, sniffing, always ready to arrest me and take another decent bite out of my limited time. Enough now. Time is up for one of us. The tomb door stands wide open. Death refuses to wait.

Ma pushes the speedometer over the eighty-kilometre-per-hour mark as we pass the perfume factory. My sweat-coated skin dries in the wind. My calloused hands grope for the shotgun cartridge that ended up on the floor.

'Use the pistols instead. Fire straight through the metal.'

I put an unlit cigar in the corner of my mouth and take the revolver in my left. I'll have to climb out onto the running board. That's hardly going to help my crummy aim. I push down the handle and open the door.

I grip around the door pillar with my right hand and place my shoe on the wide rubber-coated steel board that runs between the mudguards of the van. I lean out, and my new hat blows off.

God damn it.

Bad omen.

There's Berglund in the passenger seat, his lips curving downward beneath his moustache. He is holding his revolver in his right hand. The driver is hanging over the wheel with his face right up close to the glass. Emergency lights tear through me with their red flashes, over and over again.

Behind the houses, running along the other side of the canal, I see a big plume of locomotive steam. We are travelling at the same speed as the train. The van speeds straight along Fleminggatan, past the old fire station and lunatic asylum, with me hanging on to the side. We are approaching police headquarters but hopefully Berglund hasn't had time to stop and call for reinforcements.

My bloodstained clothes flap around my body as the van swerves to overtake. Berglund is about twenty metres behind us when I cock the trigger and squeeze out my first shot. The revolver recoils. I shoot again.

The second bullet bores through the summer evening and hits the centre of the windscreen. It passes between the two men. Encouraged by my sudden good aim, I fire another couple of shots. I miss but the Volvo slows down a little and steers into the blind spot behind the van.

I hear two bangs. One shot hits us in the rear and the other causes sparks on the pavement about half a metre from the right back tyre. They are trying to hit the wheels.

Such a dirty fucking trick.

Typical coppers.

The squad car swerves into sight again. Berglund is holding his revolver outside the side window. I take aim. The front sight trembles over the bastard's face and for one second I think I've got him. I smile as I move my finger to the trigger.

The first time I met the Detective Chief Inspector was in December 1932, when he tried to lock me up for a murder I didn't commit. Not long after that he brought me in on shaky accusations of threatening behaviour and chucked me in Långholmen for eighteen months.

My finger moves half a millimetre.

Finally, last autumn, he interrogated me over an assault, but I got away scot-free. Only now do I remember the tiepin that was among his paraphernalia on the table at the time: an enamelled trinket with a black swastika.

A gang of yelling boys run along the pavement in our wake. They're the same ones I saw earlier and the largest of them is still holding the flat cat in his fist.

'Shit!'

I daren't shoot, not with those kids in the field of fire. Berglund's revolver casts its tongue of fire along the police car. The black bodywork sparks. The bullet meets the swinging door behind me. I push myself flat against the car. The sweaty fingers of my right hand are aching and slipping on the metal. I duck back into the cab. Ma is hunched forward over the steering wheel.

'Can't get them.'

'Go for the bonnet or tyres.'

I turn my head to look forward. There isn't much traffic on Fleminggatan. We are approaching the turrets of City Hall and King's Bridge. I swing back out of the car and fire off the revolver's last shots in quick succession. One hits Berglund's side mirror and the other whistles clean past the car.

So much for my good aim.

We speed past the district court and police headquarters and their mess of law, violence and power.

A hostile area.

I toss my revolver onto the seat and fumble to get the other one out of the shoulder holster. Ma overtakes a horse and carriage. The sweat-lathered mare flinches and clops nervously to the side. Foam flies from her mouth. The driver standing on the footboard tugs on the double reins. I see the policemen being jostled from side to side in their front seat. Just then, the airspeed forces the bonnet of the van to fling open.

The car tyres screech as the cop car swerves around the horse and carriage. The bonnet flaps as the van lurches but it still won't shut. Ma stands up with one foot on the accelerator and bangs it with her fist.

It eventually slams shut.

We are approaching the end of the road. Ma slows down slightly. Either we turn right and drive towards Belzén of Birka's headquarters or we turn onto King's Bridge and risk ending up in the Klara district's maze of alleys and crowds.

Ma opts for the bridge. The tyres complain as the car turns sharply. The front door hits me hard in the back, sending the cigar flying out of my mouth.

The sole of my left shoe slips off the running board, and before I know it my heel is scraping along the pavement. My right arm is stretched to its limit but my sweaty fingers are holding fast. Inside the car Ma is struggling with that damned gearstick.

My muscles are shaking with strain when I manage to haul myself up. I take a deep breath of road dust and petrol fumes.

A boat passes under the King's Bridge coughing diesel just as the police car turns the corner. They can't be more than fifteen metres behind us. The white-puffing locomotive whistles on its way towards Central Station. We move like quicksilver over the bridge as the canal flows serenely in the summer heat. The sunset is golden-yellow with streaks of pink and red, like piss after a particularly tough fight. I squint at the sun and take aim. It's time to put a stop to these devils.

My arm whips like a snake as the revolver explodes four times in rapid succession. I aim at the tyres. My only hit gets the bumper. Berglund responds with a shot that flies past my head so close that I think I can feel the wind from it.

Two bullets left.

Somewhere nearby swells the sound of a marching band. Brass instruments wail into the wind and drums roll faster than Hiccup's machine gun. I realise too late where we are headed. I don't have time to warn Ma. She turns right onto Vasagatan, which leads past Central Station.

The bloody Olympians and spectators.

I pull myself close into the van, cock the trigger and stretch my arm out at full length. The filth are gaining on us. They are about ten metres behind. I aim at the driver. I would have preferred to see Berglund's brains splattered across the back seat but I've got no choice. I have to stop them now. In a few seconds it will be too late.

Ma blasts the horn. The marching band stops abruptly with a shrill trumpet note. People are screaming. I cock the trigger and hold my breath.

My arm wavers as we decelerate. The lead disappears into nowhere.

One bullet. No more.

I turn my head.

'Fucking athletes.'

Garlands have been hung over Vasagatan with colourful paper streamers and Swedish flags drooping from flagpoles. There are so many people crowded in front of the station's grand entrance that many are standing far off in the street to witness the spectacle. The blue-uniformed orchestra disperse before us in a flurry of shining instruments. One youth trips over an abandoned bass drum, falls and smacks himself bloody against the paving stones. Outside the vaulted entrance to the large station people are fighting to get to safety.

We speed towards the crowd. I want to close my eyes but can't. Ma is honking the horn the whole time and the squad car's shrill siren is sounding behind us. Men in their Sunday best clutch children in sailor outfits, a pair of shiny black taxicabs try to plough a passage through the throng, women scream, pimps and pickpockets plunge into the muddle on the pavement. Some are trampled, a couple fall to the ground. Three women, garishly attired in traditional costumes with yellow aprons, drop the bouquets of roses in their arms and leap out of the way. A horse rears, neighs and tries to jump free from its shafts.

Three metres in front of us a woman grabs a tiny tot from a pram. The baby's white chemise with a lace collar flaps in the flurry. The mother clutches her child close to her bosom and turns her back to us to act as a shield.

As we veer left we clip the pram with the right mudguard. It lifts off the ground and flips over in the air. I pull in my head as the pram misses someone's head by half a metre and smashes onto the police car's bonnet. The cops duck in their seats.

The van jolts as we plough through a sea of abandoned flagpoles, handbags and musical instruments. I cast my eyes across the mess of people. They are running around like a flock of sheep that can smell a wolf, billowing here and there in an unruly throng.

We catch sight of each other at the same time. For about a second, this one moment blocks out all sounds, and times stops. Lundin's skinny form is leaning on Hasse. The undertaker is standing as still and stiff as a statue in the middle of the crowd that is now little more than a blur.

Hasse is holding one hand out in front of him, stopping people who come too close. As usual, the old man is dressed in a black suit and cylindrical top hat, but with a floral waistcoat that I have never seen before, perhaps bought specially for the occasion.

Our eyes meet. A smile breaks through his bushy moustache. I raise my revolver hand straight up into the air. He takes off his hat and swings it over his head twice before throwing it straight upward. Without thinking I shoot my final shot into the sky. The bang acts as a starting shot. The noise levels return to normal and Lundin is swallowed up by the crowd.

With a thumping heart I swing back into the cab. I grope on the floor as the bell begins to ring at Tegelbacken level-crossing barrier. That makes a right turn impossible.

We pass Central Station. I look at Ma and load the sawn-off shotgun. Her eyes are half-closed. She is leaning forward with one hand on the steering wheel and the other pressed against her stomach, pale as a linen cloth. We are no more than a few blocks away from my getaway car but have to shake Berglund before we can make the switch.

'Two shots left,' I say and close the shotgun.

'More in the back.'

'What do you mean?'

'Ammunition.'

'How in the hell am I suppose to get them?'

'You're going to the States.'

'So lose them.'

'They took your daughter from you.'

For a moment the only sound is our heavy breathing.

'Slow down and keep the car straight.'

I open the door again, stick out my head and place my left foot on the seat. I shove the short-barrelled shotgun into my belt. With my forefinger and thumb I pinch the centimetre-high strip that runs around the roof and place my right shoe in the fork where the car door meets the frame.

My eyes water in the wind. I tense every muscle in my body and heave myself up. The roof is hot from the sun. The wind rages in my hair and clothes. The tyres are bouncing on the cobblestones. I slip around but begin to worm my way towards the back of the van.

My heart is pounding against the metal and the shotgun is digging into my hip. I creep along, bracing first one foot against one side of the strip, then the other. The van lurches and sends me flying over to one side. My head slides over the edge of the roof.

I meet Berglund's gaze just before he begins to reload. The police car can't be more than five metres behind us now. I peer down at the van's door handle. Somewhere deep inside I can still feel Lundin's presence: his smile and his floral waistcoat, his hat flying through the air.

If for no other reason than for that old goat's sake.

I shuffle my way a little farther and peek over the edge. I reach my left arm down as far as I dare.

Not far enough.

The gun hammers against the roof as I struggle to free it from my belt. Using the shotgun as an extension of my right arm, I

321

push the handle. The barrels slide off the chromed metal. A few centimetres farther to add some force.

That's it.

One back door flies open. It almost shuts again but I stick the barrels in between to stop it. The force of it thunders into my hand.

I slide out even farther and look up. Berglund fires. The bullet hits the vehicle about ten centimetres from my head. I flinch, Ma turns slightly, and I start to slip slowly but inexorably over the edge.

My heart stops, as if to prepare for the wild pounding of panic. I flail in the air.

I grab hold of the door's top edge, the metal cuts into my palm and my shoulder joint is stretched to the limit. My right shoe scrapes along the ground before flying off completely. I heave myself up and try to swing my legs up to reach the bumper. My whole body is vibrating as I hang from my left arm off the inside of the door, with the police motor roaring behind. They are going to ram me. Terror rages like a parasite in my blood system.

I raise the shotgun with my right. It's a lousy angle.

The barrel is moving around with each shift of the door. The weapon blasts, producing a cloud of smoke. The lead hits smack in the front of the police car.

A billow of steam immediately rises from their bonnet. The cooling system has sprung a leak and water is flooding out over the overheated engine. They drop back a couple of metres. I try to aim straight at the windscreen and fire my last shot. Most of the swarm of lead disappears over the top of the bastard car. I drop the shotgun.

The van lurches again, the back door almost slams shut and I finally reach the bumper with my left foot, then let go of the damn door and manage to tumble in among the crates in the cargo compartment. My muscles scream for fuel, it feels like I'm taking a footbath in hydrochloric acid and my heart is pounding so hard it might split my chest open.

It can't have taken more than a few seconds to climb from the cab to the roof and into the back.

It felt like an age.

I glance over my shoulder and see that the front window of the police car is now nearly completely fogged up with steam. They are still tailing us. I can only see their outlines in the front seats. I open the other door as well, turn around and slam my fist straight through the lid of the nearest crate.

With bloody knuckles I brush away a few thin splinters of wood and plunge my hand into the straw. I feel around and find a rounded object. I pick it up. I smile.

Ploman mentioned some sort of bomb attack. I am holding in my hand three tightly bound sticks of dynamite with a short fuse.

I fumble for my matches as I try to keep my balance. Maybe Berglund can see me through the fog, or maybe he just knows what the cargo compartment contains and understands where this is going. The Detective Chief Inspector leans back in his seat, draws up his legs and kicks against the windscreen with both feet to get an unobscured view.

The fool is in a panic. I am no longer in a hurry, and crouch down as the Centralpalats sweeps past.

This I want to see.

Let the fucker sweat.

I find a Meteor, put it in my mouth, wedge the dynamite under my arm and light a match. I puff on the cigar and observe the show.

Front row.

The very opposite of a tragedy if ever I saw one.

I am trembling with excitement. Hatred for the police sticks like tar to my nerves as I wave the sticks of dynamite in the air. Berglund kicks again. The driver's mouth opens as he screams something. Maybe he is trying to warn the Detective Chief Inspector. But he doesn't brake.

Their windscreen falls out with a crash and the 100°C steam flows straight into the front seat.

Finally.

The screams drown out the sirens. The hair on Berglund's head is curling up, and he lets go of the weapon to bring his scalded hands to his head. He looks as if he wants to rip the reddening skin off his face in strips. He leans his head back and roars with pain. Blisters are coming up already on his narrow lips. I laugh at him.

We all die one day.

The police car accelerates further and passes Centralpalats. I put a cigar in the corner of my mouth and bring the dynamite fuse to the glowing tip.

It crackles and flashes like a sparkler. The only thing that remains is to throw the bundle into their front seat.

I am not bowing to your sort any more.

Never again.

The fuse is burning fast and I raise my arm to throw it. The van lurches sharply to the right and back again. I stumble backwards and drop the dynamite. Pain shoots through my ribcage. I gasp for air and kick at the bundle of explosives, trying to get the bastard through the door. I can't reach it. The end is burning down and branching into three parts; its crackling changes tone.

I stare at the police car, whose driver seems to have floored the accelerator again. Their front seat is filled with steam. I kick clumsily at the explosive a second time but still can't reach it. Within two seconds we will be flying in the air.

Everywhere, since my twin brother and I split our mother in two at birth, misfortune has followed me around like a hungry dog. But there have been occasions when my miserable luck has saved my life.

For some reason I was sent to bed without supper that evening at the poorhouse. Maybe I was starving again and had stolen sugar from the box on the mantelpiece. Maybe it was some other mischief. Either way, the matron served the other paupers jellied veal for supper but mistook the bottles and poured sabadilla vinegar over the food instead of regular vinegar.

I lay awake all night listening to the paupers screaming and crying, and I thanked my lucky stars for my transgression. Two of the older ones and one young child were dead before dawn. The story was hushed up.

The van turns at the Rödbodstorget small square and tram stop, and the dynamite slides slowly towards the edge. For a moment it teeters there, perfectly balanced. The end crackles and sparkles one last time before the bundle hits the street. I get up on my knees and see the explosives disappear under the police car.

Everything is in the Lord's clear light of the summer evening. Over the engine's humming I hear the tremulous bells of St Clara ring out a blood wedding. The road dust rises and falls under the police car, as if the street itself was gasping in suspense. The faint pink glow of the sunset plays on the black lacquer. The beauty of the world makes me gasp.

'And so you die at last, you dirty pig.'

Soon your old lady will be weeping and the priest will be reading over your cold flesh.

Not a day too soon.

With an ear-deafening bang the dynamite explodes under the back end of the Volvo. The vehicle stands almost vertically on its front wheels and the back doors flap open. The car looks like the head of a black dog sniffing the street. It is about to swallow us up whole. At the same moment, the fire reaches the petrol tank.

Another explosion: projectiles with white tails shoot up into the air from a burning sea and dark skies. We are surrounded by the sound of smashing windows.

The whole high-summer heatwave concentrates into one single powerful hot blast that throws me back on the floor of the van, as limp as a scarecrow in a storm.

Debris rains down onto the van.

Everything is reduced to the simple palette of unconsciousness.

White, black and red, and black again.

FRIDAY 24 JULY

Darkness.

The smells of burnt flesh and rubber and petrol sting my nose. My broken rib feels like it has penetrated my flesh, radiating agonising pangs throughout my ribcage. My ears are ringing. A hand wipes something wet off my face.

'Now Kvist has to wake up and stand up.'

The order sounds distant, as though travelling through the long mouthpiece from the bridge to the engine room. I struggle to do as I am told. My eyelids flutter, and the familiar feeling of blood sticking in my eyelashes spurs me on, makes me feel calm. The evening light filters in, flowing like rivulets through the blackness. Slowly I pull myself out of nothingness and into merciless reality.

My head is resting on Ma's knee. She has one arm under my neck. I run my fingers over my forehead. Doctor Jensen's stitches have gone.

Shit.

I try to swallow but my lips won't obey.

With a groan I force myself to raise my foggy head and open my eyes. Ma's face is as sooty as a coal miner's. Her hand reaches for my neck to support my head. She is sitting on her backside with her legs outstretched and me in her arms. In the middle of all the grime, her eyes are shining with tears. There is some sort of affection there. She breathes heavily as she takes out her red-splattered church handkerchief and presses it to my forehead. It has long been impossible to tell whose blood is whose.

Some fucking getaway.

I blink, cough, take the handkerchief and crawl out of her arms on all fours. One foot on the street, then the other. The sirens are blaring ever nearer and drowning out the searing tones in my ears.

Where the fuck is my shoe?

I wobble and stare at the devastation where the street opens onto the small square. The dynamite cartridges have bitten substantial chunks out of the frame of the police car and scattered fragments over the street. A sooty, black skeleton remains, still smoking. A charred pile is slumped over the dashboard: the driver.

There is no visible trace of Berglund. I grunt, disappointed, and pat my jacket in search of a cigar. Then, near the car's right front rim, I catch sight of a severed leg. It's a blackened calf with the shoe pointing straight out at a ninety-degree angle, like the chopped hook of a swastika.

Angry blood and a stubborn mind are a dangerous combination, but there was spunk in the Detective Chief Inspector, I'll give him that.

'Now Kvist had better make haste. The last stretch is always walked alone.'

I turn around to see Ma holding out Ploman's brown Borsalino hat. The copper-coloured hat band glows in the fading sun.

'A man shouldn't go without a hat, even if Kvisten does look like hell.'

I hear the sirens howl up by Central Station. There are a lot of them. An approaching storm that cannot be ridden out.

'Damn it.'

With one shoe I take two hobbling steps back to Ma where she is sitting with her hand pressed against her stomach. Her wedding ring glitters on her finger among the red slime. Her entire apron

328

is wet with blood. She has wiped her face clean but the soot has set into her wrinkles.

'Give me a machine gun and I'll hold them off for a while.'

Ma gestures to the van. I put on Ploman's hat and offer her my hand.

'The getaway car is just a few blocks away,' I say. She shakes her head slowly and opens her mouth as if to protest but I interrupt her: 'No arguments.'

Her hand trembles as she takes mine. She looks me in the eye. Her gaze is crooked and she looks like she has been on the receiving end of my right fist. She gets to her feet with a whimper.

Seventy-five metres, maybe even less.

With one arm around the old woman's waist, I stumble into the side street. I pinch the gash on my forehead with my other hand, and blink to loosen the sticky clumps in my eyelashes.

Blood seeps into my shirt cuff. The sirens are hacking the world into pieces. Ma takes off her filthy bonnet and tosses it in a doorway.

We stagger past the Hotel Stora Rosenbad. The reflection in the window is of a couple of struggling swine, sooty and bloody, their clothes in shreds.

More and more sirens, even louder now, seem to be coming from all directions.

I push Ma into the doorway of number 6 and follow behind. I brace her against the oak door and poke my nose out. Opposite us is a seedy café with tobacco-stained curtains. I hazard a peek around the corner. The police cars are speeding past the Herkulesgatan junction. I try to grab her substantial midriff again but she pushes my arm away.

'I can't.'

'Of course you fucking can.'

'My time is running out.'

'Almost there.'

'Kvist can take care of himself.'

'Nearly there now.'

I drag her back out onto the pavement. She is shaking all over. Suddenly the sirens are wailing directly behind us. Someone is shouting orders but I can't hear what they are saying. I put on my sunglasses, push the hat down on my forehead and wrap my jacket around my free hand.

About thirty metres ahead of us, I see the brown roof of the Dodge poking out between two parked cars. I force my legs to run. The round isn't over yet.

'Almost there.'

A sigh, then a sudden dead weight on my arm: Ma's legs give way as she snuffs out like a candle in the wind. I manage to grab her before she hits the ground and hold her up. We are so soaked in blood that red drops are spraying around us as we walk.

There's nothing for it.

I let Ma sink down to the ground, grab her by her armpits and drag her to Paddan, Lindkvist's illegal gambling den.

My ribs smart as I slam open the door to the courtyard entrance way and drag her over the cobblestones towards the pump in the middle of the yard. The sun has melted away the pump's green colour. Flakes of paint and rust drip like tears around the stone cover. I position her head under the tap, the handle squeaks as I heave it up and a rattling sound comes from somewhere along its long throat.

Damn.

Not a drop.

This fucking summer.

I finally manage to light a cigar, kneel at Ma's side and look around. The evening smells of horse shit, printer's ink and blood. I have known Lindkvist for a long time. His gambling den has failed. The black shutters hang crooked on their hinges, covered in pollen and dust. A handwritten note on the door flutters slightly in the breeze but from this distance I can't see what it says.

Now I recall that Lindkvist was already aware of the fact that Ploman and his entourage were National Socialists last autumn. I visited after being released from Långholmen and offered to settle the bookmaker's debts but the cowardly bastard didn't dare change collector.

I roll up my jacket and lay it under Ma's head. Her eyes flicker. I pat her firmly on the cheek.

'Kvisten is here. Right here with you.'

Her apron pocket is gaping open so I reach my hand in and grope around the bloodbath until I eventually produce the glass jar. The sodden lid slips in my hand but I get it open. Fingers crossed, the powder will work like the smelling salts Albertsson used to force in my nostrils between rounds.

I press her cheeks to open her mouth. I pour a couple of proper doses right down her throat. Just then I hear the police siren getting closer and louder.

Fuck. The blasted entrance-way door. Just as open and welcoming as the door to Långholmen if I don't get a move on.

Not again.

Another stint would kill me. It would eat away at all that I am. All that I have managed to reclaim.

Pushing off the paving stones in the courtyard, I slip and fall forward. My knees throb and the sound of the siren wrenches closer. Ma whimpers as I crawl over her legs before managing to pick myself up. How many seconds do I have?

Two?

One?

I lurch forward and bang one half of the double doors with my right. There isn't much power left in my fist. Maybe that's why the bastard has the gall to hit back. My body roars with pain as I am thrown to the ground and roll into the door. It slams shut just as the police whine past.

The burning tip of the Meteor flicks off in the fall, but I pick it up with my fingertips and push it back on the top of the cigar and take a hacking puff. I see the bloody heap by the water pump start to stir. I get up, hobble back and kneel down beside her.

'Kvisten should have some too; it'll help with the pain.'

Ma wheezes and grimaces. Slimy white froth is oozing from her mouth. I hesitate but unscrew the lid from the jar and shove half a teaspoon into my own mouth. A simultaneously sweet and abrasive taste of unripened bananas fills my gob. I work up some saliva, swallow and take a deep drag.

'Now Kvisten has to listen.'

Her voice is very hoarse. I wipe her chin with the cuff of my sleeve.

'I'm driving you to Doctor Jensen. He'll stitch you up.'

'There's no time for that.'

She shuts her eyes.

'The car is ten metres away.'

I slur on the lie. My lips feels numb. A shudder moves through my body and seems to cure my limbs as it goes. Ma gasps for air.

'I'll be okay.'

'Like fuck. I'll carry you. Got an extra pistol under the dashboard.'

Ma snorts out a short laugh and grimaces.

'The cocaine has made you a touch overconfident.'

She reaches for my hand and I for hers. My fingers feel dry, mealy and sweaty all at the same time. I remember Nix's words when he shot that tramp in the guts in Klara: 'It's slow but it works, every time.'

And it does seem to be working now.

Ma breathes heavily a couple of times.

'Listen. Kvist, born into whoredom, set on the wrong track from the very beginning, must understand.' She shuts her eyes. 'Georg became something of a father to me. Maybe the black-coat in Katarina filled the same void in you.'

Her unpainted lips become a thin line but a whimper escapes them. Conviction hammers in my breast.

'Never been beaten, never even taken a fucking count,' I mutter.

Ma's hand grips mine with a strength that surprises me, and our blue eyes meet.

'We were united in revenge, you and I. I am proud to have stood by your side.' Her grip loosens and she sighs: 'It is over.'

I close my eyes and let her words settle inside me.

It becomes a caress.

It is done.

Ma stares straight up in the half-light that is stubbornly refusing to let night fall. Some delicate whispers, barely more than shapeless breath, escape her lips and I lean in close. She is struggling to breathe but manages to take a breath.

'People like Kvisten are not made for times of peace.' She sighs. 'Look at yourself. For all you lack, you have become a one-man war. Georg was the same.' She grimaces and speaks through gritted teeth. 'You don't bow down to your destiny.'

She coughs blood in something akin to a laugh.

'In any case I am glad that Kvisten is going west. It's not just my time that is running out. There is no room for our kind any more. The war that is about to rage is nothing more than death throes. The snake is biting off its own head.'

Then, through the white-foamy corner of her mouth, she says: 'May you find peace on the other side of the ocean.'

Her ribcage manages two more movements, then stops in the middle of the third. The air escapes her with a hiss.

She has made her journey.

I shut her eyes and wipe the corners of her mouth clean.

I look at her: old and weathered, but fallen in battle. I pull off my shoulder holster, lay the revolvers in her hands and close her fingers around the butts.

She will be spoken of for many years to come.

They will know that she died as she lived.

A rasping sound fills the car as I tear the sleeve off my bloody shirt, spit on the fabric and wipe my face as much as possible. I tie a tourniquet around my head and tug Ploman's hat down over my forehead. My ribcage aches as I pull on the black suit jacket I have just taken out of my seabag.

I should have thought to pack an extra pair of shoes as well.

The winding streets of the Klara district are still echoing with sirens and I hurry to get the Dodge going. My heart is pounding like a circus monkey on a drum in a harbour town. My blood is choking my veins. I smile widely. The top of my throat is numb and it is hard to swallow.

With the side window down and my elbow outside, I press harder on the accelerator. I drive faster than I should through the winding alleys and make the engine roar as soon as I reach a short straight stretch. I laugh out loud when I think of the Detective Chief Inspector boiling alive in a cloud of steam.

'Live as a pig, and you'll squeal like one!' I hit the steering wheel with my destroyed right hand. It doesn't hurt. 'When it comes down to the clinch, old Kvisten will win every time.'

I drive past Brunkebergstorg and peer up at the gigantic telephone tower. I have always been afraid of heights, and memories from last autumn when I was flailing around up there travel like electric currents through my body and make my head spin. Perhaps the blood loss is taking its toll.

The vertigo seems to take hold of my nervous system and a sudden rush flows through my limbs. I push myself down in the driver's seat in response and turn right onto Hamngatan. The contours of the cobblestones make the car shake and my hand vibrate against the steering wheel. Pain runs as straight as a bargepole through my body. I bend down and root around until I feel the steel contours of the Husqvarna, pull it free and toss it onto the leather seat next to me. I bite the end off a cigar, let go of the steering wheel and strike a match. It occurs to me that maybe Ma's powder is wearing off. My eyes flit nervously to the rear mirror.

A lonely conscript is standing by Berzelii Park, trying to earn a coin from some lovesick Östermalm gentleman. Loneliness must be carried like a badly chafing seabag wherever a man steers his course. I have rented boys here more times than I can count and got fifteen minutes of respite when I obeyed my body's desires while emptiness burned holes in my chest.

Enough of that now.

I think of Ma, the bloody heap of a corpse, and am overwhelmed by a violent sorrow. I haven't felt it until now.

The past catches up with me like a thundering echo, and I hear Gabrielsson's voice clearly in my mind: 'Every person you see is a human being doing their best to find their place in the world. Every single one.'

God knows why I am remembering this now. I glance in the rear-view mirror again.

Hell.

I flick open my sunglasses, press them on my nose, reach for the pistol and place it between my legs. All my pores open and sweat runs down my skin.

Where did that bastard come from?

The squad car is five metres behind me. I force myself to slow down and signal left. The fucker is trailing me like a bloodhound.

Falling at the finish line. The occultist's prophecy. I bite my lower lip.

Gabrielsson. The realisation hits me like a right hook. The proper sort that smacks right on target. He never would have exacted revenge. He had the strength to forgive even the worst transgressions.

I hold the steering wheel with my knees again, and hide the Husqvarna.

Maybe I am more of an Old Testament type. I look up briefly to the heavens. A hoarse whisper fills the car.

'Just let me get across the pond.'

Just like in Ma's Cadillac a few days ago, I am haunted by all the innocents I've battered throughout the years. They run begging and bleeding through my mind. More often than not my fists moved of their own accord, out of habit and muscle memory, but maybe there were times when I was trying to relive the old days too.

No one applauded.

Once I'm on the other side of the Atlantic, I will finally have the opportunity to start again. I'll take any labouring job I can find, as long as I can get out of this mess alive. Just as sure as you shed your prison uniform the day you are released. I can work. I've done it before. And they say that repentance frees the sinner.

'You have my word.'

My eyes flit between the street and the side mirror. It's two young constables. No doubt ambitious, trigger-happy and keen to show off. If I'm unlucky maybe Lundin will see me again, this time as cold as a turtle, with my body a honeycomb of bullet holes.

My foot eases off the accelerator as I force myself to slow down.

Only when I'm up at Östermalmstorg am I able to relax. The police car turns left. With one huge sigh of relief I bend so far forward over the wheel that Ploman's hat practically touches the Bakelite. I'm close to crying with happiness.

I see Gabrielsson's bloody corpse and then, like a double exposure, the Reaper's crushed head.

Not far now.

When I pass Kommendörsgatan I peer up at Ma's headquarters. I think about how quickly one family can be demolished and how long it can take for another to be reunited.

So damned close now.

I bring my palm to my chest, feel the bumps of the badly healed ribs and the fresh injury.

Somewhere inside there lives a father's love.

They say that raising children and taking care of them is women's work. Making sure they are clean behind the ears, free of lice, properly dressed and all that. But even though I was always working or training, a father misses his child – at least as much as a mother, because he is away all the time.

A dozen years, almost to the month.

I turn onto Vallhallavägen, drive past the Olympic Stadium and soon see the luminescent sign of the petrol station. I am late but

I think it'll still be all right. Hope and his word of honour are the last things a poor bastard can lose. My shoeless foot involuntarily pushes harder against the accelerator and I am gripping the steering wheel in convulsive excitement. One last look back: the city is a devastated memory, already relegated into the tangled paths of my brain, ready to be buried.

Everybody knows that America is the land of freedom. You can be who you want to be over there. They don't care who keeps you warm at night. You can even keep cool on the fire escape platforms in the summer if need be.

The petrol station's gravel yard crunches under the car wheels. I stretch my neck, hold my breath and exhale deeply. Rickardsson is sitting on an upturned suitcase in short sleeves, honouring his promise. My insides are in tumult, but it is not because of my broken ribs, or my cough. My blood rises.

At long last.

I am here now.

I am just about to honk the horn when he catches sight of me. His serious expression melts and his eyes glimmer under his hat brim. He stands up and waves. Judging by the gobs of snuff around the suitcase he has been waiting for a long time. I park at the petrol station, bounce out of the car and lean on the bonnet, trying to play it cool despite my quivering legs.

A bell rings behind me and I tread on my cigar. The attendant rattles around with his equipment.

'Full tank?'

I nod without turning around.

'We have a long way to go.'

I hear the attendant unscrew the tank lid and start to pump the petrol. Rickardsson picks up his yellow travel bag with leather-reinforced corners and walks over to me at a leisurely pace. In his cold blue eyes I see no regrets, only expectancy. He moistens his thick lips.

'Kvisten looks like absolute shit.'

'You should see the other bloke.'

'I'm happy to see you here.'

'I had no fucking idea whether you would come either.'

Rickardsson nods and goes round to stand behind the attendant. I turn around, look at him and smile. The station attendant shakes off the last few drops, Rickardsson takes his blunt-nosed revolver out of his shoulder holster and bashes the butt into his skull. He falls like a pine tree in the forest.

I make a hasty movement forward, then freeze in place and feel my mouth drop open.

Rickardsson isn't smiling any more; he looks like the killer he is. He turns the revolver on me.

'Can't have any witnesses.' He runs his tongue under his top lip, digs a snuff wad out of his gum, spits it out coolly and pensively. 'Belzén called on me yesterday afternoon. Wanted to know when you would have the van. He had four men with him. I had no choice.'

I jolt, the way you do when you fall in the treacherous void of sleep. My eyes sweep over the petrol station, see the Swedish–English British Petroleum sign, the road full of advertising placards, the round gauge on top of the fuel tank with its silent pointers: time has stopped again. I gasp for air.

'You fucking traitor.'

'You can't trust anyone in this business. This is the path we chose. We chose violence.'

'Or the bastard chose us.'

On the other side of the car bonnet, well out of my punching range, Rickardsson cocks the hammer.

I had everything in the fucking bag, but stumbled right before the finish line. As usual. I stare straight into the barrel. The prophecy flashes through my skull: don't join forces with people you don't know.

I finally admit it: they were right all along. I am thick as a fucking plank. I think with my fists, heart and cock, or not at all.

Get it over with.

Do it now.

I close my eyes. I can smell myself in a way I couldn't earlier: sweat and cigars and Fandango pomade. A gentle wind creeps around the car; some distant birds warble goodnight. A couple of lost swallows cut circles in the air with whistling wings. Somewhere far away, a door slams. My heart calms down. It is time. I give up. At a fucking petrol station on Vallhallavägen. Nothing to be done.

Born a loser, always a loser. I can't take any more.

Get it over with. I am ready. I have been for a long time.

'Pull the trigger then, you bastard.'

'You let me wait for a hell of a long time. Can I trust Kvisten?'

An ounce of hope. I lean forward cautiously and put my hands on my knees. My muscles are shaking. I turn my head to the side, spit and peer up at him from under the brim of my hat.

'We had an agreement. We spat on our hands and shook on it at my place. Only yesterday, for fuck's sake.'

'It was supposed to be an ambush of an ambush but I gave Belzén the wrong time. His rubbish trucks would have come to Hiccup's rescue only once you were finished and both Ploman and the Reaper were dead. By which time Ma and her boys would also be no more than a memory, and the city would be wide open. I ask you again: is Kvisten trustworthy?'

'You know me. I'm a temperamental bastard. But I'm here, aren't I?'

Rickardsson's revolver trembles in his hand.

'Devil take you.'

He holsters his shooter and grins.

'We definitely need to get you a new pair of shoes.'

He lifts the suitcase up onto the bonnet. The lock clicks open and he turns it to show me. There, among the underpants and trousers, glimmers one of the gold bars with the German swastika.

I feel as if I am plunging into darkness and unconsciousness again, but I get a hold of my surroundings, and cling on tight.

'Well, I'll be damned. How the fuck did you manage to get that?'

'You were the one who discovered them. Nicked one for Anna and the kids too.'

Rickardsson picks up a folded and pinned shirt, as red as love and all the fiery demons in hell. He flings it over the car and I catch it. The petrol station attendant is beginning to stir and I hear a few pitiful moans. Time to go. Rickardsson's case clicks closed again.

'You look like you need forty winks. I'll drive the first stretch.'

I nod and we meet in front of the car. For one second we are staring into the depths of each other like two opposing boxers, then I pull him by one of his braces and let it snap back. He smirks, takes me in his hairy arms and kisses me deeply. Our hat brims collide. It has been a long time since someone has taken me like this and I like it. He tastes of snuff and cognac.

For one moment I think I am going to collapse on him. He supports me and then lets me go. I look around, out of habit.

'Kvisten doesn't need to worry about that any more.'

'Always some bastard staring.'

'Since when do we care what the penal code says?'

Rickardsson moves away, and the sunset blazes over him like gold. I shade my face with my hand and look up at the golden sky. A pigeon shimmers blue as it passes overhead.

'Might be better in the States.'

He nods and pulls up a cigar from his chest pocket with a smile glittering on his lips.

'Havana?'

I grin.

'Maybe for Christmas.'

Rickardsson lets out a hearty laugh. I light the cigar and inspect it.

Not bad.

Time to trade up.

Rickardsson throws his suitcase in the car and I walk around the bonnet, stepping over the petrol station attendant. The blood is still pouring from an open wound on the back of his head but the bloke is already coming round and twitching his legs.

He'll live.

I open the door to the front seat but pause for a moment.

'Came across Oskar Olsson in Christmas '32. Runs the state police now.'

'Corrupt bastard.'

'Should drop him a word about Ploman's protection corps.'

'What the hell does that matter to people like us? A country gets what it deserves. No more, no less.'

'That's probably true.'

'They hang petty thieves like us, but lift their hats to the big ones.'

'Kvisten doesn't. Like hell.'

'Neither do I.'

'Might make a call though.'

'From Oslo, before we board.'

We get in the car. The leather creaks as I get comfortable on the passenger seat. Rickardsson revs up the engine.

'Here we fucking go, lad! Never tell me I can't make a bloody plan.'

I chuckle and take a deep puff.

'I don't even know your damn first name.'

'I'm not a first name kind of bloke.'

I laugh. Rickardsson puts his hand on the gearstick between his legs. I place my hand on his. Together we click into first and drive away with a tail of smoke behind us.

EPILOGUE

There isn't much to tell.

We drive all night. We laugh, we bicker, take a fuck break by a forest lake just outside Örebro and get mosquito bites on our arses. We sit listening to the quiet hum of the forest for a long time afterwards. No words are needed. After half an hour we go back to the car.

Rickardsson drives awhile longer. He talks about when he killed a man with a belt strap around the neck and a knee between the shoulder blades. I counter with the story of when I stabbed a copper in the eye with the broken point of a schnapps glass. I win that round.

At times I sit silently and stare at the never-ending brown line of pine trees rushing past. The motor hums and through the open window I can hear gravel crunching underneath the car tyres. Every metre brings me that much closer to my Ida, and Rickardsson farther from his children.

'Kvisten is still hanging tough.'

'What did you say?'

'That no one can really make sense of any of it.'

'Damn straight.'

'Do you know why they took my little finger with those pliers that time?'

'Half the city knows the story.'

'Maybe so.'

I yawn, light a new cigar from the old and flick the butt out the window.

'I've always had trouble remembering things. Maybe I've simply forgotten.'

We eventually swap places and Rickardsson stretches out on the passenger seat. It's not long before he falls asleep.

It's him and me now. Runaways from the law. Cut from the same fucking cloth.

If life has taught me anything it is the art of waiting. For hours outside debtors' doors in all weathers, in suspense when interrogators try to wait me out with silence, for orders from skippers and officers, and in prison, where the days, weeks and years melt into one long stagnation. Maybe all that waiting has led me here.

My thoughts are flitting past as quickly as the Värmland forests and inland lakes outside the window.

I take a look in the rear-view mirror. The new day is dawning. It is beautiful in its way. I make up my mind never to look back again.

'Thus preaches Kvisten. You can take your nation, your law book and your fucking Word of God and shove them so far up your arse that you choke.'

Rickardsson grunts. I lay my hand on his leg to calm him. It helps. I keep my hand there. There is something special about driving though the night with a snoring man next to you.

I have always liked it.

I was never struck down in all my years in the boxing ring, but if I had been, I know now that I would have got up again.

I lost a father, avenged him and gained a lover in return.

I must have done something right.

When we cross the Norwegian border without a hitch a few hours after dawn, a fine rain finally begins to fall. Rickardsson is still sleeping stretched out on the seat next to me. I brake gently so as not to wake him. I take his revolver and my Husqvarna and step out of the car. It is best not to take them aboard the boat. I sling the guns as far as I can into the forest.

The sun is shining and a gentle breeze spreads a fog-like haze on the wind. It glitters like gold flakes. I take off my hat and stare straight up into the sky to wake myself up. I feel a sense of purity, as if the warm wind is blowing the sun-rain straight through me.

We rattle over the quay paving with a couple of hours to go. Rickardsson laughs and slaps his thigh. We see her in the distance: SS *Victoria*. I laugh with him.

We park and step out to stretch our legs before departure. The wind cools; the flags whip. I have my jacket slung over my shoulder, and Rickardsson's thumbs are in his braces. He winks at me and I grin. Soon we will have a private cabin to indulge ourselves. Two dollar-millionaires.

Not bad for a couple of lowlifes.

I tell him the story of a ship's cook who kept me company the whole way to Shanghai. A big fucker who taught me to fight with a dagger. Neither Rickardsson nor I is fond of knives any more. We think similarly about almost everything.

We look, rather lazily, for a telephone. I show him the cocktail umbrella.

They are waiting for us near customs. Maybe they have been lying in wait for a long time, informed by the Swedish police. Maybe it was Thulin the forger who dobbed us in. They did say that that old bastard was in league with the police.

We are given no warning. Rickardsson takes a bullet to the leg and seeks cover behind a couple of wooden boxes but they don't offer much protection. The police shoot them and him to pieces.

A bullet to the head. His skull bursts open and Rickardsson is no more.

I stick a cigar in my mouth and run. It's not something I'm proud of. I had imagined this moment differently. The story of a country lad who was tickled to death by two farm maids flashes through my mind.

Or was it three?

Maybe I could have run faster if I wasn't so ravaged by the past week. And fuck, when I was in my heyday. Ten kilometres in three-quarters of an hour. Can't bloody well do that any more.

I smell the comforting scent of seawater. I was close. It didn't go as planned.

This is my lot in life.

This has become my final round.

The first bullet knocks the hat off my head, but it wasn't even mine to begin with. I hear a rattling winch and a seagull laughing, but I don't hear the next shots. I feel them hammer into my back. My Meteor flies out of my mouth. I think I fall on my side.

The Viking watch has fallen out of my pocket and the broken glass glistens close to my face. I cough and my mouth fills with blood but it doesn't hurt. I feel nothing. I think I reach for the photograph in my wallet.

I simply can't imagine her. Practically a grown woman.

It doesn't matter any more.

She will never hear news of my death anyway.

AVAILABLE AND COMING SOON
FROM PUSHKIN VERTIGO

Jonathan Ames
You Were Never Really Here

Augusto De Angelis
The Murdered Banker
The Mystery of the Three Orchids
The Hotel of the Three Roses

Olivier Barde-Cabuçon
Casanova and the Faceless Woman

María Angélica Bosco
Death Going Down

Piero Chiara
The Disappearance of Signora Giulia

Frédéric Dard
Bird in a Cage
The Wicked Go to Hell
Crush
The Executioner Weeps
The King of Fools
The Gravediggers' Bread

Friedrich Dürrenmatt
The Pledge
The Execution of Justice
Suspicion
The Judge and His Hangman

Martin Holmén
Clinch
Down for the Count
Slugger

Alexander Lernet-Holenia
I Was Jack Mortimer

Margaret Millar
Vanish in an Instant

Boileau-Narcejac
Vertigo
She Who Was No More

Leo Perutz
Master of the Day of Judgment
Little Apple
St Peter's Snow

Soji Shimada
The Tokyo Zodiac Murders
Murder in the Crooked Mansion

Masako Togawa
The Master Key
The Lady Killer

Emma Viskic
Resurrection Bay
And Fire Came Down
Darkness for Light

Seishi Yokomizo
The Inugami Clan
Murder in the Honjin